THE UNMASKING

She'd taken so many risks as the Brazen Angel, but none quite like this. She could hear the dire warnings, but they faded against the rising din of passion.

He met her challenge. "And if I told you what I wanted, would you give it to me?"

She swung her hips saucily. "I suppose I would have no choice."

This time when his arms pulled her close, his mouth swept down toward hers. "The choice would always be yours to make," he said, before covering her lips with his.

The searing kiss sealed her reply, as if he knew what her body had already decided.

She tried to breathe but there was no time. His lips encircled hers, daring them to open under his assault. When his tongue parried forward, his arms pulled her closer; a blazing circle of passion whisked away any protests.

In that hasty moment, she felt as if he'd stripped her of her mask, bared her to his sight, as if he sought to see her very soul.

BRAZEN ANGEL

ELIZABETH BOYLE

A DELL BOOK

Published by

DELL PUBLISHING

a division of

Bantam Doubleday Dell Publishing Group, Inc.

1540 Broadway

New York, New York 10036

The trademark Dell® is registered in the U.S. Patent and
Trademark Office.

ISBN: 0-440-22412-8

Printed in the United States of America

Published simultaneously in Canada

August 1997

10 9 8 7 6 5 4 3 2 1

OPM

Dedication

To my husband, Terry, who every day brings love and romance into my life. Thank you for giving me my island, my castle, my dreams.

PROLOGUE

London, 1793

OSWALD WENTWORTH, the Earl of Lyle, crossed his arms over his portly stomach and looked at the enticing vision next to him in his carriage.

Amazing bit of luck it was, meeting such an eager lady at such a boring affair as Lady Chilton's masquerade. With that damn Trahern and his constant interference, it had become impossible over the past few years to find a willing partner. Especially a noble one who shared his inclinations.

Well, tonight there was no one to whisper a warning in the lady's ear. Not that she appeared the type to listen.

One thing for certain, Oswald knew he never would

have stood a chance with Lord Trahern nearby. Women flocked to the man.

Undoubtedly because of all that mystery surrounding Trahern's foreign travels and his newly inherited wealth.

"Is your house very far?" his companion purred in her throaty, accented voice. "I so hate waiting." Her gloved hand grazed over his forearm.

It wasn't difficult to imagine the feel of her fingers elsewhere. "Not much farther," he told her. "Not much farther at all."

Somewhere in the distance a church bell tolled the hour. It was well past midnight.

"I'm so glad you don't mind going to your house," she said, scooting across the seat, her voluminous skirts enveloping his legs. The trim curve of her ankle slid up and down his calf. "I'm forever looking for a place to spend the night."

Despite the full moon outside, the dim light inside the carriage left her features obscured. Even in the Chiltons' drawing room her face had been difficult to discern, artfully hidden as it was beneath her black and silver mask.

That was what had drawn him to her—her morbid costume. Only a lady with a true lack of morals would come to a formal masquerade dressed as Death. Her mask, grotesque and chilling, covered most of the upper half of her face. On her skirts, a morality play had been embroidered with images of the Devil and a wicked assortment of his tortured victims.

They were images after Oswald's own black heart. He glanced at her again, trying to find a hint as to the identity of the lady beneath the costume. She would be blond beneath her towering black wig, he just knew it. He loved blondes.

And from the accent he guessed her to be French.

Probably another damned *émigré* from Paris. Newly arrived and in desperate straits. That would also explain why he hadn't recognized her when he first spied her. How he was beginning to love those wretched revolutionaries and their guillotine. Not only had they opened up all kinds of new business opportunities to exploit, now it seemed they would end up providing him with a wealth of wonderful companions.

She leaned over him again. "Lord Lyle, may I call you Ossie? That is what your friend called you as we left, isn't it?" Her hand brushed across the top of his knee. "You may call me Mignon."

"Yes, of course, my dear Mignon," he gasped. She was indeed French. He could imagine it now, her urgent cries for release in that passionate language. "I would call you Angel, my dear. For you remind me of one."

"An angel in black? How odd, Ossie."

"Angels come in many forms. Somehow I doubt you are the saving kind."

"I'm sure you'd be surprised to find out which master I serve," she said softly into his ear.

Despite the darkness he discerned the wicked slant of her smile.

"How is it we haven't met before?" he wanted to know.

"Alas, I have a wicked step-*maman* who keeps me locked away." She sighed dramatically, leaning back in her seat. "Though sometimes, when the moon is full, I steal the key and slip free. And you can't imagine the mischief I find." Her hand trailed up his knee to nearly his inner thigh before she slowly pulled it away.

"I can imagine quite a bit, my dear." He turned to her

and tugged her closer, hauling her into his arms. For a fleeting second he saw past the mask and into her eyes.

Behind the black velvet he spied something familiar.

Fear.

The lady feared him. And rightly she should.

But she didn't pull away. Instead, she reached up and lazily ran her finger down his cheek. "I wouldn't have gone with you like this unless I knew you were the type of man I wanted. I made inquiries and found out we have, shall we say, similar tastes."

Women with his type of taste usually didn't fall into his arms. Rather, they cost him a considerable amount of blunt at Madame Giselle's private club.

All he wanted to do was to free himself of his breeches, toss her skirts over her head, and empty himself into her without another thought.

Games could be played later.

But just then the carriage came to a jolting stop and his new footman promptly opened the door.

Oswald made a note to dismiss the efficient bastard in the morning.

His dark angel exited with all the grace of a duchess, her head held high, her nose pointed upward in a royal tilt. When she gained the front door she glanced over her shoulder at him and ran her tongue over the half-opened pout of her lips before she continued inside.

He followed in stunned amazement.

"What a marvelous home you have, Ossie."

Oswald waved away the footman and took her wrap from her. Tonight no one would touch her or her clothing but him. Breathing in the strange floral fragrance clinging to the fur-lined wrap, he found himself intoxicated to the point of obsession. He must have her and without any further delays.

She curled up to his side, her hand wrapping around the curve of his elbow. "Take me to the room where you spend the most time. I want to make sure you remember me often when we are not together." Then she leaned over and whispered into his ear some suggestions of how he might remember her.

Oswald licked his suddenly dry lips. How did she know that he enjoyed such things?

Guiding her up to the second floor at nothing less than a dead run, he bellowed at the footman not to disturb them, not under any circumstances.

His angel laughed gaily at his order.

Blood pounding in his ears, he stopped before the door of his study and caught her with both hands, pinning her against the wall.

"I might be a little rough," he warned, his lips grazing over her neck.

She shuddered in wanton response. "I hoped you would be. But be warned. I play rough in return."

Oswald flung open the door to his study, and after she walked in he slammed it shut and twisted the key in the lock.

When he turned around he found her exactly as he wanted her—leaning over his cluttered desk, her hips swaying back and forth in invitation.

She glanced over her shoulder again, and in a maddening pout, her gaze downcast, she whispered, "Undo me, Ossie. I've been very bad."

A strangled sound erupted from his throat as his rock-hard

groin started to give way to a presaging shudder. He choked back the release.

He looked at her in wonder. She'd nearly unmanned him without even a touch. He must hurry or he would spill himself before he had the chance to see just what Mignon considered "being bad."

She faced him now, easing her bodice to her shoulders. The pale gleam of her full breasts pushing at the top of her bodice cast a soft glow, which beckoned for his touch.

"Please, Ossie. I shouldn't be here. I couldn't help myself. Punish me."

Treading heavily on the thick rug, he started to cross the room. His breathing rasped in heavy, ragged sobs. He made it only halfway.

"That's it, Ossie." She kicked off her slippers, one of them falling at his feet. She propped her foot up on the desk, her skirts falling back, revealing her stocking-clad leg. The silk glimmered in the firelight as she rolled it down and tossed it next to the slipper. "Think of how bad I've been. A lady shouldn't be here. Not like this," she said, rolling her shoulders back so her breasts rose higher in her gown, threatening to spill out. "The last thing I want to be is a lady."

He couldn't move for fear of what would happen in his churning groin if he did. All he could do was watch in fascination as she peeled off her gloves.

Long-limbed, she reminded him of an expensive racing steed. And oh, so ready to be ridden.

Mignon held out one arm, her finger curling to induce him closer.

Oswald didn't need any further prompting. Ripping off his collar and jacket, he cared little for the threads and buttons lost in his haste. His waistcoat came next, followed by his breeches. "Ah, my Mignon. Let Ossie show you how he punishes fallen angels."

But Mignon was no longer waiting submissively at his desk. She'd darted toward the cart that held decanters of his favorite sherry and a particularly strong Scottish whiskey his Northern cousins had sent him. She poured a glass of the whiskey and pressed it toward his outstretched hands. "Drink it."

"The vision of you is enough for me tonight," he said, pushing her hands away.

She persisted, bringing the glass up between them. "You must. I want to taste it from your strong lips."

Oswald took the glass and gulped down the proffered liquor. He coughed as the fiery liquid burned his mouth and throat. "You'll taste more than my lips, you wicked creature, if you have been as bad as I think." Strolling behind his desk, he ran his hand underneath the shelves lining the back wall. He pulled the latch free and the bookcase opened up. "This is where I keep all my favorite things, my dear Mignon." Pulling out a riding crop, he snapped it on the desk.

She squealed, skittering around the room in wild abandon. "Oh, Ossie. How ever did you know?"

As he tried to catch her she darted out of reach, laughing and teasing him to follow her in dizzy circles.

Oswald came to a halting stop in the middle of the room. The floor started to pitch in a most haphazard fashion. As he blinked to clear his vision, the room spun even more wildly. Mignon's image floated toward him, her movements strangely slow and jerky.

"What have you done to me?" he choked out as he

reached toward her for support. His hands found nothing, only the floor as it rushed up to greet his rough descent.

Mignon knelt by his side, her features blurring for a second, then clearing.

He thought she was smiling.

"What have you done to me?" he repeated as he felt himself slipping into a dark sleep.

"Oh, Ossie. Now I'm going to be really bad."

CHAPTER
1

London, six months later

"O<small>H, BOTHER, GILES.</small> Look who's arrived," Montgomery, the Duke of Stanton, whispered loudly.

Giles Corliss, the Marquess of Trahern, tipped up his confounded black mask and looked first to his friend, only to find the Duke scrunching his short body behind a white marble statue in a vain attempt to go unnoticed. The stocky man's bright yellow jacket and red waistcoat made him hard to miss.

Giles should have known it was only a matter of time before the affable Monty embarrassed them.

Ignoring the Duke's precarious position, Giles turned his interest toward the entrance of the Parkers' ballroom. He knew there were few people Monty disliked enough to hide from. But spotting a glimpse of Lord Lyle's portly frame circling the crowded room, he agreed with his friend's urgent assessment of the situation, though not his method for avoiding the problem.

"Get out from behind there, Monty." Giles glanced over to where his friend had wedged himself. "If Lyle is here, he probably shares our suspicions—the Brazen Angel will be here tonight."

Monty eased out from his hiding spot. His mask perched crookedly at the end of his nose, while below it his mouth twisted in a lopsided and apologetic smile. Straightening to his full, though limited, height, he meticulously adjusted his jacket and mask.

Giles took a deep breath. It was bad enough every man in London seemed obsessed by the Brazen Angel, now even this craze for masquerades she'd launched was getting out of hand. Now every hostess in town wanted to throw a masked party in hopes of entertaining the Brazen Angel, as she had come to be known. "Whatever was I thinking when I agreed to help you find this woman?" He yanked off his mask and tossed it behind the statue.

Monty shrugged. "Boredom?"

His friend was right, boredom indeed. He should be on the continent, not wasting his time at frivolous London entertainments.

Shaking his head, Monty continued. "No, let me change that. Avoidance. Yes, I'd say you offered to help me in one last desperate attempt at avoidance."

"Why, I've never avoided anything in my——" Giles

started to say, stopping when Monty began to laugh. "Well, maybe *her*."

"When are you going to go around and meet your betrothed?" Monty's lips twitched. "And after all the trouble your father went through to arrange the rest of your life just before he died. How nice of him to pick out your wife."

Giles didn't need to be reminded that it had been his father's last wish to see his son and only heir married and settled with heirs of his own. He woke up each morning to the fact that his wedding was one day closer. If only his father hadn't extracted a promise from Lord Dryden to see the marriage finalized posthaste, there might have been some leeway in delaying the nuptials.

Monty tipped his glass in a mock toast. "And Lady Sophia, well, I can only extend my best wishes."

"Heartfelt, I'm sure." Giles knew he couldn't keep avoiding his betrothed, but when all the descriptions he'd gathered hinged on the same hesitant "best wishes" and "nice girl, that one," finding the courage to meet the future Lady Trahern failed him.

"What is it, a month away? Lucky man." Monty coughed.

"You find something amusing in all this?"

"You would if you were in my shoes," Monty continued, his lips twitching. "You have to admit the idea of Dryden going from spymaster to master matchmaker is quite humorous. I certainly wouldn't want that dour old man choosing my bride."

"I don't think the situation is as bad as all that. Besides, my father picked out Lady Sophia; it's Dryden's job to ensure the marriage takes place."

Monty shrugged. "Well, I can't say I'm looking forward

to it. Once you marry that girl you'll be off again, with your *shipping concerns*." The smaller man snorted. "As if I didn't know about your other connections with Dryden and the Foreign Office."

Giles found his mood souring, as it always did when someone pushed the subject of his upcoming nuptials. It was bad enough his father betrothed him to a girl he'd never met, now this idle life in London threatened to dull his mind.

No wonder he'd jumped at the opportunity to help Monty solve the mystery of the Brazen Angel. If anything, the exercise would keep his skills honed until he returned to duty with the Foreign Office.

He scanned the room with a practiced gaze, all but ignoring the parade of ladies in their colorful gowns edging past him.

Since his arrival in London it had been like this at every social function. At first he'd carefully cultivated a reputation for being dangerous, until he discovered that only attracted the fortune-hunting beauties in droves.

Not even the announcement of his betrothal held them at bay.

Betrothed. Giles shuddered.

"With you getting married I suppose I'll have to renew my search for my perfect duchess." Monty peered around the room.

Now it was Giles's turn to laugh. "Are you still carrying around your list?"

Monty nodded and patted his jacket pocket.

The Duke's list of attributes for a perfect wife was quite legendary around the marriage mart. Though he refused to

12

reveal any elements of what he considered a perfect wife, he claimed that when he met the woman who met all his requirements, he would spirit her away and make her his duchess. Many a marriage-minded mother had pushed her daughter in the affable duke's path, but to no avail.

Giles considered Monty's list nothing more than his friend's way of avoiding that inevitable visit to the parson. And if there was one thing Giles knew about his friend, no one was better at avoidance and diversion than Monty.

"How will we spirit the Angel away with Lyle watching every move we make?" Monty asked.

"We could still call the authorities and turn her over. After all, she did rob you." Giles didn't try to understand his friend's obsession with finding London's most notorious woman. Built like a bulldog, Monty also possessed the temperament of one. Once he latched on to an idea he refused to let go, no matter how outrageous.

"I will not turn her over to the authorities and neither will you. Not after you've seen her." Monty took a glass from a passing tray. "Besides, the money doesn't matter. Though I doubt Lyle or Rostland would agree with me."

Giles nodded. The Brazen Angel had taken London by storm over the past few months. He had thought her nothing but a foolish rumor—wishful talk to enliven a rather dull season. That was until Monty's encounter with her a month prior.

The lady was indeed brazen. Offering herself for seduction, she left her victims in a drugged stupor while she robbed them blind. Though none of her victims had disclosed that minor fact when they'd bragged in their clubs the next day about the "Angel" they'd taken home the night before.

The lady, Giles discovered, was also a master of disguise, having appeared at a masquerade as Death for Lord Lyle, at the theater as a demure miss fresh from school for Lord Wickham, and stranded by the roadside for Lord Rostland. With each of these notorious lechers she had the uncanny ability to tap into their most hidden fantasies, for her victims had bragged at great lengths that she seemed to know just what a man desired.

But in Monty's case it appeared she had meant herself for another man.

As his friend explained the day after his encounter, still clutching in his hand her trademark token—a scented handkerchief—he had met her outside the opera. Another lord had been about to assist her, but Monty, ever the gentleman where lovely ladies were concerned, cut the young man off, offering his services first.

She'd lost her companion, or so she said, and was unable to enter the opera. She confessed she had no coins for a carriage home and refused to tell her name or family connections because, she said, she'd deceived her parents to go out with a young man they found unsuitable. If her situation was discovered her reputation would be ruined.

"Could Your Grace please help me?" she asked so prettily, tears rimming her eyes.

"I still can't believe you took her home," Giles commented. "What were you thinking?"

"What was I to do?" Monty shot back. "The poor thing was overcome. I thought if I revived her with some sherry she'd tell me who her family was and I'd send for them. How was I know to that by sharing a glass with her I'd end up lying on the floor, the hapless victim, rather than her hero?"

Monty had awakened with a crushing headache, only to discover his watch and pocket money missing, along with the extra measure of gold he kept hidden in his study.

Giles shifted from one leg to the other. "A handkerchief, a hint of perfume, a potion for leaving a man unconscious, and a fondness for a full moon. And you expect me to find this woman? It sounds more like a witch hunt."

"I'm beginning to think Lord Dryden's trust in you is misplaced. It's been a month and you've got nothing. I would have thought you'd have her by now. And if you don't find her soon, I'll be a sight richer." Monty grinned again, referring to their wager. "Maybe I'll offer my services to Dryden while you're on your honeymoon."

"I could find this woman if you and the rest of her victims could refrain from waxing poetic on her beauty. Believe it or not, I need a better description than somewhere between 'just out of the convent' and 'wonderfully mature.' You might as well describe every woman in this ballroom." Giles crossed his arms over his chest and stared down at Monty.

"An accent," the Duke said, a look of surprise on his face. "I remember it now; she spoke with a slight accent. French, perhaps. But you know me and languages."

"Are you sure?" Giles couldn't help but feel skeptical.

"Yes. Yes," he insisted. "She had an accent."

Giles looked around the room. There were probably three to four hundred people filling the Parkers' ballroom to capacity. How easy it was to slip in and move about undetected. Hadn't he done the same thing in the French court time and time again? "With this crush she'd be able to meet her prey and leave without anyone noticing."

"So you still think someone in this room is her next

15

victim?" Monty shook his head. "I hate for her to take these risks. All she had to do was ask me for the money."

"This Angel isn't looking for a protector. She just wants the money." Giles studied the crowd. "But for what is the true question."

Monty took another glass of wine from a passing servant. "When you see her you'll have your answer. The dress and jewels she wore that night must have cost a king's ransom."

"No one risks so much for clothing and jewels. Any man could provide those comforts." Giles took the glass from Monty's hand. "No more of that. Clear heads prevail, and tonight we need our wits to flush out our prey." Monty frowned as Giles set the drink down on a small table. "Our best bet is to wander. Keep your ears open and listen carefully. Her voice may be the only way to recognize her."

As they worked their way through the room, Monty broke the silence between them. "Oh, this is worse than I thought!" He nodded toward Lyle, who had been joined by Rostland. The nefarious pair tipped their glasses toward Giles and Monty. "It would be a mite easier if they weren't looking for her as well."

"I couldn't agree more." Giles looked across the room at their adversaries. Being part of the Full Moon Club, as her victims were dubbed, was considered by many to be a prize distinction. Lyle and Rostland hadn't viewed it that way. They'd made it very clear to anyone who would listen that they intended to make the lady pay in their own particular manner.

The hunt for the Brazen Angel had quickly become a personal challenge, as had past dealings between Giles and the duo. There had been rumors even in Giles's father's time that Lyle's fortune had been made in illicit operations during the war with the Colonies—dealings bordering on treason, some whispered—but nothing anyone could prove. Now Lyle's fortune was on the rise again, and that in itself, Giles reasoned, warranted close scrutiny. For Lyle wouldn't allow anything or anyone to get in his way.

An icy pit chilled his gut. He couldn't think of anyone who deserved the kind of fate Lyle and Rostland planned for the lady.

"They won't find her. Not tonight." Giles nodded to a young man across the room. "Watch young Lord Harvey, my friend, but do so with some discretion."

"What is he up to?" Monty asked as the young man approached Lord Lyle and engaged him in an animated conversation.

Lyle swung around almost immediately and headed toward the door, with Rostland following hot on his heels.

"Should we go after them?" Monty's voice filled with concern.

Giles shook his head. "No. Harvey's been itching for an introduction to Lord Dryden. He'd like to go into the 'shipping business' with me. I told him tonight was a trial run."

Monty grinned. "What have you done?"

"Bait and switch, my good man. Lord Harvey told Lyle that he'd just come from a party where the Brazen Angel is attending. By the time Lyle and Rostland arrive, the fake lady will have left with Lord Harvey's cousin. It should take them hours before they discover they've been had. By then we should have this Angel creature safely hidden away."

Monty, who'd found another drink, gulped down the remaining libation. "I wish I had your confidence. What makes you think we'll find her first?"

"Because I wagered you a month's rent on my Dorset properties I would. And I never lose."

For all Giles's confidence, though, they spent the next hour searching their way through the crowded ballroom to no avail. In Giles's estimation the Parkers' masked ball had been the perfect event to attract the Brazen Angel— crowded, filled with the wealthiest members of the ton, and, of course, all the guests wore masks. In all his years on the continent working for the Foreign Office, he'd found these types of events the best to meet with contacts or other operatives. Since her work didn't appear to be that much different from his—finding a mark, making contact, and exchanging information—she should make an appearance tonight.

Ahead of him, Monty slipped in and around the guests. Giles, with his height and broad shoulders, had a slower time of it. But his height gave him the advantage of being able to see Monty's bewigged head bobbing along in front.

"Lord Trahern! Lord Trahern, is that you?" an elderly lady called as she barged her way through the ballroom.

Distracted, Giles nearly collided with Monty, who'd stopped short to allow another guest to pass by.

"Excuse me, my lady," Monty said, bowing low to the young woman.

Giles looked directly into her eyes. Though she wore a mask like everyone else in the room, behind the concealing white satin sparkled a pair of startling sapphire eyes. Her lashes fluttered in recognition, as if she knew him intimately. The sensation of it—as if she had touched him rather than just glanced at him—rocked him out of his usual composure and into a stunned silence.

She looked back at Monty, who was still blathering away with his apologies. "There was no harm done, Your Grace. If you'll excuse me," she answered softly, her voice accented.

Monty and Giles did a double take, then stared at each other before straining to catch a last glance of the woman before she disappeared into the crowd.

"That's her," Monty breathed. "Giles, it's really her."

"Lord Trahern, I must speak with you," blared an anxious voice behind them.

Giles turned to find himself facing the unmistakable Lady Dearsley. Unmistakable not so much by her formidable size, but by her ever-present yellow turban and strident tones.

He turned back to Monty. "Follow her, quickly."

Giles tried to avoid Lady Dearsley's onslaught, but he wasn't quick enough. He'd done a good job of eluding the woman and her sisters since his return, but now, of all times, she'd finally succeeded in trapping him.

Though nearing her seventieth year, Lady Dearsley moved with the speed of a young girl. She wrapped her meaty arm around his, anchoring Giles in place before he could slip into the overwhelming crowd.

"Lord Trahern, I have been trying to see you for the last three days." Lady Dearsley sent him a censorious frown. "It's time we made the final arrangements. The wedding date is a month away and you need to sign the agreements."

Curious stares followed in Lady Dearsley's wake.

Instead of cursing his father aloud for entangling him in this betrothal, Giles tried smiling graciously at his future relation. This marriage would mean his return to the Service.

But right now even that welcome thought placed a distant second to the brief image of the Brazen Angel burning hotly in his mind.

"How nice to see you, my lady." He strained to glance over the woman's feathers and turban, hoping to catch sight of Monty. "Is your niece here this evening?"

Lady Dearsley shook her head. "Sadly, she became indisposed and could not attend. She is a very delicate girl, a fact I hope you will remember when you are married. That she is *delicate*."

Giles took a deep breath. "How can I forget, Lady Dearsley? With your ever-vigilant reminders I am sure not even the King with his shortcomings could forget such an important fact."

"Just so you remember that she is delicate," the woman added one more time. "Now, since it seems you are here in London, as is my dear niece, I know you must be anxious to meet her before the wedding. Under the circumstances, though, it might be better if . . ."

Giles nodded his head in distracted agreement to whatever she blathered on about. Across the room he spied Monty waving frantically for him and pointing toward an adjoining room. Without thinking he stepped rudely around the lady. Her endless chatter faded as excitement coursed through him.

The Brazen Angel was trapped, for the room she had entered had no other exit than back into the ballroom.

Their shared glance still held him captive. He couldn't escape the notion that somehow he knew her, knew her intimately. But he couldn't recall having ever had a mistress with such startling blue eyes. Once they'd unmasked her, he'd know for sure.

But his escape came up short. Lady Dearsley latched on to his arm with the tenacity of a sailor on holiday. "Then you are agreed, my lord? I can expect your solicitor tomorrow afternoon? My niece will be so excited to know her future is to be so secure."

Prying his arm out of her iron grip, he nodded absently again. "Yes, yes. That will be fine. Tomorrow afternoon," he repeated without another thought in her direction.

Giles quickly cut his way through the crowd. He didn't care about the muffled coughs and sniffs following in his wake. Suddenly, more quickly than he expected, the milling aristocracy parted and he came face to face with his prize.

This second sight of her stunned him into an adolescent state of awe. He swallowed slowly. All of her victims' poetic, flowery descriptions hardly did her justice.

In the flickering light from the chandeliers, her artfully designed hair shimmered with a silver hue. Over this rich creation of curls sat a tall hat, the wide brim riding low over her face. Undulating white feathers dipped even lower, successfully concealing what few features her white mask didn't cover. Around her neck wound two strands of thick pearls, their luster competing with the rich glow of her creamy skin. The rounded curves of her breasts pushed to the top of her low-cut bodice. Her fashionable skirts ballooned out from her waist, ending just at her ankles. In a room filled with the bold colors of fashion, her choice of white and silver made her stand out.

She looked as fragile as porcelain, a deception he didn't trust for a moment.

"Excuse me," she said, her skirt brushing against him.

The rustle of fabric snapped Giles to attention. "May I offer you my assistance?" He held out his arm to her.

She shook her head slightly. "No, thank you."

Giles did not miss the dismissive tone, nor the slight accent to her speech. Though fluent in many languages he, too, had to admit he was stumped as to its origin. "Oh, I insist, my dear lady." He took her hand and settled it on his forearm, holding her in place. "Besides, you appear to have been left alone. I wouldn't call myself a gentleman if I didn't help a lady in distress."

She tugged her arm to free herself, but Giles only held on that much tighter.

"My lord, your reputation precedes you. My escort will not appreciate your efforts." Again she turned her face from him, obviously searching the crowd for someone.

Her next victim, Giles guessed.

"And who is your escort? Perhaps I have seen him recently."

Her sensuous pink lips pursed in concentration. "That is none of your concern. Now, if you don't release me I'll make a scene."

"I doubt that," he stated confidently. "A lady like your-self, so concerned with *appearances*, wouldn't want to attract such untoward attention." He started to stroll through the crowd, dragging her toward a side door. "Tell me your name, for I have a feeling before the evening is out we'll be old friends."

She did not reply.

"No name?" he teased. "What a terrible shame. Since I have never seen you before, I therefore must assume you are a princess from a faraway land, which would account for your accent and your shocking lack of a protector. Am I right?"

"A princess, my lord?" She shook her head. "I would have expected something much more original from you. I am hardly a princess in need of a knight's rescue."

"From your answer can I assume we have been introduced before?" he asked as they continued their halting procession through the room. As Giles towed her along he couldn't help but notice how the lady resisted each step forward.

"Oh, in a manner of speaking." She laughed, as if over some private joke.

Even as she enjoyed her jest at his expense, he began to notice subtle changes in her behavior. She still pulled against his grip, but the lady's strategy started to change.

"Perhaps in Vienna?" he asked, searching his memory of all the ladies he'd met and tarried with on the continent.

Her face upturned, allowing him a chance to study her. Her hand on his arm relaxed, while a flirtatious light sparked in the mischievous blue fire of her eyes. The enticing fullness of her lips widened to an engaging smile.

"You don't know me, do you?" she teased, leaning closer to him until her shoulder brushed ever so slightly against his arm. "I suppose I would be insulted if we had met before, but to be honest, we haven't, my lord. Not formally."

For once Monty hadn't been exaggerating. The woman was an angel to behold. And he felt himself falling under her tempting spell. Obviously, he'd been out of the field too long if some misguided member of the ton could pique his professional curiosity so thoroughly with her antics.

"Then let me be so forward as to introduce myself,"

23

he said. "With your escort unavailable to do the honors, I am—"

The Brazen Angel didn't need any introduction to the man at her side. "—You are Lord Trahern," she finished. "As I said, your name and reputation precede you."

And did it ever, she thought. Of all the men to interrupt her this evening, why did it have to be this one?

She must get rid of him, and quickly. His gaze was too penetrating and at the same time too familiar to be risked. If he saw through her painstaking costume, everything would be lost.

"While your tone sounds like an insult, I instead will be honored that such a lovely lady knows me." He smiled graciously.

It should have pleased her to finally meet the man who had puzzled her for so long. A year or so ago she'd seen a boyhood portrait of him at Byrnewood, his family home. Ever since that fateful afternoon she'd been fascinated by the determined slant of his mouth and dark eyes.

She'd often wondered what kind of man that stern child had become.

Now she knew. He was the same brooding, handsome, and devilish type of man she and her sister had giggled about and dreamed of eloping with when they'd been growing up. But in the safety of their convent school she'd never realized the dangerous passions a man like this could evoke in the corner of a woman's heart.

His fingers, warm and firm, closed over her wrist with strength and authority. Hands that could guide a woman's body into immortal danger—or heavenly release. She drew a deep breath and tried to step away from him. There were many men in the room who were handsome enough, men that attracted a woman with looks and charm. She knew enough about those types of men to be wary of their honeyed phrases and promises of undying love. Fools ripe for the picking, she discovered once she'd turned the tables on them.

But it struck her immediately that Lord Trahern may be different. Oh, he was handsome and charming, but the determined cut of his jaw and the wary look about him said that he'd seen enough of the world not to be easily deceived.

It was an expression she understood well. She saw it every time she looked in a mirror. It also meant she must be very careful.

"You seem far away, my lady," he said softly. "Perhaps it is someplace *I* could take you?" His dark gaze assessed her as if he were cataloguing and memorizing her every reaction. "A quiet room where we could be alone?"

His suggestion ruffled down her spine in an anxious flutter and settled down so low in her soul that it was indecent. Never in the last six months had a man's invitation left her like this—like she wanted to follow him.

More than flirtation lay hidden within his words. He was testing her. Trying to see if she would take his bait.

This wasn't the way it worked, she scolded herself. They followed *her*. On her terms. By her rules.

"Go somewhere alone with you?" She shook her head. "Not tonight, my lord. I have other plans." Risking a glance back up into his eyes, she found they glittered like rich, dark emeralds, revealing nothing beyond their fire.

So what had she really expected to find?

"I've never been one to interfere with a lady's plans. But I must warn you, I am not the only one in your way tonight."

She stopped short, nearly tripping over her fashionably high-heeled shoes. He knew who she was and why she was here. And he knew Lyle and Rostland were also after her. If he knew that much about her, did he also know her identity?

Though she'd weighed the risks of coming out so openly in this crowded ballroom, she'd bet her luck would hold through one more evening.

Neither Lyle, nor Rostland, nor the man at her side could stop her. Not this night, her last as the Brazen Angel.

With the money she anticipated taking from her mark, she would be able to complete her work in France and let the mysterious lady fade into nothing more than the idle memory of foolish men.

But first she needed to get rid of the nuisance Lord Trahern was quickly becoming.

And she knew just how to dispose of unwanted suitors— her dear *maman* had taught both of her daughters the trick as they arrived at the French court. With so many secluded corners in Versailles, a young girl needed to know a thing or two about deterring a man's unwanted attentions. She smiled to herself.

Heartless in her desperation to separate herself from her captor, she brought the thick heel of her shoe down on top of Lord Trahern's boot with every bit of weight and strength she could muster.

He let out a loud curse. Even better, he let go of her arm.

She didn't hesitate, cutting into the astonished crowd without as much as a glance back. "A rat," she howled. "There's a rat loose."

Pandemonium broke out. Men and women alike panicked and scattered in every direction.

Picking up her skirts, she dashed through an opening.

As if fortune smiled down at her, Lord Delaney nearly ran her over. Her mark.

But she also knew enough of Lord Trahern's reputation to realize he wouldn't give up easily. She moved on Lord Delaney without her usual setup.

"Please, my lord. Can you help me?" she begged. "I'm in need of assistance." She didn't wait for an answer, instead catching the pimple-faced lord by the arm and pulling him toward the front door. The man coughed and choked, but he didn't protest.

He went right along with her.

They always did.

Glancing back over her shoulder, she realized she hadn't underestimated Lord Trahern—the man still pursued her.

His tall form and unadorned black hair cut a distinct figure against the white powdered wigs and ornate hats of the other guests. Though he was having a difficult time getting through the chaos, she knew he wouldn't let that deter him.

Worst of all, a look of pure determination set his jaw and eyebrows into straight, hard lines.

Tugging her target's arm even harder, she guessed she probably had no more than a couple of minutes before Lord Trahern caught up with them. Escape into the dark streets of London, where it would be impossible to find them, was her only hope.

The young lord wheezed to a stop. "This pace, my lady. Can't we rest for a moment?" Lord Delaney's round eyes looked about to pop out of his florid face, and his breath heaved in and out in big, steamy clouds.

So much for saving her best lines for later, she realized.

"But my lord, I've heard it rumored that you—" Unable to stomach the remainder of her enticement out loud, she leaned over and whispered it into his ear. She finished her words with a heavy, dramatic sigh. "I do so hate to be kept waiting."

The young lord groaned, his face turning an even brighter shade of mottled red, his eyes glazing over.

No, I can't wait much longer, she thought, for your hidden treasure trove of gems and gold. She tugged him down the front steps and nearly pushed him into the carriage-clogged street. "Which one is yours?" she demanded.

Before her lust-addled victim could find his powers of speech, a deep voice called out from the top of the steps. "Are you leaving so soon, my lady?"

Trahern.

She glanced over her shoulder and realized she'd over-played her hand this time. Lanterns at either side of the door illuminated his dark figure. He loomed above her like the Devil himself. While she didn't believe for a minute he could be in league with the likes of Lyle and Rostland, his dangerous reputation was enough to send her catlike senses out in points.

Taking one last wistful look at Delaney, a man whose secreted trove of gems could have ended her charade forever, she realized the best she could hope for tonight was to escape Trahern.

"I promise we will meet again, my love," she whispered to the wealthy, though perverted, lord. Blowing him a kiss, she dove between two carriages, the horses prancing nervously in their braces.

"But you can't leave me now. . . . I'm ready," Delaney whined.

Weaving between carriages, she ran. Behind her the sound of hard-booted footsteps chased her onward.

Her wide-paneled skirts and high heels made the pace difficult, but she knew if she reached the open square at the end of the block, she'd be free. When her skirt caught on the edge of a carriage, she jerked to a stop, her fingers frantically tearing the fabric.

Glancing back, she saw that Trahern had stopped about six carriages back. For a moment they stood still. She could feel the tension rippling between them, binding them together in an ancient unity. As it had when she'd first glanced at him in the ballroom. Now she understood what the union between them was.

The hunter and the prey.

Even if she escaped him tonight, she knew this wouldn't be the last time they stood like this, at cross purposes, separated by more than just a few feet. The dark challenge of his eyes promised he would hunt her until he'd unmasked her.

"Wait," he said, holding out his hand. "I won't harm you. Just let me help."

"Not bloody likely," she muttered, shaking off whatever control he had over her and gathering up what remained of her skirt. She dashed past the last carriage and into the open square.

His deep voice boomed through the night like a church bell tolling the darkest hour. "You can't escape."

Let's hope you're wrong, she thought.

She stood in the middle of the street, looking left and right.

Oliver, she prayed silently, where are you?

Trahern's resolute pursuit echoed in the night with a steady and confident rhythm. At the corner he stopped. "It seems you have nowhere to go."

"Your overconfidence, my lord, is your weakness."

From down the street the thunder of hooves drew their attention. A plain dark carriage hurtled toward her as if out of control. She couldn't help herself. She grinned at the shocked expression on Trahern's face. With the carriage careening down the street it must have looked as if she were about to meet her demise.

The horses swerved at the last second and the carriage clattered to a halt.

"A pleasure to meet you, Lord Trahern," she offered with a flirtatious tip of her head and shoulders. As if on cue, the door swung open. Without any thought for appearances she dove in head first. The horses leapt forward, sending the coach lurching left and right, as the driver shouted at the animals.

A pair of firm hands hauled her forward, while behind her, Lord Trahern's curse followed her unlikely escape.

Bouncing along on the floor of the carriage, it took a few seconds for her to realize she had truly escaped her adversary. While relieved, she couldn't help but feel a little disappointed that she'd had to flee from him so quickly.

"Sophia, I thought we agreed to choose only targets you could outrun."

Still lying on the hard floor, Lady Sophia Maria Julietta D'Artiers pushed the brocade of her skirt off her head so she could give her chaperon the withering stare the woman's sarcasm deserved. Considering the way her heart pounded and her throat burned, she doubted she would be able to speak.

A scowl would have to suffice.

Sophia shoved back her voluminous skirts, ripped off her wig, and hoisted herself onto the tufted seat. Their driver, Oliver, had the horses tearing along at a horrible pace, their hooves pounding against the cobblestones. Clinging to a strap, she glared at Emma Langston, her hired companion.

"My, my." Emma shook her head. "Such an awful face. No wonder Lord Delaney chased you off like that. Oliver was quite clear in his information. Lord Delaney likes a woman who—"

She held up her hand to stave off the description. "There wasn't anything wrong with Oliver's information. Besides, that wasn't Lord Delaney."

"Well, I should hope not. We paid good money for that information," Emma complained as she peered out the window, trying to gauge if they had truly made their escape. "So who was that handsome rogue? He looked a fine sight richer to pinch than Lord Delaney."

Yanking off her gloves, Sophia tossed them atop her discarded wig. "We will do no such thing. I want nothing to do with that man."

"What's wrong with him? He looked rich enough."

"He's as rich as Midas." She took a deep breath and tried

to push away the last lingering sensations of his touch on her arm and the way his rakish gaze left her weak in the knees.

"So, you've changed plans before. Why not tonight? What was so different about him?"

"I didn't think it would be all that wise to drug and rob my betrothed. At least not before our wedding night."

CHAPTER
2

"Come in, my good fellow. Come in," Lord Dryden said in his usual gruff tones, ushering Giles into his private office at the Foreign Ministry. Dryden, never one for fashion, wore a plain black coat and trim, serviceable breeches. No wig for the gentleman, he wore his white hair brushed back and tied with a black ribbon. His boots glowed with a military sheen.

Where the nut-colored eyes behind Dryden's gold-rimmed spectacles usually burned with unrivaled intensity, Giles noticed at once a strange solemnity there that left the older man's gaze tired and sad. Before he could comment, the older man nodded curtly to a young assistant hovering near the windows. The nervous fellow nearly collided with Giles in his effort to escape the room.

Giles knew how he felt. When he'd first started working for Dryden at the age of sixteen, he blundered about much the same way in the man's presence. Fifteen years of experience had lessened the effect of Dryden's intimidating posture. Now Giles looked upon the older man as his mentor, a good friend, and a challenging foe in their occasional chess matches.

"I came as soon as I got your message." Giles stood patiently next to the seat Dryden offered. Pushing his hand in his jacket pocket, he fingered the scrap of fabric he'd recovered from the carriage wheel just hours ago. He traced the pattern of silver embroidery, while in his mind he tried to remember where he had seen the strange design before—a swan encircled by a *fleur-de-lis*.

He'd already decided to spend the day visiting fashionable modiste shops until he found a seamstress who recognized the unusual remnant.

Taking the seat Dryden offered, he brushed the dirt and lint off his evening clothes. Having spent most of the night with Monty searching for the Brazen Angel's carriage, he knew he probably looked less than respectable for this early-morning call. Was it his fault Lord Dryden's invitation—summons, rather—arrived about the same time he'd come home, near dawn? The older man had even sent his carriage to speed Giles's journey to the Foreign Office's building near Westminster.

"I know it's rather early," Dryden said, clearing his throat and settling down behind his cluttered desk. Though the chill fog of the Thames had yet to burn away, it appeared Dryden had been working for hours. "I take it you haven't been keeping regular hours since you decided to come home."

"I don't remember my taking up residence in London as strictly my decision." Giles dared what few men would, contradicting Lord Dryden. "In fact, I remember the words 'You'll stay put and get married if I have to order guards stationed at either side of you.' "

"Yes, well, I want to talk to you about that." The man shuffled his papers and cleared his throat several times. "Is your marriage still set for the twenty-ninth of next month?"

Giles nodded. He knew better than to ask how his superior knew the date of his upcoming nuptials.

"Good. I promised your father I would see you wed, and by all that's holy, I will."

In truth Giles had been doing his best to ignore Lady Dearsley's planning until the last possible moment. If he had to get married to return to the Service, so be it. In his heart he understood why his father had extracted the strange vow from Dryden. After fourteen generations of Traherns, Giles's father feared his stubborn son would be the last if he did not marry and sire an heir.

The call of service was too strong to keep a Trahern man at home for long, but he had one duty higher than that to his King: to see the family line continued. This, Giles acknowledged, must be done, though he disagreed with his father's methods.

"Have you met Lady Sophia yet?" Dryden asked, his bushy eyebrows raised in a fatherly gesture.

Giles twisted in his seat. How could he explain his lack of interest in his bride? And truly, did his inspection matter? "No, I haven't had the pleasure."

Why did everyone care whether or not he had met the lady? They were to be wed, nothing more. Giles understood it was to be a union of convenience between two parties to perpetuate the necessary family lineage. That type of marriage was as much a Trahern tradition as was their call to the Foreign Service.

"Nice girl. Good bloodlines. Sad situation with her family in France and all, but her English blood will keep her steady. Your father chose well."

"So I've been told." He had been more than a little surprised by his father's choice: Though noble, the girl's father was French. There had also been a huge scandal when her mother left her English betrothed to elope with the foreign rascal thirty years earlier. Her relations had been hard-pressed to forgive their errant daughter, but her husband's prestige with the French crown and rumored piles of gold and rich properties finally wore down their frayed sensibilities.

"Don't listen to the wags and their disappointment in Lady Sophia," Dryden told him, with a solid shake of his finger. "Her mother's grace and beauty were unrivaled, and just see where that left her. I've always said common sense and a good head for household accounts are worth more than looks. Take Lady Dryden, for example."

The situation was worse than Giles had imagined. Before it had mattered little to him what his wife looked like, just so she inspired enough of a response in him to perform his family duties. Now it was different.

And it had all changed last night.

Images of a silver-shrouded woman racing through the darkness flashed in his mind—an anticing smile daring him to catch her, trim ankles, and an even more daring flash of legs as she dashed between the carriages. A woman who fevered his imagination and challenged his mind.

What would it be like to share his life with such a wild, elusive creature?

His fingers itched over the fabric in his pocket. The scent of perfume clung to the threads, a hint of floral and something else. Something that dared his lungs to breathe deeply and his body to move closer. Like a sensual trap. Like the lady herself.

Monty hadn't lied when he said the Brazen Angel would capture his imagination . . . and his desires.

But one didn't marry a brazen woman.

No, one married common sense.

He looked up and realized Dryden was studying him quietly, his hands folded calmly in front of him on the assorted papers scattered across his wide desk.

Giles felt a tinge of embarrassment at being caught daydreaming like a school lad. "My lord," he began, shifting in the high-backed narrow chair more suited for an interrogation. "I assume you didn't call me here to discuss my marital state. Your note alluded to a problem of some urgency."

Dryden cleared his throat again and pulled out a tattered dispatch from a drawer. "How right you are. There's new trouble in Paris . . ." he began, handing the paper over.

The words sent Giles's toes curling in his boots, yearning for the opportunity to tread the dangerous coves and alleys of Paris again. Excitement started to course through his veins, until the lines on the paper chilled his blood.

Giles looked up, wondering if he could force his mouth to speak around the lump in his throat or the dryness of his lips.

"Webb?" he managed.

"Yes, Webb." Dryden's voice held the same trembling reluctance to say the name, as if speaking it out loud would only serve to confirm the horrible truth.

For a time the two men sat in silence, each dealing with their own upheaval of raw emotions.

Giles glanced back down at the coded words in the message. They told of a city in chaos. Grim descriptions filled the page of how the terror of Madame Guillotine's embrace now stretched out to every layer of the city.

And somehow, she'd found Webb.

Lord Dryden shook his head, reached for the dispatch, and set it aside. Removing his spectacles, he slowly cleaned the lenses with a white cloth.

"Are you sure it was Webb?" Giles finally asked.

"You saw what it said. He was seen riding in a tumbril along the Rue St. Honoré. There is no mistake."

"Send someone to verify it. To make contact with our other operatives. Surely, someone knows the truth."

"I haven't anyone to send." Dryden settled his eyeglasses back onto his nose. "We've lost four agents in the last three months. With that damned Revolution and now the war, the situation is very grave." The old man looked toward the window, obviously unwilling to meet Giles's gaze. The shoulders Giles had always thought so rock solid slumped with defeat.

Grief tore at Giles. Webb, though young, had not been inexperienced. In fact, he rivaled Giles in his skill and cunning.

After all, he had been Dryden's son.

"He's gone," the man said, as if to no one in particular, as if he were practicing the words. "Now I must tell his mother and sisters. I doubt they will ever forgive me."

"I'm so sorry, sir." The words were inadequate, but he didn't know what else to say. Dryden, his horde of children, and his overly sensible wife had been a substitute family for Giles throughout the years his own father worked for the Service. With his mother long dead, he'd gone to Dryden Manor rather than remain at his own empty estates over school holidays. It had been there that he'd met Webb. Though younger by nearly ten years, the lad always tagged after Giles, more nuisance than anything, always wanting to be included in the rough-and-tumble games they found with the local lads and stable hands.

Looking back, Giles realized that during those years he and the other older boys spent trying to hide from the younger boy, Webb had learned the persistent skills of a master spy.

It had been no surprise to anyone that Webb Dryden stubbornly followed his father and Giles into the Service.

And now it had killed him.

"Someone of Webb's skill doesn't get caught, not unless he's been——" Giles couldn't say the final word. *Betrayed.* Instead, he looked up at Dryden. "Send me."

"I intend to."

Giles was shocked by his superior's quick agreement.

"There's more," Dryden said, with a controlled voice.

Giles knew that serious tone. It meant it was time for the real business at hand.

"There is a woman in Paris called *La Devinette*. Have you heard of her?" Dryden asked nonchalantly.

Giles nodded vaguely. There were so many rising and falling factions in the rapidly changing Paris political scene that it was hard to keep them all straight. Even so, La Devinette stood out. Vociferous in her loyalty to the Revolution, she was something of a popular heroine to the ragged masses of Paris. She'd arrived out of obscurity to carve her name on the roll call of change.

"The last message I had from Webb was that he had discovered La Devinette's identity."

Giles leaned forward. "Was he sure?"

Dryden sat back in his seat. "Yes. Webb was convinced she could be used to assist us."

To other men, the notion would have left them stunned, but for Giles it made sense. Leave it to the ever-charming Webb to turn France's most loyal daughter into a double agent.

"How so?"

"Because Webb learned she's been traveling quite often between London and Paris under a different guise."

Giles's gaze snapped up as the mysterious pieces fell into place before his eyes. "The Brazen Angel." His fingers curled around the fabric in his hand, crushing it in his anger at her devious deception.

"My thoughts exactly." Dryden's eyes narrowed. "So it is true you've been making inquiries?"

Giles nodded.

"Good. You'll need all the information you've gathered." The older man sorted through his desk drawer again. "Here's something you might find interesting," he said, pulling out a pouch.

When he turned the bag over, jewels spilled onto the desk. Giles reached out and picked up a large emerald brooch to examine.

"That's been in the Rostland family for nearly two centuries," Dryden commented. "It was sold to a London dealer. The ring, that was discovered in Paris several weeks later."

"But how did——" Giles began.

"Webb sent it to me. Before——" Dryden examined the ring for a moment before tossing it back on his desk. "It was fenced at the shop of a Swiss jeweler on the Ile de la Cité."

"So you're convinced——"

Dryden waved off any further supposition. "That scandalous woman has all these addlepated idiots running around in a lather. But the truth is, she's stolen enough money to ransom half the crowned princes of Europe. I don't like it." He gathered the remaining pieces of the Rostland jewels back into the small pouch. "Good English gold going out for bad. I want to know why this booty is being taken to France." He paused, his wide jaw set with iron firmness. "If she betrayed my son for that damned Revolution, I want her captured and brought to justice."

"This might take more than a month." Giles's mind raced with plans. He'd take his own ship across the Channel. In four days, with any luck, he could be in Paris. "You'll have to explain my disappearance to my fiancée and her aunt. I'm rather sorry about all the work they've gone to for the wedding."

"Bah! Get that look of false concern for Lady Sophia off your face. I have no intention of going against my word to your father. I've taken the liberty of obtaining a special license. You'll be wed tonight. And sail on the tide at dawn."

"YOUR AUNT IS up to something. Did you see the way she practically smiled at breakfast?" A pipe clutched between her teeth, Emma continued refolding the items

41

Sophia haphazardly tossed toward the open trunk. Smoke curled around her black hair.

A tall, thin woman, Emma Langston never wore anything but the black weeds of a widow. Her dark hair and even darker eyes gave her a strict, almost puritanical appearance. It was just those straight-laced looks that had persuaded Sophia's three aunts, who shared the guardianship of their niece, to give Emma the job as Sophia's companion.

Some women do not need references, Lady Dearsley had declared in her always decisive manner. *You can see their character in the way they hold their head.*

Emma's posture was perfect. Her past was not.

But what her aunts didn't know, Sophia realized, didn't hurt them. And in the last few months her companion's less than proper past had come in very handy. Sophia found it complemented her own troubled history quite nicely.

They were quite a pair, hidden outcasts in a society that demanded virtue and modesty of its ladies.

"Are you listening to me?" Emma repeated. "Lady Effie is on to us."

Standing in the chaos of their packing, Sophia paused for a second, riding boots in one hand and dancing slippers in the other. "She's up to something, I'll agree with you there." The riding boots went into the valise next to the trunk, the slippers back into the dressing room. "But what does it matter? By this time tomorrow we will be far removed from her and her wretched wedding plans." She crossed the room and began fishing around in the tall armoire for another load of clothes.

Her rooms in her aunt's house were spacious and bright, the late-September sun pouring the last warm light of summer through the windowpanes. A fireplace took up one end of the room, while a delicately carved table and chairs sat near the windows at the other end.

Next to the chairs waited long-neglected baskets of needlework and threads. Sophia and Emma found little time for the refined accomplishments of ladies.

Returning with an armful of gowns, Sophia dumped the costly dresses into the trunk.

"I don't see how you will do it." Emma closed the lid with a firm thump. "What excuse will you give her?"

"I'll use a combination." Sophia stuffed a pair of rough-made breeches and a white shirt into the valise. "We'll tell her I received a note from Auntie Mellie this morning, and the poor dear is failing again. In her condition I would be terribly remiss if I didn't return to the country without delay. Then when Auntie Effie protests, I'll add that my heart is having a terrible time adjusting to the rigors of city life." Sophia fell back into her chair, her hand resting on her breast. She sighed loudly and patted her brow.

Emma smirked and threw a pair of thick, practical socks at her. "Considering what I saw of Lord Trahern last night, you'll need all the rest you can get. Now there is a man worth marrying."

"Don't remind me of what I'll be losing." She'd spent most of the night wishing the Parkers' ball could have been different. "Just once I'd like to spend a night like every other girl."

"You aren't like the rest of those dim-witted, simpering misses." Emma stopped her packing for a moment. "And you wouldn't want to be."

"Perhaps." Sophia wasn't so convinced. "I just wish I hadn't seen him last night."

"Him? I take it you mean Lord Trahern. Rather inconvenient running into your fiancé as you are trying to rob another man."

"Inconvenient?" Sophia sputtered. "He could have unmasked me. I would have been discovered."

Emma tipped her head and stared at her. "You've known that since you started. Why was last night any different?"

"It just was." Sophia turned her back to her astute companion. She was risking so much as the Brazen Angel, and last night as she stood next to Lord Trahern she realized just how much the discovery of her identity would mean. She'd never thought beyond her immediate plans to her own future. To what it would mean to be loved, to be married, to share his bed—all of which would be lost if anyone discovered who the Brazen Angel truly was. And until she'd seen Lord Trahern she'd never considered their impending marriage anything other than something to be avoided at all costs. Now it held a tantalizing appeal, especially the sharing-his-bed part.

But if the strict and honorable Lord Trahern ever found out that his impeccable reputation would be tainted by her misadventures, a vow to his father or not, he'd cry off their wedding and be gone from her life.

The Traherns, Sophia knew, held their family lineage to the highest of standards.

Emma reached over and nudged her. "Quit woolgathering. We still need to come up with a plan for dealing with your aunt."

"I told you, we'll tell her I've been summoned to York."

"So I suppose I'm required to stand close by, wring my hands, and add my own worries about your ill health?"

"You should know the routine." Sophia tossed the socks

into the valise. "You taught me. Besides, if we don't leave tonight we'll never make it to Paris in time."

Emma gathered odd items from the room and packed them into her own black leather bag. "I don't see how we'll pull this off. We haven't a third of the money necessary. Without Lord Delaney's gold, how will we be able to . . ." Her voice trailed off, and she looked anxiously at the door. Beyond the wood panel, footsteps echoed along the long corridor.

Sophia bit her lip and listened. She wouldn't put it past her aunt to spy on them. The hallway outside quieted as the steps resounded down the grand staircase. After a few seconds she nodded at Emma to continue.

Emma's voice fell to a sharp whisper. "Without that money we stand a good chance of finding ourselves dead." She chewed the pipe clenched between her teeth, closed her bag, and placed it next to the trunk. "There are always those plates you stole from Lord Lyle. We could use them and print ourselves a fortune."

"You know as well as I do that Lyle's counterfeit *assignats* would deceive only desperate widows and country fools," Sophia commented wryly. She'd been shocked to find the printing plates for the Revolutionary currency hidden in Lyle's study. Whatever an Englishman was doing manufacturing French bills, Sophia was of no mind to let him continue. She'd taken them to spite him, though she'd known they were worthless to her. She thought they may just come in handy, but for what she knew not. "We need gold, Emma, not worthless pieces of paper, and I have yet to find someone who could manufacture that from thin air."

"Then you should never have let go of Lord Delaney last night. His gold would have come in quite handy."

"Who said anything about leaving London without the Delaney fortune?" Sophia rose from her seat and walked over to a separate pile of gowns laid out on the bed. Selecting an especially frothy confection of white lace and ribbons, she held it up for Emma's keen inspection.

The woman puffed her pipe furiously, smoke billowing out around her. "I see what you mean. No one expects you to appear two nights in a row."

Waving her hands to clear the air, Sophia frowned. She opened the window and began fanning the room to clear the smell of tobacco.

"When are you going to give up that dreadful thing?" she chastised. "If Auntie Effie finds you smoking, you'll be out in the streets."

"She'll have to catch me first," Emma declared defiantly. "Besides, you should give it a try. It might take away some of that color in your cheeks. It's rather difficult to keep convincing everyone you are on the brink of death when you insist on staying in such fine form."

Sophia glanced over at the mirror, her face flushed from packing. Her hair curled down from the confines of her chignon, the chestnut strands glossy with good health. Where once Sophia had been proud to the point of vanity of her clear, fair complexion, the rich luster of her hair, and the light blush of rose at her lips and cheeks, now she found her attributes a true hindrance.

After all, it had been her looks that attracted men at the French court in droves to the irrepressible young beauty. She'd been foolish and unwise in her choices back then, choices that resulted in her being sent to live an ordered and regulated life in England with her aunts.

A knock on the door interrupted any further arguments.

"It's me, my lady. Hannah," a maid called out.

Sophia grinned as Emma scrambled over to the fireplace and furiously tapped her pipe out in the grate. She reached for her own shawl, pulled it over her head, and wrapped the ends around her shoulders.

Hannah, not waiting for a reply, boldly opened the door and started into the room.

Stepping forward, Sophia blocked the girl's view and halted her further progress into the room.

"What is it, Hannah?"

The maid tried to peer around Sophia to catch a glimpse of Emma. "My lady, your aunt wants you down in the day-room. *Alone.*" This comment was followed by a mincing sneer in Emma's direction. "Her ladyship wants you to . . ." Hannah's voice trailed off as she surveyed the packed trunks and discarded gowns.

Emma joined Sophia in the middle of the room.

The ambitious young maid eyed them both with a look of surprise. "I didn't think you knew."

"Knew what?" Emma snapped at the girl. There was no love lost between the two women.

Hannah used every opportunity she could to spy, looking for anything to report to Sophia's aunt. Sophia knew Emma considered it her personal mission to outwit the girl at every step. So far they'd been lucky.

"That you would be leaving tonight," the maid finished with a decided note of disappointment in her voice.

"I just made the decision this morning, Hannah," Sophia said cautiously. "I wasn't aware that my aunt knew." That explained the noise at the door they'd heard earlier. Hannah, up to her usual tricks. "Obviously, she's been informed. Is that why you're here? Has my lady aunt summoned me for an explanation as to this hasty departure?"

Confusion passed over the girl's face. "*You* decided to leave, my lady?"

"Yes, my aunt Mellisande sent around a note this morning. She is ill again and I must return to the country."

Hannah's face brightened. "So you don't know." The girl whirled around and practically skipped her way back to the door. Turning again, she bobbed her head. "Your lady aunt wishes to see you in the morning room, *alone* and without any delays." The girl raised her chin, a triumphant grin spreading across her round face. Confident in her position in the household as Lady Dearsley's personal maid, Hannah didn't spare her words. "Oh, Lord Trahern is here as well. You're leaving all right, but not to visit sick relations. He's here for your wedding. It seems you are to be married tonight."

GILES SAT ON a straight-backed chair on the far side of Lady Dearsley's morning room and wondered if this was how the condemned felt before their executioner. He would have preferred a black-hooded bloke to the lady's bright yellow day dress and feathered fan.

The morning room, a wide, airy space, had been quickly converted to a dark, vast tomb as Lady Dearsley ordered the heavy velvet curtains drawn across the sparkling windows before Lady Sophia arrived.

"The sunlight bothers her eyes so," the lady confided.

Then, like a deceitful horse trader, the crafty lady positioned him on the far side of the room. Giles decided his future relation obviously had little faith in her niece's attri-

butes if she felt the necessity to go to such outrageous
lengths to conceal the girl.

"This is a moment for which I have waited far too long,"
Lady Dearsley cooed as she poured him a refreshment.

To Giles's right, Lord Dryden smiled grimly at the lady's
words. The older man had insisted on accompanying Giles
on this prenuptial visit.

"When my dear sister proposed this union," Lady Dearsley
commented, "I wasn't sure of the connection, but Lord
Dryden assures me your family is well-respected by His
Highness, though I can't see how."

Long used to the deceptive words of informants in the
field and the honeyed tongues of London's aristocracy, Lady
Dearsley's bluntness took Giles by surprise. In the twenty
minutes since his arrival the woman had effectively insulted
his family's name at least three times, slandered half his
friends and acquaintances, and reminded him a dozen times
more as to the delicate nature of her niece's health.

Just then the door to the dayroom opened and the soft
steps of a woman whispered the arrival of his intended.
Lord Dryden rose, smiling at him to do the same. Giles followed suit, rising stiffly from his chair, suddenly unwilling
to face the woman who would be sharing his bed tonight.

"Sophia, finally. Whatever took you so long? I told
Hannah to fetch you immediately." Lady Dearsley nearly
ran Giles over as she hustled past him. "Lord Trahern, it
is my pleasure to present my dear niece, Lady Sophia
D'Artiers."

Giles turned around slowly. He still clung to the hope
that Lady Dearsley's dire warnings as to his bride's frail
condition were nothing more than the nervous tidings of an
overprotective relative.

It didn't take but a glance to see his hopes thoroughly trounced as if caught under the hooves of an entire unit of cavalry.

What meager light did filter into the room did little to favor his intended.

A white lace hood covered her hair. The dark strands escaping the lace confines hung in limp clumps to her thin, hunched shoulders. Her gown, an oversized orange-striped day dress, heightened the already yellowish tint of ill health on her face. Her affliction had taken much from her figure, for her dress enveloped her slight frame, giving no detectable sign of curves beneath. Dark circles lined her eyes, whose sharp blue color peered out in an almost ethereal light.

The unusual color struck him immediately. But any comparison to the gaze that had captivated him the night before stopped there.

As if on cue she brought a starkly white handkerchief to her colorless lips. Her long, full lashes fluttered shut while racking coughs shook her shoulders. The fringe on her shawl shuddered violently.

He knew good manners dictated he cross the room and greet his intended, but he just couldn't bring himself to close the distance between them.

When the coughing subsided, Sophia dipped into a polite curtsy. "Lord Trahern, a pleasure to meet you."

For a moment her voice stopped him. Hints of a musical French accent tinged her words.

A pleasure to meet you.

The same words echoed from the night before, but hardly from the same lips.

He shook his head and chastised himself for even making such an unlikely comparison. Mere coincidence and wishful thinking, he realized. Moving forward, he caught her hand and gently brought it to his lips.

Any lingering similarities quickly faded, as his fingers curled around hers. The icy dampness of her skin, like death's own clasp, chilled him to the bone. There was no doubt his bride-to-be was in ill health.

Whatever had his father been thinking to betroth him to this woman? She didn't look as if she would survive the walk back to her room, let alone the rigors of childbirth.

Before he could study her more closely she turned away and started to cough anew. Lady Dearsley moved between them, pounding her niece none-too-gently on the back.

"Please, Sophia," her aunt whispered loudly. "Do control that horrid racket. 'Tis unseemly." She steered her niece to the far sofa.

Lady Dearsley filled the remaining space on the narrow chaise, so Giles settled onto his well-placed and distant chair across the room.

"I must apologize, my lady," he began, having to nearly shout across the wide expanse. "You see, my business interests have made it impossible for me to stay in London, and I doubt I will be back before the date of our wedding. I have asked your aunt to allow us to be wed tonight so there will be no further delays."

Her features revealed nothing, he realized, not relief, not disappointment, not happiness. He'd seen experienced men in the field with less skills of concealment. What had he hoped to find? Reluctance? An unwillingness to marry? Anything to stop this farce from proceeding.

"If this is your wish, my lord." She coughed delicately. "Did you say you will be leaving *immediately* after the ceremony?"

The question stopped him. It would be too easy to write her inquiry off as a symptom of virginal worries, but there was something calculating about the lady's tone.

What was he supposed to say in front of everyone?

I'm sorry, my lady, but, yes, I will be taking you to my bed tonight. There I hope to get you with child so I'll never have to visit it again.

"I sail on the morning tide," Giles replied instead.

Her lashes fluttered. She acknowledged his statement with a small nod. "I understand. *Afterward,*" she commented as if it was the most distasteful thought she had ever encountered, "I would prefer to retire to my aunt Celia's home in Bath. I have a fondness for taking the waters there, and with you away it would not *inconvenience* you."

Giles shifted in his seat. "Certainly. If that is your wish."

Lord Dryden coughed and patted his jacket pocket.

Giles reached into his own jacket and pulled out a small box. It had been the older man's suggestion to stop at a jeweler on the way to Lady Dearsley's house.

"I have been meaning to send this over to you," he lied as he handed the box to the footman, who stepped forward to bear the gift across the carpeted wasteland to Sophia. "A small token of my affection."

He watched as her gaze fell demurely to the gift in her hands. As she opened the box he could see her eyes widen with awe as she beheld the diamond and sapphire necklace within.

"It's stunning," she whispered. Slowly she pulled it out and held it up for her aunt to see.

He watched with amusement as his bride-to-be turned his gift back and forth, allowing the gems to catch the light in a manner more befitting a mistress assessing the future worth of a lover's token. When she glanced up and caught him watching her, she stopped, the necklace slipping through her fingers to her lap. She reached for her handkerchief, drawing it to her lips, pulling up the white barrier of her illness.

"Oh my dear! This is entirely wrong!" Lady Dearsley jumped up from her seat. "This is your wedding day, Sophia." She pointed at Giles. "Get out of my house at once." She caught him by the arm and hauled him to his feet. "You mustn't see your bride before the ceremony. Get out, get out immediately."

He found himself stumbling toward the salon door before he could stop Lady Dearsley's forward momentum. He looked back and found his bride smiling to herself. It was a private moment, one she obviously hadn't expected him to see. She was laughing over some secret joke as she once again examined her wedding necklace. The sparkling sapphires matched her eyes, bright and glowing with fire.

To his trained gaze it seemed her posture had improved, as had her sickly pallor. For a moment something bright and alive claimed Lady Sophia.

She looked almost beautiful.

No one that ill, he thought, should look that alive. Or, strangely enough, that cunning.

He pulled himself out of Lady Dearsley's grasp and started back toward his intended.

Even as he blinked, trying to clear his vision, trying to reconcile in his mind this miraculous change in Sophia, she looked up at him. If she was startled it showed for only a second, then the lights and fire were quickly doused as she turned away and began to cough.

No, it couldn't be, he realized. Perhaps it was the jeweled blue eyes of another he was hoping to see—eyes that had teased him last night and dared him to follow her.

"I said you were to leave," Lady Dearsley complained. "This is bad luck."

He freed himself from the older woman's iron grip, no easy task, and returned to his bride's side. "I only wanted to extend my gratitude to Lady Sophia for being so understanding about this abrupt change of plans."

"Extend those gratitudes later, my lord," Lady Dearsley told him from the door.

"Until tonight, Lady Sophia," he said, bowing low over her hand. This time her fingers felt decidedly warmer, having lost most of their dampness. Her soft skin caressed his, and beneath his fingers her pulse beat solidly.

"I'm so sorry," she whispered, freeing her hand from his grasp and still unwilling to look him in the eye. "I know how much this means to you, and I don't want to disappoint you. I just hope that someday you'll understand."

Her strange words bewildered Giles just enough to allow Lady Dearsley success in finally routing him from the room.

I just hope that someday you'll understand.

Her odd confession haunted Giles the remainder of the day as he went about the tasks of planning his new mission.

Understand what?

An obvious answer, of course, was she hoped he didn't find her lacking in the marital sense, but the idea seemed too simple, even from such an obviously sheltered and inexperienced girl like Sophia. And Giles never trusted easy solutions.

No, there was something more to her apologetic statement, he reasoned. Despite the multitude of problems on his mind—making his travel arrangements to Paris, the heartbreaking news of Webb—the answer to her conundrum continued to beleaguer him, its solution dangling elusively somewhere just out of his reach.

Her odd words clung to his memory more intensely than any image of her face or features.

Not until he arrived for his wedding did he understand why his frail little bride had made her odd declaration.

She'd done her best to prepare him for the inevitable.

CHAPTER
3

"**S**EEMS THEY'VE turned out the house for your arrival, my good man," Monty commented as Giles's carriage stopped in front of Lady Dearsley's town house.

Monty wasn't far off, Giles thought. Every candle in the house blazed, light pouring into the street. From window to window servants scurried about inside. The entire house appeared in a state of upheaval.

The Duke followed Giles in climbing out. "With all this light there'll be no hiding the bride," his friend commented. "I'm sure she's not so bad, though she doesn't have half the qualities *I* would require. No snap to her, too quiet by half an ear, and no style. Down at the club they are claiming that you'll cry off before the night's over." Straightening his puce jacket and adjusting his thick woolen wig, he did his best to appear the noble duke. "I placed my money on the fact, so don't disappoint me."

Giles shot a black look over his shoulder at the shorter man, not sure that he appreciated Monty's critique of Lady Sophia.

Hell, he'd be hard-pressed to describe his future wife any other way himself after this morning's encounter.

But still, he didn't like the notion of his future wife being the subject of wagers. She was, after all, going to be the next Marchioness of Trahern.

Monty snorted. "Listen, if you had found her yourself I would expect nothing less than a bride of the first water. But need I remind you, all of London knows your father picked this little minx. And he selected her because she was sensible and solid." The Duke shuddered. "Can't imagine what my father would have chosen. Good thing he went to his reward when I was only sixteen and third in line for his titles. You should have seen the harridan he picked out for my elder brother. No surprise he died without an heir. And then with Harry's accident and the title mine, I've ended up free to choose my own perfect duchess."

"And when will that be?" Giles prodded as they made their way slowly up the front steps of the Dearsley town house. Since Monty had inherited his unlikely title through his brothers' misfortunes, it seemed they shared one thing in common: keeping the family lineage secure.

Monty came to a halt. "As a matter of fact I could very

well have found my perfect duchess." He patted his jacket pocket. "And once we capture her I'll propose."

Giles nearly choked. "You intend to marry the Brazen Angel?"

Sticking his pug nose in the air, Monty paraded past a stunned Giles. "I do indeed. I tallied up her qualifications this afternoon and found she is nearly a perfect match. Besides, one of us had to have a wife worth looking at."

Before Giles could find the words to respond, the front door was flung open.

"There you are, you devil," Lady Dearsley burst out, her fat, beringed finger pointing at him. She bounded down the stairs with the tenacious speed of a runaway bull. "What did you say to her?"

"Say to whom?" Giles resisted the urge to back up. He'd faced many dangers in his career—knife-wielding assassins, duels—but never had he come so close to being unnerved.

"To whom, he says. As if he didn't know," the lady scoffed at a plump young maid hovering just inside the doorway. "Do you hear that, Hannah? He drives my niece to a desperate end, then acts the innocent." Lady Dearsley's finger was prodding him in the chest. "You are a cruel and wicked man."

A desperate end? Giles looked up at the lit windows and servants hovering in curious knots near the curtains. "Lady Sophia? Is she all right?"

"All right?" Lady Dearsley waved and fluttered her yellow painted fan. As if on cue the maid she'd called Hannah rushed down the stairs and took her mistress's arm. After a few moments of the steadying support of her servant, the older lady recovered enough of her composure to continue her tirade. "My poor niece is probably sick and dying in some drafty carriage, or worse, the victim of some heinous crime. And it is all your fault. Whatever you said to her this afternoon frightened her poor delicate nature to the point of desperation." This time the fan smacked down sharply on his shoulder.

"There, there, my lady." Monty stepped to the forefront. "Are you telling us that Trahern's dear bride is not here?"

"Not here? Listen to these fools, Hannah. Haven't they heard a word I've been saying? Do you think I'd be in this state if my poor dear were upstairs awaiting her wifely trials?" She swung her full attention back to Giles. "After all my admonitions, after all my warnings. No, you vile man, you went ahead and terrified her. Lady Sophia not here?" The woman took a deep breath, the plumes in her hair undulating with the exertion. "Not here. That's exactly what I've been saying for the last five minutes. Sophia packed her bags and fled! There will be no wedding tonight."

For the next half hour they tried with little success to elicit details from the agitated Lady Dearsley about her niece's disappearance. When Lord Dryden arrived, having been invited to toast the happy couple, the lady calmed enough to attempt a clearer version of the facts.

"I've told you and told you, Sophia, that horrid Mrs. Langston of hers, and their driver are gone." Lady Dearsley took another large sip of her sherry.

"Mrs. Langston?" he asked.

"Sophia's paid companion. My sisters insisted we hire her. Arrogant one, that woman. I never trusted her references, not once."

Giles ignored the slight about the paid companion. "Could she have gone to a friend's house here in town?"

Setting her drink set aside, Lady Dearsley retrieved her handkerchief, letting the linen square flutter about nervously. "Sophia has no friends. She is far too delicate for such frivolous activities."

Lord Dryden leaned forward in his seat. "Then where, my dear lady, do you think your niece went?"

"I can only guess she's gone to Celia's."

Giles looked to Dryden for an explanation.

"The Countess of Larkhall," the man whispered.

"My elder sister, Lord Trahern," Lady Dearsley sniffed.

Giles couldn't believe the kindly Countess could be in any way related to Lady Dearsley. His country house, Byrnewood, adjoined the Larkhall estates in Bath. Though he hadn't seen the Countess in years, she held a dear place in his heart for having been kind to him when he was but a lad of six and his mother had died unexpectedly of a fever.

"If you'd taken any time to investigate our family you would have realized the connection. I have three sisters: Celia, Sophia's dear mother, Joceline, and Mellisande." She turned from Giles to Monty, who sat wedged in next to her on the small couch. "My sister Celia prefers Bath to London. Whatever for I've never been able to fathom. It is terribly dull out there, but Sophia is always pestering me to let her go visit Celia in Bath. I think it is why she is always so ill. She hasn't learned how to live in London. And when she isn't at Celia's . . . she goes elsewhere."

Lord Dryden coughed politely. "Do you think it's possible she's gone north?"

"It doesn't surprise me you would think of *her*, Lord Dryden." Lady Dearsley reached for her glass. "You've always had a fancy for my younger sister." She shook her head. "Good thing Mellisande threw you off and married the old Duke. Look at where it landed that poor man. Dead in a year. But Caryll's misfortune gave that mousy Georgeanne Radcliffe enough time to marry you, well before Mellie got a chance to get her claws hooked back into you."

"Your sister is the Duchess of Caryll?" Monty asked.

Lady Dearsley nodded curtly, a frown puckering her wrinkled mouth. It was obvious even the mention of her younger sister was distasteful. "Yes, she is. And to answer your question, Lord Dryden, yes, it is possible Sophia went north. She has quite an affection for my sister, as misplaced as it is. It's no wonder she pulled this ruinous stunt. I can see Mellinsande's influence all over it."

Even Giles, without his experience in the rumors and habits of the London ton, knew of the Duchess of Caryll. He wondered why he hadn't made the connection before. Mellisande Ramsey, with her odd French-tinged name and famed beauty, still left every man over fifty speaking in awed, hushed tones at the very mention of her.

To this day she was considered the reigning beauty of London, though she hadn't left her York estates in nearly fifteen years.

Lady Dearsley rose to her feet, a little unsteadily after her four glasses of sherry. She toddled over to where Giles now stood. "I don't see what all this talk is accomplishing. You must find Sophia."

Giles considered his chances of catching and holding the large lady if she teetered off her high heels.

In spite of his overwhelming relief at the delay in his marriage, he felt slightly ill at ease. Not used to having his composure ruffled, especially by some slip of a girl, Giles didn't quite know what to do for the first time in his life.

That in itself left him feeling tight-chested.

Duty dictated he go after his betrothed and drag her back to face the parson—especially since she had no male relatives to carry out the errand.

Yet bringing Webb's betrayer to justice was worth more to Giles than the misbehavior of a spoiled, misguided chit.

"Well, Lord Trahern," Lady Dearsley puffed. "Are you or are you not going after my niece?"

"That is impossible, milady. I cannot delay my plans because your niece chose to run off."

Lady Dearsley paled, her feathers quivering as she trembled with anger. Before her hovering maid could pacify her, she erupted. "Lord Dryden, I hold you personally responsible for this fiasco. You and Celia talked me into this marriage, and now look what it has done—my poor Sophia is lost forever. . . ."

From the strained look on Dryden's face Giles knew his superior was making a painful decision—send him on to Paris to investigate Webb's death, or defer to a deathbed promise.

Giles suspected he was about to spend the night searching the roads out of London.

But Dryden's choice stunned him.

"My dear Lady Dearsley," Dryden began, "your niece's actions are most regrettable. And while I am honor-bound to see this marriage secured, it appears we have not given the young lady and Lord Trahern enough time to get acquainted."

"Acquainted? What kind of nonsense is that?" She turned her anger toward the older man. "They can get acquainted just fine once they are married. Sophia suffers from an overactive imagination. I wouldn't put it past that Mrs.

Langston, with her stories of her heroic Captain Langston, to have filled the girl's head with a load of romantic blather."

Dryden cleared his throat. "Nevertheless, the girl is well on her way either north or west, and until she arrives safely at the Caryll estates or into the warm embrace of her aunt, Lady Larkhall, there is no way we can locate her. She could have taken a number of routes or be safely hidden with an acquaintance here in town. Since your niece knows Lord Trahern is leaving on the morning tide, she will likely reappear by midday, assuming her bridegroom gone."

"Bah!" Lady Dearsley huffed. "I'll not listen to any more of your speculations. What is this world coming to when gentlemen are unwilling to retrieve a young woman from the dangers of the road? Get out of my sight, all of you."

With this final exclamation Lady Dearsley threw all three of them out of her town house, Monty blustering with apologies.

Dryden pulled Giles aside. "Don't think this lets you off the hook. The only reason I haven't got you on the road to York this very moment is because the longer this situation in Paris is unattended, the more likely we are to lose the trail. If you can't find out what happened to Webb, then you will need to find this Brazen Angel woman."

Giles glanced up at Monty, who was still offering his full repertoire of inappropriate gallantries and apologies to Lady Dearsley. "I think the Brazen Angel is still here. Here in London. At least for the moment."

"Yes, that fits Webb's theory." Dryden's brow furrowed with concentration. "You've got until the morning. If you haven't found her by then, be on that ship. If it's true she's probably looking to replenish her coffers quickly before returning to Paris. If you don't find her tonight, I want you in Paris waiting for her when she resurfaces."

The sound of Lady Dearsley's thick front door slamming shut brought Giles's attention back to the matters at hand.

"What about my bride?" Giles asked, Lady Dearsley's accusations still tolling their guilt-ridden peal in his ears.

"She's traveled between her aunts' homes with only the company of this Mrs. Langston for years. Despite Lady Dearsley's dire predictions, the girl knows what she's doing and won't take any unnecessary risks."

"Still . . ." Giles thought about the frail young woman he'd met hours earlier. Her racking coughs and translucent skin belied the hardy image Lord Dryden drew.

"Still, nothing." Dryden took him by the arm and guided him to his carriage. "I'll send Lady Dryden and the girls after her. With Webb—" The man's voice broke. He glanced away, obviously struggling to recover his composure. "It will do them all some good to have something else to worry about," he managed to finish. Without another word he walked to his own carriage, his back straight and his head held high.

Giles found Monty settled into the leather seat of his carriage. "To the Duke's house, Michaels," he instructed his driver, pulling himself into the carriage.

Neither man said much as the well-lit square outside the Dearsley town house gave way to the dark streets of London. It was well past nine now, the night plunging the alleys and byways into murky depths.

"Giles, I suppose I won't be proposing to my lady now. Wouldn't seem right for me to be married and you still a free man." Monty wiped his forehead.

Giles knew he should thank the troublesome girl. He

hadn't wanted this marriage, at least not just yet, though inevitably honor would hold him fast in keeping his father's dying wish.

"Come now," Monty chided. "We've got hours before your ship leaves on this *business* trip, so why not make a night of it?" The man stuck his short legs out in front of him.

Giles knew he could never get rid of Monty now, not without a lot of questions. Just maybe his friend might come in handy. "What would you say to looking up the Brazen Angel tonight?"

Monty perked right up. "Now, that's a capital idea. Where do you propose we start?"

Giles looked out the window gauging where they were. "Delaney lives near here, doesn't he?"

Monty looked out the carriage window. "I daresay he does. Though we won't find him home tonight. His mother is visiting in the country, and with her out of town he's been seen at every wicked club from Covent Garden to Saint James Street."

"I wouldn't be so sure." Giles opened the trapdoor and gave new instructions to Michaels. A few minutes later the Trahern carriage rolled to a stop a block from the Delaney house. The street was empty. From their vantage point they had a clear view of the house. Settling back in his seat, Giles explained his plan to Monty.

Two hours later the Duke remained unconvinced. "You say since the Angel didn't get Delaney's money last night, she'd risk her neck for it tonight?"

Giles nodded. "I suspect so."

Monty waved his hand. "That makes no sense whatsoever. You said yourself that her predictability would be her downfall. She's never appeared two night in a row. Just once a month, under the light of the full moon. What makes you think she'd change her plans now?"

"You've forgotten your Angel went home empty-handed last night. She hasn't the time to find a new victim. I think she chooses her targets very carefully. She'll come back to Delaney. If the look I saw on his face last night is any indication, she knows she'll have no trouble enticing him."

"Oh." Monty shook his head. "Poor girl, the risks she takes."

The sound of carriage wheels rolling along the cobbled street brought both of them up in their seats. A fancy gilt contraption, emblazoned with the Delaney crest, rolled to a stop in front of the large stone house.

Giles took a deep breath, his heart beating with excitement. This was the part of his business he missed, the quiet waiting for the hunt to begin, then the pounding exhilaration of the chase.

But tonight was more than that, though he wouldn't have admitted it to anyone.

His curiosity to see her again ran high. He might scoff at Monty's infatuation, but he understood his friend's reaction.

The Brazen Angel was every man's fantasy. And yet, now that he knew she could possibly be connected to Webb's death, his attraction to her grew cold.

Dammit, how could he be attracted to a woman who may have betrayed his best friend and robbed another?

Down the street Cyril Delaney leapt down from his carriage. For a moment Giles thought that perhaps he had been too sure of his intuition, that Cyril was coming home alone. But halfway to the door the lady's prey stopped and looked up and down the street to see if he was being watched.

Returning to the curb, he held out his hand to the carriage's second occupant.

The street had seemed dark until she began her descent. Her white gown, the skirt billowing out in a cloud of glowing silk, illuminated the night. The Brazen Angel looked every inch the role she'd obviously chosen for the night—an innocent young girl. Her wig imitated the look of a convent maiden, falling down her bare shoulders and back in long glorious ringlets of golden blond hair.

As if sensing some unforeseen danger, she turned and looked in their direction.

Both men reeled back in their seats, but in the safety of the darkness Giles could still see her clearly. A mask once again covered her face, concealing her features. Her lips tightened into a serious line. Tipping her head slightly, she resembled a cat considering the safety of continuing into a dark cubbyhole.

She's afraid.

Giles could see her caution, the war waging inside her. Would she dare continue inside, or bolt and run?

Cyril approached her and said something. She took his outstretched hand. When he bent to kiss her fingers, she laughed, the sound rising lightly across the street and invading the deadly serious calm inside the Trahern carriage.

The melody filled Giles's ears, tantalizing him to lean closer.

Any sign of indecision or fear melted away as she took control of the situation. She wrapped her fingers around Cyril's arm and whispered into his ear. Her words, obviously of such a persuasive nature, prodded the man to leave her behind to take the steps two at a time and shoulder open the door for her entrance. The Brazen Angel continued up the stairs, her hips swaying slightly, her head held high and proud. Like a fine, well-fed feline, she sent her prey a benign yet meaningful glance as she swept past him, a look capable of enticing a man to his doom.

Monty nearly called out as the door closed, until Giles's scathing hot glare restrained the excitable Duke down to a moderate squeak.

" 'Tis the Angel, Giles. Just like you said." Monty reached for the latch on the door. "We must stop her."

Giles stopped him. "Oh, no, we won't. We're going to sit here and wait this little drama play out."

Lights appeared in a ground-floor window.

Tapping the roof of the carriage, Giles whispered quietly, "Michaels, move us slightly closer to the house and stay alert. I'm not sure how this will work, but when it does we'll have to move fast."

Monty was less willing to listen to orders. "You cannot intend to leave her inside with him all alone?" He strained toward the door. "Everyone knows Delaney's a horrible lecher. You'd think he'd have learned a lesson from his father's example. Obviously, the scandal of having one's father die the way he did in that disgraceful brothel wasn't enough tarnish for the family name. From what I've heard the young whelp fully intends to take his family traditions to new lows. He pays top money for young girls to be——"

Giles held up his hand to stave off the lurid description. "I'll wager you a month's rents from my Chester properties that our Angel will take Cyril's money in less than an hour."

Monty sat back, his nose twitching with indecision. "And if she doesn't? If . . . if . . . that wretched Cyril . . ." The poor duke appeared unable to finish his postulation.

"If she's not out in an hour we'll go after her, pistols blazing and a detachment of the King's own regiment at our backs." Smiling, Giles leaned back in his seat.

Monty's gaze flitted from the house across the street back to meet Giles's. He crossed his arms over his chest and frowned. "You're on."

They waited for nearly an hour. Giles was starting to wonder if he'd overestimated his adversary's abilities.

But the lady didn't disappoint him.

"That's what we've been waiting for." Giles pointed toward the side of the house.

Monty's eyes squinted as he stared into the darkness.

Giles was the first to make out the ground-floor window slowly sliding open. One long leg slipped through, then the next followed. With them came the *whoosh* of white glowing skirts. Their volume took some time to push through, but when they did, the rest of the lady followed quickly.

She moved to the edge of the shadows and stopped, looking up and down the street.

It was then that Giles heard the sound of hooves and the crunching wheels of a carriage as it passed by their vantage point. He recognized it in an instant. The same plain black carriage that came to her rescue the night before.

He reached for the trapdoor immediately. "Now, Michaels. Quickly. Put us between them."

The Trahern carriage sprang forward.

Giles's muscles tensed. "Move over, Monty. Give me all the room you can."

Monty scrambled to the opposite side of the careening carriage, his face white.

They passed the surprised driver of the Angel's carriage

and came to a sudden halt in front of the woman. Giles swung open the door, leapt to the walkway, and wrapped his arm around her waist.

Before she could even utter a protest, he called out to Michaels, "Get us home, now."

Giles caught hold of the outside handle and hoisted himself and his prize inside, just as the horses found their freedom. The carriage took off, and he landed hard on the floor.

His fall, however, was cushioned by the shapely Angel, who finally found her voice.

"Get off me, you great ponderous ape."

They were face to face. The triumphant gaze now belonged to him, but her eyes, blazing with fury and fire from beneath her mask, burned through him. He started to inch back.

But not before her balled fist swung hard and efficiently, hitting him square in the jaw.

Giles sat back, rubbing his aching chin. He had never struck a lady in his life, and he wasn't about to start now, but this woman was going to learn some manners.

"Oh, no, no more of that, milady," Monty interrupted as the Angel started to wind up for another punch. He shoved his cane between the two of them, as if he were separating two squabbling schoolboys. "No one here is going to hurt you," he said, his statement aimed squarely at Giles.

Giles responded with a mumbled agreement and straightened himself up and onto his seat. He lit the inner lamp in the carriage, and its meager beam gave enough illumination to watch her every move.

She still lay in the middle of the carriage, her skirts up to her knees, the breezy fabric filling the remaining space. Everything about her was in *dishabille*.

But with Giles's trained eye he knew it hadn't been his abduction that left her wig askew and the front of her dress torn. Even in the dim light he discerned the beginnings of a bruise on her fair cheek. An ugly bright blossom peeked out from beneath the edge of her silver mask.

Stark evidence of Cyril Delaney's handiwork, of which Monty had tried to warn him.

Giles didn't dare look his friend in the eye, knowing full well the censure and blame he'd find there.

Perhaps he'd been wrong to wait, to let her go in alone. Damn that fool Delaney. What kind of man would do such a thing to a woman?

He shook off the queer feelings of regret. He had to keep remembering she was the enemy. Possibly even responsible for Webb's death.

But that still didn't quell the nagging doubt that Monty had been right. They'd let her go into the lion's den alone, a mistake on his part. While she'd survived, she hadn't escaped unscathed.

The Duke appeared to reach the same conclusions. "Oh, my dear," he choked out. "You've been hurt." He reached out to help her up onto the seat next to him.

When Giles leaned forward to assist, she shrank away from his touch. Her scathing look sent him back in his seat.

I couldn't care less what you think of me, you little minx, he thought.

"Are you all right, my dear girl?" Monty continued, fussing over her like a nursemaid, straightening her skirts, sighing over the torn lace and the ruined state of her silks.

A deep sigh escaped her pink lips. "I'm fine." She brushed her skirts out and with the movement cast off Monty's hand.

Her eyes remained downcast, as if to ward off any invasion into their dark blue depths. Still, Giles noticed she was taking a furtive inventory of everything and everyone around her and, more importantly, watching the passing scenery to determine her destination.

He pulled the cord on the shade so it dropped and blocked her view.

She looked up and directly at him—a slight nod acknowledged his small victory, but also told him he hadn't yet won the war.

As the carriage careened through the empty streets, Giles knew he should be planning his questioning, considering alternatives for his investigation if the Brazen Angel refused to cooperate with the Crown. But he found himself unable to concentrate.

Instead, his gaze wandered down to catch stray glimpses of her trim, silk-clad ankles poking out beneath the edge of her skirts. He inhaled the scent of her perfume filling the carriage with its witchery and promise. Nor could he miss the triumphant glow of her eyes behind her mask.

She was plotting her escape.

It was there, so obvious, in her eyes. They burned with something so mysterious, so intimate, he felt as if she knew him, knew him like a lover, and would use that power to outwit him.

She caught him staring at her and smiled in return. At first it was so slight he barely discerned it, but then it curved at her lips, her lashes fluttered over her eyes, her head tipped slightly. Somehow, her shoulders rolled back, her breasts pushed upward against the tattered remains of her bodice.

An open invitation for him and only him. At least that was how she made him feel.

He forgot Monty, forgot why he wanted this woman, knowing only *that* he wanted her.

Looking away, Giles ground his teeth. If only he could dismiss this woman from his thoughts as easily as his wayward bride. Of course he hoped Lady Sophia was well and safe. But she certainly didn't leave him wishing for—

The carriage came to a stop.

Monty sprang out before Giles could stop him. The Duke held out his hands to the lady as if she were a princess.

She shot a look back at Giles, her brows arched above her mask, a smug smile on her lips.

You see, her expression seemed to say, *this is how a lady is supposed to be treated.*

Regally, she began her descent from the carriage.

"I hope you will forgive us for these high-handed antics, but you are in terrible danger, my dear," Monty fussed.

She paused at the bottom of her step. Giles couldn't see past her wigs and skirts, but from Monty's tone he was positive his friend was in high form.

"I hope," she stated in sweet, innocent tones, "you will forgive me."

Before Monty could respond, she whirled around, slamming the carriage door shut on Giles. The latch jammed in his hands, but he was able to jerk aside the window flap just in time to see her put both hands on Monty's chest and shove the smaller man backward into a heap of puce and green brocade. His wig rolled off his head like a top, spinning toward the gutter.

She whirled once again, this time to grin at Giles, before she was off and running.

"Damnation," he cursed as he struggled with the handle. Furious at this turn of events, he put his shoulder into the carriage door. It sprang open, the force carrying him sprawling onto the walkway next to Monty.

Giles looked up to find his butler, Keenan, standing at the front door, his mouth wide open. The man, known for his stoic features, rarely batted an eye at even the strangest of His Lordship's coming and goings. The tall man was now stuttering for something to say.

"I think . . . I mean . . . I mean to say . . . the lady . . . she's getting away, milord." The butler pointed down the street.

"Thank you, Keenan," Giles muttered as he got to his feet. She was already halfway down the block. Within moments she would turn down a side street and disappear from sight.

Sprinting down the street, he caught her just as she was about to slip into a dark alley. She twisted and fought like a cat. An alley cat to be exact, he thought as he caught her by the waist and hoisted her over his shoulder.

"You beast," she sputtered. "Put me down or I'll scream."

"Go ahead," Giles dared her, pushing aside her skirts so he could see his way clearly back to the house. "Would you like that? For the guards to come? And what name would you use? Lady Brazen? I'm sure Lord Delaney and the others would prefer the term *thief*. Or, to be more exact, Lady-soon-to-be-hanging-from-the-nearest-gallows."

She quieted her cries down to a dull roar of vile threats.

Lights came on in the neighboring houses, doors cracking

open as cautious servants peered out to witness the evening's events. Giles ignored them all.

Perhaps he should have gone after his bride, he thought with a bit of chagrin. He doubted the soft-spoken Sophia would have done anything more unpredictable than faint at her capture. And even that she would have done quietly without attracting any untoward attention.

Up ahead Keenan had retrieved the Duke's wig and was helping Monty up the stairs and into the foyer.

"Stay put, Michaels," Giles ordered his driver. "I've got one last errand for you."

The young man nodded and took his post atop the carriage.

Stooping as he entered his house, Giles found his entire staff gathered.

"I assembled the staff," Keenan said. "At the time I had thought it was appropriate for them to greet their new mistress." The gray-haired man leaned forward, his voice taking a concerned turn. "Though no one informed me, milord, that the bride was so unwilling."

CHAPTER
4

G ILES PUSHED ASIDE
the lady's skirts and found himself facing the anxious stares
of his staff.

They thought this was his bride!

Oh, Lord in heaven, how had this ever happened to him?

"There was no wedding, Keenan," he said. "Dismiss the
staff. I'll be in my study. See that I'm not disturbed." With
every ounce of Trahern pride he possessed, he straightened
his spine and made his way up the staircase to the second
floor, the squirming bundle of female fury still propped
over his shoulder.

He'd learned Cyril's lesson and wouldn't trust his captive in a ground-floor room. He paused at the first landing. Turning, he found his staff still standing in the foyer, open-mouthed and unmoving. "Keenan?"

"Yes, milord?"

"Send a doctor around to Lord Delaney's house. I have a feeling they'll find him in his study."

"Yes, milord." Having been given an order to carry out, Keenan straightened up and seemed to gain control of himself. The butler waved off the staff and tried to return the house to a semblance of order.

Giles turned to Monty, who was already halfway up the stairs. "Not so fast. I have another task for you, my friend."

Monty frowned. "And leave you alone with her? Not while I have a breath in my body."

His captive caught the protective tones in Monty's voice and latched on to them like a rope. "Oh, please," she began pleading over Giles's shoulder. "Don't leave me with *him*."

Monty nodded in agreement.

"Upon my honor, I won't lay a hand on her," Giles promised. "Besides, are you forgetting she just dumped you into the gutter? Or the condition of your wig?"

A deep frown drew across his friend's face. "You have a point there. But still, I should stay and help you watch over her. She is quite a handful."

Giles shook his head. "No, I need you to see to a more urgent matter. Take my carriage to Dryden's. Fetch his lordship personally. And be discreet."

This yanked Monty's attention away from the lady, as Giles thought it might. His friend had always hinted that he would be more than willing to "assist" in Giles's "business ventures," and now the opportunity lay within his grasp.

"If you think you can handle the situation here," Monty said discreetly, looking around to see that the servants were gone before he said anything else.

Winking, Giles continued up the stairs. "I have everything under control."

SOPHIA GLANCED FROM behind her mask at the room where she was being held captive. Tall shelves lined with books flanked the fireplace. A wide mahogany desk squatted in the middle of the room like a giant brown toad. And, of course, a tray atop a short chest in the corner displayed various bottles of libations. It was a very male domain, much like any of the other studies she'd seen in her time as the Brazen Angel.

And nothing to really help her.

Giles was at the door issuing orders to his footmen to remain stationed outside.

The ominous sound of a key clicking in the lock told her she was trapped.

She moved to the window, her fingers tracing the panes. Her mind spun with wild plans, but none seemed feasible.

"I wouldn't recommend it."

"Recommend what?" Sophia turned around slowly.

"The window. It is too high to jump and a devil of a climb. As a child I broke my arm trying to escape this room. My father had sent me here to await punishment. I had other ideas."

She looked back out at the empty street. "So am I to be punished?" Her fingers went to her sore cheek. She knew she would have a horrible bruise by the morning and no end of explaining as to how it happened.

"Is that what you expect? To be beaten again? You've been keeping the wrong sort of company, my lady."

She couldn't agree more, but she wasn't about to tell him that. For a while in Delaney's study it appeared Emma's potion would never take effect. By the time it finally did, the cruel man had already demanded his own form of amusement. Still, she didn't like the smug look on Lord Trahern's face, as if he was any better than Delaney.

"Why should I consider you different, my lord? You snatched me from the street and carted me here against my will. What is a lady to think in such circumstances?"

"And you think I am capable of the same type of obvious violence you encountered with Delaney?"

She didn't reply at once, because deep down she knew he wasn't. Though perhaps incapable of physical violence, this man could break a woman's heart if she was unlucky enough to give it to him. She knew only too well the pain of a lost love and the price a woman paid for believing in a man's promise.

Her hands smoothed out her dress and skimmed over the hidden pouch tied to her stays beneath. Inside the leather purse she'd stashed all that remained of Delaney's gold and jewelry—to her way of thinking, a fair exchange for the vile man's mistreatment.

Enough money, she hoped, to meet the demands of her Paris contact. Then she could return to London and see if Lord Trahern was a man of his word.

But first she must escape her betrothed again. There seemed no avoiding the man this evening.

Silence filled the space between them, though she could feel the weight of his gaze burning into her back. She pulled at the torn sleeve of her bodice and tried to hide her exposed shoulder. "I have found that men take what they want, Lord Trahern. Without asking. They believe it is their due, their right. And I assume you are no different."

He'd had no compunction about waltzing up to her aunt's house and demanding their marriage contract be fulfilled at a moment's notice and at his pleasure. If that wasn't bad enough, he hadn't even bothered to see his bride before making this decision. Sophia realized it didn't matter if she were as ugly as an old fishwife, so long as she was capable of being his brood mare, albeit a respectable one.

Even her obvious—although feigned—ill health hadn't been a deterrent to his selfish plans.

"I hardly think I am in the same league as Delaney," he argued, nodding toward the gaping hole in her bodice.

She sniffed. " 'Tis hours 'till dawn, Lord Trahern. I'd wager before first light you'll show your true side." Whirling around, Sophia's gaze searched anxiously up and down the empty street, looking for any sign of her carriage.

Surely, Oliver and Emma had been able to follow her.

"I wouldn't be so sure, my lady. I have no intention of causing you any harm. As long as you cooperate."

The cautious tones of his voice didn't give her much hope. A wary man was a difficult one to deceive.

Giles crossed the room toward her, candle in hand. "Perhaps you can start by telling me who you are?"

"I hardly think that would be fair, until you tell me why you've captured me, Lord Trahern." She twisted away from the window, sidestepping him and moving toward the shadows near the fireplace.

He tipped his head to her. "I think you know why I brought you here. So I would have your name, Lady—" he paused, as if waiting for her to fill in the blank.

Sophia shrugged her shoulders and tried to look bored.

His voice prodded her. "The Brazen Angel. That is what they call you, isn't it?"

She nodded to him in concession. It was futile to spend a lot of time bluffing as to her innocence. Nudging a log in the unlit fireplace with the toe of her slipper, she spared a glance in his direction.

Lord, he was handsome. Too handsome with his dark, brushed-back hair and carved features. She hadn't been able to examine him too closely in her aunt's dayroom, with him being seated across the darkened room and perched on Lady Dearsley's narrow Chippendale chair. The poor man had worn the grim look of a man being led to Traitor's Hill. Of course the distance between them had been to her advantage. He'd never gotten close enough to get a good look at his intended. With Emma's quick help they'd tinted her skin with makeup to a horrid shade of yellow, smudged dark circles under her eyes, and dressed her in an ancient, oversized orange gown to heighten her sickly appearance. A bit of ash from the fireplace and hand lotion had done wonders in dulling and clumping her hair to a dingy color and luster.

Thank goodness her aunt was so nearsighted and rarely noticed the changes in her niece's appearance.

Wherein the disappointment in his eyes when he'd first beheld her should have left her triumphant in the success of her deception, it instead had pricked her pride and vanity to see his letdown expression, as brief and quickly hidden as it had been.

No such dismay marred his features tonight. Though she wouldn't wager a shilling whether he stood across his study grinning because of his success at capturing the Brazen Angel or because he'd escaped his marriage to her.

Their wedding! Whatever was he doing chasing after the Brazen Angel when he was to be wed this evening? He should be out combing the streets of London for his bride-to-be.

"Why did your butler think I was your bride?" she asked, once again looking out the window. When he didn't answer right away, she glanced over her shoulder at him.

He looked everywhere but directly at her. "I was to be wed tonight."

She made a great display of searching around the room, ending up back in front of the window. "I see no bride. What happened to her?"

His jaw set in a firm line. "I changed my mind."

At this Sophia nearly lost her composure. He'd changed his mind? How dare he! Had he even gone to her aunt's house and discovered her missing? "You left the poor girl waiting for you at the altar? Why, she must be heartbroken."

"I doubt it," he said tersely. "I doubt she minds it in the least. It's not as if I threw her off. I just decided to postpone the date to a more convenient time."

Something in the way his words dropped from his lips like heavy stones told Sophia he had gone to her aunt's house. But that didn't explain why he was spending his wedding night with her and not out searching for his errant bride.

"Enough about my marriage," he said, his tone lightening. "I would rather talk about you and why all of London calls you the Brazen Angel. I can't believe you've gained your extraordinary knowledge of the ton through anything

but active participation, so I would call you Lady Brazen."
He held the candle up so its light fell in a dim circle around
them.

"I'm flattered you think I'm a lady," she commented.

His brows arched. "I never said that."

The words ruffled down Sophia's spine. And the last
thing I want from you, she thought quite shamelessly, is to
be treated like a lady. How incredible it would have been to
spend the night tangled in his embrace as his wife or his mistress. She could well imagine what it would be like to have
their bodies pressed together, his dark gaze smoldering with
longing.

She may have had to feign virginity as Lady Sophia, yet as
the Brazen Angel this man wouldn't care if she came to his
bed tarnished by another man's touch. Why, he'd expect it.

Sophia felt stunned that she was even considering the
notion. Still, she smiled to herself at the possibilities it
offered for escape.

"It won't work." Giles lit another taper on the desk.

"What?" she asked over her shoulder, suddenly alarmed
that somehow he'd been able to see into her passionate
thoughts. As the light flickered and glowed she turned
away, toying with a small wood box on the mantel, trying
to dismiss the lingering images of him taking her to his bed.

Giles moved about the room, lighting the various candles
in the sconces, illuminating the shadows.

Sophia circled the study, searching for the best place, any
spot where the light did not burn as brightly.

"Trying to hide," he commented as he lit the kindling in
the fireplace. "It was fine in the carriage when you thought
you might escape, but your charade is over."

She stopped behind the chair at his desk to survey her jail cell, looking for anything to aid in her escape.

Many of the lords she had . . . well . . . visited kept rooms like this for appearances, but it was obvious Giles Trahern was a man of business. She had known for some time he was connected to the Foreign Office and was involved with unspoken work, but then Lord Trahern's father had told her most of the details she needed. The old man had felt it his duty to inform his future daughter-in-law of the dangers Trahern men faced.

She had thought at the time that the old marquess might just be bragging about his son's deeds, but looking at the military posture of this Trahern and his keen, assessing gaze, she knew she faced her most dangerous adversary yet.

Her fiancé she did not fear, not when she was Lady Sophia coughing into her handkerchief. Her betrothed had wanted only to dismiss her.

This man left her trembling.

For he wanted more than anything to unmask her.

She laughed out loud as the absurdity of it dawned on her.

It was as if they had been destined to spend this night together. Either as man and wife, or captor and captive.

Really, she thought, wasn't it one and the same when you had to marry a man you didn't know or love?

Love, she knew, took time. Yet since the first moment she'd laid eyes on him in the Parker ballroom, she'd been unable to shake his image, his every word, from her mind. He'd left his impression on her as if he'd awakened some long-forgotten memory she'd always carried in her heart. A forbidden dream of passion.

"Is there something I'm missing?" Giles stood in the middle of the room, watching her warily.

Sophia brought her hand to her lips. It wouldn't do her any good to lose control. She needed to think, she needed time. She paused in front of the drink tray.

Perhaps she still had enough of Emma's potion in her sleeve. Her fingers twisted nervously at the cork in the vial.

Before she could open it, his hand, warm and hard, clamped down over hers.

"I'm not in the mood for a drink, so you can save the effort."

She tried to pull her fingers free from his grip, but he held her tight.

"I'm positive I don't know what you mean," she stammered.

"Certainly, Lady Brazen, you know exactly what I mean." He leaned closer until his lips were inches from her ear. "From what I hear you serve a rather potent blend of promises mixed with whiskey."

The words teased her senses, as if he dared her to try any tricks on him, while his fingers easily pulled the vial from her fingers. Never before had she wanted anything from her victims but their money. As her control melted away she found herself wanting to truly seduce this man.

Trapped in the Marquess of Trahern's arms, she found herself leaning closer to him, not because she wanted to dupe him, but because she *wanted* him.

There seemed to be no stopping the unexplored feelings he'd awakened the night before with only his penetrating glance and the sure touch of his hand.

He held the vial up in front of her, tipping it back and forth. "What, no denial? No witty response?"

His lips were so close, she could feel the warmth of his breath.

Shaking back the unruly emotions he brought forth, she tried to regain her composure. She'd been in similar situations with any number of her victims, but she had always been in control. She had made the rules.

"You seem to know all my secrets. What could I tell you that you don't already know?" Sophia tried to pull away, but he moved in closer, his body brushing up against hers intimately, the strong lines of his thighs trapping her hips, the maleness of his broad chest and uncompromising stance towering over her.

Hopefully, he didn't know how much he was affecting her, she thought wildly, looking for any avenue of escape.

"Not all of your secrets, Lady Brazen. But before dawn I intend to find out everything about you."

Looking up, she found his mouth was curved into a wicked smile, but she knew it wasn't from humor. From the tight line of his jaw to the arch of his brows, she could tell he was growing tired of the hunt and ready for the kill.

"Some secrets are better kept than shared," she whispered.

His head dipped lower until his lips skimmed at the tender flesh of her neck. "Who said I intended to share you?"

Everything started to happen too fast. Sophia backed away, until she found herself trapped up against his desk. "Maybe you don't want to know who I am. Most men don't. I would say they would even be a little disappointed."

He shook his head in disagreement, the wolfish look on

his face saying more than words. He knew exactly what he sought and what he expected to find.

The unyielding mahogany desk held her fast; Giles's fierce presence surrounded her.

His gaze swept over her torn bodice barely covering the full curve of her breasts. "I doubt you could disappoint any man."

Sophia cursed Emma's theatrical bindings, which propped her normally small breasts up into a wealth of false bounty for any man's lustful gaze. But his statement also gave way to another irritation.

She wondered if it would it have been like this on their wedding night. Would he have been so relentless in his pursuit of her if she were his wife?

No, probably not, she realized, her passion blazing into a pique of anger. There would have been none of this for the delicate and sickly Lady Sophia.

He would have been kind and patient and quick.

The thought enraged her. She deserved more from her husband.

She deserved his passion. This hunger he was giving so freely to a perfect stranger.

Even now she felt the riveting tension between them as his fingers stroked her bare shoulders, pushing aside the remainder of her gown. She sensed the struggle within him to control himself, even as she did the same to her jangled nerves.

"What is it you want, my lord?" she said with practiced tones.

"To see you, Lady Brazen." His fingers reached up and traced the edge of her mask.

She shook her head, breaking the contact, afraid to look

into his eyes. "What? Don't you like this costume? If I'd known you were going to extend this kind invitation to your home tonight, I would chosen something more to your taste. Something a little more daring perhaps? I venture a guess that white is hardly your color." Sophia edged away from his grasp and studied him, her hand on her chin. "Your taste would run more toward something hooded and elusive. The colors of night. Isn't that right, Lord Trahern? A woman of mystery and deception and moonlight?"

He stepped back as if her words had stunned him.

Moving forward, she pressed her advantage, for she had no idea how long it would last. Her fingers ran up his chest and she marveled at the hard, chiseled surface.

The sizzling connection between them returned, giving her back her daring, her bravado, her demanding need. The daring idea returned. If she could seduce him she might be able to escape. Outrageous as it seemed, it was not an idea entirely without its own appeal.

Most of her victims had been aging lotharios, whose sole purposes in life were to drink, eat, and wench. But this man's body told of a different life—of hard work and stringent regimens. Now it was to be hers, at least for this night.

"Why did you bring me here, Lord Trahern?" She tipped up on her toes, bringing her lips almost to his, her hands pulling at his shoulders.

He looked down at her, and for a moment she could see the warring emotions in his eyes.

Desire and need.

She was getting to him.

Her triumph was short-lived. His fingers curled around her shoulders and he set her away, releasing her at arm's reach.

She rocked back on her suddenly unsteady legs, having lost the support of his embrace.

"I can save you the time and open the strongbox. You can have all the coins you want, but I'll have some answers first, and none of your games. I want to know whose side you are on. What cause do you believe in?" His gaze turned hard and clear.

"My cause?" Sophia said in an offhanded manner. This conversation was getting too close to the truth for her comfort. "I've never heard the accumulation of jewels and clothing called that."

"Oh, my lady, you do me and yourself a disservice. We both know you care little for the things so many other women covet." His fingers flicked at the torn shreds of her bodice. "But then, you aren't just any woman." His hand reached up and brushed her cheek and moved to the edge of her mask.

Sophia ducked away. "I would think a man of your experience would prefer the mask on."

"I suppose I might," he said, stepping closer. "And of course then I could also claim bragging rights to having had you. Such as they are." His fingers clamped back down on her shoulders and he hauled her in close to his chest. "That is how it works, you give a man his every fantasy and he pays for it?"

His harsh tone slapped at her. Yet instead of lashing back, she smiled. "I need to know what his fantasy is first. And yours, I must admit, is quite tempting."

Her gaze swept from his glossy ebony boots to his tight black breeches to the severe cut of his matching jacket, as if she could assess his secret desires in only a glance.

He wore no adornments, no jewels, nothing to denote

his rank or wealth. Even his head was bare, without a wig, his midnight hair tied back in a middle-class queue, like the unwashed styles worn by those annoying Colonials.

This is what he'd worn to their wedding? She didn't know why, of all things, she'd suddenly noticed this. But now that she had she couldn't help thinking he looked more like he had been going to a funeral.

His lack of respect for their marriage annoyed her once again. Especially now that she found herself regretting what might have been between them.

She chided herself for even caring. After all, he was the one who had pressed their union, all in the name of his damned lineage.

She'd taken so many risks as the Brazen Angel, but none quite like this. She could hear Emma's dire warnings, but they faded against her rising anger at his obvious disdain for their marriage. She wanted nothing more than to desert him a second time, but not until he truly would miss her.

"It's not enough for me to know what you want," she said. "It works better if you can admit it yourself."

He met her challenge. "And if I told you what I wanted, would you give it to me?"

She swung her hips saucily. "I suppose I would have no choice." Moving closer, she reached out with one finger and trailed a slow path along his jaw.

"The choice would always be yours to make." His arms pulled her close, his mouth swept down toward hers. The searing kiss that followed sealed her reply, as if he knew what her body had already decided.

She tried to breathe, but there was no time. His lips encircled hers, daring them to open under his assault. When his tongue parried forward, his arms encircling her tighter, a blazing circle of passion whisked away any protests.

In that hasty moment she felt as if he'd stripped her of her mask, bared her to his sight, as if he sought to see to her very soul.

How had she ever thought herself experienced?

Gently, his hands ran over the length of her bare arms, as if he had all night to explore her body—in potent contrast to the urgency of his kiss, which demanded her immediate surrender and release.

The anger she'd felt at him blended with her passion for him, bringing an urgency to her response. His kiss teased her, challenged her to answer him. Beneath his eager touch her senses awakened, tingling and carrying their message downward to her very core.

His lips left her mouth and began trailing sweet kisses down the nape of her neck. He swept aside the remaining tatters of her bodice and chemise. The sweet pleasure of it frightened her as much as she welcomed the cool air it brought to her fevered skin.

Giles couldn't pull himself away from the incredible woman in his arms. He had never meant for this to happen, to fall into her sensual trap. Her flirtation seemed so harmless when she'd brought her lips to his.

He knew she didn't sleep with her victims, at least she hadn't with Monty. And since he wasn't about to share a glass with her, what other tricks could her sweet lips engage in?

And now those lips whispered suggestions to him, begging him to continue his exploration of her soft, silken flesh.

"Please," she murmured, as his fingers curled around her

taut nipple, her body arching into his. She sighed and melted under his touch.

And as much as it seemed he was controlling the situation, he now knew they had both lost control. He'd never felt like this for a woman, as if he had to possess her.

Wild, daring, brazen. He wanted this woman, even when he knew that one night would never be enough.

And yet this shouldn't be happening.

Her hand skimmed up his thigh until it reached his male hardness. Almost reverently, she began to stroke him through his pants.

He tried telling himself this was no more than a test to see how far she'd carry out her deception. Now the only thing being tested was his restraint. And it was spinning wildly out of control under her shameless touch.

He brought his mouth back to hers, seeking to gain mastery over her. She kissed him back, matching him with fire and passion, as if they'd been destined to spend this evening exploring each other's secret desires.

Pulling back, he stared at her. Her eyes glowed beneath her mask in acknowledgment of the need they shared. There could be no victor between them, for the fire engulfing their senses would only be vanquished in a mutual release.

Her breasts rose and fell with her ragged breathing. His hands plied the gentle curves until his thumbs grazed back and forth over the tender tips.

He watched her lashes flutter, listened to the soft moan escaping her lips.

Her hips pushed against his groin, seeking and demanding more.

Reaching for her skirts, he pulled at them, pulling them

up so he could find the treasured place hidden beneath. Meanwhile her hands pulled at his breeches, anxious in their need to free him as well.

The moment he touched the silken flesh of her thighs, he stopped. His hand fell away, and he pulled himself back from her trap. "This is wrong," he said, more for his own benefit than hers. "I will not do this."

She stepped toward him, a wry smile on her face. "I'll be gentle with you. There's no need to fear me."

No need to fear her? Was this how she'd led Webb to his death? Teasing the younger man to his own destruction. "I neither fear you, madame, nor do I want you. Not now. Not ever."

She tipped her head and stared at him, her gaze puzzled. "I would beg to differ, and if you'll come to your senses you'll see I mean you no harm. Come back to me, Lord Trahern." She held her arms out to him, beckoning him to step back into her trap.

What had he been thinking to let the situation get this far? That was just it—he hadn't been thinking.

Somewhere outside voices rose in argument.

She glanced at the window. "You seem to have more company. Your bride perhaps?"

The interruption below continued.

"He's taken me baby, I tell you. Give 'um back," a woman wailed.

Giles heard Keenan's smooth voice trying to calm the situation.

"I assure you, madame. His Lordship does not have your baby," the butler repeated.

"But I saw him take me little one." The woman's voice

rose to a piercing level, verging on hysteria. "He snatched 'um from the cradle, he did. I wants me little baby back."

Ignoring the exasperated sigh from his companion, Giles went to the window, opened it, and looked down to the street. On his steps stood a poorly dressed man and a woman, her face twisted with incoherent grief. She alternately pulled at her hair and dress with both hands.

When Keenan began to back into the house, she pitched herself at his feet, clutching his ankles.

"I won't let you have me little Johnny. Give 'um back. It's not fair. I want 'um back."

Her companion, probably her husband, stepped forward, his badly patched jacket marking him for a poor laborer. From his jerky movements Giles could tell he was both mortified and afraid of this unseemly outburst.

"Come away there, luv," he was saying as he caught the distraught woman by the waist and tried to pull her free of Keenan.

Suddenly she broke away and dashed inside. Giles stepped away from the window.

"Stealing children, as well?" the lady at his side commented, her fingers brushing up and down his sleeve in an attempt to guide him back to her passionate trap. "You've had a busy night."

The wailing and crying downstairs grew in volume.

Giles looked at the closed door and then back at his captive. She smiled at him, her lips swollen from his kisses. Whatever he'd been feeling a few minutes before faded, as his anger over Webb's death resurfaced.

Dryden would be here soon, and he didn't need half of London in his house when his superior arrived.

He walked to the door and unlocked it. Turning to his

captive, he looked back at her. She'd seated herself on top of his desk, her stocking-clad feet wiggling back and forth in the air.

"You won't be long, will you?" She winked at him. "I do so hate to be kept waiting."

Something like a growl rolled up from his chest. Her voice invited him to return to her arms, but this time the angelic tones fell flat on his ears, chilling his senses. How could he have let this happen?

And if she were responsible for Webb's death he should be throttling her, not falling for her lies like the rest of the fools of London. "You'll wait."

"It'll be worth it."

He didn't respond, but instead ordered a third footman up to watch the door, then strode down the staircase.

When the ragged woman in the foyer caught sight of him, her wailing stopped. Her eyes narrowed and she raised a bony finger toward him. "You evil man. You took me baby."

"Madame," he said with as much courtesy as he could muster, "I'm afraid there has been a mistake. I do not have your baby."

"Why, you lying devil," she spat out before flinging herself at him, her clawlike hands extended.

Her companion caught her before she made contact. "I'm sorry, milord, for this disturbance. Me missus isn't quite right in the 'ead, it seems."

All the while the woman fought and called out over and over for her little Johnny.

The man leaned forward. "Our baby died, you see. The fever took him. We can't make her believe he's gone to his reward. Her sister and I've been trying to get her to see the sense of it. She keeps insisting he's been stolen and she has to find 'um." The man pulled off his cap. "You won't have her thrown in the asylum, will you? She doesn't mean no 'arm. We waited so long to have the wee little nipper, and then he was only with us for a couple of months." The man looked as if he was about to break into tears. "She just took the loss a mite too 'ard."

"My condolences," Giles offered, unable to find any other words to fit the situation. He'd heard of women like this, so tormented by the loss of a child that it filled them with madness. "But you need to take her home and see that she gets the care she needs."

The man bobbed his head in thanks. "I will that, milord. Come on, luv. Our Johnny's not here. We should be getting back home, because if he's there he'll be needing his mother."

The idea appeared to snap the woman out of her dementia. "A baby needs his mother." She clung to her husband, wiping her tears with the back of her sleeve and sniffing loudly. Slowly, she allowed herself to be led from the house.

Giles followed Keenan to the door to make sure the couple made it down the steps. As they rounded the corner of the house Michaels pulled up in the carriage with Dryden.

"So you have her," Lord Dryden said when he got inside. "The fool Stanton blathered on so, I insisted Michaels drop him off before we came here. He was quite miffed, but I mentioned that his part in this evening would not go unnoticed. He cheered right up and left quite willingly."

Giles smiled. If he knew the Duke, the man would be at

Dryden's office first thing in the morning requesting a medal of honor for his meritorious duty to his country.

"Come along, sir," he said, resisting the urge to warn his superior of what was sure to befall him with the Duke of Stanton. "She's upstairs in my study."

"Has she said anything? Have you been able to find out who she is?" Dryden asked as they went up the stairs.

Giles nodded to the footmen, who stepped aside. He fished the key out of his pocket and started to open the door. "No, sir," he coughed, feeling quite guilty for his own lapse of professional judgment. "She's being quite evasive."

Dryden's features became serious. "We'll see about that."

Giles took a deep breath and opened the door, not too sure what they'd find.

He certainly didn't expect the sight greeting them.

In the middle of the room lay her skirts, in a pool of white silk. Next to them lay her hoops, and next to the open window lay her stockings.

CHAPTER
5

DUCKING INTO THE
carriage, Sophia put her back to Emma and started hunting
through her valise for her traveling clothes.

Lord Trahern hadn't been kidding when he said the
climb was impossible. So difficult that she'd discarded her
cumbersome dress, clung to the ivy-colored wall for dear
life, and ended her escape by traipsing down one of London's
most fashionable streets in only her chemise.

Across from her, Emma pinned her hair back into its
usual taut chignon at the nape of her neck. She took off the
old patched jacket she'd worn for her part in Sophia's

escape and replaced it with her usual widow's black jacket, lacing up the front with steady motions.

Sophia found the thick, interminable silence between them agitating. What must Emma think? "I know how this looks . . ." she shot over one shoulder as she pulled on a quilted cotton petticoat.

Emma's eyes widened, a smile twitching at her lips. "Looks like what?" she asked. "Is there something I'm *missing?*"

Shaking out a jacket, Sophia continued. "There was no other way out. I had to climb down. I couldn't have done it with my hoops on."

"Of course, that sounds likely." Emma nodded slowly in agreement.

"He locked me in. There was no other way out but the window."

"Certainly." Emma folded her hands primly in her lap. "But Sophia, did you have your clothes on before he locked you in?"

"Of course!" Sophia lied hastily. "Well, yes. Most of them." Unconsciously, her fingers went to her face, the memories of Giles's kiss blossoming anew.

Again, silence filled the interior of the rocking carriage.

"While I always like the opportunity to refresh my acting skills after so many years away from the stage," Emma finally said, "I find it amusing that you feel the need to continue your performance for me." Her discerning gaze fell on Sophia's bare legs.

"You think I'm acting? That I actually——" Sophia turned her attention back to getting dressed.

"I never recall anywhere in our plans the part where you

let the man have his way with you before you slip him the potion."

"He knew about the potion," she argued. "It must have been his friend, the Duke of Stanton, who warned him not to drink with me."

Emma only nodded in reply.

"I know how this looks," Sophia started again, having no idea why she felt this urgent need to continue explaining to Emma. "The point is, I didn't. In fact, if there hadn't been so much ivy on the wall and a drainage pipe nearby, I'd be there still. . . ." Sophia rambled. Be there still. In his arms, letting him remove the rest of her clothes, his lips kissing her neck, her shoulders, her breasts. Her gaze shot back up, suddenly embarrassed at the wayward direction of her thoughts. "The fact of the matter is, I was nearly out of the house by the time you and Oliver arrived."

"Oh, that's what you were doing up there. Escaping."

"Of course. What else would I have been doing?"

Emma's arched brows answered the question.

"Perhaps, well, maybe I let him kiss me," Sophia conceded. "At the time it seemed the best way to distract him."

At this, her companion laughed. "Sophia, I'm not one of your aunts. It's me, Emma. You can't hide that flirtatious delight from me. You drove that man wild and loved every minute of it." Her friend opened another valise and hunted around inside it, pulling out a pair of thick socks and sturdy shoes.

"So what if I did," Sophia mumbled, accepting the offering. She still smarted from the fact that he had been the one who'd stopped their passionate embrace. He'd pulled away from her with a startled look on his face, as if he regretted every moment, then turned positively angry at her. As if she were the only guilty party in that room.

While she finished dressing Sophia realized Emma hadn't been far off, though she'd rather die than admit it to anyone.

She was not ashamed of the power she felt when men weakened under her teasing flirtation. She thrilled at the knowledge that with one sensuous glance she could become a man's secret fantasy.

Throughout her time in the French court her schooling had consisted of just those lessons. Sophia learned early how to dodge unwanted advances and, when the time was right, allow a few liberties.

It had been during one such dalliance, one such moment when she'd thought herself in love. She'd given in to the exciting passions her lover uncovered in her as-yet-untried fifteen-year-old body.

Oh, it had been love, at least she'd thought so, until he deserted her and the shocking truth of their affair left her parents no choice but to send their hoyden daughter to live among her more rigid and regulated English relatives.

The swaying motion of the carriage as it rolled toward the coast eased the tensions still claiming her body. While Sophia knew she should be thrilled to have escaped Lord Trahern's study, she still felt strangely bereft.

If only she were like other girls—making a fashionable debut, meeting a man like Lord Trahern at a ball, and letting him pursue her while she remained aloof and out of reach, indifference masking the wild beating of her heart. And if she were like everyone else, she'd finally relent to his pleading requests for her hand in marriage.

And if she looked back on what had happened in the last twenty-four hours, her dream in some ways had come true.

But in all her daydreams and schoolgirl fantasies, she never saw herself spending what should have been her wedding night stealing down the cold street barefoot in only her shift. Or spending the night speeding across the countryside, every mile taking her farther and farther from her groom.

She dashed away the threatening tears and tried to concentrate on the miles ahead. With every passing village the Channel separating her from France drew nearer. From Dover they'd take a small packet across and once again, under the concealment of darkness, continue on to Paris.

"Emma?" she whispered into the darkness.

"What?"

"How do they do it?"

Emma looked up from the window. "Do what?"

"Make you forget everything. Make the entire world knot in your gut."

Smiling, Emma shook her head. "That must have been some kiss."

Oh, was it ever, Sophia thought, her fingers going unconsciously to her lips.

"I thought I could control him," she confided. "I thought I knew enough about him to use it as an advantage." Sophia looked away. "I would have stayed with him, Emma. If you and Oliver hadn't arrived, I would have given myself quite willingly to him. I never thought I would ever say that about any man, not ever again."

Emma reached over and patted her knee. The gesture was one of understanding. "I wouldn't have blamed you. With the right man it's hard to listen to your reason when your heart pounds so to be heard."

"Me of all people, you'd think I'd know better. Yet something happened. I can't explain it. Ever since last night when he chased me through the streets . . ." Sophia paused, thinking of the moment Lord Trahern had stood close enough to capture her. He could have pressed forward and trapped her, she was sure of that. And yet he'd let her go, maybe not consciously, but he had just the same. She looked up and found Emma watching her.

"Do you know why he even sought you out? Last night and then tonight. I hardly think it would be coincidence," Emma said.

"I agree." Sophia wrapped a shawl around her shoulders. "I can't imagine why he would want the Brazen Angel."

Emma looked at her wryly. "Do you think he suspects who you are?"

"No," Sophia answered quickly. "Though on the subject of Lady Sophia, he claimed he was the one who left his bride at the altar. Do you think he even went to Auntie Effie's house?"

At this, Emma laughed. "Of course he did."

Sophia smiled back. "I thought so as well. His pride would never let him admit someone as meek and mild as Sophia D'Artiers rejected his honorable offer of marriage. It probably rankled him thoroughly."

After patting a stray hair into place Emma nodded. "No more than the sight I guess he found in his study when he returned from my little diversion."

"Oh, I'd give the Delaney jewels to have seen his face." Sophia wanted to laugh again, but she found herself sobered by the evening's events. "You know, Emma, today when he arrived at Auntie Effie's and demanded we get married immediately, I hated him for how he could ruin everything I've worked for. And then tonight, all the same, I wanted to throw away all our plans and stay with him."

Emma shifted in her seat. " 'Tis a weakness and a curse."

"What is?"

"Being in love with a man."

Sophia sat back, stunned. "I'm not in love with him. I can't be." Even as she denied the possibility, she wondered if there wasn't some kernel of truth to Emma's assessment. . . .

Maybe she was, just a little.

What woman wouldn't be in love with such a man? Especially when he took you in his arms, his fingers unleashing undiscovered passions as if he knew every secret inch of you.

Oh, no, she realized, this can't be love.

"Love?" Sophia shook her head. She wouldn't let it be. "There's no place in my life right now for love. Not the kind you're describing."

"Maybe not in your life, but I'd say he's already found a way into your heart. Besides, if everything turns out as we've planned, we'll be back here in three weeks' time. Then you can let Lady Dearsley browbeat him into seeing your betrothal agreement satisfied, and you'll have the rest of your life to *distract* him."

"Marry him?" Sophia hadn't even considered that he'd take her back after her desertion. Besides, she saw how much her disappearance had affected him: He obviously couldn't have cared less. He'd left her aunt's house and gone looking for another woman. She wasn't about to spend the rest of her life with such a callous lout. "I will not. Besides, I won't marry any man who doesn't love me."

Emma chuckled. "Have you been listening to yourself? I don't think he could help but care about you after tonight."

"Which 'me' are you talking about? If you mean he cares for Lady Sophia, I saw no evidence of that tonight. Not three hours after I jilt him he's quite happily consoling himself by seducing another woman," she said, barely concealing her annoyance. "I think he was thoroughly enjoying himself, more so than if it had been me. Well, you know what I mean. Me, as in his bride, Sophia. Not me, this Brazen creature they all want."

Emma laughed again. "You sound jealous."

"I suppose I am," Sophia admitted. "Jealous of myself." She covered her face with her hands. "Oh, Emma, what have I done? What if my aunt forces this marriage after we return? He expects a certain type of bride—that horrid, timid Lady Sophia we've so painstakingly created. What if we marry and I have to spend the rest of my life playing that wretchedly dull role?"

Emma laughed. "If what you've told me tonight is any indication, I doubt you'd last very long as Lady Sophia in his bed."

"That's what I'm afraid of. Oh, and then there'd be hell to pay."

"I wouldn't worry about it too much until I saw the price," Emma advised. "Now, get some rest. We've a long trip ahead of us, and we have no idea what awaits us in Paris."

Sophia thought about the stubborn look of resolve on his face as he'd left her in the study. She could only guess what they'd find in Paris. She hoped it wasn't Lord Trahern.

CHAPTER
6

PARIS, TWO WEEKS LATER

"I WON'T PAY FOR bad information, Balsac." In the dank, smoky shadows of a Left Bank tavern known as the Sow's Ear, Sophia frowned through the wax and paint of her disguise at the man across the narrow table. "If you are lying to me I will not be responsible for the outcome," she croaked in the voice of an old crone.

Balsac's yellow, pointed teeth poked out from behind his thin lips. "Citeness, it is I who will not be responsible for the outcome if you continue these pointless threats. Paris is much changed since last we met. The streets no longer run with the blood of just aristocrats." The man eyed her speculatively.

While Sophia knew her facade as an old woman passed the inspection of the more inebriated patrons of the Sow's Ear, Balsac was not a man so easily fooled. The noisy boasting of the patrons, the closeness of so many unwashed bodies, combined with the permeating stench of spilled wine were part of the Sow's Ear's charm—and its appeal as a clandestine meeting place. Still, under Balsac's beady-eyed inspection, she pulled her hood closer around her features. "What would the Tribunals care about one old woman?"

"If that were the case, citizeness, I would have to agree with you." He shrugged his narrow shoulders. "These days neither infirmity of the aged nor the innocence of the young can protect one from Madame Guillotine. Remember: The wrong words in the right ear could mean disaster for you and your . . . companions."

He nodded toward Oliver, who dozed in a chair near the door, apparently passed out from drink. The small man then grinned at Emma, sitting near the fireplace engaged in conversation with a fat tradesman.

Despite the assurance of her friends' presence, there seemed a danger to this evening that Sophia had never felt before—something swirling in the smoky air, whispering over the din of the crowd, a voice urging caution.

She pushed aside the nagging premonition and gave a noncommittal shrug of her shoulders regarding Balsac's easy identification of her companions.

How could Balsac have so easily identified us in this crush? she thought.

Around them, the popular though dangerous tavern continued to fill with late-night customers, most already well into their cups, singing Revolutionary songs with great bravado.

Dressed in the rags of an old beggar woman, Sophia doubted anyone would look twice at her. Emma's theatrical artistry with white lead, yellowing agents, and wax hid any hint of fair skin and rosy lips.

Now it seemed Balsac had the advantage. At least for the time being.

"Turn me in. Is that what you're hinting? Why would you do that?" She looked around the room and then directly at Balsac. "Especially when there is so much gold at stake, *mais oui?*"

The man's thin lips narrowed. "Gold has a way of clouding the memory like too much wine. Too much gold and I can't remember where I've been or who I've seen." He turned and smiled in Emma's direction.

It seemed to Sophia that everyone in Paris shared Balsac's affliction. With the Terror reaching out to every level of Paris society, strangers were now regarded with suspicion and concern. Even at the lodgings where she, Emma, and Oliver had taken shelter on a number of occasions, the landlord had refused to house them. They found shelter at another boardinghouse Sophia was familiar with, but only after they'd offered the landlady twice her normally overpriced bill and paid three months' rent—in advance.

"Shall we conclude our business, if only to refresh your thirst?" she prompted, drawing his attention away from Emma by dropping a small black pouch on the table. It clanked down on the wooden planks with the solid assurance of good English gold. "What of the message you promised, Balsac? Our agreement was for you to provide proof that the information you carry is indeed true."

"Proof you shall have, citizeness. But first the gold. Show me my gold."

Sophia's hand shot out protectively, covering the pouch.

"In a place like this?" She shook her head. "Are you a fool? Most of these people haven't seen good currency in years. Their pockets and mattresses are stuffed with counterfeit *assignats*," she pointed out, referring to the inflated paper money issued by the National Committee in an attempt to stave off economic collapse. "Do you think your friends here will let you keep your treasure trove if you share the sight of it? Show me the proof, then you can count your coins in private."

Grumbling, Balsac dug in his pockets. After a protracted search he drew out a wadded piece of green and white brocade. Unwrapping the worn fabric, his nimble thief's fingers revealed the proof Sophia demanded.

Hidden inside the ragged scrap lay a gold signet ring. Sophia drew a deep breath at the sight of the deep rich color of the band. She reached for it, her fingers trembling with wonder and disbelief.

How long had she waited for this, her first sign that all their efforts were going to pay off?

But before she could touch the elusive proof she had sought for so long, Balsac caught her hand in a tight grasp, the strength of which defied his thin bones and wasted features.

"I mean only to examine it," she said, her eyes never leaving his face. She continued to stare directly at him until he let go of her hand. "There should be an inscription inside the band."

He nodded for her to proceed, and she picked up the long-lost ring greedily.

"You can read that gibberish, old woman? What other talents do you have hidden beneath those rags?"

"None you'll ever see," she said softly as she examined the insignia on the worn ring.

A swan encircled by a fleur-de-lis.

Her fingertip trailed over the familiar lines and curves. But this wasn't enough proof that this was the ring she sought.

Holding her breath, she tipped the band and spied the Latin motto inscribed within.

Nihil amanti durum.

"Nothing is difficult to one who loves," she whispered under her breath, the sight of the familiar words bringing chills to her skin.

Those words. How many times had she repeated them to herself through the more dangerous moments of her double life? Hearing them always made her resolve firmer and protected her when she thought all was lost.

Now everything lay within her grasp.

"And the message?" she insisted, pocketing her prize. "I was told there would be a message."

Balsac shook his head. "*Non,* madame. I've shown you the ring. Without some proof of your intentions, my memory, she thirsts like a babe for her mother's milk."

She pushed the black pouch across the table. Balsac's fingers swept down swiftly to snatch up his reward. But Sophia held tight to the purse strings.

"The message, Balsac. Or you will regret annoying me." Taking out the short dagger that she always kept concealed beneath her jacket, she prodded its sharp point into his thigh.

The man let out a nervous bleat. "There's no call for that, citizeness," he complained. "I have risked my poor neck to come here. I have a wife, a family."

Nonplussed, Sophia poked him again. The man had neither kith nor kin. At least none that would come to claim his body or mourn his passing. "Try my patience one more time and the point of this knife will make short work for your *wife*."

"Now, now, citizeness. You must not upset yourself," he fawned nervously, squirming on the point of the blade.

From his post at the door Oliver looked about to get up and come to her rescue. Sophia shook her head slightly at his anxious movements. There was no need for reinforcements just yet.

"It is these times; they make a man cautious." Balsac withdrew his fingers from the pouch, though his avaricious gaze never left the table.

Sophia pulled her knife back a bit, but remained tense. It was always like this with Balsac. These cat-and-mouse games. He had proved in the past to be an excellent informant, but one she felt deep down could never be trusted completely.

With a last glance of longing at his coveted prize, he looked up at her, his narrowed eyes nervously flitting back and forth. "Ah, I remember the message now. It is coming back to me."

"It had better," she prodded with both her tone and knife.

He flinched and continued his tale quickly. "Your acquaintance said he would meet you tomorrow night. At

Danton's salon." He paused for a moment. "For an igno-
rant old woman you keep an impressive circle of friends,
citizeness."

Sophia frowned at the probing slant of his comments.

When she refused to acknowledge his statement one way
or the other, he finished his recitation. "Once you are there,
your contact will approach you for the exchange. He said
you would understand." Balsac tapped his forehead, his gaze
focusing once again on the pouch. "*Mais oui,* I remember it
now. He said to warn you."

"Warn me? Warn me of what?"

Balsac looked around the crowded room, his cautious
sweep heightening Sophia's tension.

She'd already checked the room three times besides
arriving an hour before her appointed meeting with him to
ensure there would be no treachery.

Her uneasiness about the evening returned, rattling her
concentration.

Balsac shifted in his seat. "There is something wrong."
His ratlike nose twitched with distaste.

Someone is watching you, a warning voice murmured in
her ear.

Sophia shivered. "I'd have to agree, Balsac." Wrenching
her attention back to the man in front of her and trying to
ignore the telltale ripple of anxiety running down her spine,
she leaned forward. "The sooner you give me my message,
the sooner you can leave."

Balsac appeared not to be listening, his gaze locked on to
something over her shoulder. His beady eyes flickered and
his usual arrogant confidence withered before her eyes.
He'd obviously seen someone who frightened him. Before
Sophia could turn and determine what could make the man

go white with fear, his broken words wrenched her attention back to the matters at hand.

"You are being followed. . . . They wanted you to know . . . that until you meet with . . ." He paused and shook his head. "Caution, citizeness, proceed with caution."

The door to the tavern opened, allowing a fresh October breeze to blow through the stuffy room. A crowd of noisy soldiers elbowed their way in, stacking their long, wicked pikes next to the door, their red sashes and caps staining the room in crimson.

Balsac used the diversion to snatch up his payment and flee toward the kitchens.

Before she could cut him off, the newly arrived troops filled the space between them.

"Get out of my way, old hag," one of them complained before he clouted her none too gently to the floor.

Ignoring the sting on her shoulder, she righted herself, with every intention of dashing after the fleeing Balsac. Out of the corner of her eye she saw Emma furiously shaking the fabric of her sleeve.

Sophia looked down at her own clothes and remembered how she was dressed.

What was she thinking?

In her anxious state she'd almost forgotten that most old women didn't race through taverns like wild hellions. She glanced back at Emma, hoping her companion saw the apology in her expression. There was no need for her to risk revealing herself, for Oliver was already halfway to the kitchen in pursuit.

If there was more to Balsac's message Oliver would have no trouble getting it out of the man.

Slowly, she turned back to the soldier, groaning and

complaining. "*Sou* for an old woman. *Sou* for an old woman's meal." Her voice cracked and faded as she retrieved her bundle from beneath the bench where she'd been sitting with Balsac.

The large man scowled at her. "Get out of my sight, you old turnip. I pay money only when I get something in return." He reached for a serving girl, who, though missing her front teeth, made up for her gaping come-hither smile with a pair of ample breasts. He pulled the giggling girl onto his lap and glared back at Sophia. "If I didn't think you were as tough as an old hen, I would cart you off to the guillotine myself. But your neck would probably dull a good blade."

All of his companions laughed in loud agreement.

Sophia cackled right along with them. "Save those fine blades for the soft necks of the swine who deserve it."

Like yourself, she thought as she backed away from him and made her way toward the entrance, begging the odd *sou* from the other noisy patrons.

As she pushed open the door to leave she heard the scrape of a chair being pushed back in haste. Glancing over her shoulder, she saw a tall figure rise in the corner.

Even before she saw his face her body recognized him, with a sharp ache of longing that had never been far from the surface since she'd left London.

The heady memories of being held in his arms, of being kissed, of the way his hands molded and stroked her breasts ripped past her resolve to forget him and blazed into a bonfire in her blood.

It cannot be. How could he be here?

His patched jacket and red cap might mark him as a *sansculotte,* but his cocksure stance and the careless flip of his wrist as he tossed his coins on the table exposed him as a man of wealth and assurance.

No, she thought, staring harder. It couldn't be him. Not in Paris. Not this quickly.

For as much as her pride fooled her into believing he'd never be able to locate her in Paris, her body had longed for the sight and feel of him again.

And her dangerous passion for him hadn't cared *if* he could find her. Just so long as he found her.

Oh, she'd known he'd follow her. His pride wouldn't let him do anything less. Giles's father had told her as much over one of their chess games. He'd bragged how once his son started a mission he was methodical to a fault and unrelenting in his pursuit of the truth.

His father had thought his son's skills a blessing and a danger. Sophia now knew just how dangerous Giles could be.

The night in his study had awakened a need inside her that chased her through her sleep with wild, passionate dreams, jolting her awake and leaving her alone and empty in the dark.

She didn't need a second glance back to decide whether or not it was Lord Trahern. Balsac had already warned her that she was being followed. No matter who it was, Sophia felt the danger of this stranger's pursuit and knew she must quickly get as far away from the Sow's Ear as possible.

Slipping out the door, she clutched her bundle to her chest and fled into the dark street. Looking first in the direction where she was to rejoin Emma and Oliver, Sophia turned the opposite way, heading instead for the misty alleys near the Seine.

Detouring down the first alley and then a second,

Sophia's confidence overtook her momentary panic in the tavern. Perhaps she'd allowed her anxieties to run away with her imagination.

By the time her nose wrinkled in distaste at the growing stench of the river, she would have bet what remained of the Delaney jewelry that she'd lost her pursuer.

Standing in the darkness of a narrow alley, she looked ahead to where the new Pont de la Concorde rose across the river toward the gardens of the Tuileries and the newly christened Place de la Revolution, where the crowds gathered daily to watch the condemned die.

Confidently, she stepped from the safety of the shadows to venture across the cobbled street and over the bridge. Halfway into the open square she heard the one voice able to halt her hurried footsteps.

"Running away again?" Lord Trahern said in a low, dangerous voice.

Outwardly she froze, but inside she trembled, his words ruffling down her spine.

Slowly, she turned around to face him.

When he stepped from his hiding place and into the pale moonlight, her breathing slowed. She couldn't find the power to run as his towering black-cloaked figure loomed in front of her, his slow, even strides closing the distance between them.

Why was it that, when every bit of reason she possessed urged her to flee, all she could think of was throwing herself back into his heated embrace? She looked up at him to see if he, too, shared her traitorous response.

His dark, piercing gaze bored through her, giving no hint of the passion they'd shared.

"You may have deceived those idiots at the Sow's Ear,

but, Lady Brazen, try as you may, you cannot deceive me. Not ever again."

Having spent most of his evening hunched over a tumbler of sour wine, Giles had been about to give up his vigil. His investigation into Webb's death hadn't turned up anything beyond what he already knew from Dryden's brief missive.

Yet there were too many missing pieces to satisfy Giles, so he continued his search.

The landlady at Webb's attic apartment had let the loft to other tenants and refused his request to search the rooms. He wasn't about to argue with her, for she was a frowning giant of a woman who looked capable of taking on the National Guard—unarmed. Her dirty sleeves were pushed up on her fleshy forearms, her greasy hair haphazardly tucked into a red cap.

"What a horrible mess them soldiers left after taking him," she'd complained. "I spent two days cleaning to make it real nice again." Shrewdly assessing the opportunity, she added hastily, "He owed me for the rent, he did."

So Giles paid her two days' wages for her inconvenience and the three months' back rent she claimed Webb owed.

"He didn't have many things, some clothes that went to the poor," she'd told Giles with a rueful shake of her head.

He knew full well the clothing had probably gone on her husband's back. "Was there anything else?"

Her gaze fell to the pocket from where he pulled her first payment. "There might have been some scraps of papers and a pamphlet he was writing, maybe a book or two scattered about."

With another offer of gold, Giles obtained the papers and books. "Did he have any friends? Anyone who might have known him?"

The woman tugged her black shawl tighter around her wide shoulders. "He went to the Cordeliers' meetings near the Palais Royal. Rough lot, those ones. And there was a woman I seen him with a time or two. What do they call her?" The woman scratched her head.

Giles held up his final bribe.

The woman grinned. "La Devinette. They call her La Devinette. Up to no good, that one."

"La Devinette," he'd repeated. *The riddle*—a description that could as aptly be used to describe the Brazen Angel. "What does this woman look like?"

The woman looked expectantly for more payment. When none was forthcoming she offered her information freely, though not without a frown. "She's not as tall as me," the woman said, drawing herself up to her full height, which was nearly eye-to-eye with Giles. "She's overly proud of her eye, or rather the lack of one. Lost it in the massacre at Champ de Mars, or so she claims. Puts a big black patch and a red wrap over her face to hide the mess. You can see her for yourself any afternoon. They've got her modeled in wax down at the Salon de Cire—that is, if you have any money left to pay the admission fee." She laughed roughly, patting her now richly lined pocket.

"Was this Citizeness Devinette with him often?"

"Often enough, if that's what you mean. Don't see what he saw in her, but how's a woman to know what men will itch for?" She took a deep breath and eyed Giles as if she was sizing up what might scratch him.

"But you said they only went to meetings," he said, hoping to draw her attention back to her story.

"They went to drink at that cesspit, the Sow's Ear. He said she was teaching him politics." The woman snorted. "I have my own ideas on that notion. But long as they pay their rent and keep quiet with their *politics,* I don't care."

Giles thanked the woman for her assistance and left. He still needed to get into Webb's apartments, but he'd have to find a way past the landlady first.

The papers he'd recovered, though coded, hadn't provided any clues as to who might have betrayed his friend. Webb's notes contained vague references to La Devinette, but there was nothing damning the woman outright or any hint as to her true identity.

If Webb had infiltrated the radical Cordeliers Club, as the landlady implied, it could have been any of them who betrayed the young English agent, Giles reasoned.

The Cordeliers, their ascendancy to power in the newly formed Committee of Public Safety all but assured, denounced each other often. The rampant accusations and paranoia among the membership made it a dangerous place to harbor any secrets.

The only way he was going to discover if and how La Devinette was connected to Webb's death—and how the Brazen Angel fit into this confusing puzzle—was to find the woman herself.

He knew the Brazen Angel was in Paris, for he'd found evidence of that in a pawnshop on the Ile de la Cité. How else could a brooch with the Delaney family crest on it arrive so quickly in Paris?

To further his search he took the landlady's advice, joining the hordes flocking to the Salon de Cire to view Dr.

Curtius's wax creations. There, side by side in realistic tableau, stood the infamous and despised in a revolving display of France's political scene.

He'd silently filed past the wax version of La Devinette, a menacing Valkyrie of a woman, with her tilted *bonnet rouge* and a short sword raised over her head. Just as the landlady had described, the right side of La Devinette's face was hidden with a black patch and a red binding.

He stopped a few feet away and turned back to look at the statue one more time. From this angle he found himself staring into the passionate sapphire gaze of the Brazen Angel.

Though he'd never seen her face unmasked, he knew the curve of her cheeks, the fullness of her lips, which now mocked him from beneath a small sign that read, LA DEVINETTE.

So he'd spent the last three nights at the Sow's Ear, drinking sour wine and listening to the fanatical speeches and radical songs of the local *sans-culottes* who made up the Cordeliers Club in the roughneck Croix Rouge section of the Left Bank.

Giles knew he'd been there too long when he found himself humming *La Marseillaise*. Having concluded the money spent for the landlady's information had been offered in vain, he was about to continue his search elsewhere when his attention fell on a brief disturbance with an old hag.

Like the rest of the occupants of the Sow's Ear, he hadn't been inclined to give her a second look—until a flash of blue caught his eye.

Despite the elaborate makeup, the ragged clothing, and the twisted voice, it was her eyes, sparkling with rage as she'd scrambled to her feet, that had stopped him. The blue flash caught and held his attention.

This fire he knew, having felt its heat and seen those sapphire depths blaze with passion.

Such vibrancy couldn't belong to a woman whose bones and haggard flesh looked older than the foundation of Notre Dame.

He shook his head in amazement that no one else in the room saw through her veneer. Why, she even mocked the *fédérés* to their faces by begging coins from them. He clenched his teeth in anger at her for taking such risks.

He told himself he didn't care what she did, it was just a professional issue. A good agent never took such outrageous chances. That was, assuming she was an agent.

Parading herself before the ton in the Parkers' ballroom was one thing, but these pandering antics were insane, he thought, watching in amazement as a young soldier actually dropped a coin into her outstretched hand.

Giles wanted to laugh as much as he wanted to rattle some sense into her foolish and reckless disregard for subtlety. A good agent would use some degree of caution.

Her display raced headlong toward suicide.

Watching her make her way toward the door, he'd quickly tossed coins on the table to cover the price of his wine. He was of no mind to let her slip past him once again. But when he got outside he found the narrow street empty.

"Damn," he'd cursed.

Even as the words burst from his lips, he spotted the flap of a brown cape whipping around a corner.

And he was off without a moment's hesitation.

It had been a demanding chase though the narrow alleys and dark streets of the Croix Rouge and Fontaine de Grenelle sections. As they drew nearer the Seine the main streets widened, allowing a sliver of moonlight to filter down to the cobblestones.

Now, wary and curious, he found himself face to face with the Brazen Angel's latest deception. Wary of the treachery she represented, and curious to strip away her camouflage to see if the same woman of fire kindled beneath.

His gaze sought to look beyond her layers of deception, yet her clever disguise once again concealed her true features, leaving him with his only solid memories of her—those of her satin touch and heady kisses.

He moved toward her slowly, sure any quick motion would frighten her away. He wouldn't put it past the woman to be able to command the very air and elements to help her disappear before his eyes.

"Have you nothing to say, Lady Brazen?" he asked her in French.

"It is obvious, citizen, you have mistaken me for another," she said, continuing her charade in the cracked voice of an old woman. "For it has been nigh on forty, *non,* fifty-some years since someone called me 'Brazen.' But perhaps that is what you like, eh? A woman of some maturity, of some experience?"

He had to admit the coarse manners and country costume were perfect, right down to the large wart on her chin—so perfect that he started to doubt his earlier conviction that this could be the beautiful woman whose body so easily breached his defenses two weeks earlier in his study.

She reached over and patted his sleeve with her mitten-covered fingers. "There, there, *mon fils,* it is not so bad. You will find yourself a companion tonight. But use caution."

She looked around as if to check and make sure they were not being watched. "The Committee frowns on such pastimes," she warned with a dire shake of her finger. "Ah, this regime, they know nothing of *amour*." She wheezed out a sigh. "If you were just a few years older . . . *mais non,* I am afraid I would wear you out."

She turned to leave, hobbling in the shuffled gait of an old woman. Giles wasted no time, reaching over and catching her hand within his grip.

With one deft motion he stripped off her mitt.

The old woman howled in protest, her bundle falling from her arms. Her colorful oaths and curses continued until he held up his prize.

A hand, smooth of lines or veins or spots. Soft, tapered fingers that could only belong to a young woman. A woman capable of stroking his senses beyond reason.

He held it up in front of her face. "Now, shall we start where we left off?"

"Where we left off?" she repeated, continuing in her disguised voice.

Again, he shook her hand in front of her face.

This time the voice that answered held the same sensual charm that had teased his senses in the Parkers' ballroom and even more so on the night in his study.

"You've done well, Lord Trahern. You found me more quickly than I gave you credit for. Unfortunately, though, I haven't the time for you tonight. Return to London, and I promise one night I'll come calling." She twisted to leave, but he held her fast.

They stood for a moment, her body well within his grasp. Even now his imagination brought forth his last vision of her in his study: her ivory skin glowing by the firelight, her kiss-swollen lips open in invitation, the provocative tip of her head and smile bidding him to hurry back.

Dammit, she was a witch. Casting her spells and enticing him to forget. Forget his mission, forget Webb, forget everything except her.

The memories of her touch and the silken warmth of her skin beneath his fingers left him tight and straining against his trousers.

When he blinked aside the passionate recollection and found himself staring into the face of a wretched old hag, it was easy for him to make reason sweep aside what his body refused to. He let go of her hand and stepped back from her. "Your offer has lost the appeal that it had the last time we met."

"I suppose so," she admitted, smoothing out her worn wool skirts. "But give me my freedom and I could be anything you want." Through the wax and paint distorting her face, her blue eyes flashed with an invitation of passion.

Giles did his best to ignore her suggestion, for he well knew she could transform herself into any man's fantasy. Even his. As if she could glimpse into his soul and pluck from it the secrets of his own desires.

He crossed his arms over his chest, blocking her tempting offer. "I have no intention of letting you go, not just yet."

She sighed. "And I told you I have other plans."

Looking up and down the empty boulevard lining the Seine, Giles shrugged his shoulders. "You appear sadly lacking for a rescue tonight, Lady Brazen. No carriage to whisk you to freedom. No friends to create a calculated diversion, nor any windows to climb out." He stepped closer, aware of how she stiffened with a stubborn resolve at his approach.

Her defiance and arrogance in the face of her defeat brought out the worst in him. If she'd had any part in Webb's death, he'd see her brought to justice no matter the cost.

"You cannot escape me," he said, more of a vow to himself than a promise to her. "Not this time."

They jerked apart at the sound of footsteps. Without hesitating she turned to flee. Giles caught her by the elbow and held her fast.

"The guards," she whispered over her shoulder as she tugged against his grip. "It's well past curfew."

She turned and tried to pry his fingers open, but he clung to her, refusing to let go.

"Are you insane?" she asked. "They will not look kindly on an Englishman lurking about Paris in the middle of the night. Save yourself."

He shook his head. "I'm not going anywhere. Not without you."

She looked about to continue the argument, but her features betrayed her anxiety at the approaching regiment. "Under the bridge then. Hurry."

With agility that belied her costume she towed him down the banks of the Seine and under the Pont de la Concorde. Damp and muddy, her hiding place perched dangerously at the edge of the rain-swollen river.

Moments later the bridge above them reverberated with the sound of marching feet.

With martial law and a curfew in effect, few citizens ventured out at night. Giles knew that to walk the streets after dark invited unwanted inspection of one's papers, followed by a visit to the local committee. With a single nod by any member a citizen could well find himself riding in the tumbrils without the benefit of a trial or a hearing.

"Do you hide here often?" he whispered, lifting his once-clean boot out of the sucking mud.

She peered up at him from beneath her tattered mobcap and gray wig and frowned. "Complaining when I've all but saved your neck. If I were smart I'd be well rid of you with only a word," she shot back, nodding up above them to where the troops marched over their heads.

"It wouldn't do you much good, for I'm sure those men would find what is hidden beneath this horsehair"—his fingers tugged lightly at her wig—"not only an unlikely surprise, but something worthy of a lengthy investigation."

"You wouldn't dare. It would mean your death as well as mine," she shot back, her powdered gray brows drawing up in disbelief.

"I'm not the one in disguise. So the hand is to you. Turn me in, my lady. Turn me in and see what I'm willing to wager."

She twisted away from him, an exasperated sigh escaping her lips.

Giles allowed himself a small smile at the sound. It had been a calculated risk to see what she would choose.

If she was with the Revolutionaries she would have had no qualms about calling out to the troops. But she hadn't. So she was either waiting to obtain more information before adding him to the executioner's list, or she was the rogue agent Lord Dryden suspected—though her consistently rash behavior argued against that possibility.

As the last of the marching overhead receded, she prodded him. They scrambled carefully up the slick bank.

She reached the top first, but before she could take off again, he caught hold of the back of her skirt.

"I said I have business with you, and I meant it." But as she struggled and fought against him, Giles realized that antagonizing her would gain him neither the information he needed nor her cooperation. Perhaps it was time to turn the tables on the lady and use her own game against her.

Sophia continued to pull against his grasp, but to no avail. Why had he ever followed her? Did he suspect who she was? No, she realized, he still hadn't made the connection, for he would have said something immediately. Maybe he'd been sent by Lord Dryden for all the thefts she perpetrated. Though she couldn't believe the English government would send one of their top agents after her. She'd chosen her victims to avoid that type of scrutiny, targeting men whose vanities would never allow them to admit they'd been robbed by following their own misguided lust.

Suddenly, she thought of the one thing Lord Dryden would very well risk his best agent to uncover.

Sophia closed her eyes. How would she ever be able to deceive him about that?

Trahern's arm wrapped around her waist and pulled her toward him until her back bumped up against his chest. As he gathered her even closer within the confines of his arms, his hand slid higher, until it pushed against her breasts.

Damn you, Lord Trahern, she silently cursed, why did you follow me?

"You should be thankful your head is still attached to your neck and begone with you," she told him, trying to break free of his dangerous embrace.

Her fool costume, she realized, would make it impossible to outrun him. She stilled her struggles for a moment and concentrated. There were other ways to elude a man.

Twisting in his grasp, she turned until she faced him. Instead of smiling, she continued to frown at her captor as a new plan formed in her mind. "You have no right even being in Paris."

"Your concerns for my welfare, Lady Brazen, are duly noted."

"Don't look so smug," she snapped. "My only concern is that you'll get us both killed."

"And here I thought you'd developed a *petite tendre* for me."

Oh, the outright arrogance of the man. As if she could expect anything less from the man who'd marched into her aunt's house and demanded he be allowed to wed her immediately, sight unseen.

If he weren't holding her so tight she'd haul him out to the middle of the bridge, push him over the rail, and be done with him. Then maybe she could forget about him once and for all.

"I'm the one who left, remember," she prodded. "*You're* the one who followed *me* here." Sophia allowed herself a smug smile in this small victory.

"So I did. And since you mention it I would have certainly preferred to conduct this business in the safety and comfort of my London house," he whispered into her ear, his warm breath and innuendo teasing her senses. "Certainly, we could find someplace to be alone, rather than playing cat and mouse with the *fédérés* all night."

"Maybe you should have stayed home if you find Paris so disagreeable," she said, trying to ignore the heat of his body, which seemed to touch her everywhere—her legs, her breasts, her neck. He had a way of holding her so she knew every point of contact between them and regretted every one for the way her body angled closer to his. "Go home if you don't like it here."

Go home and wait for me, she wanted to plead. *For I will come back to you. I have no choice.*

He shook his head, his fingers toying with her stringy wig, brushing aimlessly down the sides of her neck. "Would you really want me to leave?"

"Yes," she lied, in spite of the quick, hot sensations his touch raised everywhere it brushed. And she wanted him to touch her—everywhere.

"I thought so," he said, a smile on his lips. "But first, we have unsettled business. Perhaps you can suggest someplace where we can finish what we started in London."

There was nothing she wanted more than to continue the passionate interlude in his study; it had kept her awake every night since she'd stolen out of his house like a thief. Now it was he who was trying to steal from her, robbing her of her reason and senses.

"No," she mumbled under her breath, not having meant to say the word out loud.

"I had only thought to finish our discussion," he told her in a sensual whisper that belied his words.

She shook back her tangled emotions. Emma couldn't have been more wrong. Sophia didn't love this man. Loving this man would be impossible. With his arrogance he'd take everything she possessed, right down to her soul.

Talk she'd give him.

Fall into his arms again and risk eternal damnation at his hands? Never.

She would hear him out and then send him on his way. It was the safest thing for him, and for her heart.

But the small voice that had whispered its warning to her in the tavern now changed to that of mocking laughter.

Buoyed by her newfound resolve and tamping down her doubts, she considered her choices. "I might know a place," she began slowly. Two things were for sure: She couldn't take him to her lodgings, and she had no intention of being alone in his. She didn't trust the traitorous spell he cast over her senses with his teasing kisses and heated promises.

"We'll be safe there until morning," she continued. A place sure to cool his ardor, as well as her own. "I'll *listen* to you 'til dawn, but then you have to promise to let me go and leave Paris immediately. Agreed?"

"That depends on you, Lady Brazen," he whispered as she started to lead him across the Pont de la Concorde.

She muttered a rather salty French curse under her breath, shaking off the lingering effects of his touch. "You leave at dawn, Lord Trahern. I'll not have any more deaths on my conscience."

CHAPTER
7

CONCEALED IN THE
shadows of a doorway, Sophia waited for the group of
drunken men to pass before she continued. In the meantime
she stood with her back pressed against Lord Trahern's
chest. His arm wrapped protectively around her, concealing
her in the dark sweep of his coat.

This was how she'd imagined him since her aunt informed her of their betrothal—warm, protective, strong.

How she wished it could always be.

What was she thinking? She pinched herself, as she'd
done as a daydreaming schoolgirl, to bring her wayward

thoughts back in line with what she needed to do now. She hadn't time for schoolgirl fantasies.

She glanced up and over her shoulder at him. "How did you find me?"

A wry smile curved his lips. Fishing in his pocket, he held up his evidence.

Before her eyes dangled a bracelet, one of the Delaney pieces she'd stolen. She stepped out of his protective reach and stared at the brilliants. "Damn Gauthiér. He promised me he would sell it immediately to an Italian vendor."

"Do not blame your Swiss friend too harshly," Giles told her as he returned his prize to the safety of his jacket. "He had agreed to sell it to another merchant. It wasn't until I offered so much more that he capitulated. He also seemed to think you had more jewels available, ones that I might be interested in." Tipping his head, his gaze swept her from ragged boots to the top of her tattered lace cap. "So do you? Have more jewelry?"

"Bags of it. Some pieces I think you might find quite amazing." She laughed softly to herself, relieved that she hadn't also sold the engagement necklace he'd given her. While the money it would have brought might come in handy, it wasn't essential to her current scheme.

Perhaps I'll have need of it later, she'd told herself when Gauthiér offered a handsome sum for the rich piece.

Now she realized it had been common sense and not sentiment that had convinced her to pull the necklace out of the lot of items to be sold.

It would have taken quite some explaining if he'd found his betrothal gift to Lady Sophia in a Paris jewelry shop.

Lord Trahern stared at her as if he didn't quite see the

point of her laughter. Sophia was of no mind to enlighten the man.

Looking him directly in the eye, she asked, "What do you intend to do with it?" All things considered, there was no reason why the bracelet couldn't be sold again.

"Return it."

Her mouth opened, but the words hung up in the back of her throat in a strangled sound of dismay. He wanted to return it? How could he be so thickheaded?

The drunken *sans-culottes* turned down a side street, leaving the street safe for Sophia and Giles to continue. In outraged frustration she stomped down the stairs and up the boulevard.

"You don't like the idea of seeing it returned to its rightful owner?" Giles asked when he caught up with her.

"I cannot believe you would return my bracelet to that vile man. Not after all the trouble I went to to relieve him of it." She came to an abrupt halt next to a large tree on the edge of a park. Her hands went to her hips, her elbows jutting out like exclamation points. "If you do feel the need to return it, you have to realize it will only end up in another pawnshop by the end of the month."

"Delaney selling his family's heirlooms?" Giles laughed at her. "What makes you think Lord Delaney would sell a family heirloom? With his fortune he could buy ten identical necklaces and toss them in the Thames," he said, snapping his fingers in the air.

"Then he won't miss this one, so you might as well give it back to me." Sophia found that his moralistic indignation couldn't be more misplaced. Yes, she would agree that in some circumstances stealing was wrong, but men like Delaney didn't deserve the law's consideration.

His gaze rolled upward. "Give it back to you? What, so you can sell it again?"

"Why not? I'll put the gold to better use than he will." Of this Sophia couldn't be more positive. The thought of what Delaney would do with the money disgusted her.

"I'm still not convinced Delaney has any reason to be selling his mother's jewels. After she hears her son was mixed up with you, he'll probably have to buy out Rundell and Bridge to get back into her good graces."

"How little you know," she said with a pompous huff. She started back down the street, and when he caught up with her, she glared up at him. "And what exactly is he going to use to buy his way back into his mother's heart?"

"What he's always used. Money. I don't think even you could have carted out the entire Delaney fortune under your skirts."

She stopped again. "I did exactly that. At least what's left of it."

Giles scoffed at her, shaking his head in scathing disbelief.

Oh, his utter arrogance! At least in this she could bring him down a notch or two with her better intelligence about the Delaney family. Poking him in the ribs, she closed the distance between them and rose up on her tiptoes so she nearly looked him square in the eye. "There is no Delaney fortune. It's all gone."

He shook his head. "Gone? You're starting to believe your own rumors."

She threw up her hands. "Fine, don't believe me, but how do you explain why his mother suddenly packed up and left town at the beginning of the Season?" She paused for a second. "His mother left to escape their creditors."

"Even if it were true, how could you know any of this?" Giles asked. "If Delaney's ruined I doubt even his valet would divulge something that shocking. And if he were penniless it would be the buzz of the ton."

This time she smiled. "You'd be surprised what a valet will reveal. Especially when someone else is buying the drinks."

Giles took a second glance at the woman beside him. This admission proved his theory that she thoroughly researched her victims—and explained how she so easily tapped into their secret fantasies.

They stopped at the next block. "So, you see, you can't return it," she persisted.

"If Delaney's ruined then he'll need the money the bracelet will bring."

She took a deep breath and let it out as if she were trying to restrain her growing impatience. "And you think that by giving it back to him he will use it to lighten his debts? You really don't know the man, do you?" Her hands were back on her hips, but her tone was softer, as if she wanted him to understand something very important. "More likely it will go to buying him more young girls. Since you don't seem very enlightened as to Delaney's preferences, let me explain: The man is quite partial to virgins. Young, soft girls he can break. Their bones, that is, as he beats them with a cane. Then, once they are bloody and crying for mercy, he takes his ruthless pleasures. So give it back if you feel so compelled, but know that with it he'll buy the lives of three or four girls fresh from the country. Girls, who if they survive a night with that beast will spend the remainder of their miserable lives whoring for the type of man who cares not how they look." A haunted, angry look broke through the twisted makeup on her face. Without another word she started across the street in haste.

Giles stared after her.

There had been whispers of Delaney's sports, but he had never really listened to the malicious gossip.

Though Monty had obviously known. And no wonder he'd vehemently protested Giles's decision to let her go into the Delaney house alone.

"You knew all this and still entered the man's house?" he asked when he caught up with her. He pulled her to a stop. He didn't know why he was suddenly so mad at her, and at himself.

And why it left him needing to hold her so tight.

"Tell me. Why did you go with him?" he asked again, struggling to make some sense of it.

She shook her head and looked away.

Gently, he swept away the stiff horsehair curls of her wig and found the brilliance of her blue eyes sparkling with tears. She must have been silently replaying the events from that night. With her mitt she swiped at the drops on her cheeks, wincing at the hasty movement.

In his anger over her hasty departure, he'd all but forgotten how she'd arrived at his house—her dress torn, her face bright red with the print of Delaney's hand. The resulting bruise must have been quite a sight.

He still couldn't fathom her reckless decision to rob Delaney. "Why him if you knew what he was capable of?"

"I met one of his victims." She continued to look away, but this time her eyes didn't fill with tears. A strange solemnity filled her voice, giving it a ring of truth he'd never before heard in her often teasing, playful speech. "I couldn't give him the hanging he deserved, but I could take his remaining coins and baubles to see that he wouldn't hurt anyone else. And who would protest? He's ruined as it is. No one will raise a fuss, when most would probably agree he deserved a share of what he so gleefully metes out."

The revelation sent chills down Giles's spine.

He supposed he'd always half-enjoyed her choices of victims, as had the rest of the ton. With the exception of Monty, they'd been reprobates, each and every one.

But her compassion and recognition for their forgotten victims, for the innocents they exploited to obtain their own deviant ends, gave a new dimension to the strange, mercurial woman he held in his arms.

If she was capable of this much empathy, could she in turn betray someone as honorable and kind as Webb Dryden?

As much as the evidence argued against it, he found himself believing she'd had nothing to do with Webb's death. He couldn't base the feeling on any new facts or tangible evidence, just on the unfamiliar notion that for once he needed to trust something he couldn't see or touch. That still didn't answer his original question.

"Why did you risk it?" he asked. "Yes, you might have saved another girl the fate Delaney had planned, but what of your own life? What can be so important that you'd wager your own life to steal a man's gold?" His fingers traced a gentle path down the side of her face, along the curve of her neck, until his hand cupped her chin. The silk of her skin enticed him.

He struggled against the desire to pull her closer and kiss her. To offer his protection, his assistance. Anything to prevent her from taking one gamble too many.

Didn't she know what one mistake could cost? Considering her disregard for caution, he figured her luck was already overdrawn.

She looked ready to give him the answers he so wanted. He watched the struggle of emotions in her eyes, as if she weighed whether or not to trust him.

A sigh escaped her lips and she pushed away.

Obviously, her suspicions won out, for the Brazen Angel fled his arms and continued down the street, hugging the shadows like a creature of the night. Hell-bent and reckless.

And all he could do was follow.

Pausing briefly before a small fenced churchyard, she turned and smiled at him. Her finger curled in invitation before she entered the adjoining cemetery. Around them rose the solemn monuments of the dead.

Loving mother and wife of . . .

Devoted servant of the church . . .

The prayers and names blurred in the darkness as she wove through the maze of the dead. Beneath their feet, weeds choked the paths. Finally, she stopped at the back fence, far from the street, far from any prying eyes.

She paused beside a tall, moss-covered monument, discarding her bundle at the foot of the gravestone.

As Giles looked up, he found himself staring eye to eye with a griffin held by an fierce-looking angel.

Why did he have the feeling the Brazen Angel had come home?

To the one place where life and death met every day.

"Do you see now how foolish it is for you to be here?" she said, her hands coming to rest on her hips. "Disregarding the fact that your country has declared war against France, how can you think to come here? Paris is no place for an aristocrat, certainly not one with your, shall I say, experience?"

Her statement took him aback.

While Monty liked to speculate on the nature of Giles's obligation to Lord Dryden, Giles had always wondered what his friend would say if he knew the true extent of his "business ventures." For that matter, very few knew how far-reaching his role in the Foreign Office had grown over the years.

Now this woman spouted off as if it were common knowledge.

"What do you know of my experience?" he asked cautiously.

She smiled and gave a wistful shrug of her shoulders. "More than you probably want to hear. Let us say, I would wager you didn't follow me here to return my shoes or lost clothing. You were sent."

Too close to the truth by his way of thinking, Giles decided to play the game he'd started at the bridge. "I haven't the slightest idea what you mean. Sent by whom? Why couldn't I have followed you to merely return your belongings? Men have launched wars to follow the woman they *love*."

The moment he said the word he realized the incredible weight of what he'd uttered. He'd only meant to be rash, as outspoken and shocking as she, and yet . . .

The Brazen Angel stepped back as if he'd slapped her. "You don't love me. You don't even know me," she stuttered, shaking her head in denial, as if the truth of her identity was too dangerous to even consider.

He hadn't realized his flippant statement would affect her so strongly. She feared love. Especially his.

And right she was to fear that dangerous emotion. It would hang between them with its enticing promise, obscuring their other obligations, stripping them of their reason. And instead of binding them with its promise of strength, it would destroy everything they both held dear.

Yes, he couldn't agree more. Love was too dangerous for them to share. And yet he wondered if it wasn't already too late.

He moved ahead, mindful of her wary gaze and his own discovery.

"Isn't my being here proof enough?" He leaned closer, his fingers catching her chin and tipping her head so he could bend over and whisper into her ear. "You left in such a hurry after our last . . . encounter, I was concerned you might catch cold without your shoes . . . or your clothing."

She muttered a rather unladylike French reproach and backed away from him. "Don't insult me. You certainly didn't follow me to Paris because you suddenly developed some grand passion. Play the tortured lover for some gullible miss, like your fiancée, someone foolish enough to believe your pretty speeches."

"You sound as if you don't approve of my betrothed."

"What do I care who or what you marry?" she replied. Moving around the marble monument, she used it as a shield between them. "Besides, you brought me here for business. Get on with it then, for when the morning comes I will be away from this place. Without you."

He pressed ahead, teasing her. Testing her resolve, as he tested his own. "Ah, but we have hours yet until dawn."

Her powdered brows arched in annoyance. "You wouldn't be so glib if you were caught by the Guard. . . ."

Her brows dropped, while her words seemed to catch in her throat. "You'll be tortured . . . executed."

The emotions in her voice stopped him. No one had ever expressed such a plaintive concern for his safety, not to his face, not out loud.

Giles leaned around the marker and grinned. For some reason it pleased him to hear the anxious sound in her voice. "Would you mourn my passing? Would your heart be filled with regret that we never——"

"Never what?" She tipped her head, studying him.

He leaned forward. "Never finished what we began in my study."

For a moment her breathing stilled. He saw the conflict in her eyes. And when she caught him watching her and realized that she'd dropped her guard, her pretenses came to the forefront.

Her gaze rolled upward in disgust. "You almost make me believe you are a besotted idiot. But I know who you are, Lord Trahern. Listen well. Here in Paris you are no more invincible to the quick path of the guillotine than I am the heir to the throne. And with nothing but death surrounding us, all you can speak of are regrets for what we——" She stopped abruptly, as if startled by the passion in her voice. She whirled around. Her trembling fingers picked absently at the moss on the gravestone.

"Whose heir are you? Maybe I was correct the night of the Parkers' ball when I asked you if you were a princess. One who's lost her home, her kingdom, her world." Closing the space between them, Giles reached over and gently took her hand in his. "Why, I don't even know your name. Who is this you hide beneath these shrouds of pretense?" His other hand reached over and plucked at her ragged costume.

"No one," she whispered, still looking away. "Consider me as alive as anyone else slumbering within these gates."

How strange it was that one moment she could be full of passionate outbursts, poignant compassion for the weak, and then be overcome by great sadness. Giles realized she might even be pushing him away because she sought to protect him. Yet if she knew who he was then surely she must understand that he hardly needed a guardian.

She was shaking her head. "Forget me, my lord. Go home to your betrothed. Live your life. Mine is lost."

"I disagree." He squeezed her wrist, her pulse beating wildly beneath his fingers. "You are very much alive."

At first she pulled at his contact, but he held her fast.

"Why did you follow me?" she asked in a breathless whisper.

In spite of the darkness, standing this close he could stare clearly into the deep blue fire of her eyes. Even with all her disguises she would never be able to hide her eyes from him.

Releasing her hand, he brushed aside the mobcap on her head, letting it fall to the ground. "So I might peel away your layers one at a time until you lay bare beneath me. Until I know you inside and out." His fingers twisted around a horsehair curl and started to tug her wig free. His body hardened as the excitement of discovery coursed through him.

"What you find may surprise you, Lord Trahern," she warned.

"Perhaps, but pleasantly so, I'd wager." He leaned over and laid a light kiss on the soft skin of her wrist. "How is it that you intoxicate men? What witchery do you possess to poison a man beyond reason?"

For all his chastising of Monty for his friend's wild infatuation, Giles was just as entranced. More so. Enough to throw aside his plans, at least for the night, to uncover her every secret.

And the glow in her eyes promised a willing partner.

"I doubt a man like you believes in magic." Her words became hesitant and slow. "Can you really believe that seeing me will give you your answers?"

He nodded. Of course seeing her would answer everything. Once he knew who she was, he could determine what her motives were. More than that, he needed to know who his newfound protector was, wanted to see her face uncovered.

She reached up and stroked his chin, her fingers sliding along the length of his jaw. "I possess no magic. It is all in your imagination. Close your eyes, milord. Close them and see what is hidden inside my heart." From her coat she pulled out a large linen handkerchief.

"What are you asking me to do?" He watched warily as she folded it into a long blindfold.

"To trust me." She held up the cloth as if to cover his eyes. "Trust me, milord. Let me tell you who I am in the only way I can."

Giles stepped back from the lure of what she offered. Acknowledging a hunch was one thing, but placing his life in her hands, blinding himself to her will, went beyond foolish. It was reckless.

Yet if he was to gain her trust, if he was to discover her secrets, he would have to step outside his protective circle and risk everything.

Against all his better reason he did as she asked and let her bind his eyes in darkness. At first, unfamiliar fears surrounded him, but he found them outmanned by the excitement he felt when her body slid up against his, her breasts brushing into his chest as she raised herself on her toes, bringing her lips to his.

His arms wrapped around her, pulling her closer, surrendering his mouth to hers. The kiss began so tenderly, he wondered at the tentative, almost hesitant caress of her tongue as it dallied with his.

"Let your body see," she told him. "Let your other senses trace my image."

Taking his hands, she guided them beneath her clothes until he felt the warm, smooth silk of her skin. Instead of giving them the freedom to explore, she led his fingers over her stomach and higher, until they cradled her breasts.

He heard a soft sigh escape her lips as his fingers curled around the tight and anxious nipples waiting for him. His thumbs drew slow, lazy circles around the sensitive tips.

So this was what the lady fancied. He willingly obliged her. In his mind he could see her smile, the way her neck arched back at his touch.

His lips followed the curve of her chin down to the nape of her neck, taking small teasing nips and nibbles.

Writhing in excitement against him, she suddenly took control again. Her hands sought out the warmth of his skin, pulling off his coat and shirt and finally splaying across his chest, teasing him with the whispered touch of her nails and the moist heat of her mouth.

"I told you, your eyes are useless," she whispered. "Never trust them."

She guided him to the ground, her hands tugging at

his shoulders. The tall, unmown grass choking the once-manicured plots gave them a gentle bed, enclosing and secreting them in its matted depth.

The scent of clover and grass lingered in the air around them. Giles heard stems snap and crunch as her body rolled and tossed until it melded to his. The wind played above them through the trees like the lone note of a flute. He'd never allowed his other senses to overshadow his sight. Now he found his ears, his nose, his fingers straining to fill his mind with the images she denied his eyes.

This close to her, so intimately pressed together, he found he could "see" the curve of her hips as he pushed up her rough woolen skirt to discover the tender flesh beneath. His hand cupped her rounded bottom and then moved around to the apex of her thighs.

They parted most willingly as his fingers sought to tease her there. Already hot and moist, she was ready for his touch, and more. Slowly he began his exploration, gently stroking the soft folds apart until he came to her heated core.

Sophia gasped when he touched her so intimately. The sensations came as a shock at first, so intense was the first moment of his touch. Now, as his fingers brushed in a gentle rhythm over her, she could only revel in the sweet touch. Quickly, her breathing grew more and more ragged as he continued to caress her, her hips dancing upward to meet each silken pass. His mouth claimed hers again, this time his lips and tongue matching the endless torture of his fingers.

If, as Sophia had thought, the choice of a graveyard would be enough to cool the impulsive passion between them, she'd been very wrong.

Even from the moment they'd left the dangerous streets behind, she'd considered what could come to pass within this safe corner of Paris. She knew that in the days ahead she might not live to see London again, might never have another chance to lay in his arms.

Suddenly, the price being asked of her rose too high.

What if she failed and died?

If that was to be her fate, if she should perish, then she decided in one glance at Giles's strong shoulders, in one kiss from his lips, that she could bravely climb the scaffolding if she could have but this one chance to know his love.

This would be their wedding night. The tender words she wanted to confide in him stopped in her throat. The rose-scented sheets she'd dreamed of bringing her lover to gave way to her old cloak and the sweet scent of grass.

If she couldn't profess her feelings for him or reveal her true identity, then she would let her body do what her heart and mind could not risk.

His mouth claimed her breast again, twisting from her a new torrent of need.

Oh, she wanted him to never stop. She wanted to forget her vow, her promises, and beg him to push her senses to the edge and toss her into passion's abyss.

But in this course she couldn't go alone.

If she was to carry the memory of his touch to her death, he would return to London with the same fiery gift.

Twisting in his arms, she tugged and pulled at the front of his plain workman's trousers, sighing when they opened and her hand closed around his hard staff.

Running her fingers up and down his tight maleness, she copied his own teasing touch and ran her thumb over the moist tip in a slow, tantalizing circle.

His groan of pleasure excited her further.

"I would have you inside me," she whispered in his ear. "I would have every bit of you pleasure me."

Giles needed no further encouragement, rolling her onto her back and poising himself over her. He didn't need to see the face in front of him to know her excitement matched his. Not when he could hear her ragged breathing, feel the wild pulse of her blood, taste the passion of her lips.

Anxiously, her hands sought him again, guiding him to her entrance.

"Please," she whispered. "Don't make me wait."

Nor could Giles wait any longer. With a long steady stroke, he filled her. No virginal barrier blocked his course, only her tight walls closing in around him, pulling him deeper into her.

She moaned softly as he began to move in and out, matching the frantic pace of her hips with even, steady thrusts that drove her wild with urgent desire. He could hear her murmuring pleas to go faster, go harder.

A reckless, dangerous course only a woman of passion could love.

He found her mouth and kissed her, closing every gap between them, pressing her into the grass with his fierce urgency.

"You are mine," he told her, gasping for air. "From this night forward you belong to me."

"I'll never belong to anyone else," she whispered back. Her hands caught his hips, tugging and pushing them to match her out-of-control pace. Her hips danced wildly, a final sensuous cry escaping from deep inside her.

Reaching up, he plucked aside his blindfold and stared directly into her eyes as the waves of release crashed over her. For a second he saw something he'd never seen before in a woman's eyes—an emotion so raw, so fierce, so intimate, it branded him with its intensity.

Her body continued to rack with spasms of pleasure, calling to him to continue stoking the fires. As her body closed and wrapped tighter around him, she carried him into the dark, turbulent landscape of release, his body pouring out his need and desires.

He collapsed into her welcome embrace. For a time they lay together, the spinning waves still binding their bodies together.

Pushing aside her hair, he searched for her face. At some point—he couldn't remember when—her wig had fallen free, raining down the long silken tresses his fingers now toyed with.

In the darkness he couldn't see the true color, but he felt the sleek luster sliding between his fingers.

Even so, when he uncovered her face he found her macabre makeup staring up at him. Quickly, he looked away from the wrinkles and wart.

No wonder she'd blindfolded him.

Her giggle caught his attention.

"Don't you like what you see?" she teased, rolling to one side and propping herself up on her elbow.

He looked her directly in the eyes. "I don't care what I see. I know you now."

She shook her head. "If you knew the real me, I think you would be quite disappointed."

There was something sad and wistful about how she said the words that reminded him of his little bride's haunting words.

I don't want to disappoint you.

What would his modest and frail betrothed say if she saw him here with another woman? Her undoubted dismay snapped him back to attention. He'd always been a man of monogamous tastes, one mistress at a time. In marriage he wanted to emulate his mentor, Lord Dryden. The man's respect and love for his wife was something of an oddity among the lascivious tastes of his peers. Yet the comfort of their relationship had always appealed to Giles, a man who'd never known familial stability in his life.

Giving himself to the Brazen Angel ran afoul of any solid commitment of the heart. At least he told himself that, pushing aside the intimate emotions he'd seen in her eyes. If he explored those feelings, let them creep into his heart and soul, could he ever return to his fiancée and remain only with her?

No, he realized. Never.

The notion rocked his senses. If this woman held enough power over him to forget his vows to a wife, would she also be able lure him away from his duty to uncover Webb's betrayer?

"Why all this secrecy?" he asked. "After tonight, after all this, will you tell me—who are you?"

She shook her head and looked away. "Don't ask me that. I will not, I cannot tell you."

Her words brought his distrust of her to the forefront. He would trust her to bind him in darkness, but she wouldn't offer the same in return.

Damn her and her secrets.

He reached for his trousers and hastily pulled them on. Wrenching himself away from the woman in his arms, he got to his feet and backed away from her until he bumped into a tall monument.

This mysterious woman with her siren call would claim his soul and then say she didn't want to disappoint him, refuse to tell him who she was.

Were those the words she'd used with Lyle and Rostland before she'd robbed them of their treasures?

Was it what she'd whispered to Webb before handing him over to the Committee?

Even if she hadn't turned Webb in, Giles was still standing in a graveyard with half his clothes on. The chill of the marble against his shoulder spread through his veins, robbing him of the last vestiges of heat her passion had filled him with.

What would she steal from him? She'd taken Delaney's money, possibly Webb's life. The only challenge left for her, Giles thought, was his soul.

Well, no longer, he told himself. She had been right before to insist they finish their business, but he'd allowed himself to become preoccupied with unmasking her. He'd been a fool to believe she would ever allow him to see her. She'd let him into her bed, she'd tease him with a glimpse here and there, but she would never give him what he wanted.

The truth.

Not until she was ready. And he was of no mind to dally at her beck and call, playing her deadly game.

She, too, seemed to sense the dangerous change between them and got up as well. Adjusting her clothes and gathering up her bundle, she eased away from him. Her hands steadied her rocking gait by reaching for the rusted bars of the fence enclosing the graveyard.

Sophia's heart beat a little faster. From the moment he

had stopped her at the foot of the Pont de la Concorde, she'd been trying to determine how much he knew.

Was his sudden anger evidence that he'd finally made the connection between his missing fiancée and the Brazen Angel? Had she allowed him to see past her makeup and into her soul?

If he'd discovered who she was, his jerky movements as he yanked on his clothes spoke of his apparent anger at her. And if he thought to save her, save Lady Sophia, she'd be responsible if any harm befell him. She felt the tender moments from their lovemaking fade. Try as she might, she found herself unable to gather them out of the air and hold them close to her heart. The sweet emotion, the powerful intimacy of his touch dissolved into the night, leaving her feeling as empty and cold as the heavens.

"Let us get on with this business of yours," she said. "How can I answer anything until I know what you seek?"

"If I were to ask you a question, would you answer honestly?"

It was not quite the response Sophia sought. "Yes. If I can. But first tell me, did you come here out of duty to your country or because of what happened between us in your study?"

"I have always lived my life by duty," he answered without a moment's hesitation. "And I have been instructed to discover your intentions. To find out where your *duty* takes you."

That finished her speculations.

And hurt far more than she expected. It also meant he didn't recognize that she was Sophia. He'd followed the Brazen Angel to France because of duty. Perhaps even made love to her as a means to his end.

Still, there was an edge to his voice, something that told her he wasn't being completely honest. He might be bound by his duty, but he was also a man.

One who'd left his missing betrothed for the Brazen Angel. A duty he obviously preferred to bedding his bride.

It didn't matter that she was one and the same; the insult of it prodded her.

"Then ask your questions," she said, trying to sound bored, "so we can be done with this foolishness."

His gaze jerked up, blazing with anger. "Foolishness? I speak of betrayal!"

This stopped her. Oh, it was worse than she had originally thought. He couldn't possibly think her responsible for . . . But he did, she saw it in his furious stance, his fevered gaze. It hurt to realize he thought her capable of such a crime, but what else did he know of her? She'd robbed men, she'd crossed the borders of war for her own means, she'd made love with him on what could be seen as a whim. She'd made a terrible mess of it and now she had to find a way to be rid of him. To send him home and protect him from the terrible danger surrounding them.

"I haven't betrayed anyone . . . lately," she added. "Try my patience, though, and you will find just how short my sense of honor can be."

"Honor? What would you know of——" His words cut off, as if he considered how far he dare push her. His quick gaze swept over her, measuring their surroundings.

Backed as she was into the corner of the fence, it probably appeared she was trapped.

Good, Lord Trahern. Underestimate me once again.

Sophia resisted the urge to smile at him.

"What would I know about honor?" she repeated for

him. "I suppose not much if I followed your rules. But here in France the rules have changed."

"And you change right along with them."

She nodded. "I've no choice. So will you if you want to survive." Walking over to their remaining discarded clothes, she picked up her cap and wig. Next to them lay his coat, and from the pocket sparkled a tantalizing hint of gold.

The Delaney bracelet! She glanced back, and when she realized he wasn't watching she plucked it out of his pocket and dropped it into her own.

Resisting the urge to smile, she turned back toward him.

If she'd learned anything as the Brazen Angel, it was that sometimes the most direct approach startled someone into revealing their weaknesses.

And she wanted to taunt him. Not too much, but just enough to sting his pride as he'd wounded hers.

"You want to know who I am, and whose side I am on," she said in a level voice. Her gaze locked on his, searching for a reaction. His eyes flickered, but only for a second.

Oh, he's good, she thought as she planned her next statement, but not good enough for this.

"You were sent here to discover how I am connected to your agent's death. You want to find out what I know about Webb Dryden."

CHAPTER
8

GILES FLINCHED AS if she'd punched him in the gut.

How could she know so much?

Then he thought of her strange pronoucement earlier on the bridge—about not having any more deaths on her conscience.

Had she been warning him that he, too, could share Webb's fate?

If anything, they'd more than underestimated her knowledge of the Foreign Office. Dryden would be stunned to hear of this incredible leak.

"What do you know of Webb?" he demanded. "Tell me, dammit."

"Why? So you can join him in the grave?" She shook her head. "Go home, Englishman. I'll not allow you to follow in your friend's footsteps."

"And how will you stop me?" He stepped closer to her, controlling the urge to shake the truth out of her. "As I said before, there is no one to save you tonight."

She backed up until her body pressed to the rusty bars of the fence. "I don't need any diversions or timely rescue to save myself." Her sapphire eyes mocked him. "Your arrogance that only you can solve this puzzle will be our downfall. Believe me, you will not survive Paris if you continue on this foolhardy search. Go home."

She reached over and caught hold of one of the tightly spaced bars of the fence. It groaned and scraped beneath her assault.

Only then did he notice that the bar she held was not as rusted as the others, that it appeared to have been put in place deliberately. To his horror he saw its purpose.

Beneath her grip it popped free.

Too late he realized that she was about to best him once again. He lunged for her, but not fast enough. She slipped through the opening and darted out of reach.

He tried to follow, only to find that the space was just enough for a child or small woman to escape.

His rage seethed at the unreachable lady before him. "Dammit, tell me of Webb. If you think you've stopped me you're wrong. I will find you. I will."

"Go home," she pleaded, her voice losing its mocking tone and taking on a sincere quality. "Wait for me in London. I know where to find you. If you will wait for me there, I promise to bring you the information you seek. No tricks, no deceptions, only the truth. Believe me."

Giles watched in futility as her departing figure disappeared around the corner. He saw no point in giving chase. By the time he got back to the street and around the block, she would be long gone. With her demonstrated knowledge of the city she could be anywhere from the Corn Market to the ruins of the Bastille.

Wait for her in London? Believe her?

He slammed his fist into the marble monument behind him. Pain exploded in his hand, shooting up his arm, bringing him to his senses.

He swore vehemently and thoroughly at his own stupidity, at his lust, at the way she twisted his heart. Turning to leave his grim surroundings, he nearly tripped over her jacket, which lay crumpled on the ground where he'd pulled it from her body.

While it hardly seemed worth the effort, he never left any clue unexamined. Sitting down on a grave marker, he went through the pockets one at a time, looking for any-place she could have hidden a message or coding device.

His fingers locked on to something hard and smooth, the prize he pulled out stunning him in its simplistic beauty and tremendous value.

"It seems in your haste to leave, Lady Brazen, you forgot something," he whispered toward the open railing in the fence. He hefted the gold signet ring in his palm, its weight astounding him.

A ring so rich was worn only by the wealthiest noblemen or merchants.

Stealing again, I see, he thought before turning it over to examine the insignia.

A fleur-de-lis and a swan.

The emblem sent chills up and down his limbs.

Frantically he searched in his own pockets for the scrap of fabric he'd carried with him since the night of the Parkers' ball. He held up the silver and white brocade next to the ring, shaking his head over the identical designs.

A fleur-de-lis and a swan.

Since he didn't believe in coincidence, the crest had to belong very close to the Brazen Angel's heart. He smiled to himself. "This may just give me the information I need to find out who you are," he said into the night, turning the ring over and over as he inspected it.

The ring, worn with age, was the type usually passed from nobleman to heir through the ages. And removed from the elder's hand only when he died.

He looked back at the hole where she'd escaped.

Perhaps the Angel was on a mission of revenge for a killer. Or she might be seeking the man who could claim the ring. Or perhaps she just carried it as a talisman. He could speculate the rest of the night away, but it wouldn't solve her mystery.

There was, though, one way to find some more answers.

Ignoring his body's desire to follow her, he retraced his steps and returned to the Sow's Ear.

S OPHIA PAUSED ON the third flight of stairs up to her attic lodgings. Her reluctance to continue the final flight stemmed from a strong need to sort out her conflicting feelings about the evening's events.

On one hand she was furious with Giles for not recognizing her, though it was only a further testament to Emma's incredible skills. She should be celebrating that he had yet to make the connection between the engaging Brazen Angel and the mild and meek Sophia.

But on the other hand it enraged her that he sought the company of the Brazen Angel, not that of his fiancée. He'd flirted outrageously with her, taken her as a lover, and boldly pledged his claim on her life.

What had he said as he'd brought her to the brink?

From this night forward you belong to me.

She shivered, as if he'd whispered the words once again into her ear.

It was true, she knew. She did belong to him. In a way she couldn't stop. It was as if he'd bound her with a rope, locked her away, and at the same time opened all the windows and offered to teach her to fly with the birds.

Then he claimed their night was nothing more than an act of duty.

Was this how he conducted all his missions for the Foreign Office?

No wonder he was so dedicated to his country, she thought with a huff.

And what if they did, indeed, end up married?

Would he share her bed and dream of another? Or just share his bed with others?

"The dog," she muttered before she stopped herself.

Sophia sighed, wondering how she'd let her imagination get this far.

She was jealous of herself.

Picking absently at the wax on her nose and cheeks that Emma had painstakingly applied to transform her into an old hag, Sophia realized what a horrible mistake she'd made.

She'd let her fears of the days to come divert her, allowed herself to fall prey to the false security he offered. If he knew who she was and what she knew of Webb, he'd haul her back to London and lock her away.

Looking out the hall window, she stared across the skyline, which was now turning pink with the coming dawn. Still, all she wanted to do was go back to the cemetery—convince him to trust her, beg his help in her final hours.

She shook her head and continued up the steps. It was bad enough she'd allowed Emma and Oliver to become entangled in her plans. She wouldn't allow anyone else to put their life at stake. The only thing she could do was survive so someday she could try and find a way to make him understand her duplicity.

Reaching for the childish comfort of her ring, Sophia realized she'd left it in her jacket.

And she'd left that in the cemetery. Her heart sank at its loss. By the time she returned to the churchyard it would be daylight, and the risk too great. She sighed, clenching and unclenching her fist, frustrated at the emptiness of it.

Quietly, she opened the door to their lodgings, hoping to slip in unnoticed. Emma and Oliver were probably still asleep. Two steps into their apartment, she realized sleep had been the farthest thing from her friends' minds.

"Where have you been?" Emma demanded. Between furious puffs on her pipe, she followed Sophia from the doorway to the fireplace.

So much for dodging this conversation until later, Sophia realized as she stuck her hands out to warm them in front of the flames. Even the usually agreeable Oliver sat with his arms crossed over his barrel chest, his brown eyes full of unspoken admonitions.

No help in that quarter.

"I was detained," she answered with a noncommittal shrug. She didn't want to start discussing Lord Trahern with Emma. It had been bad enough when she'd escaped his house in her underwear. Emma had teased her about that little episode for days.

Emma choked on her pipe. "Detained?"

"Do we need to discuss this now? I am very tired and I—"

"You slip in here like a thief and nonchalantly tell us you were detained? I think you owe us an explanation."

"Well, I got away."

Emma did not appear all that impressed. The clouds of smoke curled around her dark head. "That does it. You're going home." Sophia's companion began pulling their traveling bags out from beneath the narrow bed.

"Home?" Sophia protested. "I will not. Not now. Not when we're this close."

"Oliver and I can easily finish the work here. You're going home." Emma began opening the cupboards and pulling out Sophia's clothes. "Now that the authorities have seen you, there will be no saving you if you are caught again." Though older than Sophia by only five years, Emma was beginning to act like the aged puritanical companion Sophia's aunts thought they'd hired.

"I will do no such thing," Sophia sputtered, realizing she sounded like a spoiled miss in need of a scolding for sneaking out on a walk in the park unescorted.

She and Emma stood nose to pipe, glaring at each other.

Oliver broke the silence. "If you weren't caught by the Guard, then who?"

His stern, paternal voice snapped her attention and anger away from Emma. Oliver had been with her mother's family all his life, as had his father before him. He had traveled to France when her mother had eloped. Though England was his homeland, he'd never planned to return until the Comte requested that he escort Sophia to her aunt's house. He had been her only connection to France during those first lonely months in England years ago. With Oliver she shared her homesickness. He understood her jokes about her sister's desires for suitors, about Julien's boundless search for mischief, and her beloved older brother and his ever-growing family.

She loved Oliver like a dear uncle. So when she had approached him to help her with her plans, he had fought and protested over the desperate notion of returning to Paris, just like a family member would.

Her father would never allow it. She should stay safe in London and he would return, Oliver had argued.

But Sophia would not relent, and Oliver had eventually given in when she'd finally convinced him she would go with or without his blessing.

"Who caught you, little Piper?" he asked again, using a long-unused family nickname for her. "Was it Balsac or one of his henchmen?"

She looked first at Emma, then back to Oliver. She had no reason not to tell them, but she was reluctant to face what would be nothing less than an inquisition from Emma when her friend discovered who had kept her so late. "No, it was not Balsac."

"So, if it wasn't that horrid little man or the Guard, then who?" Emma prodded, her gaze boring into Sophia. Then it fell to pass over her rumpled clothing, the state of her costume. And if she couldn't see the truth behind Sophia's reluctance, she saw it well enough by the grass stains on her skirt.

The realization widened Emma's eyes. "Oh, no. It can't be. Not him."

"Who?" Oliver asked, a note of impatience in his voice.

"Lord Trahern," Sophia replied.

The satchel in Emma's hand fell to the floor with a loud *thump*. "Oh, merciful heavens. We're hanged for sure this time."

G̲ILES KNEW HE was pushing his luck by attending an evening's entertainment at the house of Georges Danton. The large, ugly man was one of the most powerful men in the new Republic, part of the group of dangerous, unshakable radicals called *The Mountain*.

The only reason Giles dared risk his neck in such company was because he'd been assured that Danton's guest list included La Devinette.

Milling near the doorway, Giles scanned the crowd.

For a group that disdained the trappings of aristocracy, Giles noticed immediately that Danton did not hide his love of luxury or wealth. Richly decorated in pastels and expensive fabrics, his salon appeared more appropriate for the home of a nobleman, not one who murdered nobles. Even the ceiling, with its bucolic country scenes, depicted a lifestyle swept aside by the Revolution. Only Danton, secure in his power with this new Republic, could dare what others would not.

"Corliss? Is that you? My favorite customer, you are back, *mon ami!*" Jacques Isnard called out, excusing himself from a conversation with a tall, darkly dressed man.

One of the few men in Paris Giles trusted completely, Isnard the merchant had provided him introductions into a wide array of powerful circles over the years. Since the last time they'd met, the man had put on a few more pounds and the cut of Isnard's suit was no longer a resplendent display of his wealth. Like the others in the room, he wore a plain-cut jacket and the new-fashioned trousers rather than breeches.

As the tides of French power rose and fell, Isnard, like the barrels he manufactured, floated along in the changing tides, always with his head above the fast-moving waters.

"Good to see you, sir," Giles said, offering his hand in greeting.

The merchant pumped his arm in an enthusiastic greeting. "Come meet the new France." Isnard escorted Giles through the room, introducing him as an American planter from Virginia. The fact that Giles actually owned a small plantation in the former colony gave credence to his story. And it helped that he had visited the place, so as to lend some realism to his ruse. A number of the gentlemen at the dinner party had fought with Lafayette during the Colonies' revolt, so their questions had been both probing and on point.

And his answers were accepted.

For now, he thought warily.

People continued to filter in, stragglers who had not been deemed worthy enough for feeding though clearly would enliven the evening's discourse. But no sign of of the lady he sought.

"You look a little tired, *mon ami,*" Isnard observed, pausing for a moment in the doorway that adjoined the salon to Danton's famous library. "Eh, too much wine last night or a good woman?"

Smiling, Giles nodded. "Too much of one and not enough of the other."

"An agreeable woman is hard to find anymore," the man said, slapping him hard on the back. "This regime is favorable in many ways, but the women, bah. They have no manners, no sophistication." Isnard grinned. "But if I know you it is not a lack of companionship that keeps you frowning this evening. Perhaps you will share your *petite praline* with an old friend, *oui?*"

"No, Isnard," Giles said with a laugh. "She's hardly your type. Much too jaded for your taste. If I remember correctly you prefer the ones fresh from the country or straight out of the convent."

"Ah, the convents." The man rubbed his hands together over his protruding stomach. "They produced such sweet morsels. And alas, they are gone as well."

"Careful what you say," Giles warned. Though they stood beyond the guests conversing in the salon, it still wouldn't do to have such talk overheard. "You sound like a man who regrets change."

"Regrets only when it comes to issues of the heart," the wily old scoundrel laughed. Isnard slapped Giles on the back. "Shake off the sour taste this whore left in your mouth and come meet our host, Danton. He is as dry and boring as a spinster's thighs, but he is too powerful to snub. A good man to have as a friend, if you know what I mean. And good timing—his guest of honor just arrived, so I will be able to say I introduced you to La Devinette."

"I've heard of this woman," Giles commented. "What is she like?"

"See for yourself." Isnard nodded across the room.

Standing next to the hefty Danton stood a slight woman. As if sensing someone was watching her, she turned and glanced in their direction.

Instead of stepping forward into the open salon, Giles took a step back into the library, concealing himself from her. Even in this latest transformation he recognized her instantly.

The Brazen Angel.

Now he possessed his final proof, he thought as he watched the lady Paris called *La Devinette* nod politely to Isnard and coolly return to her conversation with Danton.

His hands knotted into fists at his sides.

Isnard nudged him. "There's one for your adventurous Colonial blood, though I doubt she'd have you."

Giles tamped down the anger building in his gut. So she did dally with the highest members of France's Revolutionaries. Her duplicity was unmatched. Stepping farther back into the library and out of her line of vision, he asked Isnard, "Who is she?"

"Like I said, they call her *Citizeness Devinette,* for her history is a riddle to everyone. The only thing anyone knows for sure is her loyalty to the Republic."

She's certainly dressed the part of a loyal daughter of France, he thought, glancing over Isnard's shoulder as she made her way through the room, having left Danton and been joined by a young man Isnard had introduced as Louis Antoine Saint-Just.

In his mid-twenties, Saint-Just's ascendency in France had been accomplished through the young man's devoted service to Robespierre.

"They make a striking couple," Isnard commented. "The daughter of liberty and the son of the devil," he muttered under his breath.

Giles had to admit La Devinette held the attention of every man in the room. Including his, which angered him more than her alliance with the self-serving Saint-Just.

Her dark hair, so captivating the night before, now revealed a cast of chestnut under the brilliant candlelight of the chandeliers. Partially tucked into the red cap of the *sans-culottes,* the rest of the luxurious strands curled down to her shoulders in thick curls.

Her gown, of the plainest cream muslin, left her shoulders, arms, and neck bare, falling in a straight line to just past her ankles. The simple design of her dress was broken at the waist by a red, white, and blue sash, into which she'd jauntily tucked a short sword, signifying her unity with the Fraternity of the Revolution.

For all appearances she looked the Amazon warrior, confident in her cause, unshakable in her loyalty. But Giles studied her closer and saw her flinch ever so slightly as Saint-Just took her elbow, and she watched the room in stolen, furtive glances.

She was waiting for something or someone. And the waiting frightened her.

It reminded him of how she'd acted as she'd entered Delaney's house—cautious and wary.

But one question still plagued him: Where did her loyalty lie?

"Surely someone knows who she is," Giles insisted.

Isnard shook his head. "A question that has been asked by many and answered with nothing more than speculation.

Some claim to have seen her leading the people at the Bastille, others say they heard her speak years ago in the gardens of the Palais Royal before anyone dreamed of Revolution." The merchant threw up his hands. "As I said, it is all speculation, but it makes for a wonderful diversion from who is having his head cut off today."

Giles glanced in her direction.

Saint-Just bent his head over her shoulder and was whispering into her ear. Sparkling laughter followed, laughter designed to tease and flatter a man.

"And is this Saint-Just her protector?"

"Her lover, you mean?" The man shook his head furiously. "The arrogant pup would give his right arm to find himself in her bed, though he'd never admit it." Isnard nodded over to where Robespierre stood scowling from behind his thin wire-framed spectacles. "Saint-Just treads a delicate balance, pretending one moment he cares not for the vices of men, for the sake of his master, and the next—" Isnard's eyebrows raised and his gaze slowly swept over the woman on Saint-Just's arm.

"But has she taken a lover among these wolves?"

"Oh, you are a desperate man. Surely, you noticed the eye?" His voice dropped to the gossipy whisper of an old woman. "Oh, that eye . . . the wagers that have been placed on how she lost it! The most common theory is that she was used most foully by a nobleman, and when she complained of her mistreatment to the authorities, he retaliated by ordering her eyes put out so she could not identify him."

Giles held back a smile. "But only one is missing," he pointed out, knowing full well that if encouraged, Isnard would provide complete details on everyone in the room.

"*Oui*. For when he came for her, he and his henchman both found justice at the point of her sword, but not before she lost one of her eyes. It is said he was one of the first to die for the Revolution." Isnard shuddered. "I could introduce you, but I must warn you she is most fastidious about who she takes into her company. I, for one, would be too nervous with such a woman, if you know what I mean. Besides, they say she never takes off that sword of hers."

He didn't know why Isnard's announcement that she had taken lovers in the past bothered him but it did. "Who is she currently favoring?"

The older man laughed. "If I didn't know better, I'd say you're jealous. Your tastes have definitely changed, *mon ami*." Isnard glanced back in her direction. "Currently, she has no one, though Saint-Just certainly has the best chance, for he is her type."

"And what type is that?"

Isnard shrugged. "A few months ago there was an American, not unlike yourself, but younger. He had an engaging manner, a refreshing change from the rest of this morose bunch. He was quite attentive and she was—how do you say—very receptive. They were seen everywhere, until—"

"Until?"

Isnard's eyes narrowed. "This is why I would warn you not to entertain any notions about her. The woman is dangerous."

"What happened to this American?" Giles asked, already sick with dread. "Perhaps I know him." He tried to sound noncommittal, but the Angel's acknowledgment last night that she knew Webb now seemed to be confirmed.

"*Knew* him would be a better phrase. About two months ago he disappeared. It was rumored he had gone back to the Americas, but others claimed to have seen him—"

"Seen him where?"

Isnard moved farther into the library. They were alone in the room, away from the chattering din of the salon. "It is said she betrayed him. Sent him to his death."

Giles looked back toward the salon, fighting the urge to toss her over his shoulder and haul her back to London in chains. "Did he have a name, this American?"

"I'm just trying to remember that. He was only introduced to me once. . . . Your American names, they all sound alike to me. None of the beauty of our language." Isnard scratched his head. "Seth . . . no, Wade . . ."

"Webb?" Giles suggested.

The man's eyes lit up. "*Oui,* that is it. Webb. So you did know this man?"

"No, just a lucky guess." Giles swallowed back the bile rising in his throat.

What had she said the night before?

I haven't betrayed anyone . . . lately.

So it seemed she had betrayed Webb. And taunted him with her knowledge before she fled into the night. He unclenched his fists.

"You don't look well," Isnard commented. "Such treachery is always hard to stomach, but by a woman it is loathsome. Now you see why I told you she is not your type."

"I couldn't agree more," Giles said. "And you are right, I am fatigued. Perhaps I will go outside and get some fresh air."

Isnard bowed and rejoined the company in the salon,

while Giles lingered for a moment in the library. He walked over to the desk, where he found a piece of paper and a quill. Dipping it into the well of ink, he began a simple note.

Meet me . . .

"CITIZENESS," A SERVANT whispered at Sophia's elbow. "I have a message for you." He slipped a piece of paper into her hand.

She turned to her unwanted companion, Louis Saint-Just, and smiled. "It seems I have a secret admirer." Holding up the paper, she laughed. "Any wagers on who sent it?"

"You have many admirers, *ma cherie.* You bring out the spirit of liberty in men." Louis glanced back at the departing servant.

"So it seems." She knew he would question the servant as to who gave him the note, but if her contact was as careful as he had been in the past, the search for her mysterious messenger would be for naught.

Opening the folded slip, Sophia tried to still her shaking hands. Tonight's meeting was to be the first step in the culmination of months of hard work, starting with an exchange of gold in an amount that could have saved even the King from the executioner.

Best of all, it meant her deceptions were finally nearing an end.

Over Emma's and Oliver's objections regarding the threat Lord Trahern posed to their plans, Sophia had convinced them that the annoying Englishman would not find her at Danton's.

How could he? she'd asked them. He'd had nothing on her but the Delaney bracelet, and even that he no longer possessed. How could he make any connection between the Brazen Angel and Citizeness Devinette? But the best argument she'd come up with for attending the affair was that her contact would be looking for Citizeness Devinette, not Emma or Oliver. And without Sophia present they would never be able to make the transaction.

Firm in her arguments, she'd won out against the better judgment of her overprotective friends. And while she'd put on a great show of indifference that Giles would never be able to find her, she'd spent most of the evening agitated and jumpy.

What if he did arrive? What if he did find her?

If he revealed her identity before . . .

He would leave her no choice but to denounce him before he could expose her.

She'd risked everything to raise the necessary money, and now that she stood this close to succeeding, with so many lives at stake, she couldn't allow him to ruin everything.

So denounce she would. She must. No matter what her feelings for him argued. And then she'd figure out how to save his neck from the blade.

"What does it say?" Saint-Just asked, barely concealing his jealousy and annoyance.

Sophia sniffed. This man was becoming more and more of a problem. At first she regarded his indifference to her as a blessing; however, as his power expanded he seemed to believe that all of France was his for the taking, including her.

Just as he had when they had met years and years ago. But this time she had the advantage. He showed no signs of recognizing the connection between La Devinette and the blushing girl of fifteen he'd showered with his affections.

"An invitation to dine tomorrow," she lied. Tearing the note into pieces, she strolled over to the fireplace, knelt before the flames, and fed the pieces into the eager blaze. "As if I have time for such frivolous pursuits with so much work to be done."

Saint-Just joined her in front of the grate as the paper curled and darkened before it burst into flames.

Brushing her hands on her skirt, she made a great show of getting up from the fireplace and directing a scathing gaze around the room. "If he is still here I want to make sure he is well aware of my response."

"He could not help but understand your message." He offered his arm again and smiled when she placed her hand on his forearm. "I am pleased as much as my adversary is disappointed. You are a remarkable woman not to be swayed by all the attention you receive."

"It is a small price to pay for what I can do for my country."

Saint-Just nodded and they continued strolling around the room. Sophia's mind raced with excuses for extricating herself from his company. Her rescue came in the form of Citizen Isnard, an annoying but harmless barrel manufacturer who styled himself as quite in the thick of things.

"Citizen Saint-Just, a word with you." Isnard bowed low, his nose twitching. "Citizeness, I beg your indulgence in allowing me to steal the citizen away from your company for a few moments."

In past meetings with the man, Isnard had skittered around her like a nervous puppy. He probably believed the outrageous gossip about her circulating the Paris salons.

Since she knew she already frightened the man, she added a glare to her response, if only to see his bushy eyebrows flutter nervously. "Of course, citizen. I was just saying to Louis that I had heard of the problems in your jurisdiction." She turned and smiled to Saint-Just. From the smug look on Louis's face she knew he not only approved of her pricking the pompous Isnard, but probably wished he'd thought of it himself.

"Problems? *Non,* citizeness. Where could you have heard such a lie? My district is extremely loyal to the Republic. We have no problems."

"Of course you don't," Saint-Just soothed. "The citizeness is teasing."

"Ah, *oui.* I suspected as much," Isnard said. "I was just saying to my American friend that the citizeness is known for her fine humor. He sought an introduction, but I thought to spare you. He is a rather coarse fellow and hardly your type."

Sophia smiled. "And what is my type, Citizen Isnard?"

As the man coughed and sputtered she excused herself, well pleased with his timely interruption.

She strolled carefully toward the door, searching for some sign as to which of the guests was her new contact. But no one seemed to acknowledge her with anything other than the usual curiosity or cautious disdain. The note had said to meet outside, so perhaps her contact had already slipped from the crowded salon.

Near the doorway she bumped into a woman who was entertaining three rather pompous men. "*Excusez-moi,* citizeness," Sophia said politely. But before she moved on she leaned closer and said to Emma, "It is time. I am to go outside."

Emma gave no indication as to whether or not she had heard the message, continuing her animated discussion with barely a pause.

Sophia wrapped her shawl tighter around her shoulders and slipped from the salon to the hallway. Nodding to the footman at the door, she smiled at him. "If Citizen Saint-Just inquires about me, will you tell him that I stepped out for some fresh air?"

"*Oui,* citizeness," the man replied, his gaze quickly lowering to the floor, unwilling to look her in the eye or gain her displeasure in any fashion.

She knew Emma was responsible for the rumor that La Devinette emasculated her lovers when she was through with them, and she would have to remember to thank her friend for the inventive tale.

The cool night air assailed her, whipping through her thin dress. She couldn't say much for the new fashions. They might be delightful in August, but in the growing chill of October they offered little warmth or utility.

Carefully making her way down the steps, she scanned the empty street. At first she thought perhaps she had misread the note. It had said to meet him outside. Had she taken too long? Perhaps Balsac's information had been false. Or worse, this was a trap.

A ripple of fear edged down her limbs as she carefully looked up and down the street again.

There was no one in sight.

Then she heard it—a soft whistle floating on the wind in a lonely lilt. She turned toward the notes and followed.

Her senses told her this was all wrong. She had never met an informant in anything but the safety of a crowd, with Emma or Oliver watching her back.

She knew Emma would leave the salon quickly and find Oliver, who waited for them in a tavern several blocks away. The plan was for Sophia to escort the man to the tavern, where they would transfer the gold to his care.

Taking a deep breath, she rolled her shoulders back and tried to look as menacing as La Devinette's reputation allowed.

In the shadows of a doorway she spied a looming figure.

"I have a riddle for you, Lady Brazen."

The voice tangled and teased her nerves. She'd heard it interrogate her, she'd heard it whisper into her ear words of passion. It startled her tonight with the depth of its anger and intensity.

The man stepped closer until Sophia saw the wicked gleam lighting his eyes. She stilled her trembling limbs, her racing thoughts of escape. It was no use to flee.

Lord Trahern was once again the hunter, and she, his prey.

"Or should I say," he continued, "feeling brazen this evening, Citizeness Devinette?"

CHAPTER
9

Sophia's mouth went dry.

Lord Trahern!

She recovered quickly and turned on one heel to flee for the relative safety of Danton's house. Though not fast enough.

He caught her easily.

"Let me go, you great ponderous—" she gasped before his hand clamped down on her mouth. Twisting one hand free, her fingers grasped the hilt of her sword. She didn't know what she was going to do with the weapon if she got it unsheathed, but perhaps she could use it to convince him to leave her before someone saw them.

His other hand clamped down over the hilt, pinning her fingers and blade to the scabbard. "Would you run me through and be done with the deed or give me over to the guillotine for all to watch your betrayal?" he whispered into her ear.

"Both," she mumbled through his hand. Her traitorous limbs seemed to recognize his hard lines, melting into his body in anticipation of the pleasure he'd pulled from her the night before.

If his body felt the same longing he didn't show it, his hold on her deadly and impersonal in its icy grasp.

"Will you call for help if I release you?"

She shook her head.

Slowly his hand dropped from her mouth.

She gasped for air, but did not cry out. The last thing she wanted to do was explain to Saint-Just and her host, Danton, why she was being accosted by an Englishman in the street.

While he gave her the air she needed to breathe, he denied her freedom from his iron trap. She lifted her foot to stomp on his, much as she'd done at the Parkers' ball, but he anticipated her move, spinning her around until her feet tangled and she nearly stepped on her own foot. His hands wrestled her arms until they were pinned to her sides.

"Now I will have some answers, Lady Brazen." He glanced back at the house. "Or should I say citizeness?"

The sarcasm in his voice shocked her. She'd been reckless to push his limits last night concerning her knowledge of Webb, but it had been as much for his own good as it had been for her need to punish him. She'd needed him to hate her, to leave her alone.

Now she saw the terrible destruction she'd wrought between them.

She'd done more than wound him. She'd pushed him beyond his measured control.

His dark gaze drilled into her, his mouth and jaw set into hard lines as he waited for her to respond.

"Leave me be," she whispered. "You're ruining everything. Please, just let me go." What would she do if Saint-Just saw them like this?

Cold indifference filled his gaze. "How prettily you beg when you want something," he sneered. "And it must be something you need very badly to warrant such a convincing performance."

"What I want is for you to return to London. Can't you see the danger you are in?" How she wanted to touch his cheek, brush back his hair, find his gaze looking down at her as it had the night before. "I want you safe. I couldn't live with myself if anything happened to you because of me."

Beneath his arched brows, his eyes widened with disbelief. "I don't see how my death should be of any consequence to your conscience. What is another man's corpse to the likes of you . . . to the likes of them," he added, nodding at the lighted windows of Danton's house.

Sophia had never anticipated this burning hatred. Of course she'd heard accounts of his strength of character and loyalty before she'd ever met him.

But to stand at the very cauldron of Paris, at the steps of one of its most powerful men, and demand justice for his friend? Sophia didn't know whether to admire him or wonder at his sanity.

Face to face with his stubborn resolve to uncover the truth about Webb Dryden, she realized those noble characteristics that she admired so much would only lead to his demise.

And hers if she didn't find a way to get him to leave her be.

"I will tell you everything, if only you will let me go tonight."

His hand reached up and toyed with the binding partially covering her face. "And you expect me to believe you, when only last night you told me the secrets you hold would never pass your lips? Why this sudden offer to open the sacred gates?"

She glanced hastily up at the salon windows. One of the curtains fluttered as if being hastily replaced. "I haven't the time to explain. There is too much at stake right now." Sophia struggled free from his grasp, her hands going to his chest, pushing him down the street one step at a time. "Can't you believe me when I tell you, this is no place for you. I won't let anything happen to you."

Her words seemed to snap something inside him, as a look of confusion passed over his features.

Instead, he shook his head, the raw emotions so close to her own tossed aside. "No need to reach for tears to convince me, citizeness. I've seen all your tricks. *All of them*. The only thing I'd like to know is which ones you used to lure Webb to his death."

Sophia blinked, not quite sure she understood what he had said. "His death? I sent him to no such end. Why I—"

"Stop," he ordered. "I've enough evidence to see your pretty neck stretched from an English rope for what you did to him. Half a dozen people in this house could give statements that you were often in his company. I know you and Webb were very close—that is, until you turned him in."

This was why he followed her so intently: He thought her responsible for Webb's death.

Oh, what a horrible mess this has turned into.

While she could easily tell him the truth, a glance at his angry stance and glaring features convinced her he would only accuse her of lying further.

And he wouldn't be that far from the truth if he did.

"You truly think me capable of murder?" she whispered.

"I can count a dozen crimes you've committed so far in your illustrious career. What is such a sin in a list that includes theft, assault, larceny, fraud? And considering the bloodthirsty lot in there," he said, nodding toward the salon window, "murder would be probably be an evening's entertainment."

"But after last night . . ." she started, struggling to reconcile the man who'd claimed her as his and this man before her accusing her of murder. "How could you . . . have . . . how could you come to me like you did last night if you thought me capable of murder?"

"A benefit and a risk of the job, you could say." He smiled, though there was no hint of humor in the grim facade. "Nothing more."

She stepped right up to him, until she stood within inches of him. His callous indifference hurt, more than she thought possible. She'd known the risk she'd taken when she'd offered herself to him. And when he found out the rest of her deception—that she was Lady Sophia—she knew his anger and outrage would sever all ties between them.

"I have done nothing," she said. "Nothing you wouldn't have done to save the lives of—"

Lord Trahern caught her by the shoulders. "Save the lives of whom?"

Her mouth closed tightly. She looked away before she said too much.

"I've had enough of your lies and your games." He gave a short quick whistle, and from down the street a carriage pulled out from the shadows. The *clip-clop* of the horse's feet on the cobbles seemed to toll the end of her masquerade.

"Will you not believe me?" she whispered, struggling against his grip as he pulled her toward the waiting conveyance. "Webb's death . . . it was—" she broke off, as if struggling for the words, "—fate," she finished.

"Fate?" He pulled to a stop. "I call it murder when an innocent is carted off to the guillotine. You've run with this pack of vultures too long, citizeness, if you think you have the right to choose who lives or dies and call it fate."

"It isn't like that," she shot back. "I've never made that decision. Webb knew the dangers. He made his own choices—" Her gaze flicked warily toward the salon window above them. "If you would just trust me and leave this place now, I promise you—"

A voice Sophia dreaded finished her sentence for her. "Promise him what, *ma cherie?*" Saint-Just called down from the doorway.

Her captor immediately set her aside, and for that she was thankful.

"Corliss, is that you down there?" Isnard said, joining the young man on the steps. "This is the young man I spoke of earlier—Giles Corliss," he told Saint-Just. "The one from the American provinces. He has a vast number of ships to help us break these wretched English blockades."

Sophia stepped back and distanced herself from Lord Trahern. She only hoped that Louis's jealousy would not put them both at risk. Smoothing her hands over her dress, she did not look up immediately or answer Saint-Just until she was positive her face would not betray her emotions.

Please, Lord Trahern, use your best judgment. Tread carefully; both our lives depend on it.

Saint-Just was down the steps and at her side without bothering to acknowledge Isnard's chatter or this new-comer's presence. "*Ma cherie,* what is it you were about to promise this man?"

She laughed, though to her ears she sounded more hysterical than amused. "Not to prove all the rumors about me are true." She pulled her sword from its scabbard and pointed it at Lord Trahern's heart. "You know my fascination with Americans, but this one holds the most alarming viewpoint on land ownership. I told him if he left immediately I wouldn't hold his views against him, nor would I kill him outright."

Louis seemed to relax at her explanation, an indulgent smile spreading across his lips. "You are too extreme in your ideas, citizeness. This new regime is about freedom of expression for all men." He caught her by the elbow and began guiding her back into the house. "Sir," he said over his shoulder to Giles, "would you care to rejoin us? I would be most pleased to hear your ideas. You have my word that my lovely companion and her radical theories will be held at bay. I will even disarm her if you so ask."

Lord Trahern shook his head. "I have early business on

the morrow with Citizen Isnard. I think it is time I was to my bed, so I will be in top form for my negotiations."

Saint-Just nodded. "The early bird, eh? Is that not one of your Benjamin Franklin's notions?"

"Yes, it is," he agreed. He bowed to her. "If one is after a worm."

Sophia flinched at his words.

"Then happy hunting elsewhere," Louis said pointedly, his icy hand resting possessively on her elbow. "I look forward to hearing your ideas another day, for I have a feeling we shall meet again."

Sophia watched Giles climb into the carriage, pausing to catch his instructions to the driver. But Saint-Just's impatience interrupted her.

"Come inside, my dear. It is too cold out here, and far too dangerous." His grip on her arm tightened. "Whatever were you thinking to come out here alone?"

"Why, I don't remember," she replied lightly. "But you shouldn't worry about me. Of all people, you should know that I can take care of myself."

He nodded and began to guide her up the stairs.

Reluctantly, she followed Louis. She couldn't help but feel he was leading her up the steps to her own private gallows. Before she crossed the threshold she took one last glance back into the street and found it empty.

Much to her relief, Lord Trahern's carriage had disappeared.

That didn't solve her own problems. How much had Saint-Just heard of their conversation? Any of it would have been too much, that was obvious.

But if he intended to turn her in he didn't appear in any particular hurry, for once inside he released her arm.

"Rather arrogant fellows, those Americans," he commented. "I don't see your fascination with them."

"A passing curiosity," she replied with as much disdain as she could muster. "Thank you for coming to my rescue."

He smiled, then bowed. "I am always at your service, citizeness."

A servant came up and whispered into his ear, and Louis made his apologies. "*Ma cherie*, I must see to some business. Can I trust you not to threaten any more of Danton's guests tonight?"

She laughed. "Of course, Louis. I find my fit of pique is well over. Go, take care of your business. I will try to find some amusement other than politics."

As she watched Saint-Just join Robespierre in the library, Sophia scanned the lingering crowd of guests one last time.

Her contact. Could he still be here, or had he given up because of her misspent time with Giles?

She took a turn through the room, avoiding any groups that might lock her into conversation. Emma was nowhere in sight, probably waiting at the tavern with Oliver for the delivery.

She knotted her hands at her sides. All of this had been so easy until Lord Trahern entered her life. From the moment he'd taken her arm in the Parkers' ballroom, everything had started to go wrong.

For six months she'd clung to her resolve, as stubbornly as Giles held to his, and it had buoyed her through her most tenuous moments. Now she found herself doubting she'd survive the next hour, let alone the demands the next twenty-four hours would exact from her.

And with everything she had to worry about, now Giles's life was added to her shoulders.

Damn him, she thought. And damn my foolish heart for caring about the unyielding man.

Beyond the salon she saw Saint-Just in a heated discussion with Robespierre. The two men rarely disagreed, as the younger Saint-Just followed Robespierre's vision and plan for France as if it were scripture.

Something about the tense scene stilled her anger at Giles. She'd seen that look on Louis's face before, when he was to be denied something he wanted. Sophia shivered. She could well imagine what it was Saint-Just may want.

Quietly, she eased her way toward the library door. Straining to hear the conversation inside, the first words out of Louis's mouth confirmed that her safety as La Devinette was at an end.

"I agree that we need to find this American she was with tonight. Citizen Isnard will know where he lodges. I no more believe he is a simple Colonial trader than I am the Prince of Denmark. I want him found and brought in."

Sophia swallowed back the waves of fear breaking over her. Lord Trahern was in terrible danger, and it was all her fault. She should have been more careful, should have never gone out to meet him. If something happened to him—

"But what of Citizeness Devinette?" Robespierre chided. "Will you arrest her as well?"

Saint-Just did not answer at first.

Holding her breath, Sophia wondered if she could still her heart, the pounding in her chest threatening to drown out the man's answer.

"It will be no easy task denouncing her to the citizenry. They love her. I've heard her compared to that ancient English hero, Robin Hood."

"Do I need to remind you, citizen," Robespierre said, the

warning in his voice chilling the air around him and all who listened, "that even the most trusted servants of the Republic must come under scrutiny from time to time?"

Sophia knew exactly what type of scrutiny Robespierre planned.

Saint-Just cleared his throat. Renowned for his oratory skills, sometimes he didn't know when to quit. "If you are implying that I am involved in Citizeness Devinette's plots, I would have you know my loyalty is—"

Sophia turned from the doorway before she was caught eavesdropping. Her vision swam. She leaned against a pedestal to steady herself.

"Citizeness, I find this crowd quite dull, don't you?"

The voice at her shoulder made her nearly jump out of her skin.

"Pardon?" she asked, wiping her suddenly damp brow.

A rotund man peered at her from behind his small, round glasses, his owlish eyes blinking. "I said, I find this crowd quite dull."

The innocuous words might be nothing more than idle chatter to anyone else, but they were enough to snap her attention back to the matters at hand.

For they could come from only one person. Her contact.

"Yes, citizen. Quite dull. Perhaps you have visited the local tavern? The wine there is much more to my taste."

When her new friend nodded in acceptance of her expected reply, she followed him toward the door.

With one last look toward the library she realized with relief this was the last time she'd endure Saint-Just's company. Slipping unnoticed out the front door, she breathed a sign of relief to be gone from the house, whose walls had but moments ago closed in around her like a prison.

Joining her contact in the small plain carriage she'd hired, she considered how she could warn Giles of the danger he was in. He'd followed her here to Paris because he thought her responsible for Webb's death.

Maybe it was time to set him straight as to the fate of Webb Dryden.

If only he would believe her.

GILES WASN'T SURPRISED to see the Brazen Angel leave with another man. They stepped briskly down the steps and into an unmarked carriage. It left Danton's house with due haste. He immediately bid his driver to follow, though at a respectable distance. Her conveyance stopped in front of a tavern, where her companion got out and went in, while the Angel remained in the carriage.

"Quite curious," he whispered to himself, as the Angel's carriage rolled away with her still inside. He followed for some time until it dropped her not far from the cemetery where she had escaped him the night before.

He watched as she made a great show of getting out of the carriage and going up the steps of the fashionable house. At the door she waved the driver off and the carriage rolled slowly out of sight.

After it turned the corner she retreated down the steps and into the street. For a second he saw her hastily glance over her shoulder. She hadn't looked at his carriage but into the shadows behind him. When he looked back he realized that they were, indeed, being trailed.

"So you don't trust Saint-Just," Giles said quietly to himself. "Smart lady." He instructed his driver to pull past her and slow at the next corner. As the carriage made the right turn, Giles slipped out and hid in the shadows. He already knew how she was going to elude the other man following her, but this time he would be on the other side of the fence waiting for her to pop out.

In a few minutes he spotted her coming out of the alley, a sly smile twisting on her lips.

You shouldn't smile too much, Lady Brazen, he thought as she once again took him on a twisted tour of Paris. *Next time Saint-Just will send someone small enough to fit through that puzzle of yours.*

When she finally did stop at the doorway of a building, he ground his teeth together.

It was the same apartment building where Webb had lived.

She went inside the front door and he watched for which room she would enter. Sure enough, a few minutes later a candle flickered to life in the attic rooms.

Could she actually have taken the man's life and then moved into his apartment? Giles unclenched his jaw.

Well, there's one way to find out, he thought. He started down the block and slipped into the alley that ran behind the houses. Webb had picked this apartment because it offered several escape routes. Out the front, out the back, over the connected rooftops, and through a series of hidden doors in the basement to the sewers.

Of no mind to explore the Paris underground, he chose the attic entrance. He'd done this once before, on a dare by Webb. Though he wondered if in that time the landlady had done anything to improve the rotting condition of her roof.

As he climbed the tree to the adjoining building, he surveyed the roof. No, it didn't appear that the greedy woman had spent a *sou* of the money he'd paid for her worthless information for repairs. He obviously hadn't paid her enough, or she would have told him that the woman he sought lived beneath her own roof.

Well, hopefully he wouldn't find himself crashing down in the landlady's bedroom. Making her charming acquaintance once was enough, for he didn't think he had enough cash to extract himself from a second meeting.

There were lights on in the ground floor, so he decided to wait before venturing further afield. He reasoned she wouldn't go far tonight, at least not until it drew closer to the witching hour she seemed to prefer.

As he sat perched above the house, the strange stillness of Paris surrounded him. Before the Revolution, Paris at night had been a heady experience, full of light and excitement. That Paris was gone. He thought about the strained manners of Danton's guests and the strange wariness with which the Brazen Angel had moved within that dangerous circle.

Believe me, she'd asked him the night before.

He found himself wanting to believe her, as he had the night before. His body still longed for hers, despite his reason's unwillingness to believe her.

She couldn't be telling the truth. He had seen and heard all the evidence he needed.

And yet last night she'd opened his eyes by covering them, by asking him to trust what could not be seen. Something about those minutes—that incredible blindness she'd awakened him from—echoed back to him.

How could he reconcile the woman of last night with all the evidence that pointed toward her as an active participant in Webb's death?

An hour later, with no more answers than when he started and the house now dark, Giles carefully walked the roofline until he made it to an attic window without mishap. He pried open the latch and dropped into the hall. Opening his coat, he drew out the small pistol he carried for situations like this. Making sure it was primed, he stopped beside her door and listened.

Nothing but silence greeted him.

This time, Lady Brazen, I will have my answers. His fingers closed over the knob.

He hesitated for a moment before bursting into the room, pistol drawn.

The Brazen Angel jumped up from a small stool near the fireplace. She still wore her La Devinette costume, the shadowy candlelight and meager flames of the firelight offering the concealment she obviously preferred. His gaze swung from one end of the room to another, searching for any other occupants, but it appeared she was alone.

"Lord Trahern," she whispered, wiping her sleepy eyes.

He nodded to her and crossed the room in two long strides, first checking one bedroom and then the second, smaller closet. There was no one else in the apartment.

Quickly, he closed the door to the hall and turned the latch. He took a deep breath, preparing himself for the battle she was sure to pitch.

So sure was he that he would have placed a wager on her reaction. Surprise. Outrage. Anger.

The last thing he expected was this.

"Giles," she whispered, saying his given name for the first

time and saying it with relief and passion. "You're safe, you're alive."

He noticed now that there were tears suddenly streaming down her face.

She rushed to his side, throwing her arms around his neck.

"I thought I'd lost you forever." And with that final outburst she caught his face with her hands and pulled him into her eager kiss.

CHAPTER
10

N O O N E W A S M O R E
surprised than Sophia as she wound her arms around Giles's
neck and opened herself to his kiss.

Though she'd arrived home anxious for Emma and
Oliver to return, exhaustion plagued her. She couldn't rest,
not yet, not until she'd figured out a way to warn Giles of
the terrible danger. As she discarded plan after plan, the
warm glow of the fire and the quiet solitude of the room
drifted into her chilled bones, pulled her eyes closed, and
tugged her into a restless sleep.

In her dream she'd watched helplessly as Giles was led

up the scaffolding in the Place de la Revolution. She'd tried to call out to him, but the roar of the enthusiastic crowd drowned out her pitiful pleas for mercy. The cheers were so loud that they reverberated through her, leaving her shuddering at the side of the scaffolding, her hands over her ears. When she looked again for Giles, Saint-Just stood on one side of the guillotine and Robespierre the other, both men smiling down at her like indulgent fathers.

Giles stood proud and tall between the pair, his hands bound behind his back. A breeze ruffled his dark hair, his eyes looked to the west, toward the distant shores of England.

"No, please, no!" she'd cried out, trying to look away as Giles stood defiant, bravely meeting his fate. And as the crowd grew louder in their zealous anticipation, he turned his head toward her.

"Was it so difficult to love me?" Giles asked her. "Was it so easy to betray me, wife?"

As he said the words, Saint-Just pushed him into the crowd, allowing them the pleasure of killing their enemy. In a frenzy they descended on Giles's bound body, driving their pikes and stakes into his flesh. Blood stained the stones at her feet. His hand reached for her, but she was too far away to save him. Her feet froze; she couldn't save him. Try as she might, she couldn't move forward to stop the mayhem.

Sophia wrenched herself awake rather than watch anymore.

So easy to betray me, wife. His accusations tolled over and over.

She'd done nothing to save him. She'd tried, but failed him.

Startled, she'd blinked back the final horrible images, only to find Giles, alive and whole, standing in her doorway. Fighting off the last shrouds of her nightmare, she'd stumbled to him. When her fingers touched the warmth of his skin, she knew he was truly alive.

Then she'd done what any wife would do. She threw her arms around him and rejoiced.

But she wasn't his wife.

"I was so worried," she murmured, stepping back from his embrace, suddenly embarrassed at her reaction. Considering how cold and cruel he'd been in front of Danton's house, she should be chastising him. "I didn't know where your lodgings were." Sophia turned from him. "I didn't know how to warn you."

"Warn me of what?" He turned her around to face him. "What is this, my lady? More of your tricks? More deceit?"

She shook her head. "No. Never again. I overheard them . . . and then I didn't know where . . . and now you're here and safe." Sophia knew she was rambling, but she didn't know how to control her rampant emotions, the fear, the relief, the anxiety still controlling her.

His dark, restless gaze said he didn't believe a word she was saying. The realization hurt as much as his words in her dream.

And then she knew the terrible truth of it. Emma had been right all along. Sophia was in love.

No! she wanted to cry out. *Leave me be. I have no room in my heart or my life for you.* But it was too late, the damage done.

The words on her lost ring mocked her.

Nothing is difficult to one who loves.

How wrong those words are, she realized. Love made

everything all that much more difficult. Especially when one loved the Marquess of Trahern.

She struggled to regain her usual bravado, to use it to push aside her newly discovered feelings. But all she found in her heart were the leftover feelings of despair and help-lessness from her dream. She wouldn't let Giles die, not because of her.

"Please believe me," she said, touching his sleeve again to reassure herself he was alive and this wasn't another trick of sleep. "You're in terrible danger."

A hint of a cool smile twisted at his lips. "I've known that since the day I met you."

"That's not what I meant," she said, pushing her hands against his chest. "They've ordered your arrest."

Black fury rippled over his features. "And *who* betrayed me?"

The same fears from her dream resurfaced, and for a moment she saw him once again on the scaffold.

Shaking the errant thoughts away, she put her hands on her hips and faced him. It certainly hadn't been her fault that he continued to follow her, continued to ignore her warnings. "You did, you great ponderous ape. You did it yourself."

With each word his tone rose in menacing disbelief. "I betrayed myself?"

Sophia let out a large sigh. "Why do I bother? Why do I even try?" Her gaze swept back over Giles. "You betrayed yourself. I told you to return to London, not to follow me. And did you listen? No! Now you've brought yourself under suspicion. Robespierre didn't buy your flimsy story about being a Colonial. Who would? You've got pompous, arrogant English aristocracy stamped all over you. And now, if I don't get you away from here immediately, you will die like . . . like . . ." She turned away, embarrassed by her outburst, afraid of the images she'd seen.

He moved toward her so softly that when his hands pulled at her shoulders she jumped. The warmth of his fingers and the sure reassurance of his arms calmed her as he pulled her into his embrace. "What of you? What has all this done to La Devinette?"

"I am to be arrested as well. The orders will go out on the morrow."

Giles listened to her quietly pronounce her own death sentence. Where before her voice had been filled with a fiery passion for his safety, her own danger seemed to surround her with a calm resolve.

As if she'd always expected to die.

The idea of her death chilled him. He'd been furious at her earlier, sure she was part of a larger conspiracy, but now he wasn't so sure.

Her wild flight into his arms when he'd entered the small attic room felt so right, as if she belonged at his side, worried and concerned for his safety. And for the first time, the loneliness and hurt that he'd worn like a cloak most of his life fell aside to be replaced by this woman's care and concern.

His eyes saw the raw emotions on her face and in her voice. While he knew her to be an accomplished actress when she needed to be, somehow tonight felt different, as had the night before when she'd lain in his arms.

Even with all the unanswered questions about Webb, his heart told him to believe her. Trust her.

Methodical to a fault, Giles found himself considering throwing his usual sensibility and caution to the wind. And the moment he opened his mouth he did toss it aside, saying for the first time in his life what his heart held so tightly hidden from the world.

"Then we'll be away from this place," he whispered in her ear, wrapping his arms around her to ward off the chill suddenly filling the room. "I can have us back in England before anyone knows where to look."

She shook her head. "You must go, but I cannot. My work here is not yet finished."

"If you stay, I stay. You'll not be rid of me so easily."

Her stubborn features told him she would never allow it. As if you had any choice, Lady Brazen, he wanted to tell her. Instead, he asked, "What is so important that you cannot leave tonight? What is this work you hold so sacred?"

In the hallway outside, footsteps echoed.

His muscles tensed. Giles listened carefully, distinguishing three, maybe four people approaching the attic. "Who are you expecting?"

"You've wanted to know why I've chosen this life. Why I cannot leave Paris. This will answer most of your questions."

The door opened and a young boy bounded into the room.

"Piper!" his excited voice squeaked. He crossed the room like an anxious puppy, in a great, whirling streak, dashing into the Angel's open arms. "Ah, Piper, I missed you."

"And I missed you, Julien," she told the boy, tears filling her eyes.

The boy leaned back and looked at her costume. Then he broke out laughing. "You look silly, Piper. Are you a pirate now?"

Both of them laughed at Julien's announcement.

When Giles looked back at the door he saw a lanky, awkward girl hovering near the entrance. He guessed she was probably no more than thirteen. She had that coltish, uncomfortable look of a girl who thought of herself as a young lady, yet was still a child at heart. Instantly, he spotted the likeness between the two women. Copies of each other, though separated by seven, maybe eight years.

Whatever reserve held the girl back melted away and she, too, joined the boy in welcoming the Brazen Angel like family.

He remembered the Latin words on the inside of the ring he'd found in her clothing. Giles had discovered them earlier in the day when he'd taken the ring around to the jewelry shops on the Ile de la Cité hoping to identify its true owner.

Nothing is difficult to one who loves.

So the Angel had returned to Paris to save her family.

And family they had to be. The resemblances were incredible. She and the boy had the same rich chestnut hair, while the young girl's coloring ran fair and blond, but her features promised to mature into the same startling beauty as her . . . mother? No, he thought, looking back at the sentimental tableau in front of him. The Angel was too young to have a daughter that old.

Siblings.

And they'd given her a name. *Piper.* Somehow, the strange little name fit the mysterious woman.

Tears flowed down Piper's cheeks. She obviously hadn't seen her brother and sister in some time. Given her emotional reaction, she'd probably thought them lost forever.

Dressed in mere rags, the children wore the clothes of the poorest country peasants. Giles's trained eyes saw past their disguises.

Even in his excitement, the boy stood with a nobleman's pride, his back straight and his head held high. The girl, too, stood with her shoulders back, her bearing rigid.

She also looked familiar, he thought, trying to place her in the ranks of the French families he'd known at Louis's court before the Revolution. Actually, she looked more English than French, with her stiff bearing and dark scowl.

Her censorious frown was aimed directly at her brother's high spirits and antics. Julien had found his sister's sword and was dispatching his imaginary foes with the sure thrusts and parries of someone who had received the finest training.

Training reserved for the highest levels of aristocracy.

That explained Piper's seamless transition into the London ton as the Brazen Angel. She'd probably learned her lessons at the court of Louis XVI, where deception and intrigue came naturally to the aristocracy.

Piper hadn't taken these outrageous risks for her own needs, she'd taken them for her family. Giles stepped back, stunned at the chances she'd taken. And of all the scenarios he'd played out in his mind, how could he have missed this one?

The answer came to him swiftly. Because he had no family.

Actually, if he thought about it, he'd never really had one. No brothers, no sisters. Only his father, and he had been gone on his own missions for long stretches of time. Giles backed away from the threesome until he stood alone near the fireplace.

What had she said tonight?

It was a matter of life or death.

And he'd mocked her. Now he saw how real and desperate her course had been. Giles knew noble children died beside their parents every day. And the children before him were still a long way from freedom. His scene at Danton's house probably hadn't helped her plans any.

A sinking dread filled his chest. What had he done?

While this might not explain her connection to Webb, he wouldn't allow children to die because of his mistakes. With his ship at Le Havre, he would see Piper and her siblings safely to England. From there they could live in the protection of one of his country houses, until . . .

Until what? he asked himself. Until his bride-to-be found out he was keeping a mistress right under her nose? He didn't know how the meek and mild Sophia would react, but he suspected Lady Dearsley might say something about the arrangement. And just how loudly she'd lodge her protests.

Hell, he'd impose on Monty. The Duke had more property than he knew what to do with. He could spare a house somewhere.

And then Giles would have to turn his back on the Brazen Angel. Go on with his life as if she'd never existed. He'd marry Lady Sophia, since his duty to his father's choice dictated he must, and spend his years wondering what might have been. With this dreary prospect he turned from the heartwarming reunion in front of him and stared moodily into the flames.

SOPHIA THOUGHT SHE'D never see Lily and Julien again. When the countryside near their father's château exploded with Revolutionary passion, family retainers had hidden the children, shuffling them from relatives to friends throughout the surrounding countryside.

But Sophia had known none of this.

The last message she'd received from her mother had been that the youngest D'Artiers children were safe, but her mother had not said where, too fearful to reveal their sanctuary in a letter.

Not long after Sophia had received her mother's missive, the remaining family had been arrested by the National Guard.

For the first few months she'd used her money taken as the Brazen Angel to uncover where the children were hidden. To bring them to England involved further bribes and costly forged paperwork, especially after the two countries had renewed their age-old conflict and declared war against each other again.

But now everything seemed to be going as planned.

Sophia whispered a small prayer. *Please let them remain safe.*

"Piper," Julien said, "I have decided to become a farmer when we go to England. Do they like farmers in England?"

"Yes," she said with a smile. "They like farmers."

"That's good, because I like farms. Especially the pigs. They are quite social, you know. They like everyone."

She tried to ignore the haunted light in the boy's eyes or his apparent overwhelming need to be accepted. She wrapped her arms around his narrow shoulders. He was so thin.

No, the last year and a half had not been easy on her brother or sister.

Lily hovered close by, unusually quiet.

When Sophia had last seen her younger sister over four years ago, the girl had been an irrepressible chatterbox, full of questions about court life and boasting of all the dresses and suitors she would have once she had her chance to attend their mother at Versailles.

That Lily was gone, replaced by this silent shell of a young woman.

Sophia's only hope was that once the pair returned to England and were placed in the loving care of their aunt Mellisande, they'd fill out a bit and even possibly forget some of the horrors they'd witnessed.

The door to the rooms opened and Oliver poked his head in.

"The children need to get some rest. They've a long day—" he stopped abruptly when he noticed Giles in the corner.

Sophia got up. "He followed me here."

Oliver nodded to her.

Giles looked closely at the roughly dressed man in the doorway, his eyes widening with recognition. "Has your wife found her 'Johnny' yet?"

The man grinned back. "She's down the 'all looking for 'im, guv'ner."

Turning to her, Giles shook his head. "How many accomplices do you have?"

"Just one more."

"And are you going to introduce me, *Piper*?"

Sophia smiled at his use of her family nickname. "No. The less you know of us the better."

"You might have explained all this yesterday and saved us both the *difficulties* we discussed." He stepped closer to her and lowered his voice to a tense whisper. "If I've endangered your family, then I want to make sure that they reach whatever destination you have planned. My ships, my resources are yours to command."

Sophia took a deep breath, stunned by this sudden offer. The change in him was too remarkable to believe, but as his gaze moved over Julien and Lily, she knew he now understood. He knew why she'd done what she had. Not only that, he finally believed her.

"We could use a safe ship," she said. "Thank you."

"You have a ship?" Julien asked, dodging in between them.

Giles tousled the boy's matted hair. "Yes. And you will sail on it."

"I would command it," Julien corrected with a wave of his sister's sword.

"I thought you wanted to be a farmer?" Lily commented sarcastically.

Her mocking bitterness shocked Sophia. For one so young to have such anger brewing inside her—it was good that her sister was leaving France.

"I can be a farmer and a sailor. Can't I?" Julien argued.

Sophia moved forward, ignoring her sister's severe tones. She plucked the wicked blade from her brother's hands. "You can go to bed and dream of being both."

At this he frowned. "But I'm not tired."

Hugging him close one more time, she smiled over Julian's thin shoulder at Lily. "But you will be in the days ahead. You must go tomorrow with the lady you met this evening. Mind her as if she were our own *maman*. I will follow right behind you."

Sophia handed Julien over to Oliver's care and turned to her sister. "Please, go get your rest now. I'll see you in the morning before you leave."

The girl shook her head, her foot stomping almost imperceptibly. "Why did you make me leave him?" she demanded. "He was sick. He needed me. If anything happens to him . . . I'll never forgive you."

This reaction was something Sophia had never foreseen happening. Her sister sounded like a woman in love. And she had a good idea who was the object of her sister's emotional outburst.

But Lily was only a child. And this child's crush was too dangerous to be shared in front of Giles.

"He isn't well enough to travel yet," she whispered to Lily, steering her toward the door. "He will need to stay here, at least for the time being. Would you have the journey kill him?"

The girl shook her head stubbornly.

"So go on now. And sleep so you can be strong for"— Sophia paused and glanced over to where Giles stood staring into the fire—"Julien," she finished.

Lily finally relented, but not before sending another frown toward Giles and flouncing out of the room in an adolescent huff.

Sophia turned toward Giles. "You should stay here tonight. It won't be safe to return to your lodgings." She folded her hands in front of her.

He looked up from the flames. "Is that an invitation?"

"Not the way you imagine. Though I—" she looked around the small bare rooms, realizing how much smaller they were with the addition of two children and now another adult. How she wished to spend the night with him again, much as they had done last night. But it was impossible. "I'm afraid all I can offer is the floor out here."

For a moment they stood in silence, each considering the other's words.

"Thank you," she finally said.

"For what? For endangering your family? If I'm not mistaken those two are your brother and sister."

"Suffice it to say they mean the world to me. And you haven't endangered them. Not yet." Sophia sighed.

"Once they are in England no harm will come to them," Giles said fiercely, as if he'd come to a decision on something very important.

But just what, Sophia couldn't imagine. Nor would she have ever considered his next statement.

"I have a house," he began, "in Bath. It's out in the country. Byrnewood. I rarely use it, and I thought perhaps that if you needed . . ."

Sophia had never seen Giles look or sound so uneasy. Pompous, know-it-all Lord Trahern stumbling along like a stuttering schoolboy reciting his lessons. And what he offered was even more unbelievable.

"What are you saying, Lord Trahern?" she asked, wanting to make sure she heard him correctly.

"It's just that when you get to England it will be rather expensive, and you might not have planned that far ahead. . . ." He stumbled along for a few more sentences. "And you might need a place to stay while you get your bearings again, away from prying eyes."

"Are you offering me shelter?"

He nodded, obviously relieved that she was going to make this easier. "Yes, shelter. It's a small house. I never use it. But I could take you and the children there. Make sure you're settled and established without any worries."

Sophia knew Byrnewood was more than the poor cottage he was making it out to be. Considered one of the finest country houses in Bath, the lush lawns rolled from the rough local stone walls in clipped elegance. Stables, servants, endless rooms. And he offered it to her and her family as if it were nothing.

"Established?" Sophia asked, not knowing whether to be amused or angry. Here was her fiancé asking another woman to set up housekeeping with him.

"Dammit," he blustered. "You know what I mean."

"Yes, I do. And what would your charming betrothed think of this *arrangement*? I mean, you still intend to marry Lady Dearsley's niece, don't you?"

He coughed. "Yes. I've a duty and obligation there."

Sophia smiled wickedly. "And what is it we share?"

He didn't respond, his jaw working in frustration.

"And after your marriage to the lady? What will become of me then?"

"My marriage will make no difference. Don't you see that? I have no choice but to marry Lady Sophia. I'm the last of my line, and it was my father's dying wish to see me continue the family line. There is much I would give you, much I would let you ask of me—but to break a vow to my father and forsake this marriage are two things I cannot give."

It was not the answer Sophia wanted to hear. "No, I suppose you can't," she replied. "But if there is one thing I've learned, we all have choices."

"I don't. Not on this. It's a matter of honor."

"Honor?" she laughed. "Honor allows you to marry a woman you obviously care little about and hide me away in the country for your pleasures? Where is the honor in that for me?"

His gaze went to the fireplace, as if he dared not look her in the eye. "It is all I can give."

"Yes, I suppose it is." She stepped back from him, the words poised on her tongue to tell him who she was. But the images of her dream rose in her mind. No, she couldn't tell him. For if he knew he would never allow her to finish her work.

"If you were sincere about the use of your ship, I thank you for that," she said carefully. "It will eliminate some of the risk. I'll rest easier knowing Lily and Julien are sailing to England entrusted to your safekeeping."

Giles tipped his head and stared at her. "You aren't sailing with them?"

She shook her head.

"Why not? You've saved their lives; what else can you hope to achieve here?"

"I have other work to finish. I shouldn't be more than twenty-four hours behind you."

"Behind me?"

"Yes, you're going with the children. I need you to see that they arrive at your ship without any mishaps." Even as she said the words she could tell by the look on his face he wasn't going to be easily swayed.

"Oh, no, Lady Brazen, or Piper, or citizeness, or whoever you are, I'm not leaving your side. You and I still have some unfinished business. Namely, what you know of Webb Dryden."

Sophia had hoped to avoid that sticky situation tonight. "I've told you my position on that subject. I'll bring you all the evidence you need in London. Not a moment before." She saw the storm clouds brewing in his dark gaze, but her own anger at his continued stubbornness about his marriage to Lady Sophia provoked her. Her hands in two tight fists, she spoke. "Go ahead," she dared him. "Bring down the house. Rant. Rave. Call the local guards. I'll not tell you another word about Webb Dryden until you are safely back in London."

"Then I stay here in Paris with you."

Silently, she cursed his stubbornness.

"Besides," he asked, "what could be more dangerous than tonight's escapade? What could be more dangerous than deceiving every member of the National Committee?"

Sophia took a deep breath. Pulling herself up to her full height and squaring her shoulders, she told him.

"Tomorrow I intend to break the remaining members of my family out of Abbaye Prison."

IN THE QUIET of the small bedroom Sophia listened to her sister's even breathing. When she'd come into the room Julien had awakened and insisted on sleeping in the outer room with Oliver and Giles.

In case they needed an extra guard, he'd argued sleepily with his sister.

Sophia gave in rather than start another disagreement.

Her head pounded from her battle with Giles. They'd spent a good two, three hours arguing over her plan to rescue her family. And in the end they'd reached a stalemate.

The morning promised to see the fight continue, until she'd convinced him there was a prayer in hell that under the right circumstances and despite the warrant for her arrest, her incredible plan just might work.

"Emma," she whispered. "Are you awake?"

"How can I sleep? Your little sister told me smoking was vulgar and all but ordered me to put away my pipe."

Sophia laughed softly. "And did you?"

"Yes. The little brat threatened to complain to your

aunts the moment she returned to England. You'll have your hands full with that one when you get her home. If she doesn't happen to *accidentally* fall over the ship's rail during the crossing."

"I know what you mean. You didn't hear what she nearly said in front of Giles."

"I heard, all right. The entire pitiful story. You are truly a wicked sister to wrench her away from the man she loves. She'll never forgive you." Emma chuckled.

"*Maman* did the same thing to me when I was nearly fifteen. I had a rather unsuitable affection for one of the gardener's sons. That was when I was sent to Versailles."

"Did you forgive her?"

"Yes, eventually." Sophia remembered when she forgave her mother. It had been the moment she'd fallen under the spell of Louis Antoine Saint-Just six months later. His dark clothing and ardent passion had inflamed her fifteen-year-old sensibilities.

She'd learned only too late that Saint-Just had none of the strength of character that surrounded a man such as Giles like an ancient knight's armor.

"Well, I suppose Lily will forgive you," Emma commented.

"In time."

Emma lit up her pipe, the familiar scent of her tobacco filling the small room.

"Giles offered me a house," Sophia whispered. "A place for me and the children."

"How generous," Emma commented. "Is he going to put it in your name? That was always my mistake. I never got it in my name before I said yes."

"Emma!"

"Well, he intends to make you his mistress, am I correct?"

"Yes, I would assume that's the arrangement he has in mind."

"Then get the house in your name," her friend advised.

"And what name do you propose I use?"

The pipe glowed with a furious puff. "That is a problem."

"That isn't the only problem," Sophia said. "I think I'm falling in love with him."

Emma rolled over and stared at her. "I can see that falling in love with the man you are supposed to marry would be a problem."

"Oh, you know what I mean. He's in love with her, with the Brazen Angel, or La Devinette, or everyone else, but he's not in love with Sophia. And it will be Sophia he marries."

"So tell him the truth."

Suddenly the words from her dream made complete sense.

Was it so easy to betray me, wife?

She wasn't *going* to betray him, she already had. With her deceit and her elaborate plots. Giles Corliss, Marquess of Trahern, could never marry the Brazen Angel. And if he did marry Sophia and her dual identity were ever discovered, the disgrace would be insurmountable.

He and his heirs would be shunned from polite society, all because of her.

"I can't tell him. Nor can I marry him."

Emma tapped out her pipe. "Then become his mistress."

The idea held more appeal than Sophia cared to consider. But Giles needed a legal wife, a respectable woman to bear his children and ensure that his lineage continued untainted. "I'll disappear. Maybe go to the Colonies."

Laughter followed this response. "Sophia, is it a nice house?"

"What house?"

"The house Lord Trahern offered."

"Yes. I visited Byrnewood often with my aunt while the old marquess was still alive."

"Then take the house." With that, the ever-practical Emma rolled over and went to sleep.

CHAPTER
11

THE CHILL OF THE
October morning penetrated Giles's rough wool uniform.
Standing in the mews behind Webb's old apartment
building, he waited with Piper for Oliver to arrive with
the horses they'd been able to hire and the cart they'd
purloined. Behind him he heard her fidgeting with her
sword, rattling it in its scabbard. Every few moments she
would peer down the alley, searching the narrow byway for
Oliver.

"He should be here any minute," she said, pacing back
and forth in a steady rhythm with the peal of the distant

tocsins. They'd started before dawn, calling the people of Paris to hear the latest news. "I suppose with this morning's tidings it will take Oliver longer to get here."

Giles nodded, though he was hardly anxious to see the poor cart come rambling down the lane. Oliver's arrival would be the first step in this suicidal plan. Though he should know better, he had to give his arguments one more try.

"This is insane. Abbaye? Why not just try to steal the Crown Jewels?"

"If you think of a better way let me know." She sniffed and looked down the alley. "I agreed to let you go with us on the condition that you wouldn't argue with me. That you follow orders. If this is a problem . . ."

Shaking his head, Giles shoved his hands in his pockets and said nothing. What could he say that he hadn't already voiced? But he wasn't about to let her go in alone, not after he'd realized he was responsible for ruining her position of trust with the National Committee. Even with his admission and apology, it had taken most of the night and into the morning to convince her that he could be of assistance.

The woman was too damned stubborn.

The children and Piper's companion, introduced only as "Emma," had left before the first hint of light. The woman's face was shrouded in mystery, for she'd worn a hood and scarf wrapped tightly around her head and shoulders. With Lily and Julien also dressed in rough country clothes, Emma towed her unwilling charges on foot toward the city's gates.

Once outside, Piper explained, they'd be met by an accomplice who would carry them in a freight wagon to Le Havre.

Down the alley the rattle of wheels and the whinny of a horse caught his attention.

"Now, explain to me once again how you propose to keep us from being killed," he said as she clambered up into the front seat of the cart next to Oliver, who also wore the uniform of a National Guardsman.

Piper grinned at his question. "I don't know. That depends on how well you follow orders," she said, nodding at his newly acquired uniform. "So get in." She jerked her thumb toward the back of the cart.

Relegated by his lower rank, Giles climbed into the back of the cart. He grimaced and scratched at the ill-fitting coat and trousers. Barely settled in his seat, he found himself jerked backward as the cart lurched forward, the wheels crunching over the cold cobbles.

Giles wondered what Lord Dryden would say about the report from this mission:

16 October. Helped the Brazen Angel free family members imprisoned in the Abbaye while Paris celebrated the death of its Queen.

It was bad enough he voluntarily agreed to walk into the most heavily guarded prison in all of Paris, never mind that they were doing it under the guise of *fédérés*.

A swift death by the guillotine would be too much to hope for if they were caught.

Breaking into Abbaye, Giles assumed, and masquerading as *fédérés* guaranteed nothing less than being drawn and quartered.

So despite all his protests, all his arguments, he and Oliver ended up spending the wee hours of the morning finding a pair of suitable guards from whom to steal uniforms. Their choices had been less than ideal, but the clothes had been obtained without too much of a fight.

Well, a bit of a fight, Giles thought as he rubbed his bruised knuckles.

"I still say you should dress in something else," he said, nodding at her La Devinette costume. If anything, he considered it his duty to inject some sanity into her impossible plan.

"And how am I to get into the prison without it?" she shot back. "If they think I'm on official business we'll be allowed to enter the yard unrestricted. Otherwise we won't make it through the gates."

Giles remained unconvinced. "Tell her," he said to Oliver. "Tell her this is nonsense. No one will believe her."

Oliver clicked the reins and laughed. "Better to tell today's crowd they should spare the Queen's life. Why do you think we called her 'Piper'?" The man's wide face split into a smile.

Giles smelled a good story and perhaps a clue to her true identity. Besides, the story might take his mind off the impossible task ahead of them. "Ah, so she was always good at leading the other children into trouble, eh?"

Piper and Oliver exchanged glances. Her face colored slightly at the question, while Oliver grinned even wider.

Intrigued, Giles persisted. "Come now. Out with it. I want the entire tale."

She crossed her arms over her chest. "It's just a childhood nickname. Nothing more."

Oliver laughed. "If you won't tell him, I will."

She muttered a rather potent curse. "If you must, but be

216

quick about it." She glanced over her shoulder at Giles and then at Oliver. "No embellishments."

Oliver leaned back in his seat, obviously enjoying his mistress's discomfort. "When she was quite young she decided she wanted to be a shepherd when she grew up."

"Not a shepherdess?" Giles asked.

Oliver responded with raised eyebrows and a slight shake of his head.

Giles studied Piper for a moment. "I see what you mean. A shepherd it is."

"A noble profession," Piper said, interrupting Giles's muffled laughter.

"And so she set out to learn the necessary skills. She dressed like a shepherd, learned to tell all the sheep in the herd apart, how to lead them to the best pastures."

"And she did this with great skill, I assume?" Giles asked.

"Of course," she snapped back. "Suffice it to say I played at being a shepherd as a child. There, you've heard a charming and amusing story about my childhood. That should satisfy your curiosity, for this story is at an end." Her tone brooked no resistance.

Oliver winked at Giles and continued quite merrily. "There was, however, the matter of the pipes. A good shepherd should be able to while away his afternoons playing his pipe. The sound soothes the little beasts and keeps them close."

To this, Piper "harrumphed" and turned away.

"Our little shepherd never quite mastered the instrument. In fact, she was ordered out of the fields. Her playing agitated the poor sheep into a state of revolt. They found some of the distressed animals several fields away cowering in the shadows of the local parish. Some said the beasts were praying for the hellish racket to end."

Giles laughed out loud this time, ignoring her outraged glare.

"Enough," she said between gritted teeth.

"Oh, but it just begins," Oliver said. "Our poor little shepherd enlisted the help of everyone in the village to teach her how to play the pipes."

"Did you finally master the instrument?" Giles asked.

At this, Oliver laughed so hard that Piper had to pick up the story and the horses' reins.

"No, I didn't," she said in disgust. "I'm tone deaf. I failed horribly."

"Then why are you called 'Piper' if you can't play the instrument?"

"That's the irony of it," Oliver said, finally having stopped laughing enough to finish his tale. "Everyone in the village trailed after her, trying to help. Soon, people from other villages heard of her predicament and came to offer their advice. Crowds would gather——"

"Crowds!" she muttered with disbelief. "Next he'll be telling you the King sent royal musicians to instruct me."

Oliver retrieved the reins from her hands. "As if that could have helped."

Giles laughed at this, until Piper turned in her seat and frowned at him.

"I suppose you can play better?" she asked.

"As a matter of fact, I can," he told her, crossing his arms across his chest. "Someday I'll prove it," he added in response to her look of disbelief. "This still hasn't answered my question. Why are you called Piper?"

Oliver clucked at the horses. "Because she attracted so

much attention and so many people came to hear her play so badly, we called her Piper, like the piper in the children's story. Only instead of stealing all the children of the village, she drove away all the sheep and anyone who stopped to listen."

Giles nodded his head in triumph. Coyly, he glanced over at her. "And what was your name before they called you Piper?"

"Nice try," she muttered. "Believe me, it's better you don't know our identities. It would only endanger you further."

"Perhaps. However, it would give me something to tell the Tribune when they put me on the rack to confess."

"That isn't funny."

"I didn't mean it to be."

They fell into silence as Oliver turned off the quiet streets of the Place Vendôme and joined the processions heading toward the Rue St. Honoré.

The crowds thickened around them, slowing their progress. The air of Paris thrummed with the somber, steady sound of tocsins, calling the people to the streets.

"They truly are going to murder her, aren't they?" Giles asked in disbelief as a pair of boys dodged in front of the cart. They held aloft a burning effigy of the Queen, Marie Antoinette.

Piper nodded, her gaze fixed on the flames. "Balsac came by after the bells started. The jury handed down her sentence at about four." She shook her head. "She isn't the first." Her wary gaze continued to watch the burning wax and crepe as it caught in the breeze and lofted far above their heads. "Nor will she be the last."

She shuddered. "I've feared this. The streets are about

219

to run with blood. If the Assembly thinks her death will appease the people's thirst for revenge, they're mistaken. This murder will unleash a fury of the worst demons. A plague against the innocent."

Her words brought a chill to his spine. So softly spoken, with such utter conviction, he couldn't help but think she was looking into the future. "But your family will be safe."

Piper turned to him. The deep remorse in her gaze stunned him. "And I should rejoice in their lives while so many others will lose theirs?"

"You cannot save them all."

"No, I suppose not." Her gaze drifted far away, as if she were contemplating how she could free all the captives locked away in the Paris prisons. "How will I rest in England, knowing this continues?"

Giles couldn't answer. He would tell her to stop because he wanted her to live; he wanted her to be a part of his life.

Yet what part of his life could he offer? The only part he would feel right in offering already belonged to another.

He tried to think of Lady Sophia's face, some feature he could hold close to his heart, but nothing came to mind. The only thing he could "see" was the feel of Piper's skin beneath his fingertips or the way she met his embrace with her own passionate claim.

The cart lurched along in the seething Paris traffic. It seemed as if every citizen in France filled the ancient city's streets to witness the death of their hated Queen. The mood swung between a festival atmosphere, with parents and young children carrying wicker baskets of food, to the dark, scowling faces of the *sans-culottes,* triumphant in their vindictive revenge.

Now his misgivings about her costume resurfaced two-fold, as the crowds around them swelled and the mood turned more and more turbulent.

The Paris crowds were a fickle lot, Giles knew from experience, and while he'd seen and heard of their affection for La Devinette as a heroine of the new Republic, such fond regard could change in a matter of moments.

There was no predicting the often ugly humor of a *sans-culotte* mob. If they were not satisfied with the death of Marie Antoinette, they would quickly look for fresh victims to fill their boundless appetites for murder.

If the order she'd overheard Robespierre issue last night had reached any of the forty-eight Paris *section* commanders, their allegiance to the lady they revered as an icon of Revolutionary spirit would be forgotten. They'd tear her to shreds, stick her severed head on a beribboned pike, and take it to the Salon de Cire for a new wax modeling. She'd be the latest attraction in Dr. Curtius's hall of horrors before the end of the week.

If Piper felt the tension surging around them, he could not tell. Her eyes were set straight ahead, and she barely nodded at the cheers of recognition that were raised as she passed.

Occasionally, the crowds closed around them, dirty hands stretching out to touch the infamous Citizeness Devinette. He marveled at her control and ingenious manipulation of her adoring fans. Piper neither smiled nor acknowledged her fans. Instead, when the press of people became too thick she'd reach into her pockets and toss out a handful of coins, scattering the crowd as they fought for the tokens.

"Vive La Devinette!"

"Vive La Republic!"

If he could prove to Dryden and himself that she wasn't involved with Webb's death, as she claimed, they ought to consider recruiting her. With her natural talents and chameleon skills at disguise, she was the best agent he'd ever come up against.

"Is there some way you could lessen your appeal with the citizens of this city?"

"Why?" she asked. "I find them charming."

"You say that now, but what if they find out . . ."

Piper frowned at him. "And you make your living doing this? I can't see how you have survived for so long. My condolences to your wife. You'll make her a widow before she has time to stitch a nursery sampler."

Giles pushed back the red tricorn on his head. "I don't make a habit of parading myself in front of a bloodthirsty crowd when I have a death sentence hanging over my head. That's akin to inviting your good friend Robespierre to an underground Royalist meeting."

Her brows arched in challenge. "Where's your sense of adventure, the challenge of the hunt you English love so much?"

"We love the challenge because we are the hunters, not the hunted."

"All the same, if you find my plans so objectionable you can always hurry and catch up with Lily and Julien. Back to your sweet and deserving bride."

Giles silently simmered. The woman truly needled his pride like no one else.

It was bad enough that her face screwed up into a sour countenance every time she spoke of Lady Sophia. But what really needled him were her sarcastic tones, which revealed that she found his choice of bride a great source of amusement—at his expense.

How could a woman like Piper, so full of vitality and sensuality, a woman to whom men flocked, belittle his betrothed as if she were a worthy opponent?

Perhaps Piper knew as well as he did that she would make a far better wife than Lady Sophia.

And Piper loved him. Giles knew it as much as he feared it. Her kiss last night had been evidence of that.

But was her love enough to toss aside Lady Sophia to marry a woman who would be regarded with scorn? His honor, his reputation, his place in society, all lost if he followed his heart. Not to mention what it would do to his heirs.

Marrying Piper was as crazy a notion as walking into the Abbaye. Impossible and against every grain of reason he possessed.

Yet here he was following her into the impossible.

Could he take that next step? Giles knew he couldn't. Never.

Still, he didn't like her superior tone, as if she knew his own struggles with his emotions.

"I think you should reconsider," Piper said over her shoulder.

"Reconsider what?"

"Coming with us. The poor girl. First you throw her off and leave her on your wedding day, and now you spend what would have been your wedding holiday with me." Piper shook her head woefully. "But she is rather a plain little creature, isn't she? The type to be very understanding and accept you back into her good graces. After all, what other matrimonial chances would a girl like that have?"

At this insult Giles decided a lesson in humility was in order. "I'll have you know my fiancée holds me quite near and dear to her heart. Besides, she is a lady and will accept whatever I tell as the truth."

"Yes, I suppose she will." She rubbed her chin, as if pondering the inconceivable notion of such an arrangement. That is, until a wicked gleam lit her one uncovered eye. "If you find her again. Correct me if I'm wrong, but didn't *she* run away from your marriage bed?"

Giles sat bolt upright, clinging to the sides of the rocking cart. "How did you know that?"

She shrugged. "A lucky guess."

Oliver shot her a censorious glower, as if she'd gone too far.

"Some night," he grumbled. "You were as faithless as my bride."

In a moment her face softened into the charm and romance of the Brazen Angel. Her voice teased and softened into sensual tones as she leaned over and whispered into his ear. "It could have been quite a different night if you hadn't been so resigned in turning me over to the authorities." She laughed merrily, the sound bubbling with promise and adventure. "But I won't hold that against you, if you promise to hold me one more time."

Giles witnessed a glimpse into the real woman as her emotions rippled past her disguise—the heated desire in her gaze and the lingering touch of her hand as it curved around his chin.

The tenuous ties from their night of lovemaking rekindled as though they'd never been extinguished. Giles's chest tightened, and he drew his breath in deeply. He could well imagine how her touch felt elsewhere, how she could command him with her desires.

She, too, appeared affected by the moment. Her face glowed, almost blushed, as she probably remembered her daring, unabashed enjoyment in his arms. She looked away and then back into his eyes. The glance promised much, vows Giles would bind her to, no matter the price, no matter the risk.

Damn his honor, damn his father's last wish.

He'd spend the rest of life with this woman and no other. A woman who risked her life for what she believed in, a woman who loved so deeply. And once they'd survived this day he'd tell her what was in his heart, carry her away from this wretched city, and give her and her family the safe home they deserved.

Sophia watched the strange change in his features, as if he had struggled with a great problem and finally found the solution, but what it was she didn't have time to ask.

"Caution," Oliver whispered. "We are being watched."

Ahead at the next intersection she spied three toughs in the uniforms of their local *section* police, lounging. Their churlish expressions scoured the crowd, obviously searching for sport.

"Trouble." Sophia took a deep breath. "I can feel it."

Suddenly, one of the guards whooped out in anger. She jumped in her seat, thinking all had been lost and they knew of her warrant, but they halted not ten steps in front of her.

It was then that she saw their intended victim, a elderly man wearing the ribbons of an officer from the *Régiment du*

Roi, standing at the very fringes of the crowd. Former officers of the King's armies were so universally despised that most had either gone into hiding or emigrated, and he looked old enough to have been pensioned off long before the first troubles.

The scream in her throat stuck as the first of the louts descended on his victim like a rabid dog, the others following in a maddened pack.

Giles leapt from the cart and started to rush forward.

Before she knew what she was saying, she turned to Oliver. "Stop him," she ordered. And to her horror she realized she hadn't meant the murderer. She'd meant Giles.

Oliver caught the back of his collar and held him fast.

"Let me go," Giles raged over his shoulder, swinging wildly at the larger man's grasp.

Sophia shook her head, unable to let him do what was right, what was honorable. For if he stepped in, if he intervened, they would be the next victims.

Neither the pensioner's age nor his feeble protests stopped the growing crowd. They raised their pikes and started the slaughter.

"Blood. Blood. Blood," they chanted. And it ran from the man's body, pooling in bright contrast to the dirty mud of the street.

Sophia struggled to look away from savagery. As in her dream she sat frozen in the moment, unable to move, unable to intervene. Bile rose in her throat, bitter, and she choked back the sobs that wanted to tear from her chest.

What had she just allowed?

Giles wrenched himself free of Oliver's grasp and started forward again.

"Leave be, my friend," Oliver warned. "Remember who you are."

One glance at the old man told him it was too late to help the poor misguided soul. His time had ended.

"How can you be so callous?" Giles shot back, this time directing his comments to Piper. Oliver, he knew, would do nothing without his mistress's permission. So it would have been her decision to intervene.

"Get in the cart," she ordered, her gaze never leaving the grisly scene in front of her.

"Not before—"

"Get in or be left behind."

Defiant, Giles considered a number of angry retorts as he stared down her challenge. Until he realized how wrong he was about her.

Her cheeks and lips were colorless and drawn, the blood drained away. Her hands trembled slightly, and as if sensing his gaze upon them she clasped one over the other to still their wavering.

She hadn't been watching a stranger die, she'd been watching what could happen to the members of her family or the three of them if they were caught.

The ignominious and brutal death of being cut down in the street and left.

Unburied, unknown, unmourned.

The enormous responsibility she carried weighed down heavily on his shoulders.

And how had he helped? By jumping out of the cart and calling attention to them. Without a word he climbed back in and sank into his seat, humiliated by his behavior and his own stupidity. He could have killed them all.

He barely heard her quiet order to Oliver.

"I think we should take another route today."

Without comment Oliver turned the cart from the wide paved boulevard and picked his way through the deserted side streets.

SOPHIA TOOK ONE deep breath and then another.

What had she just done?

She'd sat immobile while an old man was slaughtered. The events happened so fast that it was as if she were back in the nightmare, her cries unable to reach the surface, her limbs unresponsive and weighted.

Nothing. She'd done nothing.

Had it been a crippling fear of discovery or cowardice that held her to her seat, unable to lift a finger to help the man?

Giles suffered no lack of morals. He'd leapt forward without a moment's hesitation. One nod from her and Oliver collared him like a petty thief, holding the man back from doing what was right. Held on as if their lives depended on it.

And they had.

The notion repelled her as much as it frightened her.

She'd traded their lives for that of an unarmed old man. Reason told her the decision was sound, but her heart mourned the inequity of it.

Giles's accusations echoed up from her dream. She'd betrayed the old man, as she would Giles if they failed to free her family and were captured in the process. Would she stand mutely by if he were caught? Would she have the courage to step forward and save his life?

"We're here," Oliver said quietly.

Sophia looked up at the gray, stained stones of the Abbaye.

To hazard this final deception and see her family freed, she needed her ruse and skills in persuasion firmly in place, her mind focused, her thoughts consistent.

Before her eyes the dark soot and years of grime coating the prison's walls turned a brilliant shade of red, bright deadly blood, until the image blotted out everything else, her ears roaring with an ominous chant.

Blood. Blood. Blood.

Their blood. Her hands gripped the wooden plank beneath her.

When Giles leaned forward and nudged her, she nearly jumped out of her seat.

"I apologize," he whispered. "We would have been lost if I'd tried to stop them."

She shook her head violently, clearing the fearful images from her mind. Blinking once or twice, she saw the walls return to their unimposing gray. "Never apologize for trying to do what is right. It is I who should be apologizing, to you and to that man. May his soul find peace."

Giles caught hold of her by the shoulder and shook her gently. "They would have killed us right along with him. And where would that have left your parents? Your brother and his family? No, your instincts do you credit."

"Credit? I did nothing because it was all I could do." Panic started to rise within her, all her doubts and fears pushing it to the forefront. For this moment she'd taken any number of risks, and now . . . "I've changed my mind. You're not going in with us. Get out of the cart."

He shook his head. "No. I made a mistake back there, but I will not interfere again."

She jumped from her seat down to the street. "No, it was my mistake, and look what happened—that old man died. Get out of the cart. I won't kill you as well," she continued, her fears and emotions getting the better of her. "You've been right all along. This plan is foolhardy and has no place for you."

Giles climbed down and caught her hand. "You can't start reconsidering alternatives now. While I agree your plan is preposterous, it's just brazen enough to work." He turned his head back toward the Seine. "It may sound callous, but the Queen's death will give us the additional diversion we need to make this work."

"If it works." She pulled her hand free from his.

"It will succeed because you believe it will," he answered. "What if something happens to you or to Oliver? With me along there is that much better of a chance for your family to reach England. But you must let me help."

The guards at the front gate started to move toward them. She didn't have much time.

Giles glanced over at them and back at her. "You, of all people, know how important it is to give someone their fantasy." He saluted her. "Go in there, Citizeness Devinette. Make them feel the wrath of your displeasure if they don't follow your orders immediately. Believe you have every right to march in there and demand the release of those traitors. Believe it, and those guards will follow your orders without hesitation."

She had no choice; there was no time to dismiss him in front of the Abbaye guards.

Sophia nodded to Oliver, who turned the cart and horses

toward the entrance. Two guards stepped forward, while several more stood at attention inside the closed iron gates.

Straightening her shoulders, she adjusted her sword before marching forward to met the guards at the entrance.

"I am Citizeness Devinette. I have a direct order from Citizen Robespierre on a matter of urgent business. Attend to this at once."

CHAPTER
12

"WHAT IS THIS?"
the guard said, looking down at the paper in Sophia's outstretched hand. "An order. I haven't heard of any new
orders."

The other guard shrugged his shoulders.

Sophia bored a glare into the first man until he looked
away, obviously uncomfortable. "Do I have to repeat
myself? This order is signed by Citizen Robespierre. I
watched him sign it myself not an hour ago." She shook the
paper under the man's nose. "See for yourself."

She handed him the paper upside down, and when the

fellow began to act as if he could read the words, she knew she had scored her first bit of luck. Sophia hoped none of the rest of his comrades could read or knew Robespierre's signature very well. While it was an excellent forgery—for Emma's skill was unequaled—it was still a fake.

"Will this take long?" she asked, tapping her foot. "I hate to be kept waiting. The Tribunal is most anxious to hear these cases. They hope to have them over by noon so justice can be dispatched without any further delays."

"We haven't ever done it like this, citizeness," the first guard said cautiously. He tipped his head and looked at her. "They've already hauled away today's lot. We don't usually get an order twice in one day. Besides, we haven't the guards to spare to make the journey. Everyone's off to watch the widow lose her head."

"That is why I brought my own guards," she replied, jerking her thumb over her shoulder at Oliver and Giles. "Now, step aside and open the gates or I will add you to this list."

The man's mouth opened to protest. The second guard backed away, distancing himself from anything hinting of treason.

"I'll have to get my commander to approve this," he muttered.

"Then take me to him at once." She marched up to the entrance, where the second guard fumbled with the locks. Finally, the large iron gate swung open, the metal grating and creaking.

She turned to Oliver. "You there, quit loafing the day away and get that cart inside. My patience is thin enough as it is without having to wait half a day for you two as well."

"Yes, citizeness," Oliver said, snapping the reins. The

horse pranced forward nervously, jolting the cart over the uneven stones.

"Don't envy you two none. Not even if you get to see that Austrian whore's execution," the second guard muttered as Oliver and Giles pulled up to the gate.

Sophia came to an abrupt halt in the courtyard. She swung around, her gaze falling on the man who'd spoken. "Did you have a comment you want shared with everyone, citizen?"

He shook his head, his entire body trembling. "No-o-o . . ." he stuttered.

"I would suggest keeping it that way." With her curt nod of dismissal the man skittered away.

So far, she thought, so good. No one seemed to have heard of a warrant for her arrest, for if they had they would have seized her at the door.

"Take me to the commander of this cesspool," she barked to the next guard. With any luck he would be as easily intimidated as his men.

A half hour later she found it was not to be so easy. The commander of Abbaye Prison, a pinch-faced man by the name of Augustin Lamude, held his position against her from behind the relative safety of his massive oak desk. He was anything but cowed by her demands and threats.

"I don't know how you continue to claim you are a dedicated servant of the Republic if this is how you run this hovel," she said, her voice level and filled with distaste.

She heard Oliver, who stood just behind her at the door to the commander's office, take a deep breath and shift from foot to foot. The office was stiflingly hot, and the cheap wool of his suit probably itched. Glancing over at

Giles, he appeared nonplussed by Lamude's reluctance to release his prisoners.

Sophia knew as well as he did that time was running out.

Lamude had dispatched a runner to verify the order in her hand, and it wouldn't be more than another fifteen or twenty minutes before the young man returned.

It was a race against the clock, now more than ever.

So as Citizeness Devinette she continued her full frontal assault to get what she wanted.

She tested and pushed Lamude, seeking an opening capable of cracking his rigid exterior. Some fear, some fault in his loyalty where she could push her agenda through and open a hole wide enough to let every single occupant of the prison go free.

Yet no matter the threat, the depth of her insult, the slander of her statements, the prison's commander took each one with the same squirming smile.

"*Oui*, citizeness."

"*Non,* citizeness," was all the wormy little Lamude seemed able to mutter in his high-pitched whine.

Sophia knew she was out of avenues—save one. Down to her last card, she decided to play it. She turned to Oliver and Giles. "Both of you go down to the courtyard and wait for me there."

Giles opened his mouth to protest, as she knew he probably would. Forestalling that, she turned until her back was completely to Lamude and drew a small vial from her belt. With a nod and a wink, she saw the light on Giles's eyes acknowledge that he understood.

"Yes, citizeness." He bobbed his head and followed Oliver obediently out the door.

"Oh, and close the door," she called after him. "I would

be *alone* with the Commander," she said, letting the sultry purr roll from her lips.

Returning her full attention to the man behind the desk, she smiled her best Brazen Angel offer. "I must apologize for my temper. With so much work to be done I am afraid I have been neglecting my manners of late. I would like to find a way to make up my rudeness to you."

"I disagree, citizeness," Lamude said, his words coming out like the final wheeze of a hand organ. "I find a woman of your, shall we say, temperament quite stimulating, if you know what I mean." His nose pinched up and down like a rabbit, while his hands squirmed in his lap.

"Then perhaps you should have offered me some wine. I have a terrible thirst, and you have been most rude not to offer me a drink before this," she scolded.

Lamude smiled a nasty grin at her admonishment, as if it were high praise.

Leaning over his desk, she pushed aside all his papers, clearing the space between them. "And after we've had our drink I will find a fitting punishment for your insubordination. What do you say to that?"

"*Oui,* citizeness," he replied, as he scurried across the room and fetched a wine bottle and two glasses from a locked cabinet.

As he poured the deep claret-colored liquid into the fine crystal glasses, he squinted over the rim as he offered it to her. He raised his in a toast.

The glasses touched and Sophia tossed hers over her shoulder.

Lamude's eyes grew wide.

"I would rather taste the wine from your lips," she told him, closing the space between them by crawling across the wide open expanse of his desk top, the oak smooth and cool beneath her. Rolling her shoulders forward and tipping her head, she smiled her invitation at Lamude as he greedily took in the view down the front of her muslin gown.

It took all of two seconds to empty the vial into the unsuspecting man's glass.

"Drink it, Lamude," she ordered. "Drink the wine and share your passion with me."

"Fire!" the cry came. "Fire!"

Giles looked up to see black smoke pouring from the Commander's third-story office. Chaos broke out in the courtyard, as soldiers from the gates and others from all four corners of the walls ran to stop the blaze.

Acrid smoke billowed out Lamude's window.

"Never one for subtlety, is she?" Giles asked Oliver.

"Never will be."

Seconds later he spotted Piper tearing down the steps, yelling orders at the top of her lungs.

"You men, quickly, to the Commander's office. Hurry." She looked up and grinned at Giles, then held up a ring of keys.

"You there," she snapped at a youthful-looking officer, whose eyes widened as she drew out her sword and pointed it first at him and then at the gates. "Get those open. Wide open. How is the watch to get in if you've got them locked out?"

The befuddled man shook his head and then nodded, trying to find an answer to please her.

"Open them now," she barked. "Move it."

And move he did. He raced to the prison entrance and threw the gates wide open.

"Wait with the horses," she said to Oliver as he tossed her a bundle from the back of the cart. "Come on, Englishman," she whispered to Giles. "Prove to me you were worth bringing along."

Together they raced into the prison. After three tries with her pilfered keys she found the right one.

"Do you know where they are?" he asked as he stepped into the hall and made sure the way was clear.

"Yes, I think so. Before I started the fire I got a chance to look through Lamude's directory. Efficient little bastard, though his handwriting is atrocious. He's taken to moving everyone every couple of days to prevent them from being rescued. My family is listed on the second level down."

They entered the first hallway, darkness closing in around them. Giles pulled a torch from the wall and held it aloft. With his other hand he drew out his pistol.

Piper looked left, then right, as if reacquainting herself with a childhood home. She grinned at him and set off to the left.

For the third time in as many days, all he could do was follow. "How do you know where you are going?"

"I've been here before."

Why hadn't he guessed that outrageous notion?

She continued down the hallway, cautiously hugging the shadowed walls. "I also obtained a copy of the floor plans the last time I was in Paris," she grinned over her shoulder. "I've been memorizing them ever since. I know every inch of this place as if I laid the stones myself."

"How can you be sure the plans are correct?"

"We'll soon find out," she said with a fateful shrug of her shoulders. "And what I don't know I'll make up. It's worked before."

Not as reassured as he would have liked given that they were moving deeper and deeper into the Abbaye's depths, Giles had to admit that following the Brazen Angel was akin to dueling with pistols—taking aim and wondering whose bullet would find a home first. It thrilled him more than he cared to realize, especially after all his lectures last night on caution and careful planning.

At the top of a curved, narrow staircase she abandoned her bundle before they descended into the bowels of the prison. The stench was incredible—like an open sewer in the heat of August. There was little air left to breathe, and what there was hung heavy and damp with the foulest of odors.

Before they could start their check of the cells, a large guard stepped out of the shadows, filling the hallway with his massive bulk and frame. "What do you think you are doing?" he asked, rubbing his sleepy eyes. He'd obviously drunk himself into a stupor, his breath rank with sour wine and the overturned flask next to his chair evidence enough of his inebriated state.

"What are you doing down here?" she asked back. "The prison is burning down around your head and you sleep away the day like a babe."

"Fire?" he said, the fear evident in his voice and his fat, crooked nose sniffing the dense air.

"*Oui*, you fool. Fire."

"Gotta get out of here," he mumbled, trying to get past them.

"You would leave your post?" She stabbed her finger into his chest, backing him down the hall with her fearless intimidation. "I will ignore your dereliction this time, citizen, but any more of this insubordination and I will bring you before Lamude for discipline. Now, get on with your duty. Show my guard that all the cells are secured. Then you can assist with the fire."

"*Oui.*" The big fellow turned and lumbered down the hall, his keys rattling at his waist.

She flattened herself against the narrow hall, giving Giles the room he needed to pass by.

Retrieving the man's lead bottle from next to his chair, Giles clouted the big lug over the head with it. He fell like Goliath, in a heap at Giles's feet.

"Is he dead?" she asked.

Giles knelt at the guard's side. "No, he's breathing."

Piper grinned, hopped over the body, and was off like a shot down the dark hall. "Lucien," she whispered loudly, first to one cell and then another. "Lucien, where are you?"

"Piper?" came a dazed answer.

"*Oui,* Lucien. It's Piper." She waved to Giles. "Hurry, I've found them."

"Oh, sure. Hurry, she says," he muttered as he tried for a third time to flip over the giant guard. The narrow hall didn't leave much room for maneuvering, but with a mighty heave and shove he was able to pry the man over enough to snatch the keys from his belt.

He tossed them to her, then joined her at the door as she tried key after key. Turning his back to her, he held his pistol out in front of him, mindful that at any moment her fire would be put out and the forces would start looking for them.

"Piper, what are you doing here?" a male voice asked from within the cell.

"Rescuing you, Lucien. What does it look like?" she shot back hotly.

Giles smiled at the sibling bickering. It reminded him of Dryden's brood.

She shook the ring again and selected another key. This one worked and the door opened.

Two small boys tumbled into the hall, followed by a woman with a babe in her arms. A tall, thin man, obviously Lucien, followed, catching hold of his sister and hugging her close.

"I prayed you wouldn't be so foolish to do this, and I prayed you would," he said.

"How like you," she teased back, "to hedge your bets."

"I hate to interrupt this reunion," Giles said, "but there's still a garrison outside to slip past."

Piper let go of her brother and went back into the now-empty cell. "Where is *Papa? Maman?*"

Lucien shook his head. "Aren't they with you?"

"Why would they be with me?"

"They left here this morning. Under special orders. We thought for sure it was because you'd been able to obtain their release."

"No!" She backed farther down the hall. "*Maman, Papa!* Are you here?"

Pleas for help were her only answers.

"Release me, I have much gold."

"Take my children, for the love of God, take my children from this place."

Giles started pushing Lucien and his family down the hall. He handed the emaciated man a torch and pointed toward the stairwell. Catching Piper by the hand, he towed her along after her family.

She fought him every step. "No, I will not leave them. I know they are here."

He stopped and grabbed her by both shoulders. Rattling her back to the present, he shook her until her wild-eyed gaze finally focused. "You must save your brother and his family. We will find your mother and father, but not now. As La Devinette you have the best chance of getting us out. Now start acting like that Revolutionary she-bitch."

Sophia nodded her head and faltered up the dark stairwell.

At the top the light was better, and she saw the radical changes imprisonment had left on her brother and his family.

Lucien, once broad of shoulder and full-framed, now resembled a gangly youth, so thin and brittle did he appear. His wife, Noël, renowned in the Bourbon court for her sweet temperament and fair beauty, wore a wary look, holding her child close to her breast and humming a discordant tune. Her once long blond hair had been cut to her shoulders in ragged clumps.

The twins, Félix and Lucien-Victor, clung to their mother's bedraggled skirts, their noses dirty and their eyes wide in their gaunt faces.

The shock of their appearances prodded Sophia back to her duty. Untying the cords from her discarded bundle, she pulled out odd pieces of clothing. Handing a cloak to Giles, she told him, "Wrap it around her, and make sure it covers the babe."

Turning back to her brother, she handed him a uniform not unlike the one Giles wore. "Get into this, the jacket at the very least." Outside, the shouting and cries were still going on in full force, the bells of Abbaye pealing with the news of the fire. They hadn't much time left.

Kneeling beside her nephews, she topped their heads with bright red caps.

"Who are you?" Félix asked.

"I am—" She was about to say, *your tante Sophia*, but stopped herself. "I am Citizeness Devinette. And we are going to play a game." She picked up Lucien-Victor and handed him to Giles, then she gathered Félix into her arms and gave him a quick kiss on the cheek. "Now, the first step in this game is to be very, very quiet. and then we are going to hide. . . ."

And with Félix in her arms she sprinted along the inside wall of the courtyard, with Lucien pulling Noël along and Giles bringing up the rear with Lucien-Victor.

Oliver had moved the horses nearer the entrance. The moment the family scrambled into the cart, Oliver snapped the reins. The horses took off just as the alarm raised.

"Escape! Escape! The prisoners are escaping!"

With no guards at the gates, there was no one stop them. From behind, gunfire broke out. Giles returned fire, yelling at her, "Get them down. Get them all down."

She did, scrambling to cover the children. The cart careened into the square and turned down the first side street they came to. Zigzagging through the narrow streets of the Unité section, Oliver drove the horses like a man possessed.

"Does he know where he is going?" Giles shouted.

"Yes. Not much farther," Sophia said, a twin tucked beneath each arm. She held them tight as the cart rocked back and forth. She looked back toward the high walls of the Abbaye, regret and fear filling her heart. Her parents—what had happened to them? How could she have been too late?

She found Giles watching her, a grim look on his face. "We'll find them. We'll find them together. I promise," he told her.

When the jolting ride came to a thundering halt, she looked up and found they were still far from the city's gates.

Oliver glanced over his shoulder. "I can't push them much faster," he said, nodding at the poor nags. "And if we continue at this pace we'll only draw attention to ourselves."

She agreed. "The word of our escape will spread quickly. We'll have to use our alternative."

Giles stepped down from the cart. "I take it you have another plan?"

At this she shrugged her shoulders. "When have you known me not to?"

He grinned and began helping Noël and her baby down from the cart.

Digging through the straw, Sophia pulled out two more bundles. "Get rid of those uniforms." She pointed at a pile of trash in the middle of the alley. "Bury them in there and then put on these," she told them, once again doling out more clothing.

For herself she'd stowed away a modified version of her old-lady outfit. Since she would be unable to have the complete makeup to twist her face into the aged contortions Emma usually devised, the cape fitted with a hump on her back would have to do. If she kept her head down, most people wouldn't bother looking for a face.

Once everyone changed they abandoned the cart and horses several streets away and set out on foot for the banks of the Seine.

Giles leaned over to her. "This pace isn't fast enough."

"I know," she said, looking back at her brother and his family. With the children and the combined ill health of their parents, it was difficult to get them to move along quickly enough.

"Go ahead," she told Oliver. "Make sure our friend is ready."

Oliver took off, a look of pure determination setting his grim features.

Around them church bells pealed, and the Guards' tocsins seemed to cry out for retribution.

Blood. Blood. Blood.

Stopping at a corner, Sophia realized the streets were too empty. Most of Paris had gone to the Queen's execution. Everyone else was shuttered in their houses, fearful of the celebrations or rioting that could follow. They stood out, obvious in their haste and number.

Giles stood at her elbow. She looked up into his eyes and saw the same concerns.

"We have to split up. It isn't much farther, but together we stand out." If she expected him to argue with her, his answer surprised her.

"I agree. You take your sister-in-law, the baby, and one of the boys. I'll go with your brother and the other son."

"Exactly my idea." She smiled at him. "There is a small blue boat near the Pont Neuf. The boatman is an Italian called Aldo. He has been paid in advance, but more than likely he will demand additional money before the city's walls. Pay him with half of this," she said, handing Giles a pouch. "Pay him no more until you are well outside Paris."

He tried to hand the pouch back to her, but she pushed it away. "You'll be there. You pay him."

"In case I don't make it. There should always be a contingency."

Giles agreed, yet there was something about the way she'd said it.

In case I don't make it.

He noticed that she hadn't included her sister-in-law in her gloomy prediction. After she got done explaining everything to her brother, she turned back to Giles.

"You aren't planning on going back with them, are you?" he asked.

"Of course I am." She frowned at him.

Giles didn't believe her. Catching hold of her, he pulled her close into his arms. "Promise me you won't do anything foolish. Promise you will be on that boat."

She shook her head. "I can't make that promise. I have no control over what will happen between here and the river."

He looked down into her face, tempted to tear off her ridiculous patch. From there he would brush back her hair and stare into her features—features he'd never seen in their entirety or under the light of day—to memorize her entire face.

This incredible woman teased his senses, challenged his mind, and never stopped surprising him. He would hold her like this for the rest of his life given the chance.

Dipping his head, he brought his lips to hers, sealing his promise. He allowed his kiss to memorize her as his eyes could not. First, he explored her lips with a single request.

Willingly, she opened herself to him. He continued his exploration onward. The warmth and depth of her response called to the deepest levels of his soul. He no longer felt lost, like a man without a map, but instead found himself remembering every nuance, every tiny detail of her as if he'd known her through the centuries.

He peeled aside the masking layers of clothing until his hands brushed against the warm satin of her bare arms. He deepened his kiss, her tongue meeting his in conquest. Their rising needs found the familiar fire and demanded fulfillment.

The clatter of hooves down the street yanked them apart. The only thing still holding them together was their gazes, which locked in a passionate understanding.

"We will finish this soon," he whispered to her.

"I'll be waiting." She caught his hand and squeezed it. "Promise me, Giles. Promise me this: You will see my family safely to England."

"But—"

She shook her head. "If something happens to me, do not come after me. Lucien and his family's safety must come first. They must get to England. Promise me."

"Nothing will happen between here and the—"

"Don't say such things. You tempt fate. Just promise me."

He smiled, leaned over, and kissed her quickly on the lips. "I promise. And there is something I would ask of you in return. I would—"

She placed her finger on his lips and stopped his words. "There is no time. Save your words for another time." She turned to her brother and whispered privately to him. Lucien did not seem pleased with her instructions, but accepted the pouch she handed him.

Giles was wondering how many plans she had hidden across Paris.

With some coaxing, the twins were divided and Giles found himself carrying an unhappy Félix. The boy's father was too weak to carry his son, almost too weak to keep up, but they managed to make it to Aldo's boat in less than an hour after having to take two detours to avoid patrols.

When they arrived Aldo greeted them with a wide smile. "Good, now everyone is here." He ordered a boy, a miniature of the swarthy and tanned captain, to start untying the lines.

"Where are they?" Giles asked.

"Below," Aldo answered, jerking his thumb at a hatchway. "Send those two down with everyone else. You can stay up here and help my boy with the lines so we can get under way."

After the boat had left its moorings and started down the river, Giles went down into the hold, only to find Noël and Lucien stowed comfortably in a wide berth, their children sound asleep between them.

But no Piper and no Oliver.

"Where is she?" Giles demanded.

Lucien shook his head. "She would not leave without finding out what happened to our parents."

Anger surged through him.

He tore back up topside and stood at the edge of the boat, staring down at the brown water of the Seine. Up ahead the river was packed with boats, as they drew closer to the Place de la Revolution. Giles guessed it was nearing midday, and gauging from the crowds it seemed the Queen had yet to be brought to the square. Crowds lined the banks, and for a moment he thought he saw Piper and Oliver.

A hunched-over crone hobbled along beside a looming giant. The woman looked in his direction before pushing her way into the crowd and out of his sight.

A hand on his shoulder kept him from jumping into the river and swimming for shore.

"She gave me a message for you," Aldo said.

Giles nodded, his gaze still fixed on the crowded shores.

"She told me to say that you must keep your promise."

"Why should I? She never promised me anything in return."

Aldo shrugged his shoulders. "Women are strange, my friend. They don't understand honor as we do."

"I disagree," Giles commented. "I think they understand it all too well." Just as he'd vowed to marry another for the sake of honor, she'd made him promise to keep her family safe, because she knew he would do it. She'd mocked his obligations and steadfast dedication to his beliefs in honor and then used them to see him safely back to England.

And to England he must now go.

Giles knew enough of her operations to realize that this time she would disappear deep into Paris, making a search useless.

Yet eventually she would have to return to England, return to rejoin her family. She'd known he would come to the same conclusion and see the reason behind her refusal to make a promise. He'd go to England because it was the one place he could count on finding her again.

Damn, she was good. Too good.

Aldo called out an order to his son and turned back to Giles.

"There is one other thing she said to tell you."

Giles looked up, resigned to one more of her lectures.

"She said to tell you that you've been looking in the wrong city for the man who betrayed your friend. This Webb, she spoke of, he was betrayed by an Englishman."

CHAPTER
13

London, two weeks later

STROLLING INTO THE
St. James gaming hell, Sophia paused at the doorway and
surveyed the lively crowd before her from behind her black
mask. Her masked appearance hardly stood out, for if a lady
dared to show her face in such a low place, she did it prop-
erly concealed.

As far as she knew this place had no name, and entrance
required payment of "dues" to the tall, elegant Persian,
Namir, who ran the establishment. The clientele consisted
of the wealthy and the worst kind who clung to their
fringes—schemers, aging mistresses, and cheats.

Though putting on the Brazen Angel's mask had always lent itself a secret thrill, tonight the strings binding the silken covering to her face felt too tight.

Emma had argued against this plan, as had Oliver, but now more than ever Sophia needed to raise money quickly. She'd been unable to locate her parents, and she'd promised a fortune to Balsac if he could find the Comte and Comtesse D'Artiers before Madame Guillotine did.

Tonight she intended to raise that fortune.

"Ah, my lady, it is a pleasure to serve you," Namir said with a low bow.

She nodded to him. "I am looking for a gentleman."

"So many ladies are," the host laughed. "Is there one in particular you favor?" He offered his arm and they began to stroll through the room.

"Yes. Lord Selmar."

Namir stopped. "You cannot be serious, my lady."

Sophia took a deep breath. "If you don't mind, which table is he at?"

Her host gave his head a rueful shake and led her to a private room in the back. The walls were lined with red velvet curtains, the rich, deep color shaking her reserves.

This time she stopped Namir.

Blood. It seemed to be everywhere. Her nightmare, which was now a nightly occurrence, began to repeat before her eyes.

"Are you all right, my lady?" Namir asked.

Pinching her fingers at the bridge of her nose, she shook off her fears, for there was no turning back now. "I'm quite fine."

Glancing around the small party filling the private room,

she spied Lord Selmar. For him and him only, she smiled seductively.

Arrogant and vain, Selmar preened under her attention. "Won't you join us?" he asked.

She nodded and took the seat he offered.

Now in his late forties, Selmar had been married years before, sired an heir, and promptly shipped his wife to the country, where she'd died a few months later under mysterious circumstances. Still a handsome and virile man, he'd taken a mistress or two, though the ladybirds never lasted long. Selmar wasn't known for his generosity or gentle regard for the fairer sex.

Namir's hesitation to make the introduction, Sophia knew was because Selmar was reputed to be ruthlessly jealous in both love and business as well as a deadly shot if his honor was affronted. There were few who dared cross him. But what did she care if he could shoot? He'd be unconscious and on the floor before he could find a pistol.

She cared only that the man was horribly rich, his holdings consisting of an extensive collection of gems and gold. Some had been inherited from his late wife, others amassed through cheating at cards.

A perfect, irresistible target for the Brazen Angel. And more than enough to pay off Balsac's greedy demands.

"Ah, my dear lady, do you play macao?" Selmar asked, leaning over his cards, more interested in staring at the low cut of her gown than the hand he held.

"I love any game of chance." Beneath the table her foot slid up Selmar's leg. "I'll wager just about anything if I think I can get what I want."

"And what do you offer for the stakes?" He winked at the other players.

"Myself."

For a moment he stared at her in stunned silence.

One portly gentleman nearly choked on his aperitif. "Did she say—"

Selmar held up his hand to stop the man. A slight, greedy smile pulled at his lips. "Would you like to deal the first hand?" he said smoothly, handing her the deck.

And so her evening began—handily winning the first hand and then proceeding to lose the next five. Selmar staked her losses, so obviously determined to collect her "marker" before the evening's end. His assessing gaze as he looked at his cards and then at her sent chills of revulsion down her spine. But she had no choice—this was her best bet for taking a boundless fortune in one night.

But she did have another choice—go to Giles and ask for his assistance.

That had been Emma's suggestion. After all, the man had offered her a house to become his mistress. Her engagement gift was proof the man was anything but tight-fisted. Emma urged her to demand a bevy of presents up front and use them to finance her parents' rescue.

As much as she wanted to, Sophia couldn't do it.

Giles would help, that she knew only too well. But he'd also demand she stay in England while he returned to France. Alone.

The thought of him in Paris, in danger, with her so far away and unable to help, left her resolved to the only course open to her. The dream had become too real, and there was nothing she wouldn't do to prevent it from coming true.

He'd already risked too much, having guided Lucien and his family to the French coast, where his ship, along with

Emma, Lily, and Julien, awaited them. From what Emma had told her, it had taken a hefty exchange of gold, Giles's gold, to get the ship cleared by the port authorities for sailing. With such a *noble* cargo, a delay was not unexpected, but even Sophia had been staggered by the sum the marquise paid to save her family.

Emma and Lucien had followed her directions and slipped away from Giles not twenty-four hours after they reached London. Emma had hidden outside London at a small inn they had used in the past for just such purposes. Lucien and the D'Artiers brood presented a larger problem, since they would be easily spotted traveling on the roads to Bath or York, so instead Sophia had told him not to venture outside the city, but instead to take their family to Lady Dearsley's town house near St. James's Square.

Sophia assumed it was the last place Giles would venture.

Her aunt had welcomed her long-lost family with open arms and accepted their unlikely tale of escape as nothing less than a miracle. Already, the twins were starting to fill out, and Noël—well, the damage to Noël was, according to the doctor, a matter only time would heal.

She hadn't confided her current plan to Lucien, for he, like Giles, would insist she stay at home and allow him to return to Paris.

Then there was the subject of her engagement. Auntie Effie had accepted Sophia's tearful apologies for running away from Lord Trahern. Now the old dear fully intended to see her niece wed to Lord Trahern, if she had to haul him to Gretna Green and perform the ceremony herself.

There would be no hiding Lady Sophia from Giles this time. It would take more than yellowing agents and an ill-fitting dress to conceal her identity if Lord Trahern was to arrive at Lady Dearsley's house to call on her.

It was time indeed that she push forward with her rescue plans.

She glanced down at her hand and realized she held the perfect cards.

Damn, she was supposed to be losing. As she tried to consider a way to throw away her best cards without appearing obvious, a strange air surrounded her, not unlike the whispers of caution she'd heard in the Sow's Ear the night Giles had found her in Paris.

Someone was watching her.

She twisted in her seat and scanned the room, disappointed not to find his dark gaze studying her from a corner.

Disappointed and relieved.

It was bad enough she'd failed to save her parents; now this added guilt over Giles left her feeling that she was betraying him as well.

And maybe she was, in manner of speaking.

Selmar was saying something to her, and she realized all eyes were on her to lay down her cards.

". . . what do you think?" he was asking.

Startled, Sophia looked up, struggling to concentrate. "What ever you think, milord," she replied, hoping that was the desired response.

"I think it's time we departed," Lord Selmar leaned over and whispered. "I can't afford any more of your losses."

She took a deep breath and forced a dazzling smile. "I said I'd make it all up to you. And I am a woman of my word." Tamping down the urge to flee from this man and head out the back door, she instead rose from her chair and moved closer to him.

"It's not your words I want," he replied as he laid her wrap over her shoulders.

"Then I doubt you will be disappointed."

S INCE HIS RETURN from Paris Giles had been unable to locate any information based on the Brazen Angel's cryptic clues. Even the lady herself had not been seen or heard from. Though he'd expected her to return to her family, even they'd disappeared.

He'd given Lucien the hospitality of his home, which the exhausted family used for a day. Giles arrived home from his club in the early evening, only to find them missing, with no word of where they'd gone.

Back to where he started, without any idea of where to begin, Giles resorted to the only course of action he understood: a methodical reexamination of the clues, and a relentless search for new ones. He'd hired runners to watch the docks and men to question all the coaching stations leading out of London to determine where Lucien and his family had fled.

He'd spent his days prowling near the mercer's shops on Ludgate Hill, haunting the bookshops near St. Paul's, and dining in the cafés where *émigrés* congregated. No one seemed to have any clue as to the identity of Piper or her family.

In fact, the only thing he'd been able to turn up in the last month was that his missing fiancée had arrived safe and sound at her aunt's Bath estate two days after she'd fled their wedding.

This evening he'd promised to join Monty in a search of the round of parties that were scheduled for the ton's entertainment. With the full moon on the rise Giles couldn't shake the feeling that *she* was out there somewhere and up to no good.

As he was finishing dressing he heard a great pounding on his front door. Going out to the foyer, he found a dripping wet Lord Harvey anxiously waiting for him.

"I've found her, my lord." The young lord's face burst with a grin. "I mean, His Grace found her. He sent me to tell you."

"Where?" he asked, bounding down his staircase two steps two at a time.

"The gaming house run by that Persian bloke. Namir, he's called." Lord Harvey shook his wet hair like an anxious puppy in from the rain. "His Grace sent his carriage, because his driver knows the way." He pointed at Monty's carriage waiting for him across the street.

Giles nodded to Harvey and dashed into the rainy night, without a coat or hat or a look back at Keenan's astonished face. Much to his consternation, the younger man followed.

"My lord, if you please," he asked as Giles was about to climb into Monty's carriage.

"What do you want?" Giles barked, his patience clearly at an end.

"An introduction," the fellow stammered. He blushed and then straightened. "To Lord Dryden, that is. I want to serve my country."

Nodding, Giles smiled at him. "It's yours. I'll make the introductions, but you'll have to do the rest, young Harvey."

He barely heard the lad's gleeful "Thank you, my lord" as he began barking orders to the driver to make haste.

The wild ride through the wet and dangerous streets only matched Giles's unruly emotions. He'd gone from anger to relief back to anger by the time the driver pulled the horses to a stop in front of the gaming hall.

"What took you so long?" Monty demanded as he shot out from under the dripping eaves of the gaming house. He didn't give Giles a chance to get out of the carriage, only called out directions to his driver and climbed in.

"Where is she?" Giles demanded. The carriage jerked to a start.

"Gone. At least an hour ago." Monty shook the rain from his coat and hat.

He couldn't believe this. She was truly back in London and up to her old tricks. "Why didn't you follow her?"

"Without you?" Monty snorted. "You would have had my hide."

Giles took a deep breath. "So that's it? You just let her go?" He couldn't believe this. After all his searching, all the dead ends, Monty finds her in a St. James Street gaming hell.

"What was I supposed to do?" Monty's jaw set like a bulldog. "Why excuse me, madame. Remember me? Would you mind leaving this man you are about to rob and come with me?"

Giles shook his head. "Of course not, but you could have at least followed her." How could he come this close, only to lose her again?

"Why, when I know perfectly well where she is headed?"

His patience at an end, Giles reached over and caught his best friend by the collar. "Why didn't you say so in the first place?"

"You didn't ask." Monty glared back until Giles let go. Leaning back in his seat, he crossed his arms over his chest. "Brace yourself, for I don't think you are going to like this."

Giles ground out each word. "Where has she gone?"

"It's not the where that is the problem," the Duke pointed out. "It's the who she went with."

This stopped Giles. What kind of fool danger was she chasing now?

Giles knew the answer to that only too well. Something dangerous.

From the first moment he'd found her in Paris, her only thoughts had been to convince him to leave, to save himself. He still bristled at the idea of being treated like someone's doddering aunt to be shuffled off to quiet corner where he'd be safe from harm.

Damn her and her stubborn independence. Didn't she see she'd never be able to save her parents alone? She needed him. Needed someone to bring order to her dangerous schemes.

And the fact that he needed her was something he still had to come to terms with.

"Who did she leave with?" he asked in a quiet, steady voice.

"Selmar."

Stunned, Giles didn't reply at first.

The carriage began picking up the pace, having reached a wider street.

"He'll kill her, given the chance," Monty said despondently, clinging to his seat, his rain-soaked wig drooping.

"He won't have the opportunity if I have anything to do with it," Giles said. "That privilege belongs to me."

NOTHING WAS RIGHT. Sophia knew that the moment she'd entered Lord Selmar's house.

Instead of taking her to his study, she found herself in his private armory. She could only wonder what one man needed with such a collection.

Pikes, swords, cutlasses, and shields were mounted in ordered designs around the high walls. One wall, devoted entirely to guns, looked as if he were expecting a simultaneous invasion from both the French and Spanish. There were no paintings, no ornaments, other than those devoted to war. Lacking in any furniture, even a chair, the room resembled a medieval hall, complete with two suits of armor standing guard in opposite corners.

She felt their round, empty gaze on her as if they were living, breathing men ordered to watch her every move.

They certainly weren't going to point her to where Lord Selmar kept his jewels and money hidden.

"Damn," she muttered under her breath.

"What was that, my dear?" he called out, crossing the room from where he'd been selecting an ancient Spanish sword to show her.

"I was saying, my, what a big collection you have," she replied, turning from the row of axes. *Though not nearly as big as your colossal arrogance,* she wanted to add. He'd seemed interested enough in the carriage. Once they'd arrived at his house, though, he'd dragged her to this cold, lofty room and made her look at his "children."

Her information had seemed so clear: He loved danger and thrills. Mysterious women were his forte. He was an accomplished swordsman and rumored to be the deadliest shot in London.

Deadliest bore, she would now add.

Worst of all, he'd refused to share a drink with her,

stating it was too late in the night to imbibe. He wanted a clear head to discuss her "repayment."

"It's taken years to amass my toys, if you will," he was saying. "This one is my favorite. Late sixteenth century, an incredible piece of work. I came by it in a rather unorthodox manner."

His finger passed over the piece with an eerie devotion that sent goose bumps up and down Sophia's arms.

"What do you mean?" she asked.

He smiled. "I had it stolen. The family who owned it refused to sell it to me. So I found other means to obtain my treasure."

She smiled back in complete understanding. "Did you accomplish the deed yourself?" She moved closer, hoping to use this opening as a way to rekindle his interest.

He sidestepped her approach, his eyes widening in horror. "Of course not! I hired the work done by those more suited to such a despicable task."

Hypocrite. He loved the idea of possessing the stolen sword, not the thrill of the heist. He wasn't just a hypocrite, he was a coward as well. One in need of a lesson.

"Examine the inlay, the gems encrusted in the hilt," he said, pulling her toward the fireplace. "You won't see a finer work of art anywhere."

Sophia's breathing stilled at the sight of the large emeralds and fat pearls. Now, this was something she understood. Why, the gems alone were worth a fortune, not to mention what the silver and gold work would bring.

He held it out to her. "Try it."

Sophia didn't need any urging. She slipped her hand into the hilt. To her surprise she found it fit. Balanced and deceptively lightweight, the blade molded to her grip as if it had been made for her. She twisted her arm back and forth, the sword moving gracefully like an extension of her arm.

Selmar grinned. "I thought you would find that amusing. It was made for a lady. A pirate of some note."

"A pirate's blade," Sophia repeated. She knew the rumors well enough to know better than to provoke Selmar, but she didn't have all night to view his collections. She had business to finish.

"Is it sharp?" she asked, eyeing the edge.

"Very," he cautioned. "I keep all the blades in my collection well-honed. Best you hand it back to me."

"Not just yet." She stepped back, pointing the deadly weapon at his chest. "Now, Lord Selmar, you say you love a game of chance. What say you to raising the stakes on the matter of my debts?"

WHEN MONTY'S CARRIAGE pulled to a quick stop in front of Lord Selmar's Mayfair house, the place was ablaze with light and activity. Servants dashed about.

"What do you think happened?" Monty asked as he followed Giles out of the carriage.

"Something has gone wrong."

Just then another carriage wheeled up. A somberly dressed man climbed out, a black bag in hand.

An older servant, probably the butler, came bustling down the stairs. "Doctor Riverton, if you please, follow me," the stern fellow asked. "Your patient is in grave need of your services."

The two men hurried up the front steps.

At the doorway the butler turned around, his brows arching at Giles's uninvited approach.

"Is this man with you, Doctor?"

The physician looked up from checking his bag. "No, I've never seen him before."

The servant eyed Giles warily. "Who are you?"

"I am the Marquess of Trahern, and this," he said, turning to Monty, "is the Duke of Stanton. We have business with His Lordship. Take us to him immediately." Giles tried to push past the man, only to find his way blocked not only by the butler, but by the two other younger, much bigger footmen.

"I will do no such thing. His Lordship is quite busy right now. The doctor is needed to see to the situation."

The door started closing again in his face. Giles shoved his boot into the crack. "Listen well," he said. Reaching into the space in the doorway afforded by his boot, he grabbed the annoying man by his throat. "Let us in, or you're the one who is going to need more than a doctor to put you back together."

Monty squeaked something behind him. Giles didn't care. He'd left his careful, cautious ways back in the carriage. If Piper was inside this house, if she was hurt . . . he'd be damned if he'd let anyone stand in his way.

"L-l-let me go," the man begged.

"When you let me in," Giles said, each word full of venom and promise.

The butler waved off the footmen, his arms flailing about, his face turning a bright shade of purple.

Giles released him, pushed the door open wide, and marched in as if he owned the place.

"Where has the doctor gone?" he barked.

The servants stood silently at their posts.

Pulling out a pistol from his jacket, he cocked it. "Where is the doctor?" he asked the youngest footman.

"This way," the boy stuttered, leading them up the staircase.

Monty brought up the rear. "Is this a good idea?" he asked. "Terrorizing Selmar's staff?"

Giles shot him a black look.

"What has gotten into you?" Monty persisted, trotting along to keep up. "Are you out of your mind? I've known you since we were children, and I've never seen you act like this. What is going on?"

"If he's harmed her, I'll kill him."

Monty grinned. "Have you considered that it might be Selmar who is being attended by the doctor?"

Just then Monty got his answer, as the footman led them into Lord Selmar's bedchamber. The man lay on his bed, wailing and carrying on as if he were mortally wounded.

The doctor pulled out a bottle and a compress from his bag.

Even from the door they could see that Selmar's wound was nothing more than a nick, though by his thrashing and complaints it was hard to even see it. One thing neither Giles nor Monty missed was the pistol in the wounded man's hand.

"Now, you'll have to put that down," the doctor said, attempting to take the weapon from his patient. "You've done enough damage for tonight."

Giles backed out of the doorway pulling Monty and the young footman with him.

"What the devil happened?"

The young man looked glad to have someone to tell. "His Lordship brought home a lady. Haven't seen one around here for years. Most of us kinda thought he'd forgotten how." The boy grinned.

"Then what?" Giles growled, his tone wiping the smile from the boy's face.

"Well, see, I don't rightly know. They was in the armory, alone, and then he started yelping that he was dying. We all came running. Before we got to the room all hell broke loose. His Lordship firing his pistol like the French was invadin'. Well, none of us was going in that room 'til he stopped his firing. When we finally went in, the lady was gone and the room was all shot up."

"The lady, what of her?"

"No one seen her leave. I imagine she lit out of here right about the time his nibs there started firing at her."

Giles felt sick. "Where's this armory?"

"This way, Your Lordship, Your Grace."

The boy showed them to the vast room. Giles set to work immediately, looking for clues.

The footman, now having warmed up to his story and the prestige of telling it, showed them all around. "I think she went out the back," he offered, showing them a side entrance.

Giles asked her for a light, and the boy fetched a candle. Holding it up to illuminate the dark passageway, he saw the one piece of evidence that he'd dreaded.

Bright red blood stained the wall at different intervals as far as the light afforded.

It sickened him. Terrible images rushed forth of Piper—injured, helpless, and dying.

Why hadn't she just come to him in the first place? Believed him when he'd promised to help her find her parents?

Monty pushed forward, gasping at the terrible sight, his usually florid face turning pale.

"Was His Lordship brought this way?" Giles asked, though he doubted the slight wound he'd seen on Selmar could have caused this mess.

"No, we took him up the front stairs. Do you think he actually could have hit her? He's such a terrible shot." The boy gulped, realizing he'd confided too much.

Giles looked at the boy. "What are you saying?"

"Well, I'll deny it if you say I said it—His Lordship can't shoot. He can't see more than a few feet in front of his face. If he hit her it was blind luck."

Looking at the fresh bloodstains, Giles realized whatever it was, luck hadn't been on the side of the Brazen Angel.

CHAPTER
14

FOR THE NEXT WEEK
Giles's search for Piper or any clue of the Brazen Angel
turned up nothing. Worst of all, he feared she might have
raised enough money to finance a return trip to Paris, but
Selmar claimed she'd taken nothing.

Not that he believed the arrogant man.

It wasn't supposed to be like this—he was a trained and
experienced agent, and yet a mere slip of a girl had out-
witted him, as if she knew his every move.

To add to his woes, Lady Dearsley kept sending around
notes insisting he go visit his betrothed at Lady Larkhall's

estate in Bath. He'd politely declined with every conceivable excuse he could muster, but knew he couldn't avoid Lady Sophia or her aunts forever.

Stepping out of his carriage, Giles entered the small bookstore in Covent Garden. It was an odd place for a bookseller, stashed between two theaters, but the owner had a reputation for being both an eclectic collector of French texts and a devoted fan of the ladies of the stage.

He opened the door, making his way into the dark recesses of the shop. In the far corner a hunchbacked man bent over a candle and a large tome.

Giles stood for a moment, waiting for the man to assist him. The old man did nothing to acknowledge his new customer.

"I beg your pardon," Giles said, coughing, more from the dust than as a polite distraction. "I was told you collect old French texts."

"Eh?" the man muttered, finally looking up from his book. "What's that?"

"I said I'm looking for a specific French text."

The man climbed down from his stool and hobbled over, using a knarled wood cane to support his crooked steps. "French, eh? What kind of text?"

Giles reached into his pocket and pulled out two objects, laying them on the counter.

A gold signet ring and a piece of silver and white brocade. Each emblazoned with a swan and a *fleur-de-lis*.

The man hopped the last few steps up to the front counter, his nearsighted eyes blinking at the objects. "May I?" he indicated, his hand poised over the ring.

Giles nodded.

The man snatched up the ring, poring over the design.

His flitting gaze didn't seem to miss a thing, for a second later he tipped the ring toward the candle and peered inside the band to read the words inscribed.

"Nihil amanti durum," he muttered. He leaned back and examined Giles. "Don't suppose you need this translated?"

"No, I know what it says."

Nothing is difficult to one who loves. Words he was starting to believe were nothing but a contradiction in terms.

"Thought as much. Then what is it you do need?"

"I want to know who claims this crest and motto. I don't think it belongs to a current title. I suspect it is an old family name, long since discarded. The motto, I believe, is used only with the family name."

The man nodded in understanding.

Under the weight of loftier and more prestigious titles, a French nobleman's ancient surnames were often all but forgotten, known only by direct family members, if even by them. Names so old, they went back to the times of Charlemagne.

Of late there had been a resurrection in using these surnames, for they offered a readily familiar disguise for the aristocrat seeking a new identity.

"I may have something to interest you," the man said, his eyes twinkling with the challenge and the opportunity to show off his more prized books. He hobbled from the front desk back to the high back wall, which was lined with books from floor to ceiling.

He climbed up a small ladder, his narrow thin fingers latching on to a thick book. "Here it is."

Carrying it over to the counter, he carefully turned the brittle pages of vellum.

Giles leaned over, stunned by the amazing colors that

nearly leapt from the pages. Brilliantly detailed hand illus-
trations of family crests crowded the Latin text.

The man glanced over at the ring again, smiling. "Here it
is." He pointed down at the page. "Laurent. That mean
anything?"

Giles shook his head.

"Doesn't surprise me. Good at confusing the issue, the
French. We aren't through yet." The man returned to his
stacks, muttering titles and names, more to himself than his
customer.

Four books later Giles had his answer.

Laurent was the ancient family name for the Comte
D'Artiers.

His future father-in-law.

Which could only mean that Lady Sophia was—

Damn her, he thought. Damn her duplicity to hell.

He paid the man for his help and left the shop without
another word.

Monty poked his head out of the carriage, where he'd
been waiting for Giles to return. The Duke had insisted on
offering his "assistance" in the search for the wounded lady.

"Where to, Trahern? Another one of those dreary French
coffeehouses or another dressmaker?" Monty asked as Giles
climbed into the carriage.

"Neither. We're going to Bath," he answered. "I suddenly have the strangest urge to visit my betrothed."

Two NIGHTS LATER Giles's carriage stopped at the
gates of Larkhall Manor.

"Looks as if they've brought everyone out from town,"
Monty commented. "Could be quite a party."

Giles glanced up at Larkhall Manor. Carriages stood waiting in the front drive, and soft candlelight glowed from most of the windows. He'd sent a note to Lady Larkhall advising her of his arrival at Byrnewood and requesting to dine with her and her niece.

And he'd asked the lady to keep his impending reunion with his bride-to-be a surprise.

"I'd have to say, I'm in the mood for a party." Or a hanging, he thought, still furious at the way his "meek and mild" betrothed had played him for a fool.

He knew she lived, that at least she'd survived Selmar's gunfire. But how, he didn't know.

Considering that Dryden and Lady Dearsley had spent most of the last three weeks urging him to travel to Bath and see this marriage matter settled, Giles felt all that much more frustrated. If he'd heeded their unwitting advice he would have discovered Sophia's deception before she'd had the opportunity to don her Brazen Angel costume again.

As the carriage rolled along the gentle curve of the drive, he recalled the first time he'd ever visited Larkhall Manor. His mother had died the fall before. The winter had been a miserable ordeal as he'd spent his first year away at school. Lady Larkhall had suffered a similar loss: Her husband had died of a fever during the winter. By summer when he returned home, she still wasn't receiving guests. But that hadn't stopped the six-year-old lad, lonely and without a mother, from wandering across the property lines.

Compared to the dark, lonely halls of Byrnewood, Larkhall Manor seemed to him a fairy castle, and Lady Larkhall, the queen of merriment.

She listened to his stories, laughed at his jokes. She sympathized with his complaints about the endless studies his tutor assigned. She helped him with his lessons under the wide oak that marked the property line between the two estates. The kind lady filled a void in his empty life, and looking back he realized he may have provided her a diversion from her own grief.

"Lord Trahern?" the butler asked, as Giles once again entered the house he'd always loved.

He nodded and handed over his coat to the man. "This is the Duke of Stanton," he said, introducing Monty.

"Dinner has already started, Your Grace, my lord. Lady Larkhall's instructions were to see you announced the moment you arrived."

Monty and Giles followed the man down the long hallway to the dining room.

"My lady," the butler intoned in a deep, rich baritone. "The Duke of Stanton and the Marquess of Trahern."

Twelve pairs of eyes turned to them. He heard a deep intake of breath at the end of the table and could only imagine who it might be coming from.

Lady Larkhall rose from her place at the head of the table. "Lord Trahern, I am so pleased you've finally arrived." She came forward, her hands outstretched. "And you've brought a guest, how wonderful. Your Grace, please, if you would take this seat here," she offered.

While Lady Larkhall called for another setting for Giles, he studied her.

She was in many ways the same woman he remembered. Her chestnut hair had gone gray, but her blue eyes still sparkled with the familiar warmth he'd always loved. As a child he'd thought her a tall woman, but found that his childhood memories had been outgrown. He now towered above her.

"We have quite a crowd tonight," she whispered, as she turned back to him and took his arm. "But I know who you are most anxious to see again. . . ." She led him down one side of the table toward the place setting the footman was rapidly squeezing in on the crowded table. The high-backed chairs hid the guests to his immediate right, but across the table he vaguely recognized some of the people: Squire Fischer and his wife; Reverend Harel, the local parson; Mr. and Mrs. Whitcombe; and a young girl, who by her long nose and red hair could only be the squire's daughter.

Monty was placed between the squire's daughter and a severe-looking woman in widow's weeds. Giles recognized her at once.

Emma!

So, Sophia's companion, Mrs. Langston, was also the harridan who diverted his attention the night he'd captured the Brazen Angel, as well as Julien and Lily's companion back to London.

If she recognized him she did little more than nod politely, but when he glanced back a second time, she had a wry smile and an amused flash to her dark eyes.

Before he could comment, Lady Larkhall was saying, "Now, here we are." She squeezed his arm. "The real reason you've come to visit. My dear niece, Lady Sophia."

The young lady rose from the chair on Lady Larkhall's right. As she turned to greet him Giles forgot about everyone else in the room.

The young woman was dressed in the height of fashion, à la Turk, complete with feathers in her dressed hair, a striped gown, and starched fichu. Despite all the fashionable trappings, he saw what he'd come for.

The indignant flash of blue eyes, the gentle curve of her

jaw, and her full lips, which were currently pulled into a strained smile.

Beside Lady Larkhall stood the one and only reason he'd come to Bath.

The Brazen Angel.

It seemed his search was over.

FOR SOPHIA, GILES'S entrance into the dining room left her gasping for air. Startled, she'd looked to Emma for help.

No help there, for Emma was being introduced to the Duke of Stanton.

The Duke of Stanton! Why, she'd robbed the man!

Whatever was Giles thinking in bringing him to Larkhall Manor?

She gulped again for air. His unlikely arrival in Bath could only mean he'd discovered who she was. No, he couldn't have—she'd been too careful. Short of a sudden fit of apoplexy, there was little hope of her avoiding detection now. Frantically, she pulled the feathers in her hair forward, hoping they offered some mask against detection.

Lady Larkhall coughed. "Sophia. Get up, girl, and greet His Lordship."

Struggling to her feet, she kept her gaze fixed on his gleaming boots while she extended her hand in greeting. "My lord," she murmured.

"Lady Sophia, it is a delight and a sincere pleasure to see you again." With that he brought her hand to his lips and laid a gentle kiss there, his thumb caressing her fingers in soft, languid strokes.

The contact brought back flashes of the passion they had

shared. Her turbulent feelings for him tossed anew, clamoring to respond. But as Lady Sophia she could hardly throw herself into his arms and beg his forgiveness.

She pulled her hand away. "Yes, I suppose it is." Allowing him to assist her into her chair, Sophia refused to meet his gaze.

Once he took his seat the meal began again. He leaned over his plate and studied her. "I see you have recovered from your unfortunate accident."

Accident? Sophia looked down at her bandaged hand and dropped it to her lap. When she finally risked a glance in his direction, there was no doubt in his dark gaze that he recognized her. And worst of all, he knew about her robbery of Lord Selmar.

"Accident?" Lady Larkhall commented as Giles turned and held her chair for her. "Sophia, you were in an accident? I don't recall you telling me anything about this."

Giles's eyebrows rose in mocking challenge, as if he couldn't wait to hear her answer.

"A minor incident only, Auntie," she replied quickly, holding up her bandaged hand. "I cut myself on a vase while arranging flowers for Auntie Effie," she said slowly, for Giles's benefit. "Auntie Effie was worried I would have blood poisoning. Lord Trahern, you are too much like Lady Dearsley, and make far too much of a simple accident."

He shook out his napkin and paused for a moment. "Lady Dearsley made a point of telling me about your delicate constitution and the great care that must be taken with your health."

"Delicate?" Lady Larkhall eyed Sophie. "Whatever is he talking about? You haven't been ill a day in your life."

Sophia patted her aunt's hand. "You know Auntie Effie;

she quite exaggerates." She shot a glare in Giles's direction and seethed when he grinned back.

What was he up to? All too soon she found out.

The squire's wife, Lady Fischer, an ambitious woman who liked to consider herself in the forefront of Bath's smartest sets, was seated next to Giles.

"Lord Trahern," she said, leaning over his elbow as if they were the oldest and dearest of friends, "I find your concern for our dear Lady Sophia quite touching. There aren't many men who take such an intimate concern for a future wife's welfare. How considerate you are, sir." She smiled across the table at Sophia, the feathers in her towering wig waggling with annoyance. "And you, Lady Sophia, how lucky for you to be gaining a husband who will so obviously watch over you so carefully." The lady sent Sophia a prodding nod meant to encourage her out of her moody silence. "I know if my Dorlissa found such a man," the lady said pointedly at Monty, "he would be blessed with a wife's sincerest devotion."

"How right you are, Lady Fischer," Giles told her, leaning over toward her as if they were conspiring in some plot. "I've every intention of watching over Lady Sophia day and night from here on out. I say it is my duty and obligation as her future husband to safeguard her from harm." He paused, a serious expression on his face. "Would it be quite medieval of me to lock her away in Byrnewood's tower and keep her all to myself? At least until we've secured an heir or two."

"Ooh, you do tease, Lord Trahern." Lady Fischer tittered at the wicked intimacy of it.

"Who said I was teasing?" He looked directly at Sophia.

She wanted to gnash her teeth. Lock her away like a brood mare? The utter arrogance of him.

The young parson coughed, obviously uncomfortable with the discussion of locking away young ladies for the sole business of procuring heirs. The poor man blushed and sputtered. He finally recovered enough to smile kindly at Sophia. "Perhaps we should be discussing when this blessed union is going to take place," Reverend Harel stuttered. Folding his hands over his plate as if in prayer, the nervous man tried to look as if he were providing a moral focus to the meal.

"Next summer——" Sophia answered.

"End of the week," Giles corrected.

Under the table she knotted her napkin and considered how she could possibly stuff it down his throat without creating too much of a scene.

"End of the week," he repeated.

End of the week? Try the end of the next century, Sophia wanted to tell him.

"Oh, you are an anxious one, Lord Trahern," Lady Fischer bubbled.

"Anxious doesn't even begin to describe what I feel when I look across this table at my intended, my dear lady."

"And what do you say, Lady Sophia, in the face of such ardent admiration?" Lady Fischer asked. "Aren't you the least bit excited about becoming the mistress of such a fine house as Byrnewood?"

"I'd say the Marquess has expressed his intentions quite clearly." Sophia stabbed at the food in front of her.

"I know if my Dorlissa were becoming the next mistress of Byrnewood," Lady Fischer said, waving her hand at her daughter, "I'd be there right this moment redecorating a suite of rooms for myself right next to the nursery."

Sophia couldn't resist. "Well, perhaps you'll get lucky and I'll cry off my engagement, Lady Fischer. I'm sure Lord Trahern wouldn't do any better than Dorlissa for his bride."

The unwitting girl had chosen this moment to stuff her mouth too full of food, and she blushed furiously upon finding every eye at the table staring at her. Under the strain of such unanticipated attention she began to choke.

Monty, seated next to Dorlissa, pounded the hapless girl heavily on the back, while the lanky parson tipped over a water pitcher while attempting to pour the unfortunate girl a drink.

"How you tease, Lady Sophia," Lady Fischer said loudly, drawing the attention away from her daughter's ungainly mishap. "I would think at your age and in your situation you wouldn't be so apt to throw off such a fine man as Lord Trahern. Not many men will take a penniless bride."

Sophia smiled back, trying to decide if she had enough napkin to choke both Giles and Lady Fischer. Before she could think of a reply, she found her rescue in a most unlikely corner.

"Lady Fischer," Giles interrupted. "I have no concern for dowries or my betrothed's current circumstances. My father sought this marriage because he found the lady to be engaging and intelligent, her kindness to an old man trapped in his infirmary unequaled. I've placed my faith in Lady Sophia because of his high regard, for I know such praise from him would not be misplaced."

Sophia was taken aback. She'd never known the old marquess had thought so highly of her. Even when he'd proposed the betrothal he'd done it in his usual gruff and terse manner.

You'll marry my son and be mistress of this house, he'd ordered one day over a game of chess. *I don't want some chattering debutante and her harridan mother coming in and ruining the place.*

Sophia wondered if the old crank had envisioned Lady Fischer and Dorlissa when he'd issued his mandate.

"Your father was not a man known for his generosity in compliments," Sophia said quietly, suddenly realizing how much of a debt she owed the old marquess. The hours listening to his tales of espionage and tactics had been her training ground. "I'm pleased to know he enjoyed the time we spent together as much as I did. Byrnewood will be a different place without him."

"The whole neighborhood is different without him," Lord Whitcombe blustered at the end of the table. "Good man, he was. Good one to take fishing. Knew his way with horses as well. Good man, he was."

Whitcombe probably would have continued his litany if it hadn't been for Lady Whitcombe giving him a sharp jab in the ribs.

The dinner continued quietly for a time.

That was until Lady Fischer and Mrs. Whitcombe started arguing over who should give the newlyweds their first ball.

Sophia started to feel as if she'd fallen into a play near the Palace Royal, one of the comical farces her mother had been so fond of—only this time it was one of her own making.

She knew her aunt had been watching her closely ever since Giles's comment about her "delicate constitution." Lady Larkhall was right—she was never ill, at least not when she was in Bath. Emma had warned her that the varied deceptions she was juggling between the aunts would one day start tumbling to earth.

Tonight, Sophia realized, the first one fell.

At Lady Dearsley's, Sophia used a constant state of ill health to explain her extended need of the waters in Bath under the gracious care of Lady Larkhall. To extract herself from Bath Sophia confided to her kindhearted aunt how lonely her younger sister was. And from the Duchess's home in York Sophia pined for the amusements of London.

Since none of the sisters communicated with each other, having had a tremendous falling out over how to raise their niece, they relied on Sophia to carry messages between them. Using this advantage, she'd been able to travel to Paris whenever she needed to without any of them becoming the wiser.

Lady Larkhall rang the bell for dessert and turned to Giles. "Lord Trahern, when you last saw my niece did you have the opportunity to meet Mrs. Langston, Sophia's companion?"

Sophia held her breath, her wineglass frozen in midair.

"No, I haven't had the pleasure of a formal introduction. Mrs. Langston, how lovely to meet you." He tipped his head graciously.

"And you, my lord," Emma answered in an amused tone. "Sophia has told me *so* much about you."

Sophia glared at her.

"Mrs. Langston, I hope you don't think me impertinent," Giles said. "But have we met before?"

Sophia sputtered on her wine.

"I don't believe we have," Emma answered. "I'm certain I'd recall the acquaintance."

Lady Fischer jumped right in. "Mrs. Langston is being

too modest, Lord Trahern. Her late husband was the naval hero Captain Langston. Surely you've heard of his brave deeds in the war with the Colonies and in the earlier Dutch campaigns?"

It was Emma's turn to cough into her napkin.

"Is that so, Mrs. Langston?" Giles scratched his chin. "Wasn't Captain Langston the commander of the *Nemophila,* or was he on the *Southern Cross?*"

Emma paused, dabbed her lips with her napkin, and looked around the table.

Sophia held her breath, silently praying Emma would get it right. Up to now they'd never met anyone who'd actually known Captain Langston.

Hell, she hadn't even thought there *was* a Captain Langston.

"It was neither, my lord. My dear departed husband commanded the *HMS Righteous.*"

Giles nodded, as if acknowledging her small victory on this bit of information, but his look said that this was only the beginning of his inquisition.

"And what a brave inspiration you are, Mrs. Langston," Lady Fischer broke in, "to the rest of us foolish creatures, who haven't had to give up a loved one for the sake of our country."

"Yes," Giles added, with a serious nod. "What sacrifices a woman of your quality makes. I can only hope you'll continue in my wife's employ after our marriage. Your fine moral example would only be a credit to our household."

"Thank you, my lord," Emma said, turning toward Sophia with a gracious nod.

"Oh, don't you even consider it, Mrs. Langston." Lady Fischer poked over her pudding with a delicate sniff. "I'd hoped to lure you away from Lady Sophia once she was wed. My Dorlissa could use the influence of someone of your character." She nudged her husband, who up to this point had appeared to be dozing. "Wasn't I saying, Lord Fischer, we must have Mrs. Langston for our Dorlissa. Whatever the cost."

Lord Fischer huffed and puffed at the mention of money, his bloodshot eyes opening and blinking as if this were the first time he'd realized he was in the middle of a dinner party. "Whatever you say, Lady Fischer. Price is no object. Always spend top dollar for cattle, I say, and you'll get top stock." When everyone stared at him in wonder, he shrugged his shoulders and started a close inspection of his dessert.

"Oh, do say you'll come to Fischer Castle, Mrs. Langston," Lady Fischer implored.

Giles grinned at Sophia before turning to Lady Fischer. "I'm sure you'd find Mrs. Langston's influence on your dear daughter a wonder to behold."

Sophia watched her aunt look first at Giles and then in her direction, as if she were trying to determine what exactly was the undercurrent traveling between them.

Nevertheless, the perplexed lady rang the bell for the dishes to be cleared, and she rose from the table to excuse the ladies.

"Gentlemen, please enjoy a glass or two of port. And when you feel inclined I bid you to join us in the Rose Room." She withdrew from the table, the ladies rising and following her in en masse.

Mrs. Fischer caught Sophia by the elbow. "Don't look so forlorn, my dear girl. If dinner was any indication of your betrothed's feelings, I'd predict he'll be joining us in record time."

"That's what I'm afraid of," Sophia muttered under her breath as she glanced back to find Giles tipping his glass of port to her in a mock salute.

Lady Fischer's prediction, Sophia found out, did not prove true. It seemed the men were never going to join the party in the Rose Room. Meanwhile, Sophia paced about the room in an utterly unladylike fashion, until she looked up and caught her aunt watching her. Dropping into the nearest chair, she tried to concentrate on the inane chatter flowing mostly from Lady Fischer.

"As I was saying, Lady Larkhall, I have it on the best authority, and through only the most confidential of sources, that it has been said by a certain lady who shall remain nameless that . . ."

Sophia glanced over at Emma, who sat trapped between Lady Fischer and the ever dear Dorlissa. She'd never seen her companion look more miserable, her fingers lacing and unlacing in her lap.

Emma was probably plotting right now how to escape to her room, light up her pipe, and start drafting a resignation letter. Effective immediately.

A few minutes later, unable to stand the suspense, Sophia found herself back on her feet, stalking the room again.

While Giles hadn't said anything at dinner, it was only a matter of time before he would confront her. She could take the fact that he hadn't denounced her outright at dinner as a good sign, but this insistence of his that they be wed immediately was preposterous. She'd ruin his reputation if they were married and her dual identity ever revealed.

Male laughter in the hallway stopped Sophia in her tracks. The men paraded into the room—Lord Fischer mumbling to no one in particular, Lord Whitcombe espousing to the young parson the finer points of hounds, and, finally, Giles, trailing along with an indifferent smile tacked on his face. In fact, he barely looked in her direction, instead heading directly for the empty seat next to Lady Fischer.

If he was anxious to confront her it didn't show from his obvious lack of interest or his languid pace.

Sophia promptly turned her back to him and stared out the windows into the moonlit shadows of the rose garden.

"Oh, what a splendid idea, Lord Trahern," Lady Fischer exclaimed. "You are a romantic and daring fellow. If only I was but a few years younger."

Sophia glanced over her shoulder, suspicious of anything the odious lady found splendid.

"Lady Sophia, where are you?" Lady Fischer called out, craning her head back and forth until the feathers in her wig became a blur of pink and white. "Oh, you sly girl, there you are. Hiding over there as if you didn't care a bit about Lord Trahern's arrival." The gregarious lady poked Giles with her fan. "She's been pacing the room like a fox since we left your charming company. Pining for you, she was. Come on, girl, His Lordship has a favor to ask you."

Sophia gritted her teeth, turned around, and tried to smile. Crossing the room, she stopped several feet shy of the couch where Lady Fischer held her impromptu court.

"I would have no objections if this were my dear

Dorlissa——" She paused and sent a poignant look in the Duke's direction, hoping he'd take the hint. Monty seemed oblivious to the woman's matchmaking. Lady Fischer gave up on the Duke for the moment and returned her attentions to Sophia. "I am sure your aunt will agree with me, Lady Sophia. Lord Trahern would like to take you for a stroll in the orangery."

Shaking her head, Sophia struggled to find a polite way to say no without making it come out like an emphatic *hell, no.* Alone with Giles? Not if she could avoid it.

"I'm afraid I left my shawl in my room, and the orangery has such a terrible chill this time of year . . ." She stuttered along, searching the room for support from someone, anyone.

"Pish and nonsense," Lady Fischer said, reaching over and stripping Dorlissa's wrap from her narrow shoulders in a quick snap. "This should be adequate. Now, go on with you. Your aunt has no objections, do you, Lady Larkhall?"

"None whatsoever. Go on, Sophia. The lively air might put some color back in your cheeks. You look rather pale this evening."

The unmistakable challenge in her aunt's words left Sophia in a quandary. If she continued to back away from Lord Trahern, she'd spend the rest of the evening undergoing a lengthy interrogation by her aunt as to what was going on between her and Lord Trahern.

Taking another tack, she turned to her companion. "Emma, would you accompany us? You've always taught me it is immodest and improper to accompany men unescorted."

Emma leaned forward to get up, until Lady Fischer raised her fan in warning.

"Stay right where you are, Mrs. Langston," she said.

Emma's eyes widened, and then a bemused look passed quickly over her face. She inclined her head to Sophia as if to say, *You're on your own with this one.*

Lady Fischer rose from the sofa and caught Sophia by the elbow. "I'll hear no more of these missish excuses from you. This isn't London. Here in the country we are free from some of the restraints society places on young lovers. Take the liberties where you can find them, my dear girl."

Before Sophia could utter another protest she found herself being propelled toward the now-open door leading toward the orangery.

Giles beamed at his complete and utter rout of her safe position in the salon.

Before releasing Sophia into the care of her betrothed, Lady Fischer added her final piece of courting advice.

"Maidenly virtues and reticent manners are fine indeed," she whispered none too quietly. "But do you want the man to think you aren't interested? You've led a sheltered, sequestered life with your aunts. Live, Lady Sophia, take some chances with your life. He might even be inclined to steal a kiss if you'd smile a bit." The lady winked at Giles.

With those words ringing in her ears, Sophia found herself being pushed out the door and into the waiting arms of her betrothed.

CHAPTER
15

"**L**ET GO OF ME, you great ponderous—" Sophia sputtered the moment Lady Fischer closed the door.

Giles noted her quick use of the insult the Brazen Angel favored, then saw the realization dawn on her face as to what she had nearly said.

Her mouth snapped shut, and when she spoke again, her tone changed to the sweet and even-tempered tones of a lady.

"Please, my lord," she continued, "be so kind as to unhand me."

Giles did just that, depositing her quite nicely on a padded bench positioned under the gloomy portrait of a Larkhall ancestor. He had no desire to hold the traitorous female in his arms any more than she wanted to be held. At least not until he had some answers. And honest ones at that.

For a minute they stood there, facing each other in stormy silence. Absently, she started picking at the wrappings on her injured hand.

He dropped to his knees beside her. "He did hit you. How bad is it?"

"Whatever do you mean? I wasn't hit. As I said in the dining room, I was arranging flowers when—"

Giles shook his head. "Stop the act. I know who you are."

He had to admit that behind the fashionable clothing, the elaborate headdress, the feathers, and the copious amounts of lace, he might have been deceived once again, but this close to the lady it was impossible not to know her. The sapphire eyes, the curve of her chin, the glorious hair.

Why hadn't he seen all this before and recognized her deception earlier? The timid, mousy Lady Sophia he'd met in London was nothing like this styled, accomplished woman before him. It seemed she had a persona for every occasion.

He reached over and pushed back the feathers dipping into her face. "You've pulled quite a feat, haven't you, Lady Brazen?"

She tipped her head and stared at him. "Are you well, my lord?" She laid her hand on his brow. "I'm your betrothed, Lady Sophia. Don't you remember me?"

"And here I was starting to wonder if there even was a Lady Sophia."

Her brow furrowed. "Who else who I be but your betrothed?"

She really had some nerve playing the innocent miss, and he was of no mind to continue her ruse any further. Reaching into his coat pocket, he pulled out the signet ring the Brazen Angel had lost in Paris. "Does this look familiar?"

Her hand trembled as he placed the ring into the warmth of her palm, but her face never betrayed her.

Her lips pursed in concentration. "I'm supposed to know this?"

"You should; it's your family's crest."

She looked away, as if trying to find some plausible excuse, some other deception with which to continue.

"There is also this," he added, pulling the scrap of fabric from the Brazen Angel's dress he'd retrieved from the carriage wheel the night of the Parkers' masked ball. "Odd coincidence how they match, isn't it? Now, do you start telling me how badly you were shot, or do I go in and ask your aunt to unwrap these coverings?"

She tried to scramble up to her feet. "Why, you—" She stopped halfway.

"Uh, uh, uh," he said, shaking his finger at her. "We're being watched."

He pointed over her shoulder to where Lady Whitcombe, Lady Fisher, and Dorlissa stood, their noses pressed against the panes of the connecting French doors. When the snooping threesome realized they'd been caught, they backed away, leaving only a trio of small smudges on the windows.

Sophia muttered something in French, the translation of which made him cringe. She straightened to her feet and started down the gallery toward the orangery in long, impatient strides.

"Are you coming along or not?" she asked over her shoulder.

Giles followed, taking his time. He wondered if he'd ever see the real Sophia—for she played each role with the skill of an accomplished actress—or would life with this woman be a never-ending drama?

"Isn't this putting your reputation at risk, my lady? I mean, running away so quickly to be alone with me. Where are the protests for your virtue?" he asked, finally catching up with her as she mounted the marble stairs to the glass-enclosed orangery Lord Larkhall had built thirty years earlier. Lamps burned at the entranceway, a tradition that Lord Larkhall had begun when he finished his glass-enclosed marvel and that his widow continued to this day. "Your virtue and honor mean far more to me than I can express," he teased.

"As Lady Fischer would say, pish and nonsense," she shot back, crossing the small open-air room and settling down primly on one of the stone benches. "You weren't too concerned about my virtue before."

He laughed. "Neither were you."

His words brought her back to her feet. "Oh, you—"

"I don't know what you're so aggrieved about—you act like I stole your virtue." Come to think of it, he realized, the woman he'd been with in Paris had hardly been a virgin, which meant that Lady Sophia . . . He looked at his bride-to-be again. "Speaking of virtue . . ."

Her cheeks turned crimson, as if she'd followed his silent reasoning. "That is none of your business," she snapped.

"Some men would disagree, but I'm not of a mind to

debate that point tonight." He paused. "I think we have more immediate concerns to consider. Like whether or not you are carrying my heir."

Her hands on her hips, she glared at him. "I'd sooner——"

"You'd sooner what?" he interrupted. "Take it all back? If only it were so easy."

"Everything would be much easier if you would return to London and leave me be."

"You didn't answer my question."

"Then no, I am not. Will you leave now?"

He settled down on the bench and stretched his legs in front of him. She frowned at his action and took a seat on the opposite bench.

"You heard me at dinner," he said. "I'm not letting you out of my sight. Not until we are married."

"Why are you persisting in this marriage? 'T'would be ruinous for both of us." Sophia folded her arms over her chest.

"I don't think so. I find we suit."

"Well, I disagree."

Giles threw his hands in the air. "I'll never understand you."

At this, she smiled. "Would you want to? I thought you rather liked the mystery."

She had a point, and it bothered him. The mystery of the Brazen Angel had possessed his mind, and now he had come to the conclusion that it wasn't enough to know who the woman beneath the mask was—he wanted to know everything about her. And he wanted to spend the rest of his life exploring those secrets.

He didn't understand how she could possess him so completely, unable to put a name on the emotions she stirred.

She rose from the bench, letting her shawl slide over one shoulder. She held the other end up in front of her face and continued to wrap it like a harem slave's mask around her face. By the time she finished, all he could see were her eyes. Slowly, she approached him. "Is this what you wanted, the lady of the night?"

" 'Tis a dangerous game you play." He met her in the middle of the room. "Choose carefully who you are. Act like Lady Sophia and I'll treat you as such." He moved even closer, until he caught her in his arms. Tossing aside Dorlissa's wrap, he pulled her into his embrace. "Act like the Brazen Angel, and you'll go back into that house in a state of such *dishabille,* Lady Fischer will be booked for the next three seasons with malicious people anxious to hear her tale." He brushed back a stray lock of her chestnut hair and looked directly into her eyes. "What will it be, my Lady Brazen?"

"Sssh," she warned, though she didn't struggle against his embrace. "You shouldn't call me that. What if someone heard you? They'd have that pimpled person out here and we'd find ourselves married before midnight, if only to save my reputation."

"And would that be so bad?"

She took a deep breath, as if to launch into another argument. Instead, she let out a long sigh and stared at the marble floor. "I don't know anymore."

He realized it was probably the most honest admission she'd ever made to him. "Then let me decide, for I never want to face another sleepless night not knowing if you've been hurt or worse. When I arrived at Selmar's and saw the blood, I could only imagine—"

Her gaze shot up. "You were there?"

"Of course I was. When will you realize? Wherever you go, I am destined to follow." Giles brushed at a stray curl of her hair. Dammit, he should be furious with her for the risks she'd taken, for the deception she'd pulled.

But holding her in his arms, knowing she was alive, the only thing he felt was relief. "I've been trying to find you for weeks. Monty saw you leaving that gaming hell, and we followed you to Selmar's. I've been out of my mind since I saw that room, the blood in the hallway. I didn't know where you'd gone or how badly you'd been hurt. I only hoped Oliver retrieved you in time."

"I'm sorry you were worried." She held up her injured hand. "Truly, it isn't so bad. Selmar, for all his bluff and foul reputation, is a miserable shot."

Sophia couldn't help but feel a bit guilty that Giles had been worried about her. And over an arrogant nitwit like Selmar; really, the man was too much.

He shook his head. "Whatever were you doing to get yourself shot at?"

"What do you think I was doing? I was robbing him."

He groaned and set her out at arm's length. "How did you plan on accomplishing this? Remember, I know how your little scheme works, and Selmar doesn't imbibe."

"A fact I found out a little too late," she shot back. "It was touch and go after I realized I was going to have to rob a fully conscious man. But, really, you could say he handed me my prize, and who was I to say no?"

"Out with it," he ordered. "I want to hear everything."

So she explained about the sword and how Selmar bragged about having it stolen from the rightful owners. "He's pilfered most of his possessions." Crossing her arms over her chest, she shook her head. "At least I don't rob innocents."

"Unlike the Duke?"

She pursed her lips. "He was an exception. I didn't want to steal from him, but he cut off my intended mark."

"Who was?"

Sophia laughed at this. "Some things a lady doesn't disclose." As if she had any intention of revealing that bit of priceless information. Besides, the man in question had just arrived in Bath to take the waters, and Sophia knew the time had come to pay him a little visit. "Suffice it to say, I carried away only what I thought the Duke could spare. The Stanton jewelry is famous and priceless, so you should be proud that I took only his coins."

"Such nobility," Giles scoffed.

"I have my standards."

"Standards that are now at an end, as your misadventure at Lord Selmar's should have taught you."

She didn't like the direction of this. It was starting to sound like another one of his lectures on caution and care. Didn't he understand that the time for caution was well past? The news out of Paris spoke only of the horrifying rise in executions, and her parents were still unaccounted for.

"You promised to contact me," he continued. "I've had runners searching everywhere. Did you think I would just give up and forget?"

"It would be better for you if you had."

"Well, it's too late for that now. I've found you."

Now Sophia definitely knew she didn't like the course of this conversation. Hadn't he all but said he would follow her to the ends of the earth? It was worse than she thought. Since the death of the old man, she'd awakened each night in the throes of the nightmare where Giles was led to the scaffold. And after she'd convince herself it was only a dream and return to sleep, her sleep was filled with images of him being cut down by rabid groups of *sans-culottes,* their long, wicked pikes tearing and ripping his flesh.

His days of following her were over. She must put an end to them now.

He stopped for a minute and studied her. "You intend to go back there," he said aloud as the realization struck him.

Damn, she hated him for his keen insight.

"You had no intention of coming to me for help," he continued, his mouth tightening with anger. "You were going to gather another fortune and disappear again. And soon, if that failed robbery of Selmar was any indication."

That brought her gaze up, and she studied him. He didn't realize she'd been successful that night, that she'd carried off Selmar's prized pirate sword along with a small cask of jewels and several jeweled daggers. Or that she knew a buyer in Paris who would readily buy the lot. "Whatever do you mean? Return to Paris with a warrant on my head? I'd have to be insane."

He caught her by the shoulders and gave a gentle shake. "As insane as robbing Selmar? He could have killed you."

"But he didn't. He missed." She grinned at him. "Missed by at least a good foot or two on the first round. By the second one I was well out of range." Sophia laughed a little, hoping to tease him out of his indignant concern.

"Then how do you explain this?" he asked, holding up her hand.

She shrugged her shoulders. "A piece of paneling caught me when his shot hit the wall. Emma fixed it up with one of her potions."

He released her, his arms crossing over his chest. "I won't stand for this. I forbid you to continue this dangerous charade."

"You forbid me?" she repeated. "You have no rights over me."

"I will once we are wed. Believe me, if you thought I was joking over dinner about hiding you away, tomorrow I will order extra locks installed at Byrnewood and all the ivy trimmed from the outer walls. You'll stay bolted in the fourth-story tower until you are so heavy with child the stairs will be a challenge."

She backed away. Her voice lowered to an angry whisper. "What would you have me do? Stay here? Marry you while my parents are murdered? I cannot. I will not."

"I promised you in Paris I would see your family to safety." He paced once or twice in front of her, then stopped. "I have every intention of bringing them here to England. I've already started inquiries as to where they are being held."

Catching his hand, she tugged at it. "Have you found anything?"

He paused for a second too long. "No."

Something about the catch in his voice told her he was lying. But she knew there was nothing she could do to convince him to share his information. If he told her anything, they both knew she would be on the next ship across the Channel. And without him.

"This isn't your problem," she said, so softly that at first he barely heard the words. "I will not ask you to risk your life any further. Have you forgotten the warrant for *your* arrest?" She couldn't bring herself to say the next words out loud. *Or have you forgotten what I let happen to that poor old man?* No, she couldn't allow that to happen to Giles, not even if it meant she had to turn her back on him, spurn him to get him to forget her.

"Have you forgotten the warrant for La Devinette?"

"No one will ever see her again."

And would he see her again if she went to Paris without him? Giles didn't want to consider the notion.

"Sophia," he whispered. "Please, leave this to me. Let me do this for you. Consider it a wedding gift." His lips rained down kisses on her face, her neck, and finally her lips, trying to use the passion between them as a way of convincing her. If her mind refused to see reason, perhaps her body would.

For a moment he lost himself in the passion of their kiss. He tried to let his lips and mouth explain to her what his heart could not.

He saw the struggle in her incredible eyes—a mixture of indecision and passion as she weighed the choice before her. It had been like this every time he'd held her, but tonight he would find a way for her to acknowledge the tenuous yet fiery bond between them.

Bending his head, he kissed her again, his lips asking his question anew.

Her mouth opened tentatively, almost shyly, as he'd expect from the more demure, virginal Lady Sophia. But he knew that wasn't the true nature of the lady in his arms, so he deepened his search for her, allowing his tongue to gently move over her reluctant lips, opening them and allowing him entrance.

The moment their kiss deepened, he felt her acquiescence, as if the tinder between them suddenly found a match. A soft sound of longing mewed from deep inside her, answering his question.

She needed him as much as he yearned for her.

Her arms twined around his neck, her fingers tangling in his hair. Sophia pulled herself closer, the brocade of her wide skirts and the doeskin of his breeches thin barriers compared to the rapid heat spreading between them.

Yet it wasn't close enough. His hands ran down the length of her bare arms, his fingers sliding over the sleek skin. She flexed like a cat, moving closer to his heat, to his touch. As her hips rocked back and forth against his groin, Giles felt himself tighten, his need for her sending his blood pounding.

"What are you doing to me?" she gasped, as his lips nibbled and caressed her neck. "I can't think, I can't remember anything when you do this."

"Good," he told her, knowing full well he'd reached the same state. "Then it's working. For once, listen to your body."

How could Sophia hold fast to her earlier vow to cast him away when every nerve blazed with the need to be touched, to be caressed?

This was what frightened her so much about this man—his power over her body, over her heart. Before she could start the mental argument he'd told her to forget, his hand curled around her breast, his fingers teasing the tip through the thick brocade of her dress.

"Ooh," she whispered, her knees suddenly buckling as his hand pushed her bodice lower, exposing her flesh to the chill of the air and the warmth of his touch. Where his fingers before had caressed, his mouth now covered, his tongue teasing the overwhelming sensations from her.

He knelt in front of her. Their mouths met again, but they both seemed to realize it wasn't enough. Her hands tugged first at his jacket, and then, having discarded it next to the forgotten wrap, her fingers plied the buttons of his shirt. Splaying her fingers over the warmth of his chest, she ran them through the dark mat of hair.

Sophia allowed herself to fall into the incredible passion rising between them. It was exactly how it had been in Paris. And just as easy to allow the fire of his touch to engulf her senses, his hands running over her shoulders, his fingers trailing a tingling path down her arms.

The more he caressed her body, the deeper his hold on her became.

Where in Paris she had thought she might never be with him again, now his touch branded her.

Left her under his control. Made her forget.

"We can't do this," she said, struggling to the surface of sanity, her hands pushing at his shoulders. "I cannot."

He moved back, his face puzzled. "What is this?"

"You can't do this to me. If you think to use my body against me, it won't work. I will not be lulled away from what I must do by mere kisses."

He pulled her back into his arms. "I've never thought of my kisses as 'mere.' And I was of a mind to do more tonight than kiss you." His head dipped lower to claim her lips anew.

She shook herself free from him, her heart beating wildly from the passion that clamored to be answered and from her own anger at allowing her love for him to divert her so completely. She remembered what he had said earlier, half-teasing—he would send her back to the Rose Room in a ruined state, the implication being they would have to wed.

"No, I cannot. You would make me forget what I need to do. What I *must* do."

He ran his fingers through his hair. "But I told you, I've already started making the necessary inquiries. I'll have them here before the blade finds them. So forget about stealing any more fortunes. And I will hear no more talk of you returning to Paris."

"It will take more than a fortune to get them out. I can't ask that of you. I won't accept it." Accepting his offer would be akin to taking blood money. His blood. "Go back to London, Giles. Forget me. Forget my family." Tears welled up in her eyes, the final proof of her decision. She wouldn't give up until her family was free. And she would do it without him.

Giles's mouth set in a grim line. "As I said at dinner, we will be wed within a week. There will be no more robberies and no more talk of your returning to Paris. Your misadventure at Selmar's was your last performance as the Brazen Angel, and from now on you will be Lady Sophia. And that is final."

With that he took her arm and all but dragged her back to the Rose Room.

For the next few days Giles made good on his promise to Sophia and stuck to her side throughout the days and evenings. He knew his constant presence annoyed her, but he couldn't care less. He filled her schedule with visits to Byrnewood, shopping in Bath, and entertainments.

Despite his assurances that he was doing everything possible to save her family, he knew that beneath her silent acquiescence she was not about to be pacified by mere words or the frivolous amusements of Bath society.

"What the devil is wrong with your fiancée?" Monty asked as they waited in Lady Larkhall's salon for Lady Sophia to finish dressing for a concert at the Guildhall. "She looked as if she wanted to end your life when you suggested tonight's entertainment."

Mrs. Whitcombe, Lady Fischer, and Dorlissa arrived just then, having earlier offered the use of space in their carriage.

"I haven't the vaguest notion what you mean," Giles replied, getting to his feet to greet the ladies.

"Oh, Lord Trahern," Lady Fischer cried, "I think you are winning over your reluctant bride. And tonight's entertainment is just the romantic choice to soothe her nerves." The lady leaned closer, her plumes waggling in his face. "I've made arrangements for our second carriage to be brought along. I thought it would be most wicked if you and Lady Sophia rode alone together in your carriage. The Duke and Dorlissa could ride with Mrs. Langston in ours, and the third carriage can carry all of us older folks, who are in the way when it comes to young love. What say you to my plans?"

Giles grinned at her. "I think it sounds as if you're not as old as you make yourself out to be, Lady Fischer."

"Where is Sophia?" Lady Larkhall asked as she entered the room.

"She has yet to grace us with her presence," Giles told her, enjoying the annoyed look on her aunt's face.

While she asked one of the servants to see what was taking Sophia so long, Giles rejoined Monty near the fireplace.

His friend frowned at him. "I don't see why you're going

ahead with this marriage. While I admit the country air has improved her looks, that sullen expression chills my bones."

Giles laughed. "Don't worry about my bride. I have a fine wedding present in store for her. She'll cheer up."

Monty didn't look so convinced. "You won't catch me marrying some sour little chit. I've learned a thing or two from your lesson book."

Giles couldn't resist teasing his friend. "Still intent on marrying the Angel?"

Monty looked shocked. "Oh, heavens, no. She would never do. Not now. Not when I've found the perfect wife right here in Bath."

This hardly surprised Giles. Monty usually found his perfect duchess everywhere he went. "You have?" he asked in mock seriousness. "Did I miss the banns while I was out of town? Has the lucky bride been informed of her impending good fortune?"

"Laugh all you want," the Duke shot back. "But my choice is made, see for yourself." He nodded toward the knot of women, who were being joined by Mrs. Langston. Just then Lady Fischer and Dorlissa turned toward the fireplace.

When Lady Fischer caught the Duke's gaze in their direction, she prodded her daughter to smile.

The girl did so, but it was obvious her heart wasn't in it.

Monty beamed with pride at his intended bride.

Dorlissa? Giles glanced hastily back at his friend, stunned at this rapid change of events. "Are you sure?"

"Of course. She's perfect. Picked up the special license this morning." He patted his jacket pocket—the one usually reserved for his list of qualifications. "She'll be the next Duchess of Stanton by the end of the week."

"Have you considered this carefully?" Giles warned, thinking of a life with Lady Fischer as one's mother-in-law, but also shocked by this rapid turn of events.

"I spent all night listing her qualifications."

"And she fits the list?" He couldn't quite see Dorlissa fitting any list for the perfect duchess.

"Eminently so. Well, she's—"

"Oh, this will ruin everything," Lady Fischer began to wail. "I have everything perfect, and now that selfish girl goes and ruins it. I won't hear of it. Lord Trahern, you must insist."

"Insist on what?" Giles asked, distracted from Monty's dissertation on Dorlissa's qualifications.

"Lady Sophia. She has gone and taken ill. Why, she's begging off, and now all my plans are ruined."

CHAPTER
16

SOPHIA WAITED NER-
vously for Emma to return. She would have bet the blade
she'd stolen from Selmar that her companion would arrive
with not only her aunt, but also Giles.

Ducking under the covers, she pressed her forehead
down on the hot bottle they'd hidden beneath the covers.
Meanwhile, she clutched a cold rag, hoping it would add a
chill to her hands. With Emma's help and a few tricks,
Sophia felt confident their deception would fool even a
physician.

From the hallway, Emma's protests echoed in advance

warning. "My lord, 'tis highly irregular to have a gentleman in a lady's bedchamber, and given her frail state it may just push her fever higher."

Sophia bounded out from beneath the covers, ran her fingers through her already tangled and matted hair, and lay her head wanly on her pillow. One nearly guttered candle wavered beside the bed, adding to the miserable ambience of her sickbed.

"Nonsense," Giles's deep voice answered. "I will see her immediately."

The door began to open as her aunt added her opinion. "Mrs. Langston, I don't think Sophia will mind knowing that Lord Trahern is concerned about her welfare."

Sophia's lashes fluttered heavily. She opened her eyes slowly, as if the exertion pained her. Tossing her head from one side to the other, she finally allowed her gaze to focus on her aunt's concerned expression.

Aunt Celia sat down on the edge of Sophia's bed. "Sophia, dear, you look feverish."

"I can't be," she whispered weakly. "I'm so cold." To emphasize her point she caught her aunt's warm hand in the icy grip of her own.

"Dear goodness, child. You're freezing."

Nodding her head in agreement, Sophia reached with her other hand for her companion. "Emma," she called out. "Did you bring the extra coverlet? The chill is terrible." Sophia didn't dare lift her gaze to see if Giles was buying any of her performance. From her vantage point all she could see was the disbelieving tap of his boot.

While Emma went to the dressing closet to retrieve another blanket, Sophia's aunt laid a gentle hand on her brow.

"Just as I thought. You've a terrible fever. That explains these chills." Lady Larkhall glanced over her shoulder. "She shouldn't go out. Not until this fever breaks."

Giles made a noise in the back of his throat. "May I?" he asked, gesturing toward the bed.

Lady Larkhall conceded her spot, and Giles leaned over the bed.

Sophia opened her eyes again, just enough to find his dark gaze examining her with a skeptical air.

"I'm so sorry, my lord," she whispered. "To have ruined your evening."

"Nonsense. My evening will be spent here watching over you," he told her, his voice filled so much concern that he sounded as if he'd just received news of her imminent demise.

At the doorway Emma stood frozen, obviously unsure of how to intervene in this turn of events.

Smiling up at Giles, Sophia tried to look brave. "Would you? Stay with me? I would feel so much better if you did."

Her answer obviously took him aback. He tipped his head and looked at her anew. "You want me to stay?"

Before Sophia could answer, her aunt came unwittingly to her rescue. "Stay here? With her so ill? 'Tis neither proper nor cautious. Fevers like this can be highly contagious, and I wouldn't want to see you, my lord, fall ill before the wedding. Besides, if she is to be in perfect health in two days' time, she needs rest, not company." Lady Larkhall caught Giles by the elbow and tugged him from the bedside.

Sophia whimpered a little for effect.

"No, no. None of that, my dear," her aunt scolded. "You

rest quietly. If you need anything, Mrs. Langston will be right here."

Emma nodded to Lady Larkhall and went to work spreading the coverlet over her patient.

Peering through her half-opened lashes, Sophia watched in victory as her fiancé was pulled from the room, guaranteeing her freedom this evening.

By the time the parade of carriages rolled down the drive, Sophia was out of bed and frantically searching through her wardrobe for a particular dress.

Emma sat at the dressing table picking through her satchel of paints and powders.

"Do you think he believed me?" Sophia asked.

"He didn't have a choice."

Dropping her armload of silk skirts and undergarments on the bed, Sophia paused. "Do you think he will forgive me?"

Emma glanced over her shoulder, her face strangely sad. "I hope so. For all our sakes."

BATH SOCIETY, GILES discovered, was every bit as boring as the company in London. Probably because it was made up of much the same silly, pointless people.

The spacious room at the Guildhall was crowded and packed with a wide variety of spectators. In Bath, unlike in London, anyone with money for a ticket could vie for attention in the public room. It made it all that much more comical to watch the people aping what they assumed was the behavior of their betters.

Even after the music began, people continued talking and seeking out advantageous introductions to whomever was new to town.

Monty, though for the most part protected from the worst of the fortune hunters by the territorial Lady Fischer, quickly became the most sought-out guest. As a duke without a duchess, he was a catch that had even the most reserved mothers pushing their awkward daughters forward.

Giles nodded to the occasional friend and every few minutes glanced moodily at his pocket watch. If only he could come up with an excuse to leave early and return to Larkhall Manor.

Though Lady Larkhall's opinion carried a great deal of weight with him, he also knew that his little bride-to-be was the leading mistress of deception. He'd seen her play her illness role before, only that time he'd believed it. Now he wasn't so willing to fall for her trap.

There was only one way to find out, he reasoned, as he started for the door.

"I say, my lord," an older gentleman called out. "Is that you, young Trahern?"

Giles turned to find Admiral Griffey pulling his angular frame out from a chair.

The old man, one of Giles's father's best friends, held out his weathered, wiry hand in greeting. "It is you, you young rake! Look at you, you remind me of your father when he was your age. Back when we first met in the troubles with the Dutch."

Giles nodded politely. He respected the Admiral too much to be rude. "It's good to see you, Admiral. I didn't know you were here in town."

"I've come to take the waters. My lady wife has it in her head that after forty-some years at sea, more water will cure my aches and pains." The man nodded to an elderly woman in a starched lace cap and an even stiffer dark dress. "I try to tell her it was all those years adrift that put these blasted agues in my bones and more water is no solution. And these baths? Bah, nothing more than a public exhibition of bare limbs. Not anything like being at sea. Why, I remember old Captain Langston from the *Righteous* used to say—"

"Did you say Captain Langston?" Giles interrupted.

"Why, yes. Captain Howland Langston. You know him?"

Know him? Giles felt another piece of the puzzle falling in place. "No, I never *knew* him," he answered carefully.

"Knew him? What are you talking about? I had dinner with him and his latest bride just last month in Dover. Won't travel outside the sight of the sea. Have you heard something different?" Admiral Griffey leaned forward. "I warned the man that taking a third wife was asking for trouble, but the man can't resist. This latest one is young enough to be his granddaughter. The old goat. Watch him if he doesn't sire a whole new batch of children with the silly little chit."

"Must have been my mistake," Giles said. *Believing anything either of those two women said,* he wanted to add.

He wondered what Lady Fischer would say about finding Mrs. Langston's husband returned from his watery grave. He had a feeling it wouldn't be much of a shock to Emma.

Admiral Griffey continued his gossipy monologue while Giles chewed this latest piece of information.

So if Emma wasn't the Widow Langston, who was she?

It seemed to Giles that every time he answered one question about the Brazen Angel and her entourage, ten more popped up in their place.

"Admiral," he interrupted again. "I'm afraid I was just

leaving. My betrothed was unable to attend this evening due to a sudden illness. I was returning early to see how she fares."

"I heard you were to be married, and to the daughter of one of the Ramsey sisters." The old man grinned and jabbed Giles with his elbow. "I hope she favors Mellisande. Ah, what a beauty, that one."

Giles knew all the signs. The man's eyes glossed over and he was about to launch into a long-winded tale about the legendary lady and her nefarious misdeeds.

What had his staid and stoic father been thinking to align him to such a family of hoyden women?

But then again, Giles reflected, life with Sophia would never be dull.

After politely listening to another half hour of the Admiral's requisite tales, Giles was finally able to excuse himself and return to Larkhall Manor.

Quietly, he passed through the house. When his knock at Sophia's door went unanswered, he pushed it open a few inches.

"Sophia? Mrs. Langston?" he called out, already pretty sure of what he would find.

An empty room.

He looked first at the unmade bed, covered in discarded items of clothing, then to the chaos of powder and pots on the dressing table. She'd left in quite a hurry.

Crossing the room, he unknotted his fists and laid a finger on the pane of glass. Why had he let this happen? He should have insisted that he stay behind—if not in her room, then somewhere in the house.

Now there was no telling where she'd gone or with whom.

He shook his head and looked around. He knew one thing: She planned on returning, and before her aunt and the rest of their party was due to arrive home. She had no choice, because the first thing Lady Larkhall would do was check on her condition.

But she wouldn't be returning to a cold and empty room, he decided. Pulling up a chair, he settled in by the window to watch the driveway. She'd have to come home soon, and then there would some explaining to do.

THE ROBBERY OF Lord Percy went off without a mishap.

Well pleased with her success, Sophia climbed out the window and tiptoed through His Lordship's prized rose garden. Slipping out the back gate that let into the alley behind his fashionable town house on the Crescent, she grinned as Oliver brought the carriage out of the shadows.

Jumping in, she settled down across from Emma and smiled.

Emma didn't look all that happy.

"Don't look so glum," Sophia chided. She held up her prizes. "More than enough to see my parents released."

"I just think . . ." Emma crossed her arms over her chest and she looked out the window.

"Think what?" Sophia had never seen Emma like this. Since her first outing as the Brazen Angel, the woman's confidence and experience had given Sophia the necessary nerve she needed to complete some of her more daring robberies. Leaning back in her seat, she began stripping off her elaborate finery, starting with her mask.

"You think I should allow Lord Trahern to find my parents, don't you?"

Emma nodded. "I have one of those black feelings about this trip. I don't like it. Let the man do what he was trained to do. His own father told you he was the best, and you've seen it with your own eyes. Let him do this. Don't take this final risk. Let the man help you." She paused. "I fear it will be your last."

Closing her mouth to halt a quick denial, Sophia instead turned away.

"Every night I see the scaffolding in the square. I see the tumbrils rolling down the streets. But the only person I see being harmed, being torn apart by those fiends, is Giles. I can't let that happen. He musn't return to Paris."

"Then don't go alone. Take me with you."

Sophia took a deep breath. "Emma, I know you're concerned, but you also know why you have to stay behind. You must convince Giles I've gone to York to gain my aunt Mellisande's assistance. He might believe you, and he may just travel there before he learns the truth. That will put him three, maybe four days behind me. I'll be in Paris and have my parents free before he can cross the Channel."

Emma looked unconvinced. "I don't like the idea of you leaving without me. Why not wait? By the time your aunt arrives home you'll have only a few hours of darkness to hide your trail. You'd be better off waiting for tomorrow evening. You could plead off early, and we would be long gone before anyone discovered us missing. With eight to ten hours of night in which to travel, Lord Trahern won't have any idea in which direction we've gone."

"No. I can't allow you to go any more than I can let Giles."

Emma's dark eyes flickered. "Sophia, if you don't take me, I'll tell that man the truth. I'll tell where you are going, what route you are taking." She paused, her jaw set in determination. "I'll tell him you're carrying his child."

Sophia gasped. "That's a lie and you know it."

"It might be, but he'd catch you before you left the shire." Emma leaned back in her seat. "Now, which plan do you want to follow?"

Knowing full well that Giles would have her locked in Byrnewood before dawn if Emma carried out her dire threat, Sophia decided to acquiesce. At least for the moment. "Yours. I suppose you may be right, Emma. If I'm home tonight, maybe he'll relax his guard enough to give us the time we need to get away. 'Tis a better idea."

Emma nodded her head in agreement, looking well pleased at not being left behind. She tossed over a cloth. "Best get that mess off your face. We'll be home soon."

By the time Sophia removed most of her paint and powder, Oliver had brought the carriage near the house, depositing Sophia and Emma on the road not far from the Larkhall wilderness. The pair stole silently across the garden and into the house through a side door they'd left unlocked.

They bid each other good night, and Sophia made her way back to her sickbed, while Emma took up her post in the library to await Lady Larkhall's return.

While she'd agreed in principle with Emma's plan, she had no intention of following it. Emma would remain safe, just as Giles would, Sophia decided as she made her way up the staircase.

Once her aunt and Giles looked in and determined she

was resting comfortably, she would sneak back to the carriage and be off to the packet ship waiting at the coast.

With luck, Emma's assurances that Sophia was sleeping soundly and shouldn't be disturbed would stave off the need for another performance.

Into her dark room she crept, realizing as she tripped over a discarded gown that she would need to clean it up a bit before getting into bed. She froze in the middle of the room when a tall shadowy figure rose from the corner.

"Feeling better?" Giles asked, stepping into the light.

Sophia looked down at the expensive gown she wore and the telltale mask in her hand. "I thought perhaps a walk might—"

He cut her off by crossing the room, catching her by the arm, and holding up the hand that still clutched the white mask. "Don't insult me. Now, where is it?"

"Where is what?" she asked.

"Whatever you stole tonight. Where is it and from whom did you take it?"

Her mouth closed into a tight line.

Giles knew that expression. It meant it would be difficult—it not impossible—to get the information he wanted. He let go of her and crossed the room closing the door and twisting the key in the lock. "Now tell me what you've planned or I will cart you to Byrnewood tonight and see you locked in the tower room for a month."

She stood rigid and silent, the gold embroidery on her gown shimmering in the candlelight.

She was infuriating in her stubbornness. She refused to trust him enough to allow herself to accept his help. He could not let her endanger herself any more than she could turn her back on her parents.

Then the truth behind her family's motto struck him.

Nothing is difficult to one who loves.

His anger dissipated as he realized he'd driven her to this—sneaking out at night to secure her own ends because of her misplaced fears for his safety. She thought nothing of risking her life to save those she loved, including him.

But it was time she learned that love was worthy of such selfless sacrifice only when it was shared by two people.

"If you insist on going to Paris, I'm going with you."

Her face turned, her suspicions evident in her narrow gaze. "No."

"Then I'll follow you," he said. "Isn't it better to know where I am than to wait tensely for me to appear out of nowhere? I could blunder in and destroy your cover as I did at Danton's. So, you see, you have to take me with you."

Sophia shook her head, sadness filling her every word. "If I do, you'll perish."

And you'll think I betrayed you. Images of her dream circled around her. She closed her eyes, trying to blot out the terrifying images.

Even with them closed, she couldn't wipe the image of his blood-soaked body from her tortured imagination.

"And what of yourself, Sophia?" he whispered into her ear. "Who will keep you safe? Who will keep your neck free of the blade's wrath?"

Her eyes fluttered open. He stood within inches of her. "I won't let you die," she said.

"I have no intention of going to Paris to be killed. *We're* going to save your parents." His hands gently plied her shoulders, turning her to face him. Playfully, he plucked at the wig on her head. "From this day forth it will always be *us*. Not just you or just me, but us. We are bound together as surely as if we were wed. But if I were to die, just once before then I would like to see you unmasked, unclothed, and free of these layers you use to shut me out."

Sophia's nerves tingled under his touch, her body recognizing his request by leaning closer to him. How could she help but want to be with him?

His hand cupped her chin, tipping her face upward so his lips could join hers in a kiss.

The moment his mouth touched hers, Sophia knew she was lost. She'd give him anything if he would never stop kissing her. His lips nibbled at hers until his tongue moved forward, tangling with hers.

Oh, she wanted one more night in Giles's arms. She tried to tell herself it was only to thank him for saving her family, it was only for his offer to come with her to Paris, but it was more than that.

She wanted to tell him that she loved him, pure and simple.

The words stopped in her throat, for if she uttered them they would bind her to him with the promise they carried. If she admitted out loud that she loved him, she would have to let him into her life.

Right now, loving Giles meant leaving him behind.

But she could tell him with her kisses and with her touch what she dared not say.

Her arms wound around his neck, her kiss deepening in a tender response. For a time they stood in the middle of the room, kissing, as if they had the rest of their lives.

Yet Sophia's passion for Giles wasn't satisfied with just a kiss. She needed to feel his bare skin, caress his muscled limbs, feel the heat build between them when their bodies met.

Pulling back from his kiss, she pushed her hands inside his jacket, easing it off his shoulders.

"I would see you, Lord Trahern," she said, mocking his earlier request. "I would see you unclothed."

"I am but your willing servant, milady. Do with me as you please."

A daring thrill ran over her as she accepted his submission to her desires. Slowly, she continued to undress him, kissing his arms and chest as she pulled the shirt from his body. Her hands worshiped the knotted cords in his arms, knowing how they would feel wrapped around her when he entered her.

She glanced up to see his reaction as her fingers freed his tight breeches.

His eyes were shut, but a wicked smile curved his chiseled features.

Her hands ran over the length of his naked thighs, the hard lines of his calves, pushing aside his stockings and boots. Now he was naked, and entirely hers.

And very much ready for her further pleasures.

Slowly, she led him to the bed and bid him to lie back.

Stepping just a few feet away, Sophia leisurely undressed herself, her gaze never leaving his face.

With each layer, with each piece of finery, she saw in his eyes what he would do to the flesh she bared for his inspection.

As she eased off her bodice, freeing her breasts, his eyes lit up. She remembered how it had felt to have his mouth tease and torment her there, her nipples puckering tight in anticipation.

"Come to me, Sophia," he whispered. "You tarry too long."

"No longer," she answered, joining him in the bed.

Their naked bodies fused together. In the hurried moments that followed, it seemed they couldn't get enough of each other's touch.

Sophia discovered quickly that he had all but read her mind as she'd undressed.

Giles's mouth immediately claimed her breast, teasing it with his tongue while his thumb rolled over the other tense nipple.

She writhed beneath him, the rocking sensations leaving her aching with tender need. In answer to this, his hand dropped lower, easing open her thighs and teasing the rigid nub hidden away in the soft, wet folds.

A moan erupted from her lips, calling for more, pleading with him to take her out of this tender torment and to that blissful lover's reward.

She rolled onto her back, her expression heated and anxious. "Don't make me wait. Please, Giles, love me. Love me tonight."

Giles hovered over her, his hips rocking forward, pushing his manhood toward the warm, moist spot his fingers had moments before teased to this blind, aching need.

He tried to enter her slowly, but her hands caught his hips and pulled him into her.

She nipped at his shoulder with her teeth and whispered a brazen challenge into his ear.

"Follow me if you dare."

Her body wrapped around him, setting the pace. Her fingers plied his back, his bottom, while her hips rocked against him.

He felt the desperation in her loving, this reckless need

for him. He wanted to tell her how he felt, that he loved her. Loved her for her vitality, her layers, her mysteries.

And so, like she, he loved her with his body. Stoking her requests, pushing himself farther and farther into her. Following her as she beckoned him to come closer, to go faster, to catch her.

Even as her lashes fluttered and her mouth opened in surprise at the shattering explosion of her release, he felt his own body answer in kind, pouring from him wave after wave of passion.

It flowed out of him and into her, this love. The waves carried them as one into a blissful peace the real world rarely offered.

For a time he held her tight, rocking her through the last, lingering shudders.

The fireplace crackled; a log falling apart sent a shower of sparks up the chimney.

"That's how I feel," she said.

"How's that?"

"Like those embers in the grate. Hot, spent, and still on fire. Like I'm floating up into a great unknown. 'Tis frightening."

He brushed back a strand of her hair. "But you aren't alone. You brought me with you."

She smiled. "I'm glad. I'd hate to go alone." Even as she said the words she realized the implication, only to hope he wouldn't take her literally.

But obviously Giles did. "So you'll let me go with you to Paris?"

She looked into eyes. "Yes," she lied.

He smiled and wrapped her tight in his arms. "You'll see, I'm right. It's better that I go with you."

Smiling her agreement, Sophia stayed in the warmth of his arms until he fell asleep. Even then she waited until his even breathing reassured her he was truly asleep.

Then she eased out of his embrace and slipped from the bed, shivering in the chill of the room.

Making her way by the fireplace, she watched as the last glowing ember went out. She wondered then and in the days ahead if that hadn't been an omen of the disaster to come.

CHAPTER
17

EMMA HEARD THE
first carriage arrive just past dawn. She didn't pay it much
heed—until a second and then a third conveyance arrived
not an hour later. The noisy din of voices downstairs rose to
her second-story room. Curious, she got dressed and stole
down to the main floor.

The open foyer at the main entrance of the house was
stacked high with trunks and traveling pieces. Children
darted through the maze of boxes, while the voices of their
elders argued in the dining room.

Moving slowly to the open door, Emma peeked in. To her astonishment the room overflowed with Sophia's Ramsey aunts, as well as her brother Lucien and his family. Even Aunt Mellisande, who never left her York estates, sat ensconced in the place of honor, directing the servants as if the house were her own. Lady Dearsley tried to catch a racing Julien, who darted from one aunt to the next, laughing and teasing his relatives.

At the far end of the table sat an older man whom Emma didn't recognize. His ramrod-straight posture and his severe, dark coat added the only order to the chaotic room. At his right sat a dimpled, plump woman, who smiled and nodded to the other guests.

"I have no idea what you are talking about, Effie," the Duchess said to Lady Dearsley. "Sophia visiting my house last month? Preposterous. I distinctly remember her saying she intended to stay here with Celia."

Lady Larkhall looked from one sister to the next. "I think you're both confused. Sophia remained in London last month. She arrived in Bath not a fortnight ago."

Lady Dearsley frowned. "I don't know what in heaven is going on, but I demand an accounting for all this. She always mopes around my house begging to be sent to the country, and now I suspect her behavior is nothing more than an act. I should never have let her out of my sight. I knew it was a bad idea to pass her around our homes like a tray of chocolates. She's been ill-influenced by both of you. And that Mrs. Langston. I never trusted her. I told each of you her references should be carefully screened. No, you wouldn't hear of it. And now our girl's ruined, I tell you. I just know it." The lady looked from one side of the room to the other. "Where is my Hannah?" she bid the footman. "Have Hannah fetch my niece immediately."

Emma nearly choked. She backed away from the door and hurried up the stairs. She hustled into Sophia's room without pausing to knock. Throwing open the drapes, the early-morning light illuminated the dark chamber.

"Get up," she ordered. "We've got trouble in spades downstairs. And Hannah is on her way to deliver the bad news."

The bundle in the bed rolled over, pulling the covers along.

"Did you hear?" she prodded, nudging the sleeping Sophia. "The entire family is downstairs. All of them. And let me tell you what is for breakfast. Your recent history."

Emma headed to the closet, tossing out first her well-worn traveling bag and then her clothes. "I don't know about you, but the back door may be my only chance. I can't think of another excuse to try to foist off on them. And whatever we come up with, I doubt they'll believe it. Do you hear me? Your aunts are down there right now comparing calendars. And they are none too pleased as to how the days are adding up." She stopped and stared at the bed. "Well, did you hear what I said or are your ears still asleep? Feigning death won't save us now; we're finished for sure. Now get up and help me come up with something to tell them."

She marched over to the bed, caught hold of the bed-cover, and gave it a good yank.

"How about starting by telling *me* the truth?" Lord Trahern answered.

As Emma tried to stutter out an answer, Hannah did her one better.

The girl screamed.

HANNAH'S ALARM BROUGHT the entire household running to Sophia's bedchamber.

A hysterical Hannah kept sputtering her rendition of finding Mrs. Langston and Lord Trahern in . . . in . . . such a . . . oh, the overwrought girl couldn't even say it.

Lady Dearsley shoved her way through the gathered relations and made her way to the bedside. "What is going on?"

From there, Giles decided, the discussion went downhill.

With Emma's quick help he'd retrieved his shirt, but his breeches were an impossibility. He found himself in the ridiculous position of entertaining his future relations in his betrothed's bed with the bedcovers pulled up to his waist.

"This is worse than I thought," Lady Dearsley cried, wedging her wide hips into the closest chair. "I never trusted you," she said, waggling her finger at Giles. "Nor you, madame." Her censorious gaze flitted over Emma before giving her a nod of dismissal.

Giles had to hand it to Emma—she stood her ground well in the face of the storm. But he couldn't let her take any portion of Lady Dearsley's censure that she didn't deserve.

"I think you are under a misunderstanding, my lady," he told her. "I didn't spend the night with Mrs. Langston. I spent it with your niece."

Lady Dearsley swung around to where Lady Larkhall stood hovering near the door. "This is all your fault, Celia. You knew why she was sent to live with us, and yet you allowed her freedom she did not deserve. It was our job to find her a husband and see her ruinous tendencies stomped out. Now look what you've done. Why I—"

"Stop your caterwauling immediately, Effie," the Duchess of Caryll said, bringing her walking stick down on the hardwood floor like a magistrate's gavel. "For the moment I don't care if the King slept here. I want to know, where is Sophia?"

Everyone looked around the room, as if stunned by this request. In all the confusion, everyone had forgotten Sophia.

"Gone," Giles commented. The incredible beauty parting the crowded room could only be the Duchess of Caryll.

Mellisande Ramsey, London's most legendary diamond, outshone every woman in the room. Forty-some Seasons since her debut, her figure still held the charms and curves to make a man forget she was probably nearing her sixtieth year. Alabaster skin showed none of the wrinkles or ravages of age that claimed Lady Dearsley's face or whispered at the edges of Lady Larkhall's complexion. The lady towering over his bedside held everyone's attention, but not for any other reason than that her iron will demanded it.

She caught him staring at her, and one gray eyebrow arched.

He couldn't help himself—he grinned at her.

How many times had he seen Sophia do the same thing? Now he knew where his little bride had inherited her tenacity and a good dose of her daring.

"That was just what I was about to ask Mrs. Langston," he told the Duchess. "Before that one"—he nodded at a tearful Hannah—"started her keening and wailing."

"It's just they was . . . and he was . . . the covers were . . ." Hannah sobbed out her protests, while Lady Dearsley patted the girl's hand.

Thump!! Thump! The Duchess's cane pounded on the floor. "Enough of this. All of you, out of this room so this man can make himself decent. We will discuss this matter in Celia's library. Lord Trahern, you will attend me there"—her imperious eyebrow arched a little higher—"once you are decently clad." She turned to leave.

"I don't mean to be rude, Your Grace," he replied. "But I have no intention of spending the morning discussing this matter. My bride is missing. I'm leaving immediately to find her."

The Duchess turned to Lady Larkhall. "Is he always so impertinent?"

Lady Larkhall smiled at her sister. "Let's hope so, for Sophia's sake."

Nodding, the Duchess turned her stony blue gaze back to Giles. "Nevertheless, I will hear this story told first, and then you may leave—with all the facts firmly in place and a good idea of where to begin your search."

The Duchess pointed her cane toward Emma. "Mrs. Langston, you will follow me, *now.*" The woman marched out of the room with such military precision, Giles thought, even Dryden would be envious.

Dryden! Giles caught a glimpse of his mentor at the very fringe of the crowd. "Sir," he called out. "I hadn't expected you."

Dryden stepped inside and closed the door. "Lady Dryden and I escorted Lady Dearsley here for your nuptials. From the look on Mellisande's face, I think I'll have the parson sent for immediately."

Giles got out of bed and started to get into his breeches. "I think that is a little premature. Once again I am without a bride, so I don't think the parson will be needed."

Dryden laughed. "I wasn't calling him to marry you. I just wanted the old boy around for your last rites once the Duchess gets done with you."

GILES ARRIVED IN the library to find that the Duchess's interview included the entire family. She'd even asked Lord Dryden to sit next to her and consult as he saw fit.

Emma walked to the middle of the room and began her confession.

"Sophia met me at a coaching station two years ago. I was penniless, without a home, without any legitimate references."

"Did you ever have references?" the Duchess asked.

"No."

Lady Dearsley started to protest, but the Duchess's cane ended any interruptions. "Who are you, then?"

"A lady—at least I was until my mother threw me out. Lady Sophia and I have a lot in common. However, her indiscretions got her sent here to England. Mine landed me in the gutter." Emma's head rose a little higher. "None of that mattered to your niece."

Giles shook his head. "What do you mean by this?" He turned to the three sisters. "Why was Sophia sent to England?"

They sat stone-faced, until finally Lady Larkhall spoke up. "It wasn't to protect her from the changes in France, as we told everyone. Sophia was a headstrong girl. At fifteen her unrestrained behavior resulted in a disastrous alliance with a rather unsuitable young man. He promised marriage, then ran away. The affair ruined her chances of making an advantageous marriage . . ."

Lady Larkhall turned to her sisters. "He deserves to know everything." She glanced back at Giles. "There was a child."

The admission stunned Giles. "A child? What happened?"

"It died at birth," Emma answered, her gaze downcast, her hands folded in front of her. "Like I said, Sophia and I have much in common. She felt she could never live up to your expectations of a worthy bride."

Not worthy? He couldn't disagree more. But he had one more question. "Did my father know this when you proposed this betrothal?"

The Duchess nodded her head. "We told him everything. I think that was why he liked Sophia so much. She hadn't allowed her disgrace to ruin her. Your father didn't tolerate self-pity."

Giles searched his own heart. Did it matter that years ago his bride had fallen in love and followed her heart? He had to admit it was the part of her that he cared for most—her reckless and headstrong devotion to those she loved.

His fingers toyed with the ring in his pocket, which he'd found on the nightstand when he was dressing. In his mind he retraced the inscribed words.

Nothing is difficult to one who loves.

It seemed his father had known this and chosen wisely.

"It all makes sense now," he said to no one in particular. He looked up at Lady Larkhall. "Thank you. Thank you for helping me understand."

The lady's eyes brimmed with unshed tears.

"Well, now that we have all this out in the open," Lady Dearsley said with a harrumph and a grumble, "shall we continue? None of this explains why Sophia has gone missing or where she has been spending her time."

Emma shuffled her feet. "Sophia has been—"

"Sophia has been parading around London as the Brazen Angel," Giles admitted very matter-of-factly.

All three aunts sat open-mouthed.

He smiled at them. "Now it's my turn to drop a cannon-ball on this little party."

"My salts, my medicine. Where is Hannah?" Lady Dearsley called out, her hand flittering in the air. "My heavens, you lout, what kind of nonsense is this?"

Emma picked up the story from there, leaving out nothing and including, it seemed, every detail.

Besides, the sharp-eyed Duchess demanded instant clarification of anything that seemed at the surface vague.

Giles had to give Emma her due: She told the story with her head held high, bestowing credit to Sophia for the girl's triumphs and taking full blame for their shared failures.

A more loyal friend one couldn't ask for. And it was evident she was just as worried about Sophia's disappearance as everyone else in the room.

The Duchess then allowed the entire family to add their own version of events to her *ad hoc* hearing, so, as she said, the truth could be muddled out.

Oliver had been sent for, but the stable boy returned with a message that he could not be found, nor could Lady Sophia's carriage.

The Duchess turned to Giles. "You see, this process is adding some valuable information to your search. So please quit fidgeting and listen carefully."

Even Julien took the floor to tell the story of his rescue. He finished his tale with a royal bow worthy of a presentation at Court.

"Lucien," the Duchess said. "Why didn't you inform me that your sister planned to return to Paris?"

Sophia's brother shook his head. "She promised to wait for me before attempting another rescue."

Out of a corner, Lily stepped forward.

Giles hadn't noticed the young girl until this moment. She looked as petulant and unhappy as she had in France.

"Sophia did not go back to save our parents," the girl announced. "She went back to save her lover."

The room stilled until all Giles heard was the pounding of his heart.

Lily stomped her foot. "She stole him from me. He was mine first. I took care of him, and I would have continued to do so if she hadn't made me leave him. She wants him for herself, and I'll never forgive her." The girl burst into tears and started to run from the room.

Lord Dryden, seated near the entrance, rose from his chair and caught her. "Who, child? Who has Lady Sophia gone back to?"

"He's mine, I tell you," she insisted. "I'll love him all my life."

"I know you will," he continued in a fatherly tone. "But you need to tell us this man's name."

"Webb."

Giles watched Lord Dryden let go of the girl, the color draining from his face. Stepping forward, he spun Lily around. "Who did you say?"

"Webb. His name is Webb."

"He's alive?"

"Yes," the girl answered almost indignantly, as if everyone in the room had gone daft. "Of course he's alive. At least, he was when she made me leave him in Paris."

Dryden stared at the girl and then at Giles. "He's not dead."

Instead of relief, Giles felt a wrenching anger. Sophia had known Webb was alive and let him believe his friend was dead.

"Why?" he asked Emma. "Why wasn't I told?"

"Webb insisted. Agents were being betrayed. He knew he was next. If it looked as if he'd died, then he could uncover whoever had infiltrated your network." Emma looked to Lord Dryden. "I'm sorry for the pain this caused you, but your son said to tell you that he did it to protect the others, and he thought you would understand."

Lady Dearsley got to her feet and tottered over to Giles. "I know this is all your fault. Somewhere in all this it is your fault. Why didn't you stop her?"

But Giles wasn't listening. He dodged past the lady and headed toward the door.

"Just where do you think you are going?" Lady Dearsley demanded.

"To fetch my runaway bride."

"Well, it's about time you did something right," she replied.

"My lord, my lord," the young stable boy called out as Giles mounted his horse.

"What is it?" he asked.

"Oliver, he asked me to give you this 'iffin you were to go tearing out of here." The boy held up a scrap of paper.

Giles leaned over and snatched up the note. "Thanks."

Opening the paper, he read the three words and offered a small prayer of thanks that Sophia had more than one wise and loyal friend.

Tucking it into his pocket, he gave the horse its head and went tearing out of the yard.

The note contained the three words he needed to find them.

The Sow's Ear.

SOPHIA'S DANGEROUS AND rough journey to Paris ended a week after her reluctant flight from Giles's arms. Since the death of the Queen the city had undergone a startling change—her murder had unleashed the horrors Sophia had predicted. Suspicions ran high, and not even the oldest allies could be trusted. Still, Sophia had to find her family, and she knew the one man who could locate them—for a price.

During the day she and Oliver had joined the crowds choking the squares around the executions. Scanning the tumbrils' unfortunate passengers, Sophia feared that each passing cart would contain her parents. She couldn't even be certain they still lived—but something told her they couldn't have died, and that something or someone wanted them alive.

One thing was certain: Every day the parade of victims grew longer and longer.

She cursed herself for not having saved them earlier.

Knowing that Robespierre's spies may have located her usual apartments, she and Oliver took rooms not far from the Sow's Ear. A festive air held the small neighborhood in thrall. It was as if the noisy rabble felt the world's gaze upon them and rejoiced in their newfound recognition.

"Can we trust him?" Oliver asked as they slipped from the lodgings and headed to their meeting with Balsac at the Sow's Ear.

A dangerous silence filled the darkened streets as they worked their way through the shadows.

Sophia glanced up at him. "We have no choice. Webb is nowhere to be found. That leaves only Balsac." She didn't like the wary look on Oliver's face or his constant nagging that they needed to wait for Webb.

At least he hadn't dared to make the same statements about Giles.

She could only hope Giles had become so angered by her disappearance that he stayed behind in Bath. If he still cared for her—which she doubted after this latest betrayal—she prayed Emma had convinced him to travel to her aunt's home in York.

A block away from the tavern Sophia stopped. "Wait here," she told Oliver. When he opened his mouth to protest, she held up her hand. "You must. If that weasel bolts with our money again, I want you out here waiting for him. If he thinks I'm alone he'll be more cocky."

Oliver let out a deep breath. "I don't like this. I won't allow it."

"Have you a better idea?"

He crossed his arms over his wide chest. "I go in and you wait here."

"He'll deal only with me. I have to go in." She reached over and squeezed his arm. "What harm can he cause an old woman?" she asked, her voice cracking with age. Pulling her ragged shawl over her shoulders, she hunched her back and bent over her cane. The makeup wasn't as good as Emma's work, but it would have to do.

Hobbling down the street, she made her way to the Sow's Ear.

Nothing appeared out of the ordinary when she entered. The same sour stench of spilled cheap wine and rancid cooking from the kitchen filled the air. Near the smoky fire a group of young men sang a particularly bawdy song about a noble lady on her way to the guillotine.

She spied Balsac sitting in the far corner, his back to the wall, his ratlike gaze flitting nervously over the crowd. He nodded to her to approach his table, and she made her way slowly to the seat he offered.

Even as she sat down, Sophia felt the tension. Tamping down every sense that told her to flee the smoky room, she stared at Balsac and searched his features for any sign of treachery. But in this man, she knew, she had only to scratch the surface to find deceit.

"What have you for me, citeness?" he asked, his hand already outstretched.

She squeezed back in her chair, just out of his greedy grasp. "Nothing—until I receive what you promised."

He shook his head. "Not this time. Payment first. I no longer can afford the generosity that has marked our past dealings."

Sophia nearly laughed. "Generosity? Is that what you call it? I would call it by another name." She started to pull her knife from her pocket, but beneath the table she heard the distinct *click* of a pistol being cocked.

He'd anticipated her maneuver.

"No more of your tricks," Balsac sneered. "This time I'm in charge."

"No longer, citizen," a male voice said over her shoulder. A pouch landed on the table between them. "The woman is mine. Just as I instructed."

Sophia whirled around and started to bolt for the door. Robespierre, flanked by two of his minions, stood blocking her escape.

She turned again, this time thinking to head for the kitchens. The young men near the fireplace jumped up from their seats, cutting her off. The largest of them grabbed her by the arms, wrenching them behind her back and hauling her over to where Robespierre waited.

Pain shot through her arms as the lout yanked her arm harder.

"Unhand me!" she argued in her disguised voice. "I am an old woman. I have done nothing!"

"You are no such thing," Robespierre said, his voice edged with impatience and triumph. His hand snaked out and wrenched her wig from her head. "Citizeness Devinette, or should I say Lady Sophia D'Artiers."

Her hair spilled from the confines of the wig. Shaking it out of her face, she twisted at her captor's hold. This nightmare couldn't be happening.

"I have done nothing," she repeated, even though she knew her words were worthless.

Near Robespierre's elbow, Balsac grinned as he pocketed his reward. "The warrant for your arrest tells another story, citizeness," the little informant crowed. "As a loyal son of France I was shocked to discover your duplicity."

Robespierre looked unimpressed. He nodded to one of the other thugs. The man caught Balsac by the collar and rifled through the man's coat until he retrieved the money pouch.

Before the man could protest, Robespierre pulled out a stark white handkerchief and held it to his nose. "Then as a loyal son of France you never should have asked to be paid for what was your duty to report in the first place. Take them both."

Sophia struggled at first, until Balsac received a hard crack to his head when the little man tried to bite his guard in an unsuccessful bid for freedom.

She took his lesson to heart and resisted the urge to fight. She'd need her strength and wits ready for any opportunity to escape.

Outside, she stared at the ground, unwilling to turn her head in Oliver's direction. She knew Robespierre watched her, waiting for any clue as to where her companions lay in wait.

A satisfaction he would never receive.

Oliver, she prayed as they led her toward a large black carriage, *please stay hidden. Don't intervene.*

Balsac, she noticed, didn't receive such preferential treatment. Instead, they herded him into a cart and tied his hands to the railing.

"Why the favor?" she asked Robespierre as her captor nudged her toward the carriage door.

"Because I asked for it," Louis Antoine Saint-Just answered, leaning out from the carriage.

SOPHIA SAT SILENTLY in her seat. Across from her, Saint-Just looked relaxed, almost jubilant in her capture. In his lap lay a pistol. Outside, a guard rode on the step, clinging to the side of the carriage and preventing any attempt at escape. Robespierre followed in his own carriage.

"It's amazing, is it not?" Saint-Just commented. "How you deceived so many people. The heroine of the Revolution turns out to be the daughter of the infamous Royalist Comte d'Artiers. Impressive." He reached across and took her hand in his. Smiling, he brought her fingers to his lips and kissed them.

Snatching her hand away, she wiped any trace of his touch on her skirts. "Not so difficult when you have an audience of fools to perform for."

"Except one. Me. You never thought to encounter an old lover, did you? How did you think to deceive a man who knows you better than anyone?"

She tipped her head and studied him. "You never said a word."

"Why should I? It was too amusing to watch. Besides, I know you—and what you'll risk. So I bided my time and enjoyed your company again." He looked over her costume. "Once we've removed that paint and wax, I look forward to seeing if the promise you held at fifteen has come true."

"You think I would . . ." She reeled back in her seat. "You've been lapping at your master's feet too long, Louis. The filth has infected your mind if you think I'd ever return to your bed."

He laughed. "I'm glad to see you haven't lost that outspoken tongue of yours. I hope you haven't forgotten the other things I taught you to do with it."

Sophia seethed in silence. How had she ever thought she loved this man? He'd been visiting her family's estate for the summer, and they'd stolen away every chance they could. He'd made her promise to tell no one of their affair, and she hadn't, believing in his promise to take her to Paris with him in the fall. Then he'd abruptly left after her parents discovered the truth of their relationship.

Talk of a possible marriage dissolved when Louis denied ever having touched Sophia and claimed to have seen her with a gardener's son.

Sent to a convent for her confinement, Sophia spent her time writing note after note to her lover, begging him to save her and their unborn child. Through the agonizing trials of labor at the hands of an inexperienced midwife, she'd thought she would perish along with her child, born still and blue.

Of Louis Antoine Saint-Just, she'd heard nothing over the years, until she'd returned to Paris as La Devinette.

He'd risen to a position of power as Robespierre's right-hand assistant. And he'd been pleasant and attentive whenever their paths crossed in the tight circle of Paris's ruling party.

"Sweet Sophia, what happened to you? I tried for a year to find you, but your family shut me out, refused to give me any idea of where they'd sent you." He brushed back his jet-black hair so the gold ring in his ear twinkled at her. His concerned smile dazzled.

It was his handsome, dangerous manners that had attracted her as an innocent girl. Older and wary, she said nothing to his lies.

"You don't believe me," he told her. "Perhaps in the days to come I will have the opportunity to make up this bitterness that passes between us. Because of my position and power, I've secured but one chance for you. I've convinced the Committee not to have you publicly tried or executed. You're still a heroine in the eyes of the people. If you denounce your family and turn in your accomplices, you'll survive. At least for as long as I can continue to convince them you are worth keeping."

His words sent chills over her skin. The carriage rolled to a stop and the guard opened the door. "And what would you receive in return for all this?" she asked him.

"You as my mistress. And if you agree I will see that your parents are kept alive, as long as you continue to please me." He leaned back and sighed. "We have much time to make up for." He studied her, his arms crossed over his chest. "Look outside, Sophia. See where you are—La Force is not known as one of Paris's most hospitable prisons. One word from you and I will order the carriage to return to my house, with you at my side. Say the word and your life will be spared."

She shook her head, unwilling to consider either notion.

He reached over and stroked her bare arm. "It won't be quite like our summer together, for I imagine you may well be the teacher now, and I, your most willing student. That is, given your reputation and what I hear of your exploits in London. But you always were a hot and willing bitch when it came to men."

Sophia considered her reply carefully.

She spit in his face.

CHAPTER
18

GILES STOOD IN
the gallery of the Paris courtroom, watching the Public
Prosecutor, Antoine Fouquier-Tinville, dispense his brand
of swift Revolutionary justice. The thin-lipped man offered
little emotion with his sweeping summations and far-reaching
conclusions. Yet with each accusation, with each vague fact,
the jury nodded in ardent affirmation.

Today's docket of defendants moved through the courtroom quickly, as if the prosecutor felt the crowd's restless
anticipation for the one defendant whose case had filled the
hall with spectators.

La Devinette.

Giles's search for Sophia ended even as he passed through the city's gates. The entire city buzzed with the news of La Devinette's arrest.

Some claimed she spied for the English, others the Austrians. The only point the gossips agreed on was that she would be executed within a day or two.

Packed into the courtroom with the other "lucky" citizens who'd won the daily lottery for seats, he waged a war within himself as he discarded one plan after another as to how to rescue her.

He hadn't slept a wink the night before, spending most of the night in the Sow's Ear hoping to find Oliver.

When the man didn't show up he'd sought a different course of action, but the name of the prison where they'd locked her away couldn't be bought for any amount of money.

With no idea if Oliver faced the same fate as his mistress or if he remained free, Giles searched the crowd for the man's wide shoulders and peppered hair.

The hapless defendant at the bench listened to the jury's unanimous verdict—guilty. The downcast man left to the accompanying cheers and jeers of the hostile crowd, the noisy din blocking out the announcement of the next case.

That was, until the door behind the prosecutor's table opened. An uncharacteristic hush fell over the chamber.

An older man and woman stumbled into the room, pushed by their grinning guard. The man, dignified in both his height and bearing, meticulously helped the lady regain her footing, then sent a withering stare at the insolent lout.

The guard, smaller in stature, sheepishly backed away

from his captive. The nobleman acknowledged his small victory with a wry smile.

Suddenly, the pair was joined by a third defendant, a small woman in a plain white gown. For a brief second Giles felt he had her all to himself, recalling the rich color of her hair, the stubborn tip of her chin, until the crowd's recognition sent them clamoring to their feet, cutting off his view.

Their heroine, their victorious symbol of Revolution, whom they'd memorialized in song and effigy, had arrived. Instead of the adoring plaudits, the courtroom filled with venom.

Whistles, catcalls, and insults hurtled toward her.

"Austrian bitch!"

"Whore!"

"Traitor!"

"Let the razor shave her neck!"

Vehement and angry, the crowd decided her verdict before the prosecutor uttered a word. And from the smile on Fouquier-Tinville's face, Giles knew this was the type of case the man loved, his narrow gaze bearing down on his next victim like a bird of prey.

The crowd's hatred for her tore at Giles as much as his love for her grew.

Giles shoved aside the man in front of him to gain a better vantage point.

Amidst the terrible onslaught, Sophia stood proudly defiant.

In that moment he knew why he loved her so much. Reckless and brave, she acknowledged her detractors with a bright smile. Her hair, loose and unbound, hung in long curls down her back and over her shoulder. Her face, scrubbed of makeup or paint, held a quaint blush of innocence against her fair porcelain skin.

He didn't think he'd ever seen her like this. Stripped of every layer, her armor of makeup relinquished. How was it he could know every inch of her body, every curve, the way she moved against him, and yet never see her face so untouched, so pure?

The idea made him want to laugh. For all her accusations of his being superficial, he had truly fallen in love with her in each of her varied guises. Now for the first time—and perhaps the last—he saw the real woman he loved.

It was like regaining his sight after years of blindness.

"We have before us, citizens, the woman once known as La Devinette. Today I put before you the heinous solution behind her riddle. Her crimes. All of them, treason against the Republic." Fouquier-Tinville, warming to his duties, politely bid Sophia to join the other couple at the defendants' bench.

Jeers and cries for revenge drowned out the pronouncement of the other defendants' names and crimes.

She crossed the courtroom with the posture and deportment befitting a debut at Versailles. The grace of her movements was lost on the rabble before her. Joining the two other defendants in front of the Tribunal, she looked toward the galleries as if she sensed Giles's gaze upon her.

For a moment her eyes looked wistful, full of regrets.

The hint of emotion, so real and honest, hit him hard. Never before had she asked anything of him, and now when she needed him most, needed his strength, he could only stand by in frustrated defeat.

He remembered her lesson on the Rue St. Honoré as the crowd butchered the old man before their eyes.

She'd sat by and watched in impotent silence.

Now he understood the bitter gall she'd swallowed. To preserve her life she'd remained quiet, and now he must do the same if he was to save her.

The head of the Tribunal banged his gavel on the table, calling for order in the mayhem of anarchy.

"Please, citizens," Fouquier-Tinville advised the crowd. "This is a courtroom. We must respect the sanctity of justice in our new society. Be seated and silent."

The crowd muttered their displeasure at having to behave, but they righted their overturned benches and settled in for the afternoon's entertainment.

The prosecutor continued by reading the remaining charges against Sophia.

Guards stood ready at every door. The room was filled with loyal Revolutionaries, every one burning with hatred at her apparent betrayal to their cause.

Giles racked his wits to find a way to save her. He could wait outside, then follow the cart that would return her to prison. From there he could bribe a guard or find a way to rescue her. But what if they ordered her sent to the guillotine immediately, as was often the case?

There would be nothing he could do to stop it. He buried his face in his hands, blocking out the horrid image of seeing her die.

He needed more time—even just a few hours—to set a plan, any plan, into action.

Another man pushed his way onto the bench, interrupting Giles's thoughts. "A pretty little head on that one. Almost a shame to cut it off. Wouldn't you say, citizen?"

Giles froze. The voice, so familiar, so long lost, called

him out of his reverie. His head twisted, and he looked into the eyes of his childhood friend, Webb Dryden.

Thin, with a haunted look about his hollow eyes, the young man smiled.

Too well-trained to acknowledge this miraculous resurrection with the outburst and handshakes it deserved, Giles shrugged his shoulders in a nonchalant gesture. "What's another head if it belongs to an aristocrat?"

Webb nodded in agreement. "It must be real inconvenient for the likes of her staying at La Force."

So the younger agent knew where they were holding her. He'd have to put Webb in for a promotion—that is, after his father got done demoting him for "dying" in the line of duty.

Giles looked at Sophia, wondering how she'd survived the foul conditions in Paris's worst prison. Considering her great deception, fooling even the members of the National Committee, her imprisonment in La Force made sense. Communication with prisoners inside the walls of the two adjoining buildings, Petite-Force and Grande-Force, was impossible. Built with thick, impenetrable walls, high facades, and surrounded by the worst hovels of poverty in Paris, a stay at La Force made even the guillotine look hopeful.

"And such a bargain today," his friend continued. "Not just La Devinette, but the foul couple who spawned her, the Comte d'Artiers and his *sow* of a wife."

Stunned by the realization that the couple with Sophia were her parents, he almost missed Webb's clue. Now he saw what had intrigued him before about the couple. In her father he recognized the strong resemblance between the d'Artiers men—the Comte, Lucien, and Julien—the bearing, the stance, the hawklike features. Sophia had obviously inherited her mother's Ramsey blue eyes and vivid coloring.

"A sow, you say," Giles replied. "No, you're wrong. I think she has the *ears* of a donkey."

Webb glanced back down at the defendants' bench. "My mistake. I see what you mean now. My eyes aren't as good as they used to be, but I would say in *a couple of hours* I will be seeing much better." He leaned closer and whispered. "Stay with her, my friend. She needs your strength."

With a thousand questions still unanswered, Giles watched Webb get up and push his way out of the crowd.

For the next few hours Giles listened as the witnesses trotted out and gave their coached testimony. Finally, after Webb's former landlady gave her damning evidence that Sophia was prone to keeping odd hours with strangers and never paid her rent, Fouquier-Tinville asked the jury if they had heard enough.

The threesome looked to each other and nodded in agreement.

"And what say your verdict?"

Stilled and tense, the crowd leaned forward, all eyes on the Tribunal.

"Guilty."

Pandemonium erupted. Cries for liberty and justice filled the air.

Fouquier-Tinville waved his hands once more, calling for silence. "I ask they be sent to the guillotine in the morning, so they can have the night to consider their grave sins against our fine Republic."

"So granted," the first man on the Tribune acknowledged.

Giles used the opportunity to slip out, while everyone

else began congratulating themselves on the prosecutor's stunning victory.

Outside the courthouse he waited near the gated entrance to the courthouse yard, where the guards transferred the prisoners into the carts that carried them back and forth from the jails scattered throughout Paris.

The shouts and singing continued inside, while in the courtyard the guard started to move about quickly.

Giles stepped back as he saw Robespierre and his dangerous assistant Saint-Just cross the cobblestones toward one of the waiting carts.

Sophia and her parents, all three in chains, were being escorted by a tight knot of guards toward the nefarious pair.

Saint-Just moved forward and said something to Sophia, but Giles couldn't hear his words because of the distance.

Whatever the man said, Sophia must have found great distaste in it. As if her chains weighed nothing, she kicked the man, connecting sharply with his shinbone.

He toppled back in pain while Sophia grinned over his writhing form.

At first it looked to Giles as if Saint-Just, who'd crawled out of her range and struggled to his feet, was going to retaliate by striking her. A barked order from Robespierre brought the young man back in line. Recovering some of his famous stoic composure, Louis Antoine Saint-Just turned his back to her in scorn and trailed into the courthouse at the heels of his master.

Sophia's mocking laughter chased his every retreating step.

She might still wear her chains, but she looked every ounce the victor. Stripped of her liberty, her freedom, and now even her life, whatever sway the man once held over her was powerless against her disdain for him and everything he represented.

Giles remembered her aunts' startling revelation—she'd made an ill-advised alliance. And he remembered the night at Danton's house, how Saint-Just's hand rested on Sophia's arm in a manner more befitting a possessive lover.

He'd thought even then that they might be lovers, before he'd known the truth about her.

Now he wondered again and thought perhaps they had been. A long time ago.

He didn't know why he thought that, but there was something about their interaction and Sophia's savage delight in the man's defeat and humiliation, albeit small, that told Giles her youthful indiscretion had come full circle.

And she'd exacted a lover's revenge.

The guards pushed her into the caged cart where her parents waited. As the metal lock snapped shut, the driver guided the horses out of the yard.

Crowds from inside the courthouse now lined the avenue around Giles. As the cart rolled down the street, he fought his way to its side.

Thrusting his hand through the rails, he grabbed Sophia's arm. At first she fought him, until their gazes locked and recognition set in.

She shook her head violently. "No . . . go back."

He didn't answer, but ran alongside the cart, clinging to her hand. He pried her fingers open and pressed the signet ring into her palm, just as the guards started to push the press of people away.

She looked down at his gift, shaking her head. "No, don't do this," she cried.

For one last moment the connection between them held, their fingers intertwined, as their bodies had done so intimately before. He squeezed her hand and whispered his vow to her.

"I love you, Lady Brazen."

Slowly, as the cart gained speed, their hands separated, until finally only the tips of their fingers brushed together and then parted.

"Now I understand what your ring means," he called after her, as the horses picked up speed and pulled the cart away.

He couldn't tell if she'd heard him, for she knelt in the middle of the cart, sobbing, her fist closed over his gift, clutching its promise to her heart.

"So you saw her," Webb commented as Giles slid into the dark corner of the tavern.

Giles glanced up. "How can you tell?"

"You look like you've stared death in the face."

"I could say the same of you. Where the hell have you been?"

Webb leaned back in his chair. "Dead, unless the news of my demise never reached you."

"Oh, it reached us. Your family had a nice ceremony for you, even put up a headstone." Giles leaned forward. "You young fool, what were you thinking, leading everyone to believe you were dead?"

"It worked, didn't it?" Webb shot back.

"It most certainly did, but why the elaborate hoax?"

Running his fingers through his golden brown hair,

Webb looked away. "It was not by choice. I was betrayed and imprisoned in the Abbaye."

"By who?"

"I'm still working on that one," Webb demurred.

The grim look on Webb's face told Giles not to press the issue. "So how did you escape?" he asked instead. "Your father's information was very clear: You were seen on your way to the square."

"I thought I was destined for the razor too. Until one night I heard the voice of an angel whispering through the doorway."

Giles didn't need much help with this one. "Sophia."

"Yes, Sophia." Webb's voice turned wistful. "I have to admit I've spent a fair amount of time envying your good fortune. I could never hope to have my father bequeath a bride like that as a dying wish."

"So I've discovered," he answered, less than comfortable with the tenor of Webb's admission. He remembered Isnard's description of the young American who had been rumored to be La Devinette's lover.

Webb started to laugh. "You can stop those foolish thoughts, my friend. Your bride has eyes only for you. She spent most of her time asking me all about you, what you liked, how you spent your time, what type of women you preferred. I don't know why, considering all she'd ever seen of you was that wretched portrait your father made you sit for when you were seven, but she's been half in love with you for ages."

The final pieces—how she knew so much about him—fell in place. It wasn't just her time with his father, but also her ongoing interrogation of Webb.

The sneaky little minx.

"You were saying, she found you in the Abbaye?"

"Yes. Foolish girl blamed herself for my arrest. Though I would have told her it had nothing to do with her."

"Wouldn't matter," Giles grumbled. "She'd have sought you out anyway."

"You know Sophia."

Giles nodded. "Only too well."

"She arranged for a diversion when I was being transferred at the courtyard after my trial. A small fire in the records room."

At this, Giles laughed. Would she ever learn to be a little more subtle?

"In the confusion," Webb continued, "I slipped free and she helped me get out of the city."

A serving girl sauntered forward and placed a bottle of wine on the table. She gave them both a welcoming smile and then flitted off to her duties.

Suddenly, Giles remembered the day they'd broken Lucien out of the prison. Sophia had told him she'd obtained the floor plans of the jail from a former prisoner. He lowered his voice. "You gave her the plans to the Abbaye."

"So she told you of that."

"No, not really, but it's all starting to become much clearer." Giles reached for the bottle of wine and poured himself a drink. "Where have you been for the last few months?"

"In hiding mostly. Spent nearly a month stowed away in the countryside with her brother and sister until the furor died down and I healed up a bit. My jailers didn't find my sense of humor very amusing. Especially the one about the regicides at the gates of hell."

Giles could well imagine what the *sans-culottes* would think of Webb.

"I always liked to go to the country as a child, but those thirty days of hiding were almost worse than jail."

"You made quite an impression on young Lily," Giles teased.

Webb held up his hands. "I never touched the girl."

"I believe you, but I don't think Lily preferred it that way."

"Those Ramsey women." Webb shuddered. "Mother told stories of their licentious behavior to my sisters as examples of how *not* to act. Have you noticed that all their husbands seem to die early? They wear them out utterly and completely if you ask me. I'll stay clear of Lily until that little vixen is married and toothless, with a passel of children clinging to her skirts. Give her time, she'll make Sophia look tame."

Giles would have argued the point, since he thought no one could outdo his future wife, but he didn't have the time. "Well, I would ask your indulgence and aid in seeing me to my early grave. I have every intention of marrying my little hellion and spending the next fifty years damning the consequences. Will you help me?"

"Do you even need to ask?" Webb glanced over his shoulder. "Since I figured you wouldn't heed my advice and head home alone, I asked someone to join us." He waved his hand at a man entering the tavern.

Giles watched Oliver shoulder his way through the crowd. Relief flooded him to know that the good man hadn't been captured.

"See you got my message," Oliver said, nodding to Giles.

"And I owe you a great deal for your faith in me. More than she had." He caught Oliver's hand and shook it hard.

"Don't judge her too harshly," Oliver said, looking almost embarrassed. "She thought she was doing what was best for you, as I did when I left the note with the lad in the stables."

Giles nodded. Sophia would protect those she loved fiercely, without regard for her own safety. He'd have to get used to the notion of having someone looking out for him.

Webb poured the remaining wine into the glasses before them. "If I know you, Giles, you've already got a plan in mind."

He smiled at his companions. "I do. Let me explain."

LED FROM HER cell in the morning, Sophia saw her parents waiting for her at the end of the dank hall. She tried to smile at them, but her thoughts were elsewhere.

Giles.

Against everything she'd wanted, he'd followed her to Paris.

Damn him. She'd sat up the entire night, her ears straining for any hint of rescue, but none had been forthcoming. Now it was too late, and some part of her was glad of that. That meant he would stay free of danger.

If only she could have told him that she loved him with all her heart.

Sophia glanced down at her hand, where her family's ring encircled her finger. He'd given it to her like a wedding band—one she'd never wear.

Her hand tightened into a fist. She'd cling to the warm metal until the life drained from her body.

Outside, the sun made a rare appearance for November. She blinked at the unaccustomed light, raising her hand to her eyes as she and her parents were led into the courtyard.

"Get up there, you traitorous bitch," one of the guards spat as he pushed her toward the waiting cart.

Sophia noticed that her father was about to turn and elbow the man in the face. Quickly, she reached out and stopped the angry motion.

"*Non, Papa.* It isn't necessary."

"I won't allow this swine to treat *my* daughter in such a manner."

She shook her head and nodded to where her mother stood alone at the front of the cart. "Go to her," she told him. "She needs your strength. I can take care of myself because I am your daughter."

She turned to the guard and glared. "Help me up, citizen, and be polite about it. You might think me unable to harm you, but I have yet to name my accomplices, and you could well find my finger pointing at you before I die. So be polite to me and my family. For it could very well be your turn tomorrow."

The man backed away from her and crossed himself.

Instead, her father did the honors. "I forget how grown up you've become," he whispered to her. "And how proud I've always been of my little Piper."

Tears brimmed in her eyes. One of the last times she'd seen her father was when she'd been sent from the house for her confinement. After that she'd gone directly to England, without seeing either of her parents. On that horrible day of leaving her home in disgrace, she'd begged her father to allow her to stay. His mouth was tight at the corners and his dark eyes were full of what she thought was shame, as he shook his head and watched Oliver all but carry her to the waiting carriage.

Now she knew better. He hadn't been ashamed of her. His heart had instead cried out with sorrow. He couldn't let her stay and have her condition become common knowledge, for that would have resulted in her being shunned for the rest of her life. So he'd made the impossible decision to send her away. He'd watched her go, knowing that even he couldn't bear for her the pain she faced.

Just as he couldn't bear the agony she faced today.

Beyond the gates the milling crowds were already thick, waiting like alley dogs for today's scraps to be tossed into the streets. She heard the catcalls and names, but paid no attention to them. The guard tied her hands to the cart's railing.

Even as they started on their slow journey out the heavy metal gates, she ignored the taunts and violent threats, searching the mottled, angry faces for any sign of Giles's dark, glittering eyes.

There was still no sign of him, yet his vow in the orangery came back to haunt her.

Wherever you go, I am destined to follow.

But not in death, she prayed. Not today.

But follow her he would. It wasn't in his nature to give up. It frightened her to think of what type of foolhardy rescue he'd plan. Foolhardy plans were her specialty, not his. She didn't want to be rescued, not if it meant he might face this same terrible fate.

Better he got back to England, marry a Dorlissa, and live out his life in the safety of the countryside than risk his life for hers.

Go home, she whispered. *Leave me be*. Even as she said the words she heard a familiar sound rising up over the heads of the crowd, teasing her with its simplistic notes.

A shepherd's pipe.

Hunched over and limping gamely at the edge of the crowd, Giles danced, pipe at his mouth, playing a notable rendition of *La Marseillaise*, the fervent battle cry of the *sans-culottes*.

He glanced in her direction, noticed her eyes on him, and raised two fingers from his pipe.

His emotional version of the uncrowned national anthem drew the crowd's attention away from her cart.

Two, two, what could it mean? she thought wildly, looking ahead toward the Rue St. Honoré to determine how much farther they had to go. Two blocks.

Two blocks? Was that what he'd meant?

"Papa? Maman?" she whispered. "Do you see anything unusual?"

Her father glanced over at her. "What do you mean?"

"Anyone you recognize?"

Her mother's gaze scanned the crowd. "No, but does this have to do with that man who accosted you yesterday?"

She nodded. "He's here. I don't know what he hopes to do, but we must be ready. Look for Oliver, or a young man about Lucien's height with golden brown hair."

They neared the corner where the street would join the wider, more accessible Rue St. Honoré. Around them the shops leaned precariously into the streets, stacked together like a child's toy blocks. It became so narrow, she lost sight of Giles as the press of people closed in around them.

A voice in one of the windows above her head cried out, *"Vive La Devinette!"*

The crowd stilled, and she looked up, but the sun blocked her sight. She blinked and stared again, the cry growing louder.

"Vive La Devinette!"

As she finally was able to see the face, she also saw Webb's arm sweep in a broad gesture, and the air sparkled with gold and silver coins.

A fortune in hard currency showered down on the crowd from both sides of the narrow street, clanging and jingling onto the paving stones. Opposite Webb, she spotted Oliver leaning out an attic window, tossing coins and paper *assignats* into the air.

The crowd paused, almost stunned by the strange turn of events. The money continued to fall—buckets of it—showering down like a hailstorm. Instead of running for cover, they entered the streets in a chaotic crush.

People dove into the discarded refuse clogging the gutter, digging with their bare hands to scoop the precious coins out of the clutter and filth. Fights broke out, as greed turned the fraternity of the people into a free-for-all.

Sophia discovered that her guards had deserted their posts and joined the swarming tide. Her driver looked to his passengers, shrugged, and jumped from his perch into the teeming horde.

"Quickly," Sophia said, pulling at the ropes binding their wrists.

A pair of strong hands closed over hers, a knife snaking forward.

She reeled back—until she realized the hands belonged to Giles. He caught her with one arm and pulled her close for a quick kiss on the cheek. "I hope you realize all of this is coming out of your betrothal trousseau," he teased, nodding

358

at the seemingly endless shower of coins. His knife cut through her ropes in a second, and in a heartbeat the Comte and Comtesse's hands also sprang free under the assault of the sharp blade.

He wrapped his arm around Sophia's waist and swung her free from the cart. This time he kissed her on the mouth, his lips quickly branding her, finishing his hasty declaration from the day before. "I love you with all my heart. And if you ever do something like this again, I swear I'll build a tower so high at Byrnewood that you'll never see land again."

Stunned by his pronouncement, she wanted to tell him what was in her heart as well. When she opened her mouth to reply, he shook his head.

"We haven't the time. And I already know." He turned and nodded in respect to the Comte. "Into this shop," he told them.

Sophia and her parents followed as Giles led them into the weaver's display room. The spindly man frowned at first, but when Giles tossed him a large pouch the man grabbed a bundle by his chair and walked out the front door, leaving his still-strung loom behind, his fireplace and lamps still lit.

She glanced up at Giles for an explanation.

"He expressed an interest in visiting Italy," Giles explained. "Now he'll live out his days fishing at the shore and drinking wine."

Through the back of the shop they dashed, Oliver joining them as they entered the alley. There a cart and horses waited in the narrow byway.

"How's the gold holding out?" Giles asked the man as he climbed up into his usual driver's seat.

"I think Mr. Dryden has a few more sacks left," Oliver grinned. "Plenty to slow down the guards at the front door of his shop.'

"We can't leave him behind," Sophia protested.

"We aren't going to," Giles said. "Now, get down under the cover," he told her, pushing her into the cart where her parents had already scrambled. "There are clothes there. Change as quickly as you can."

He joined Oliver up top, and the cart lurched to a start.

They drove in a wild path, down one street, up another, zigzagging through the Paris maze of streets and alleys.

Sophia poked her head out from beneath the cover. "I won't leave without Webb!"

"We aren't. Now, if you love me, stay under cover," he said, pushing the top of her head down.

She wiggled out of his grasp. "I do love you, but how do you plan on getting us out of the city?"

Giles groaned and yanked the cover over her head. Picking up one corner, he whispered down to her, "Who said anything about leaving?"

They rounded another corner before turning into the large, open delivery yard of a warehouse. The workmen, anticipating their hasty arrival, closed and barred the thick oak gates to the street, blocking out any view.

Oliver drove the horse and cart directly into a cavernous warehouse stacked with barrels.

"My friend, you are right on time," Citizen Isnard called out as he left his adjoining office.

Giles glanced up and smiled at his friend. "I've come to see about the order we discussed last night. Six to be exact." He glanced over at Oliver. "Make that five and one very arge one." He prodded the large man in the ribs and they all aughed.

Sophia was already out of the cart, her hands on her hips. "You mean to ship me back to England in a barrel?"

"An Isnard barrel, my dear lady," Isnard said, coming orward to help the Comte and Comtesse out of the cart. "A nore comfortable and safe journey you could not ask for. Times being what they are."

She shook her head with a stubborn tilt and looked back t Giles. "This is the best plan you could come up with? I hought you were a seasoned professional."

Giles laughed and pulled her into his arms. How he loved his woman. With all his heart. "I learned everything about his line of work from the master. Blame her."

She looked back over at Isnard and grinned. "Can you nake that a very large barrel for two?"

C H A P T E R
19

G ILES ROSE FRO his bed at Byrnewood, his bare feet treading quietly acros the cold hardwood floor. A clear winter sun streamed ray of light through the open curtains. Around him the hous was still, although he knew from the sun's position it wa probably well past noon.

"Everyone is so quiet," Sophia said sleepily from th warmth of the bed. "Do you think they've gone home?"

Giles laughed at the hopeful tones in her voice. "The must all be tiptoeing around this morning to allow us som measure of privacy."

"Wonderful," she said. "Dinner should quite interesting. I can hear my auntie Effie already. *And how did you sleep last night, Sophia?*" She shuddered and pulled the covers over her head. "Maybe I'll tell her exactly how I found my rest. That ought to make for a rousing discussion."

Shaking his head, Giles teased her in mocking tones. "Lady Trahern, you should have more respect for your position as hostess." Not that he didn't agree with her. He, too, longed to be alone, just the two of them.

She peeked out from beneath her hiding spot. "I know it was nice for everyone to want to see us married yesterday, but aren't they all supposed to leave afterward?"

"What would you have me do? Throw out your family? Toss out Lord Dryden and his brood?"

She shook her head. "No. It was wonderful to have everyone here. It's just that today . . . well . . ." She smiled like a lazy cat, one bare leg slipping out from beneath the sheets and wiggling invitation. "I want you all to myself."

Giles rejoined her in the bed, pulling the covers over his head. Sophia giggled as she slipped under the covers to meet him.

Sometime later he rolled over and pulled at the stray strands of her rich chestnut hair.

How thankful he was for his father's choice of brides. To wake up with Sophia each day, to see the light of her bright smile. He couldn't believe his luck.

Now, if she would only forgive him for what he had planned for the rest of their honeymoon.

"Just be thankful Monty wasn't here," Giles commented as he reluctantly got out of bed. "He'd have had us all up at first light for a ride. You wouldn't know it by looking at him, but he's quite willing to stay up all night gambling and dancing and then at dawn saddle his mount for a long, vigorous ride. The man never sleeps." He laughed. "Must be his pirate heritage."

"The Duke of Stanton is descended from pirates?" Sophia leaned forward, intrigued.

"Yes, a quite famous lady pirate, if you believe Monty's stories. For two hundred years her sword sat mounted over one of her descendant's mantels—until it was stolen about five years ago. He put out all kinds of rewards, but it was never returned."

Sophia frowned. "What did this sword look like?"

"Of Spanish make, with pearls and emeralds in the hilt. A fancy gold and silver basket over the hilt," Giles told her, wondering at her sudden interest in Monty's lost heirloom.

"Was it made for a woman?"

"Why, yes." Giles looked back at her, puzzled.

Sophia scrambled out of bed, pulled on her peignoir, and raced over to the dressing closet where her clothing had been hung the day before. Throwing open her traveling trunk, she pulled out a long bundle. "Did it look like this?" she asked, unwrapping a sword.

Giles's mouth opened. "That's it! Monty's blade. How did you come by it?"

"I stole it from Selmar. I thought to pick the gems out and sell them. But I was arrested in Paris before I had the chance. Oliver brought it back and gave it to me yesterday as a final memento of our adventures." She saluted Giles with the blade. "I think I would rather see it back with the Duke, where it rightfully belongs."

Giles crossed the room and pulled her into his embrace. "Monty will be your most devoted servant."

Sophia stepped back. "You don't mean to tell him how I

came upon this, do you?" The entire family had been sworn to secrecy regarding Sophia's double life. Everyone agreed it best to allow the Brazen Angel to fade into obscurity.

"Certainly not. Monty can't keep a secret to save his life," he said. "No, we'll find some other way to return it."

Sophia snapped her fingers. "I've got it. We'll have the word delivered anonymously from the Brazen Angel. The note can say that because of his kindness to her, she wanted to see him rewarded." She walked over to the small desk and proceeded to pull out a blank sheet of paper and the necessary writing instruments.

Giles laughed, thinking about his friend's original idea to marry the Brazen Angel and Giles's own incredulous reaction to such a preposterous idea. Perhaps it was better Monty didn't know. Giles would never hear the end of it. "His new bride might not like to have his affections for the Brazen Angel revived."

"The Duke got married?" Sophia asked, looking up from her note.

"He was telling me the night of the musical in Bath that he'd found his perfect duchess at Larkhall Manor."

"But who?" Sophia asked.

"Dorlissa."

Now it was Sophia's turn to stare open-mouthed at her groom. "No. Dorlissa and the Duke? Are you positive?"

"Lady Fischer claims the Duke carried off Dorlissa and the pastor two weeks ago, and no one has heard a word from them since." He strolled to his dressing room.

"And Lord Fischer isn't out looking for his daughter?"

Giles leaned out the doorway. "Lady Fischer won't allow him to. She'd never let him hear the end of it if he ruined Dorlissa's chance at becoming a duchess."

"Nor will the Duke," Sophia commented when Giles rejoined her in the bedchamber.

At this they both laughed, the shared companionship of the moment touching Giles with its intimacy. This is what he had missed most of his life.

He walked over and ruffled her hair, then placed a gentle kiss on her forehead.

"What was that for?" she asked.

"For being my perfect marchioness."

While Sophia set to work on her note, he began to dress for the day, watching her emotions dance across her face as she composed her words.

She stopped abruptly. "Whatever are we going to do about Emma?"

They'd arrived back in Bath only to find that Sophia's aunts had turned Emma from the house. There was no word of where her companion had gone, much to Sophia's distress.

Giles crossed the room and kissed her again. "We'll find your irrepressible Mrs. Langston. Despite all your dire predictions of her starving or freezing at the roadside, she seemed to me to be a woman who could land on her feet."

"I know, Giles. I'm just worried. And I want her here at Byrnewood where she belongs."

"So now you want more people in the house? I thought a few minutes ago you wanted me to clear everyone out from the rafters to the cellars."

She shook her head. "Just for today. Then tomorrow we'll throw the doors back open and let everyone back in." Her gaze traveled to the window. "Lucien and my father are already talking about going to the Colonies. Just when I get my family back, they start talking of leaving me."

"That may be my fault," Giles commented as he pulled on his black breeches. "I've offered them a half stake in my plantation in Virginia. I need someone there to manage it, and your brother thought it would be a good place to start over. Your father was also of the same mind. The house there is large and needs a big family to make it feel more welcome when we go to visit."

Sophia's eyes glowed with her appreciation. "No wonder I've loved you for so long. I knew what kind of man you were."

Giles turned away from her emotionally charged words, unable to find the right way to respond to her praise.

What he hadn't mentioned was that he intended to send her to the Colonies with her family. Dryden's visit to Larkhall Manor had also been of a business nature.

There was trouble brewing in the Russian court of Empress Catherine, and someone was needed to review the situation immediately.

What would Sophia say when she found herself being shipped to the Colonies with her family? She'd curse him and hate him.

Atlantic crossings held their own danger, but less so than traveling the perilous steppes of Russia. And it was the only way he knew to make sure she didn't follow him.

He edged his way to the window and looked outside. To his surprise a strange carriage turned up Byrnewood's driveway and rolled toward the house.

As the carriage drew closer, he assumed it was one of Sophia's Ramsey aunts arriving from Larkhall Manor to see if their "poor, dear niece" survived the night.

Reaching for his shirt, Giles pulled it on hastily. If this

was Lady Dearsley, he wouldn't put it past the woman to barge into the bedroom to make sure Sophia was still alive.

The carriage pulled to a stop and a footman stepped forward to open the door. A cold chill—a premonition of anger—swept through Giles as first Lord Lyle and then Rostland climbed down.

He looked back at Sophia, still hard at work on her composition.

"Are you going to be much longer?" he asked.

"I thought I would bathe and wash my hair. It might take some time." She smiled. "You're famished, aren't you? I can't imagine why." This was followed by a sensual laugh. "Go on ahead and eat. You'll need the fortification."

Giles glanced one more time out the window. "Take all the time you want."

AN HOUR LATER Sophia ventured out of the master suite, having taken great care with her appearance on this, her first full day as Lady Trahern. She wasn't more than halfway down the hall when Webb stepped out of an alcove.

"I thought you were never going to come out of there. We've got trouble brewing."

Sophia stepped back. "Is it Lily again? I told her to stop pestering you. If you want I can speak to *Maman* and ask her to—"

"No, it isn't your sister. It's worse."

"What is it?"

"Do you know who your husband has been closeted with in the library for the last hour?"

"No. We aren't expecting any more guests."

"Don't know that I'd call them guests. It's Lyle and ostland."

Sophia took a sharp, deep breath, stunned. "What?" she whispered.

"That's why I've been out here pacing for the last half our. Lily came tearing into my room to tell me Giles was a trouble."

"Trouble . . ." Sophia didn't really need to ask what kind f trouble; anything wrought by those two evil men would bell disaster.

"Oh, don't get that look," Webb told her. "It scares me. esides, Giles is holding his own. For now. If I know that air they've figured out who you are—or rather, were—nd now they want to blackmail your husband into keeping he secret."

"Giles won't give them a shilling." He'd better not, she hought fiercely.

"He might not have a choice. They will ruin your reputa-on, ruin the Trahern name."

Webb's statement stopped Sophia. After her rescue in 'aris and her subsequent return to England, she hadn't even linked before Giles pulled her in front of the parson and aarried her. Flush with her own selfish happiness, she'd orgotten her vow to go to the Colonies in hopes of keeping he stain of her misdeeds from tarnishing the Trahern name. This is all my fault."

"There is a way out of this, if you have the stomach to ace those old lechers. Besides, I think Giles needs to learn hat his independent days are over. He needs us."

To save Giles's honor and his family's name she'd face he very demons of the underworld. After all, this disaster vas her fault. "Tell me what you want me to do."

"Do you still have those items you 'borrowed' from
Lyle's safe?"

She nodded. "Yes. It's just about all I have left."

"Good woman. No wonder Giles snapped you up. Now
this is what we'll do."

SEATED AT HIS desk, Giles slammed his fist down on
the cherry-wood surface. Ignoring the pain shooting up his
arm, he glared at the two men in his study. "I won't give
either of you the coppers for your eyes when I kill you."

Lyle looked down at his nails, obviously bored with the
amount of time this meeting was taking. "You'll pay, Trahern. Every bit of it."

"Never."

Rostland stretched his long, thin legs out in front of him,
his Hessians gleaming. "And why ever not? The amount is
more than fair. Especially when you consider what is at
stake."

Giles didn't need to be reminded what was at stake. The
two vultures had made their position very clear.

Lyle studied the document in his hand and laid it back
down on the desk. "The court record is rather clear—
Sophia D'Artiers, known as La Devinette. And the drawing
from the pamphlet is quite good. See for yourself."

"La Devinette?" Rostland asked Lyle. "My French is terrible. How does that translate again?"

"A whore," Lyle said, his gaze never leaving Giles.

Giles restrained himself from killing the man outright for
the slur against his wife. He would be well within his right
to call the man out and kill him for the insult, but he knew

before Lyle died, the man would wreak havoc for Sophia and her family that wouldn't be undone for generations.

And there was also Rostland. Giles looked over at the reed-thin man in his fussy, fashionable clothes.

Giles would kill them both if he had to.

"I see the murder in your eyes," Lyle commented, his hands resting comfortably on his fat belly. "It would be a poor decision. For if I meet with an untimely demise, an accident, anything, my solicitor has been instructed to publish a full account of Lady Trahern's activities. And he will hand out certified copies of the affidavits we've collected to anyone interested in reading about her exploits as La Devinette and as the Brazen Angel."

Rostland leaned forward. "We actually considered selling the idea for a novel, but no one would believe it."

"Then what makes you think they'll accept this pile of lies when you are dead?"

"Because they're the truth. You know it, I know it, and if you don't pay what we ask, then the entire world will learn of your wife's true proclivities," Lyle said.

Giles scrambled to his feet, fully intending to come around his desk and kill Lyle outright.

Just then the study door opened. In walked Sophia, a covered tray in her hand. Bumping the door shut with her hip, she smiled apologetically as the tray tipped precariously in her hand. "I'm not much of a domestic," she explained. "With such important business being discussed, my lord husband, I thought you might like me to bring in refreshments for our guests so as to keep these matters private."

He could well imagine what arsenic-laden cups she had in mind to serve their guests. And he doubted either man would drink willingly anything she offered.

She continued into the room, all but ignoring Lyle and Rostland, who had risen at her entrance. Placing the tray on the table between the two men, she lifted the silver dome.

She stepped back, allowing Giles to see what poison she offered their guests.

"Is this what you gentlemen are hoping to find?" she asked politely, coming around the desk to stand at Giles's side.

He looked at the contents, unsure of what he was seeing.

"Printing plates," she explained. "For French *assignats*. Your guests have been counterfeiting."

"I deny this," Lyle said, backing away from the evidence. "What proof do you have?"

"I stole these from your safe months ago."

Her statement stopped even Giles. What could she be thinking? Publicly announcing she was the Brazen Angel? After he'd spent the last hour denying the possibility.

But the plates did explain why the pair had hunted her so ruthlessly.

"So you admit you are the Brazen Angel?" Lyle said, closing in, a nasty smile on his face, as if he couldn't be more pleased at her hasty admission.

Sophia leaned over the desk and met Lyle's stare with a deadly one of her own. "Why deny it?"

Giles had to admire her bravado. It seemed to be working. Her opponent backed down slightly, obviously surprised and unsure how to proceed when the lady seemed more than willing to ruin herself.

Lyle pointed down at her evidence. "So what if I printed French money? What is any Englishman going to care if I contributed to the downfall of that horrid Revolution? Counterfeit money has made their economy so unstable, they won't last but another season."

"And just in time for you to have bought up as much French land as you can with your worthless bills," she responded.

Giles stared at his wife in amazement. How did she know this? Then he remembered her claim that Webb had been betrayed by an Englishman. Giles knew Webb's investigation had involved checking out strange transfers of English money into Switzerland. There had also been the disappearance of several other English agents looking into the situation.

It was one thing when the English government sanctioned foreign operations by their agents, but rogue ventures by greedy civilians were frowned upon. Especially when they caused the deaths of English agents.

"Buying land in France? Why ever would I do that?" Lyle scoffed, though to Giles's trained eyes the man looked uncomfortable at her latest accusation.

Sophia had the truth of the matter, and Lyle didn't like it one bit.

"Why indeed?" she said. "With land going so cheaply and you able to print your own money to buy it, it sounds like quite a worthy investment to me."

"Perhaps I should look into it for you," the man countered with a mocking smile.

"You already have, Lord Lyle." Sophia's hands went to her hips.

Giles knew that move. It meant she was quickly running out of patience for the man in front of her.

"You've been snapping up French holdings for a song," she accused. "And if the poor *émigrés* make it to London, you sell them back their own family lands for gold or what-

ever hard currency they can scrape together. I'd say you ha
quite a business going—that is, until you were caught."

"I don't know what you are talking about. Considerin
your reputation for veracity, Lady Trahern, this story is a
fanciful as your masquerade as that Brazen tart. At least
didn't rob anyone. I bought land that was freely for sale an
resold it at a profit. There is nothing wrong with a littl
commerce between gentlemen."

"Profit made with counterfeit bills?" she countered.

Rostland stepped forward, joining in the fray. "Profit i
profit. We took great personal risks to buy the land. Wh
should we risk our money as well?"

"That may be," Sophia agreed. "There is nothing Englis
law can do to you for counterfeiting French currency, bu
I'm sure English law does take a dim view of treason an
murder."

"Murder?" Lyle burst out, his face mottled with rage
"You have no proof."

Giles wondered at the man's quick and angry reaction
Only guilt drove a man to snap like that, like an anima
trapped in a corner.

"But I do," his wife shot back. "When English agent
started investigating the uncommon rise in aristocrats bein
turned in to the Committee, both here and in Paris, the
started to look into your misdeeds. You would lure unsus
pecting French nobles to Paris with the offer to secure thei
lands on their behalf, and then you'd have them betrayed
And collect a tidy sum for the reward on their heads. Whe
their lands came available you snapped them up and sol
them back to the grieving widows in London."

"English law has no authority over these transactions
Your arguments are meaningless."

Sophia shook her head and moved forward. "That might be true, if you hadn't done this to the Duc de Lemoine."

Lyle paled visibly, but recovered quickly. "The man's death was unfortunate, but hardly a matter of English concern."

Giles realized all too quickly the point Sophia was making. Now he knew he could step in and bolster her attack without destroying her masterful plan. "That would be true, but Lemoine wasn't a French citizen. He was an Englishman. And an English agent."

Rostland stepped back from Lyle's side. "You said he was of no concern."

"Quiet!" Lyle ordered. "There is no proof."

"Yes, there is," Sophia said with firm conviction. "There was one other man involved in your dealings with Lemoine."

This time Lyle smiled. "The man you speak of, unfortunately, followed Lemoine to the guillotine. Unless you have by some miracle the means to reattach a man's head."

Sophia smiled at Giles. "Should I show him my latest amusement?"

Giles nodded. "Please, with my blessing."

Sophia strolled past Lyle's pompous stance and opened the door to the study.

"May I introduce my miracle," she said, curtsying to her new guest. "Webb Dryden."

Rostland sputtered and staggered back. Pointing his narrow finger at Lyle, he spouted out his accusations. "You said he was dead. That there would be no proof. This is all your fault."

"Quiet!" Lyle shot back. "You'll hang us for sure with this blathering."

Giles shook his head at how quickly the two fiends fell upon each other when they finally faced their reckoning.

"I think hanging will be the least of your worries," Webb said, walking into the room. "Arrest these men," he said over his shoulder.

A detachment of local soldiers marched into the room, subduing the crying Rostland and the still-protesting Lyle.

"I'll not keep quiet, Trahern," Lyle threatened. "I'll tell the entire world the truth about this trollop you married."

Giles stepped in front of Sophia to shield her from the man's vile statements. "And who will believe you, Lyle? You are obviously insane. Not to mention a traitor and a coward. My meek and mild bride masquerading as the Brazen Angel? Why, the notion is preposterous. I find her quite pleasing, but she is hardly a diamond of that order." He turned to his wife. "My apologies, my dear."

"Apology accepted. I'm not vain about my appearance," she said with a strained look on her face. "I know I'm rather plain and could certainly never venture out alone like that daring creature."

Giles smiled, knowing he'd pay for his statement about her looks. He turned back to Lyle. "You'll only look all that much more vindictive and foolish if you start spreading more lies."

Lyle wrestled free from his captors. "I have proof. I have statements. I have the court documents."

"From a man who freely admits he counterfeits money to steal land from noblemen?" Giles crumpled the papers in his fist. "Manufactured to blackmail my family once you realized your treachery had been discovered." Giles turned to the captain of the guard. "Take this filth from my house.

Lord Dryden will instruct you later as to how they are to be dealt with."

Lyle and Rostland were dragged from the house by the soldiers.

Once everyone had left, Webb pulled up to the cart of liquors at the side of the room. "This calls for a toast."

Sophia stepped forward. "Allow me to pour."

Considering what he'd said about her plain looks, Giles thought better of having her offer the drinks. "I'll do the honors."

Her eyes widened. "What, don't you trust me?" A saucy smile, reminiscent of the Brazen Angel's, lingered on her lips.

"Utterly and completely," he lied. "Still, allow me." After he'd poured two glasses of whiskey and a glass of sherry, he looked back at the two co-conspirators. "Quit gloating. Both of you. It's becoming annoying." He offered Sophia her glass, and then Webb his. "I had everything under control."

Sophia's eyebrows raised in disbelief.

Giles muttered something under his breath as he returned to his chair behind the desk. "Yes. Perhaps your interruption was rather timely."

"And?" Webb asked, a bemused smile on his face.

"Fine. Without the two of you, none of this would have been settled. I needed your help."

Sophia bounced up and deposited herself in his lap. Wrapping her arms shamelessly around his neck, she kissed him boldly in front of Webb. "You see, now you can't go to Russia without me. I'm indispensable."

Giles leaned back. "Russia? What do you know of that?"

"Everything. Including the fact that you were planning to leave me behind."

She glanced over at Webb, who suddenly had become very interested in the bookshelf behind him.

Giles could well imagine who'd told his bride his secret plans.

She crossed her arms over her chest. "I think I've just proved how much you need me."

Arguing with her was useless, Giles knew, when she furrowed her brows up in that peculiar Ramsey slant. There would be no leaving her now.

Pulling her closer into his embrace, he thought perhaps the cold St. Petersburg winter wouldn't be so bad with Sophia curled up next to him.

"You can go."

Sophia laughed triumphantly, kissing him anew.

Webb coughed and got up from his chair. "I think I'll leave you two alone." As he approached the door it opened, nearly hitting him in the face.

Lily rushed in. "Sophia," she asked. "Have you seen Webb?"

Webb poked his head just out from behind the door and shook it furiously, holding up his hand to stave off the girl's discovery of his whereabouts.

Giles grinned. "Why, yes, Lily. He's right behind the door."

LATER THAT SAME afternoon Lord and Lady Fischer arrived at Byrnewood to offer felicitations to the new couple and make an announcement of their own. The anxious lady all but towed her husband into the sitting room where everyone was gathered.

"I had word this morning from my dearest Dorlissa," she said, waving a piece of paper in her hand. "She's married! And to your good friend, the Duke of Stanton."

Sophia and Giles exchanged bemused glances.

"You'll have to extend our best wishes to the happy couple," Giles offered.

Lady Fischer settled on the sofa. "You can extend them to my daughter, the Duchess, in person. Her note says they will be stopping here at Byrnewood this very afternoon."

Sophia plastered her most gracious hostess face on, preparing to endure an entire afternoon of Lady Fischer's gloating.

"So you've forgiven her?" Lady Larkhall teased.

"Forgiven her?" Lady Fischer asked, her tone incredulous. "What ever for?"

"For eloping," Lady Dearsley pointed out, sending strained looks at both her sisters, who had eloped in their wilder youths. "It leaves such a question of decency about the marriage."

"There was nothing indecent about this situation," Lady Fischer sniffed. She reached over and selected a cake from a nearby tray. "The Duke, such a gentleman and so concerned about Dorlissa's reputation, insisted they take a chaperon, and I have you to thank for that. When you cruelly threw out Mrs. Langston, the Duke asked her to accompany them to Scotland to add a measure of respectability to the arrangement. They even took the parson to make sure there was no doubt as to the validity of this marriage."

Sophia straightened up. "Emma? She's with the Duke and Dorlissa?"

"Why, yes," Lady Fischer said. "Such a lovely woman and such a good example for Dorlissa."

Giles leaned over and whispered into his wife's ear. "I told you Mrs. Langston would land on her feet."

For the next few hours the family endured Lady Fischer's descriptions of the Duke's properties. Giles egged her on by correcting her mistakes and adding greatly to the Duke's holdings, until the lady's eyes glowed in rapture and awe at the detailed accounts of each of the houses.

Just before supper the Duke's carriage rolled up to Byrnewood.

Lady Fischer could barely contain herself as her daughter bounded into the room, her face glowing with marital bliss.

"Mother!" the new bride cried out. "I didn't expect you here."

"Where else would I be when I knew you would be stopping here first?" Lady Fischer held her daughter at arm's length to examine her. "Or should I be calling you *Your Grace*? Oh, I've been practicing saying it for a fortnight now. Your Grace. How I love the sound of it."

Giles looked up at the door and found Monty and the young Reverend Harel smiling at this happy reunion. His friend could grin now, because he didn't yet know what his new mother-in-law had planned for him.

"But, Mother," Dorlissa said, looking back toward the doorway. "Why would you call me that?"

"Your Grace? Why shouldn't I? I might be your mother, but you're a duchess now."

"A duchess?" Dorlissa frowned. "I'm not a duchess."

"Of course you are. The Duchess of Stanton. That's what happened when you got married, you silly girl."

Monty and the Reverend stepped forward, almost in unison. But it wasn't Monty who wrapped his protective arm around the confused Dorlissa, it was Reverend Harel.

"Get your hand off the Duchess," Lady Fischer demanded, swatting the Reverend's offending arm with her fan.

"He hasn't got his hands on the Duchess, my lady," Monty corrected.

"Not the Duchess?" Lady Fischer wailed. "How can this be? You're married. Why wouldn't Dorlissa be the Duchess?"

"Because I didn't marry Dorlissa. Your daughter married Reverend Harel." Monty paused for a moment, a wide smile on his face. "Please allow me to introduce you to *my* bride." With a wide sweep and bow, he stepped out of the doorway.

Framed in the opening stood Emma, the new Duchess of Stanton, resplendent in a brightly colored dress, fur-lined wrap, and what Giles might have guessed were a good portion of the Stanton jewels at her neck, wrists, and ears.

The room fell so quiet, it seemed to Giles that everyone had forgotten to breathe. Including him.

Everyone but Lady Fischer, who sank to her knees and broke out in a flood of tears. "You faithless woman," she shot at Emma. "I offered you a job in my house, and this is how you repay me? By stealing my Dorlissa's groom?"

Emma smiled and wrapped her arm around Monty's. "You could say I had a better offer."

EPILOGUE

St. Petersburg, 1794
The Winter Palace

"Really, Lord Trahern," the English ambassador to Russia said, his voice dropping to a low whisper. "I was surprised to see that you brought your wife with you to Saint Petersburg. Isn't that highly unusual in these cases?"

"My wife is highly unusual. Besides, I thought she offered a brilliant cover." Amused more than annoyed by the man's patronizing tone, Giles watched the whirling crowd of Russian nobles. Princes, princesses, grand dukes, and generals gathered this evening to celebrate the fiftieth year of their Empress's arrival in Mother Russia. The gilded room glittered with the rich fabrics and jewels of Russia's elite.

What Giles didn't tell the less-than-discreet man was that his wife was his best ally in the tempestuous tides of Russian politics. She'd already charmed most of the men at court, as well the cagey old Empress herself.

"Yes, I suppose that might work, but . . ." The man shook his head as if he didn't quite agree with the notion.

Giles might not agree either, and he knew Dryden had his reservations about the situation, but what else could he do? Leaving Sophia home wasn't an option. He knew she would just follow him, and then there'd be hell to pay when she found him.

No, he'd taken her as his wife and his partner.

Though perhaps it was better that she'd stayed in their apartments tonight, he thought as he looked over at the enormous tables of food and enjoyed the smell of ham and fish filling the air.

Lately even the slightest odor sent her racing for her chamberpot.

The doctor had advised them that the sickness would pass in a month or so, then in another five months the first Trahern heir would arrive.

Yes, he thought, it was better she stayed in bed and got some rest.

"I say," the ambassador commented, "have you ever seen the likes of such a creature?"

Giles glanced across the room. Parting the crowd was an elegantly dressed woman, clad entirely in black. In a room filled with white and gold and pink frothy dresses, the stark black costume caused quite a stir.

He recognized her in an instant and didn't know whether to be angry that she wasn't back in bed resting or bemused by the attention she attracted.

Her bare arms glowed against the dark fabric, while diamonds sparkled at her wrists and neck. Her towering, powdered-black wig twinkled with strings of white brilliants, like stars on a clear night set against the deep, dark mysteries of the heavens.

People whispered about who this late arrival could be, for no one could identify the masked lady as she picked her way through the crowd.

The ambassador coughed. "Now, there's a reason not to bring your wife, young man."

"Exactly my thought," Giles answered, caught between the excitement coursing through him and his concern over her risky return to her costumed capers.

What the hell was she up to?

The lady in black made her way through the astonished crowd until she stood in front of Giles and the ambassador.

For the benefit of those nearby, Giles smiled politely. "I believe we've met before."

At this the ambassador's mouth dropped open in amazement. He looked first at Giles, then back at the woman before them.

"Have we?" She tipped her head and studied Giles. "I think I would remember such an acquaintance," her voice purred.

The floral scent of her perfume, the one that ravaged his senses with its sensual promise, surrounded them.

He caught her hand and brought it to his lips. "Does this help?" he murmured, more than willing to play her game.

She shook her head. "Sorry, but I don't recall the introduction. Now, if you will excuse me, I'm looking for my escort." She went to step away from him.

Giles caught her by the elbow. "I think you've found him."

At this, she laughed. Bringing up a pair of quizzing glasses, she peered through them, studying him from the top of his dark hair down past his black frock coat and along the lines of his tight breeches. Her devilishly bright gaze strayed back up to his groin. "I suppose you will do."

In a court used to the lustful gaze of their Empress, no one seemed shocked at this flagrant behavior—in fact, they quite enjoyed it. However, the more staid English ambassador started to cough.

Seeing how she enjoyed herself, Giles joined in her game. Besides, her antics were giving the pompous ambassador a case of jealous apoplexy, as the stuttering man watched Giles win over this beauty with barely a word.

"Perhaps you could use some air?" Giles suggested.

The masked woman smiled. "I have a delightful balcony in my room. The night breeze there is quite invigorating, if you dare try it." She reached inside her bodice and pulled a silken ribbon from between her breasts. Attached to it was a key. She swung it before him. "Join me if you are of a mind. But don't tarry, because I do so hate to be kept waiting."

Giles held out his hand, and she dropped the silver key into his open palm.

She turned and strolled from the room like a dangerous feline.

Giles shrugged his shoulders at the ambassador and followed the Brazen Angel back to their suite of rooms.

Once inside with the door bolted, they caught each other in a crushing embrace, their mouths fusing in a hot, heated kiss. In a mad rush, they removed each other's clothing.

"And here I thought I'd lost you," he said between kisses. "I thought you'd left me."

"Who do you think I am?" she asked.

"A woman I searched for sometime ago. I last saw her in London and thought I would never find her again."

She purred softly in the back of her throat and shifted her body closer to his. "Maybe you just didn't know where to look," she answered. A sly smile curved her lips as her hips rocked gently against his hard manhood. "If you like, I could help you."

"I'll offer you some clues. She should like this," he said, trailing the tips of his fingers from her shoulder, down her arm, and over the curve of her hip. Her playful expression urged him onward.

"And if I needed more hints?"

"She would never protest if I did this."

His lips nuzzled at her neck, her head and neck arching back to allow his kisses full access to the tender flesh.

"Mmm . . ." she moaned. "I think I'm starting to see what you mean. I suppose if I were the lady you sought I might do something like this."

Sophia's fingers massaged his chest, raking and dividing the thick curls. Lower and lower her hands worked, until they brushed over his flat stomach.

The sensation of her touch left him spellbound. For a

moment she paused right over his aching staff, as if she wanted him to beg, to plead with her to touch him there, to ease his needs. When he said nothing she passed over his groin, her fingers whispering over his thighs and down to almost his knees.

Shaking his head, Giles nipped her on the shoulder. "I don't think the woman I'm looking for would ever tease a man so unmercifully." His hands copied her earlier movements, curling around her breasts, skimming the sensitive ends, and then moving lower. His fingers worshiped her thighs in light, feathery touches, but never came close enough to give the needed touch at her core.

She tossed and moaned at his mistreatment. "I see what you mean. I think you are looking for someone a little more daring . . . perhaps a little brazen." She yanked off his jacket and all but tore the rest of his clothes off.

He dipped his head to her breast, taking her erect nipple in his mouth, teasing it. His hand curled around her bottom, pulling her up and against him.

The sensations in her breasts spread his message through her nerves in quick, urgent waves. As he continued to lave the rough surface of his tongue over her nipple, she found herself unable to think beyond the pulsing need settling in her very core.

When his manhood rubbed against the tight curls at the apex of her thighs, she opened her legs quite willingly.

"What is it you want?" he asked in a smoky voice.

"You," she answered, her tone urgent and tense.

His hand reached down until his fingers glided over the moist welcome of her body, which arched to meet his welcome touch. As his fingers found her center and began to stroke her, she writhed in enjoyment at the building sensations he provoked.

As she climbed higher under his gentle ministrations, his mouth reclaimed her breast, adding to the rising fever boiling though her blood.

Release. She needed release. How he did this to her, she didn't quite understand. How he seemed to know just where to touch and how much to tease her.

Even now, as she neared the frenzied state where her vision blurred and everything focused on the places where his body met hers, he pulled back, leaving her tottering on the brink.

"Giles, don't tease me further. I need you so badly," she pleaded, feeling herself sliding back from that soaring pinnacle.

"Like this?" he asked, the rapid motions of his fingers guiding her back up the steep course.

"Yes . . . yes . . . no . . ." she panted, her hand reaching for him. She stroked him, mimicking his motions.

Giles groaned, the need for more than this teasing play pushing him to pull away from her. Catching her by the shoulders, he gently laid her back in the downy recesses of the mattress. Positioning himself over her, he gazed down into her eyes. She blinked once or twice, her eyes both stormy blue and lazy with passion.

She didn't say anything; instead, she reached up with both hands and brushed back his hair. They traced a path along the edge of his face, her thumbs reaching around and following the curve of his lips, the touch gentle and exploring, as if she wanted to memorize his face.

Moistening her lips, she pulled him closer until their mouths could meet.

The moment lost all the playful teasing of their earlier play as their tongues met, loving each other in a warm, tender embrace. At the same time he slowly entered her, taking his time to move first in and then out, each time pushing himself a little deeper into her, stroking her with loving, gentle promises.

Sophia shuddered. How she loved this part of their lovemaking. With each slow thrust he told her what his heart could no longer deny: He loved her.

Rocking against his hardness, she wrapped her legs around him, pulling him closer inside her, so that she, too, could give him love with every rising motion.

Together they found the best pace, first one that gave them the quick, thrilling rush, then a slower one to enjoy the tenderness of their joining.

Sophia's release welled up, bubbling over and taking her by surprise with its beauty, overflowing with wave after wave of relief.

She felt Giles's body tense over her, then with several long, slow thrusts he, too, found his release, gasping for air while his seed spilled into her body.

For some time they cradled each other, murmuring soft, private words for their hearing only. Their hands retraced the earlier reckless paths, but this time with whispered, skimming touches, as if to reassure themselves that the sensations hadn't been imagined.

Pulling back for a moment from the warmth of his arms, Sophia looked into his eyes. "Did you find her?"

"Find who?" he asked, his lips brushing over her forehead, her brows, and ending at the tip of her nose.

"The woman you seek. Did you find her tonight?"

"No," he said with a sad shake of his head.

"No?" she asked, looking more than a little disappointed.

"I suspect it will take a lifetime to find her."

Sophia grinned and burrowed deeper into his arms. "I can wait."